Outside the Rules

ALSO BY DYLAN JONES

Thicker Than Water

OUTSIDE
THE RULES

Dylan Jones

St. Martin's Press
New York

ISBN 0-312-11873-2

First published in Great Britain by Century

First U.S. Edition: March 1995
10 9 8 7 6 5 4 3 2 1

For Eleri, Gruffudd, Caradog and
Brynach, my kings and angels.

With thanks to David Rouse MRCPath, DMJ(Path) for his expert guidance, Keith, Sue and Melody for their local knowledge and Val whose librarianship remains unparalleled.

Chapter 1

At six thirty-five, just as he did every morning, Meredith walked slowly to the male employees' changing room and clambered out of his soiled whites. Next to the tiny sink, a large blue canvas bag hung from an aluminium holder. It overflowed with stained white trousers and overalls that spilled out in a heap on to the floor. By eight the bag would have been removed for laundering, but at this time the stale smell of sweat and cooked food that tainted the clothes drifted up to join the mouldy stink of cigarette smoke and feet that pervaded the inadequate room's atmosphere.

Meredith was alone, just as he desired to be. His shift finished at six thirty and most of his colleagues, the chefs and the other dish stackers, had gone ten minutes before. But Meredith was in no hurry. It was still dark outside. He changed slowly into light-weight chinos and a sweat shirt. He would freeze on his way to the car, but it was of little concern to him.

Slowly, he washed his face, using the cleanest part of his thin jacket to wipe himself dry before he threw it into the bag. He turned back to the mirror, not really wanting to confront the image there. As usual, his pallid face looked strange to him, his hair short and poorly cut by his own hand, the bunched vertical lines between his eyebrows suggesting constant pain. But there were no aches in his limbs, and the minor headache he suddenly felt was, he knew, merely the fumes from the dryers and ovens and would wash away in the morning air.

Even so the lines remained, a constant reminder of a pain that although no longer physical, was nonetheless intractable. He glanced at his watch: five minutes had elapsed. It was time to begin.

He left the changing room and walked back through to the gleaming kitchen. Someone was whistling; a radio droned echoingly. Meredith walked quickly, staying on the narrow side of the big dryers, keeping his head down. If anyone saw him, they would not bother to hail him because they knew he would not reply. At the end of the tiled room, he entered a small annexe. The air was fresher here, exchanged constantly with the air-conditioned space in the seating area of the big Flamingo restaurant. In the door that swung both ways to give the waitresses and crockery collectors access, a six-by-ten glass pane allowed views in and out so that collisions could be avoided.

Standing well back, Meredith peered out into the seating area. His view was restricted, but it was the best he could manage. After a couple of minutes, he spotted only two possibles. The first sat in the smoking area, a tall, fair-haired man busy scribbling in a diary. His white shirt and flowered tie, added to the rigid-framed briefcase, smacked of rep.

Still, it could be *him*.

The second sat alone in the corner. Casually dressed, two days' growth of stubble above an Iron Maiden jacket. Meredith watched as he eyed a woman with two sleepy children. There was nothing exceptional about the woman except for a too tight T-shirt that showed up a pair of full breasts.

Meredith glanced between the two men. Neither seemed in any hurry. Neither fitted the physical profile the police had told him about. But it didn't matter to Meredith. Although the place was beginning to fill, they were the only single male travellers there at that time.

He glanced at his watch again. Six fifty.

Quickly, he turned and strode back through the kitchen. At the rear was a fire exit. In the summer they held it open with a galvanised bucket. But this wasn't summer, this was February. He depressed the crossbar and pushed the heavy door out into the dark morning air.

Swiftly, he walked to the corner and stopped. He watched the light from inside the kitchen fade as the sprung door closed itself.

With a mechanical clunk, the latch engaged and he was in darkness, crouching slightly, letting his eyes adjust, feeling the freezing air seep into his bones.

Ahead were some steps up to the level of the main car park. Behind him was the lorry park. To his left, twenty yards away, the main entrance to the restaurant and shop spilled light out into the black morning. In his ears, the hiss of traffic on the M4 cut through the air. This far west, three lanes constricted to two before continuing west as the A48, completing the connection between London and Wales's west coast, the ferries and Ireland. Out of the corner of his eye, across the man-made mounds of greenery that contoured the car park, he could see the Texaco sign at the filling station red against black. But his retinas were glued to the entrance.

No one came out.

He glanced behind him. The exit, too, remained tight shut.

Satisfied, he strode towards his car. The Escort was ten years old, but it started first time. Meredith drove towards the petrol station, continued right through and stopped at the exit. From there he could see both the slip road from the service-station car park and the filling station.

He sat for four minutes, his engine revving as the choke over-ran in the freezing air.

He saw no sign of either the Iron Maiden jacket or the smooth rep.

At six fifty-five, in the knowledge that by the time he got home dawn would be breaking and there would be light, Meredith drove off.

There was no security in the knowledge, merely a slight lessening of the pain that never totally left him for any minute of his existence. For the day would end and yield once again to the night. And with the night there would always come the darkness that fed and nurtured his fear.

Chapter 2

On that same freezing, clear Monday morning in February, Assistant Chief Constable Martin Tindal stood in the small living room of 21 Wesley Gardens, Bitterne Park; Southampton, a nondescript Victorian terraced house in a quiet residential area favoured by students and first-time buyers. He had never been to Hampshire before in his life and found himself wishing to God that he wasn't there at that moment. The house that was once a cosy haven now felt desolate and empty. The sweet smell of decay assailed his senses, yet had he been asked to describe it, it would have emerged merely as the faint odour of potpourri emanating from the spilled perfumed shavings of a pewter bowl mixed with the coppery odour of the butcher's shop.

Tindal was not a tall man. In stockinged feet, he had measured five eight and a half at his last medical. The bedroom mirror at home showed a midriff on the losing side in the battle against middle-age spread, as his wife liked to whisper it. He retained a full head of silver-streaked hair parted on the left in the style he had adopted on entry into the force twenty-six years before. The white shirt and Rotarian tie were spotless under a jowly, ruddy face from which two flint-grey eyes stared out above puffy lower lids that always lent Tindal the deceptive appearance of a man in need of sleep. But there was no thought of sleep in his head as he surveyed the living room.

The scene-of-crime officer had been hovering in the lobby when Tindal arrived, wittering on about how extensively they were going to fingerprint the house. Tindal, who had completed the three-hour trip from the Midlands without a hitch, received the SOC man's starchy greeting without enthusiasm. He knew he was trespassing in making his presence felt at the scene like this, but he had to know. They would have sent in a video man immediately, and the local investigating officer would have this to work with until the Scientific Support Unit were happy to let him trample over everything. He suppressed the urge to tell the intense, white-suited men not to bother wasting valuable time and resources in fingerprinting; it was not within his remit. He would let the Hampshire police have their head despite knowing in his bones that it was likely to lead nowhere.

Above, on the first floor, he heard creaking boards and muffled voices. Soon more officers would arrive; more man hours wasted in the investigation he had led fruitlessly for what seemed like years and which was beginning to cast a long, dark shadow over his every waking minute. But, for a moment, he was alone in the room. And so he stood and surveyed the jumbled array of inanimate contents as he had surveyed so many other rooms.

Across from him stood a mahogany-effect wall unit cluttered with pot plants, photographs of a family flanked by separate portraits of two girls in caps and gowns, and a battered midi hi-fi system next to an untidy stack of tapes and CDs. Beneath the small bay window, a bookshelf groaned under the strain of a hundred paperbacks, copies of *Nature* and, on either end, heavier tomes in the shape of textbooks on human biology and zoology, various cookery books and travelogues.

Behind the door stood an ancient upright piano, lid open, keys yellowed with age. On top stood the pewter bowl, its contents disgorged by some act of violence.

In the centre of the room, on a small round table, a bundle of papers lay scattered next to a Liberty-print shopping bag lying on its side. Tindal moved forward into the room and looked down on to the table, stepping over an upturned chair as he did so. A red felt-tipped pen was open next to a handwritten answer paper. The script looked immature, the word *proteen* underlined in red. It didn't take a Mensa membership to see that she had been marking when the intruder disturbed her.

Footsteps clattered down the stairs. Tindal turned and saw

Superintendent Jack Lyons enter from the hallway where a uniformed man hovered uncomfortably, his radio crackling intermittently. Lyons was only a couple of inches taller than Tindal, but his large frame looked muscular and well tended. A moustache sprouted on his upper lip. Like the receding hairline, it seemed incongruous in his otherwise boyish face.

'Morning, sir.' Lyons' greeting was perfunctory.

'I don't suppose there is any real doubt, is there?' asked Tindal wearily.

Lyons shook his head. 'First time in a victim's home, admittedly. But otherwise everything's the same.'

'Where is she?'

Lyons made eyes over Tindal's head. 'Kitchen, sir,' he paused fractionally before adding.

'They're waiting to take the body . . .'

'I'm sure,' said Tindal dismissively. 'How did he get in?'

Lyons sighed. 'Back door. She was marking answer papers. The hi-fi was still on. My guess is she didn't even hear him come in through the kitchen. No doubt about it. Looks like he hit her with the Mace in here as she stood. She fell back and he overpowered her before dragging her through to the kitchen.'

Tindal followed the path traced by Lyon's finger. 'Anyone see anything?'

Lyons shook his head. 'There's a small cul-de-sac behind. Couple of lockups, otherwise it's just an empty space. There's a high wall at the back of this terrace. Not easy to see into the lane at the best of times. But surprise, surprise, the streetlight was vandalised a couple of weeks ago.'

'No prizes for guessing who by,' said Tindal sourly. 'Any sign of forced entry?'

'None. Either the door was open, or he had a key. My guess is that he's been here once already. Inside even. Neighbours said she kept a spare over the lintel. He probably used that, or got a spare cut.'

Tindal was shaking his head and massaging his eyeballs. After a short pause he asked, 'Who found her?'

'Couple of colleagues called at eight. They used to give her a lift to work at the local comprehensive. Couldn't get an answer so they assumed she'd slept late. One of them came round the back. There's a door from the garden into the lane at the rear. The kitchen door was open . . .'

'It would be,' said Tindal bitterly. He swivelled round and pointed at an opaque glass door recessed into a narrow archway. 'This it?'

Lyons nodded.

'OK, let's get it over with,' he exhaled.

Lyons pushed past him and opened the door, which was already ajar, with the tip of a ballpoint he took from his pocket.

She was lying on a worktop peninsula that jutted out from the far wall two-thirds of the way across the room. With a flashing glance, Tindal took in neat spice racks, gleaming sink and pans hanging from butchers' hooks in the ceiling before his eyes were drawn to the shrouded body. She had been laid out, legs propped on a stool, arms neatly across her chest. It looked as though an undertaker had been there, but Tindal knew that no one had touched the body. This was the way he liked to leave them. All ready for the police inspection.

The metallic smell of blood was stronger here, and there was a lot of it. A large square table against the opposite wall was coated with it. Tindal saw four ragged splinters evenly distributed where he had used the nails to pin her. He dragged his eyes away, but blood was everywhere. It had run in slick rivulets down the sides of the peninsula into a thick, congealing lake on the floor.

Stepping gingerly around the black pools, Lyons went ahead along the sterile path marked out by the SOC team so that the scene would not be contaminated. As Tindal looked on over his shoulder, Lyons pulled back the sheet that covered her face. There was little or no resemblance to the graduate photograph of the young girl so full of hope and expectations. Death by asphyxiation was inevitably gruesome. Here it had bloated and inflated her head and transformed the peaches-and-cream complexion into a dusky, livid plum. The ligature marks were dark deep crevices in her neck, the ligature itself absent, as in all the other cases. Probably a favoured instrument, well kept and cherished by its owner. Mucus and slime matted her upper lip, but Tindal's gaze had already shifted to her eyes. The lids were puffed but open and between them, where there should have been sightless eyes, there glistened pools of black blood. His trademark. As if, in death, he could no longer bear for his victims to witness what there was left to do. And so he would remove them and fill the sockets with blood that poured from countless wounds and let it clot there. Like black, viscid pennies.

'Bastard,' said Tindal and automatically looked up, searching the walls. It was there over the sink. A single, large, curving figure. The experts said he used his nondominant hand just to confuse. This time it was a six.

'They've already bagged the hands,' said Lyons.

Tindal glanced down at the large plastic bags secured around the hands and forearms.

'They weren't happy about leaving the head – I thought the Scientific Support Unit people were going to throw a wobbly – but the pathologist understood. I told him you'd want to see.'

'Put it back,' he said numbly.

Lyons hesitated. 'Don't you want to . . .'

Tindal was already turning away, but he shook his head slowly. 'He's done the same, hasn't he?'

'Exactly,' said Lyons.

'Then I don't want to see it. I've seen it too many times already.' Tindal was a hardened veteran, but he had no desire to see this young girl without nipples, nor search in her throat for her eyes, nor examine her intestines splayed out . . .

He walked back into the living room and stared at a screen print of a girl on a beach under a lowering sky.

'Is there anything here worth me knowing about?' he asked without turning round.

'She's taller than most of the others. More like Jilly Grant if you ask me.'

Tindal swung round, his eyes narrowing. 'You sure?'

Lyons nodded. 'Looks like she put up a bit of a struggle too. Bruises on her forearms and at least three broken fingernails. Pathologist said there might be some skin.'

Tindal smiled for the first time that day. 'Get it pushed through as quick as you can.' He turned again to contemplate the room. 'But why did he come here? In her own house of all places. It's bloody risky.'

'Not for him. He will have done his homework, sir. And', he added darkly, 'it's been a long time. Perhaps he was hungry.'

Tindal was brooding, still unconvinced. 'But to come in off the street like that.'

'I've already spoken to the psychologist. He used a word, uh, decompensation, something like that.'

'Don't come at me with that stuff, Jack. It's too early in the morning.'

'OK. Then my opinion is that he did it just to show us he could.'

Tindal nodded grimly. 'Who is the local man?'

'Chap called Stamper. Ex-Met. Bit excitable but decent enough.'

'Right. I'd better pay my respects before I go and face the music in London. I don't mind telling you, Jack, I've been dreading this. There'll be a backlash and it'll bring out the worst in people. Sensible coppers I've known for years are going to come out with the most ludicrous stuff. I'm just waiting for someone to suggest a bloody clairvoyant.' Tindal walked towards the door but stopped on the threshold, remembering something he hadn't asked.

'What was her name?'

'Terry. Alison Terry.'

The seminar room at the Ellison Institute of Psychiatry, nestling unprepossessingly in the shadow of the Post Office tower in West London, was two-thirds full. Dr Natalie Vine, Reader in Forensic Psychiatry, sat near the rear of what had originally been the Regency building's drawing room. She was thirty-nine years old and managed to keep her five feet eight inches reasonably trim thanks to a disciplined approach to circuit training at an Islington gym. She used her heavy-lidded hazel eyes to scan the ceiling for the hundredth time, trying her best not to get irritated by the inane questioner who currently held the floor and was buttonholing the speaker. There were still some very attractive ceiling roses in the building, and there was no doubt that the huge windows were original. That was obvious from the chilly draughts of February air that gusted through them, despite the heavy, lined curtains.

She let her gaze fall to the audience again and caught the eyes of one of the psychology students, who had been watching her, flick away. She let a tiny smile curl the corner of her lips. She had no idea of his name but he was tall and loose-limbed with longer hair than she herself had. She had noticed how the three girl students always hung around him and she supposed she should be flattered. He could not have been more than twenty-two. Young enough to be her –

Oh, come off it, Natalie. There was no way on earth you were ever going to have a child at seventeen.

True. Then she would just have to accept that the good bones she had inherited from her father still held a modicum of attraction. She let her eyes drift across the rows of seats arranged five deep, with a central aisle for access to the projection area behind. It was not a bad turnout for a cold February lunch time.

The twenty-odd audience consisted of a handful of hollow-eyed final-year zealots from University College, with which the Institute had been summarily amalgamated three years before. They sat in the front with notepads open. In the centre rows a group of eight senior clinical lecturers were clustered attentively, their presence no doubt due more to the constant threat of further departmental cuts than to academic enthusiasm. Both senior lecturers were there. It would be unthinkable for them not to be since one of them was responsible for organising these post-graduate seminars and the other was a personal friend of the speaker. With them, in front of Vine, were the six psychology students who had been hanging around for two terms trying to glean some clinical experience. They included the boy who seemed to be finding Dr Vine more interesting than the lecture.

As Reader, Dr Vine's presence was a welcome bonus. Her status was such that no apology for her absence would be either expected or given. But she did make an effort to attend whenever circumstances allowed, which was more than could be said for many departmental members. However, in this instance, there was a genuine element of interest involved. Dr Richard Glazer PhD was a criminal psychologist from Towerlake State Hospital in Massachusetts and had academic links with *the* clinical psychiatrists in Harvard. 'Neuropsychological and Organic Predictors of Murder and Extreme Violence' was his brief. This was not the usual lightweight slide show and the talk had been excellent, which was more than could be said for the insistent questioner who now had them all squirming in their seats.

The two notable features about the audience were the absence of the departmental head, Professor Falkirk, which was not surprising, and the presence of Professor Johan Zilvan, which was. The latter, a cantankerous, opinionated goblin of a man from King's, had dined out for years on one abortive consultation demanded of him by Scotland Yard in the Hindley case. Natalie knew that he felt a misguided obligation to turn up at any venue where the topic under discussion verged on excessively violent crime and his welcome absence from recent Ellison programmes had lulled everyone into a false sense of security. Nearing retirement, he alone continued to consider himself an expert. His colleagues and peers had long ago relinquished this opinion and his only redeeming feature as far as Vine was concerned was his loathing for Falkirk. Zilvan knew him for what he was, a leech who lived off the hard work done by other members of the department, and on more than one occasion had seen fit to voice his feelings. But then, thought Natalie, it took one to know one.

So far, the meeting had been an enjoyable one, made all the more pleasurable for Natalie by Falkirk's absence. The lecturer had been a little dry, but had adopted only a moderately didactic style that had been almost without flaw. Certainly nothing Natalie had felt obliged to pick up on.

Zilvan, however, had harboured no such reticence. Once Glazer had thrown the floor open for questioning, Zilvan had waded in with sabre drawn. To his credit, the lecturer was holding his ground, but Zilvan was relentless in his attempt to draw

Glazer out of his sphere of knowledge towards his own speciality. So far, Zilvan had yet to allow a question from anyone else.

He was leaning forward in his chair, his large, protuberant eyes ablaze as he fired another question at Glazer.

'Your implication seems to be that substance abuse is therefore a direct predictor of antisocial behaviour. I would argue that this high correlation is purely a North American phenomenon.'

Glazer grinned. 'I can't comment on your rates of abuse. All I can say is that in our study the correlation was approaching 40 per cent. You will know, too, that other workers have suggested that substance abuse may interact with specific neuropsychological impairment to substantially increase the likelihood of violence.'

Zilvan was shaking his head and smiling a sad smile that showed his tobacco-stained teeth.

'Then they are not syringe-toting, Neanderthal school dropouts?'

'Intelligence is another matter altogether. It seems to be no safeguard against antisocial behaviour. Of the eighty or so in our study, their crimes ranged from aggravated assault to recreational murder. The intellectual levels show mid-range scores across the board.'

Zilvan's eyes glittered. The fish was beginning to take the bait.

'So you are not suggesting we arrest everyone with a flat forehead and mishapen teeth who has ever sucked in a lungful of marijuana?' He laughed at his own joke before adding venomously, 'It would not be original. The Third Reich had similar ideas.'

At least half a dozen people in the audience turned round to stare at him incredulously. Zilvan lapped it up.

'So tell me, Dr Glazer . . .'

Here it comes, thought Natalie, the part we've all been waiting for.

'. . . does your research throw any light on the neuropsychological predisposition that some individuals might have towards being the victims of acts of violence?'

Glazer frowned, 'Uhhh, not really, I –'

'You see,' continued Zilvan, 'in my own small field of investigation into lust murder – uh, you did have one or two lust murderers in your studied group, I believe?'

Glazer nodded, the smile beginning to fade from his lips.

Zilvan pressed on. 'In my own small field, I have come to the conclusion that organic dysfunction is distinctly lacking. Moreover it is my opinion that it is the interaction between victim and murderer which is the key trigger. I would go so far as to say that in some instances it is in fact the predisposition, neuropsychological or otherwise, of the victim that triggers an otherwise sane if paraphilic individual into extreme violence. What would you say to that?'

Glazer had reddened visibly. 'I know that there is some evidence to show that –'

'There is a Darwinian element,' continued Zilvan. 'One can see it developing in the schoolyard. As early as five or six it is possible to detect those children who will bully and those who will be bullied. I would go so far as to suggest that the true sociopath has developed traits by the age of two. Likewise the victim. But without the weak to prey on, the sociopath has nowhere to go. Perhaps we should be turning our attention towards eliminating the weak as opposed to punishing the excessively strong.'

Glazer was staring, completely nonplussed by Zilvan's bizarre statements. They were so unbelievably crass that he felt like either laughing or screaming. Instead, a slow smile spread across his face as he pushed himself off the table he had been perching on.

'Much as I would love to answer your question, I feel a little out of my depth. However, I am aware that we have Dr Natalie Vine at the rear, and knowing too of her acknowledged expertise in the field of psychopathy, I wonder if she would care to comment?' Glazer searched the audience until his eyes locked on Natalie's.

'Uh, Dr Vine?'

Good for you, Dr Glazer.

Natalie kept her eyes on Glazer's, although she could feel Zilvan's boring into the side of her head.

'Thank you, Dr Glazer. I'm sure that Professor Zilvan's experience in lust murder is well known to us. However, I can only assume that he continues to propound his theory so as to be deliberately controversial and to trigger meaningful discussion. In that sense, I applaud him. But we cannot ignore the fact that hereditary and hormonal factors as well as abnormal family dynamics all play a part in predisposition. True, there are some overlaps with recurrent head trauma in certain cases, and in general with neurotic disorders such as compulsive behaviour, and indeed with antisocial dysfunctions. But in the context of sexual sadism we are playing semantic games when we use terms such as sociopathic since by its very nature sadism is antisocial.'

Natalie took a breath. She was on a roll and she knew it.

'Regarding victims, admittedly the NIMH studies in your own country have suggested that victims of sexual assault may have higher rates of mental disorders. But again, when applied to lust murder the figures are meaningless. If the questioner is implying that we can ever predict who is likely to be the victim of lust murder, I would say that this is ludicrous. Unless you consider gender as a predisposition. But as yet, I do not think that being female is classifiable as a neuropsychological disorder.'

The audience laughed. Glazer beamed. Zilvan sat with his arms folded staring straight ahead. She hoped she had not been too sardonic. Zilvan was a dangerous man to make an enemy of.

One of the psychology students had raised a hand and Glazer was speaking again, safe on familiar ground. Behind her, Natalie saw the door open and a secretary stick her head round. A beckoning finger pointed at her and she crept out.

'Message from Prof. Falkirk. Could he see you please?'

'What, now?'

The secretary nodded. 'He said it was urgent.'

Natalie thanked her and glanced back into the seminar room. Glazer would have to fend for himself for a while.

Chapter 3

Tindal sat legs crossed in Falkirk's office at the Institute. The Professor was vainly attempting to disguise his disappointment at learning that it was Dr Natalie Vine who Tindal was there to see and not himself. Professor Falkirk's welcome had been effusive and the policeman had received the uncomfortable impression that he was in the company of a man who had been expecting the director of a nationwide murder enquiry to walk through his door any day for the last thirty years.

Of average height, wiry and with the whining remnant of an Edinburgh accent, Falkirk was approaching his late fifties. A large part of his life's ambitions remained unfulfilled. He had pale, freckled, waxy skin that was almost translucent above the orange goatee that was there, at least in part surmised Tindal, to hide a generously protuberent chin. Washed-out pale blue eyes kept scanning Tindal's face for the moment when the policeman would admit that it was all a huge mistake and it was, of course, Falkirk they wanted. The eyes scanned in vain.

'You, ah, do of course understand that almost all of Dr Vine's work has been in collaboration with myself? I do not include my name on all publications for fear of, ah, appearing, how shall I put it?, avaricious. The academic world is full of such, ah, venal behaviour.'

'That's very generous of you, Professor,' Tindal smiled graciously, 'but our people also think that a female approach might be more suitable.'

Falkirk's bland smile never slipped. He stared into Tindal's eyes, daring him to reconsider, before saying, 'I see. It appears that in this instance the weaker sex has the upper hand. However,

I do feel I should point out to you certain of my misgivings, since I would not wish for such an important investigation to be put in jeapardy because of any misguided loyalty towards Dr Vine on my part.'

'I would expect you to be nothing but candid,' said Tindal.

'Natalie has a complicated personality. She has difficulty sustaining relationships. Her colleagues find her, ah, challenging.'

'Are you telling me she's not up to this?'

'Far be it for me . . . Academically she has shown signs of brilliance, but on a personal level there are problems. She had a difficult childhood. I have had the opportunity of glancing at her medical files – part of my brief in employing her, you understand. Her, ah, mother was, ah, an alcoholic with mental complications. Under stress, there may be a tendency to over-react . . .'

You bastard, thought Tindal.

'But you must make up your own mind. I feel I have, ah, discharged my duty. And I shall simply add that if there proves to be a problem, I would be only too happy to advise. Shall I send for her now?'

'If you wouldn't mind,' Tindal had remained impassive, but he couldn't help the uncomfortable feeling he had under his suit. The last time he had experienced anything similar was in the reptile house at Regent's Park.

Falkirk backed out of the room. 'I'll get my secretary to provide you with some, ah, coffee. I'm sure Dr Vine will not be long.'

While Falkirk made arrangements for refreshments, Tindal was left with his own serpentine thoughts. The meeting that morning in London had proved as frustrating as he had expected it to be. No one had any new ideas apart from the psychologist. He was the one who had brought up Vine's name and the consensus was that they had nothing to lose by talking to her. So here was muggins having to pander to a lot of trick cyclists. They made him nervous at the best of times, and if Falkirk was anything to go by –

His thoughts were interrupted by the Professor himself, who

24

entered with a tray and two mugs. Tindal had barely had time to spoon in a couple of sugars when the door opened to admit the woman he was there to see. He saw a thin, polite smile break open a broad face made striking by excellent bones and severe eyebrows three shades darker than her short fair hair. The smile arrived fractionally late, allowing an ill-humoured frown to accompany the woman into the room. Tindal had the distinct impression that the delay had been no accident.

'You wanted to see me, John?' Her voice was curt, the potentially pleasing tone edged with irritation as if she was there on sufferance from something much more important.

Falkirk had risen to greet her. His reply came with an apologetic laugh that, Tindal perceived, might become irritating in the extreme should their contact be prolonged.

'Ah, Natalie. Sorry for the royal summons.'

The woman's smile was fixed. Tindal saw anything but amusement in her eyes. If Falkirk saw it too he decided to ignore it and turned to begin a faltering introduction.

'Ah, Dr Natalie Vine, this is Assistant Chief Constable Tindal of, ah, West Midlands Police.'

She took his hand in a firm, dry shake, her fingers long and ringless. Tindal smiled in greeting, wondering if it was the heavy lids that gave her an air of defiant coldness.

'I've, ah, been telling Mr Tindal all about you. Although I needn't have bothered. Your fame, it appears, has spread and gone before you,' Falkirk beamed sycophantically.

Tindal grimaced inwardly at the patronising tone and found himself sympathising easily with Vine's frown.

'Really?' said Vine aridly.

'Perhaps', interjected Tindal, 'it might be better if I explained exactly why I'm here, Dr Vine.'

'I'm all ears.' The smile remained politely dry.

Tindal turned to Falkirk. 'Is there somewhere Dr Vine and I could talk in private, Professor Falkirk?'

Unbelievably, Falkirk blushed before blurting, 'Uh, of course, by all means stay here. Stay here, ah, use my office. Take as long as you like.'

'That's most generous of you.'

Falkirk's smile had become almost a grimace as he carried the charade of politeness through to its conclusion. 'My secretary will bring some coffee for you, Natalie.'

Tindal nodded and watched the door close behind Falkirk. When they were alone, Natalie said, 'Could you make him jump through a burning hoop as well?'

Tindal suppressed a smile. 'Dr Vine, I'm sorry to have to take up your time. I appreciate how irritating it must be to have your work interrupted, but I'm afraid there was no opportunity to arrange an appointment.' He smiled and then added, 'Pulling rank is a perk of the job.'

'Obviously,' said Vine.

Tindal studied her momentarily. The data he had on her had suggested a plump bookworm to his imagination. The colouring was the same, but thirty or so of the hundred and forty pounds hanging on a tallish frame had been shed. The effect was disarming. 'Aren't you even the slightest bit intrigued as to why I'm here?'

'I've been meaning to pay those parking fines . . .'

Tindal laughed and saw a perfunctory smile touch her lips. He thought about adding a retort of his own but forgot about it when her smile disappeared and she said impatiently, 'Could we get on with this? I have two lectures to prepare for a conference next week.'

'Frankfurt?'

Vine's eyes narrowed suspiciously. 'What is this all about?'

'Thomas Meredith.'

'Meredith?' Her eyes widened.

Tindal nodded. 'It would be fair to say that you are familiar with his case?'

'Of course.'

'He is, you'll agree, a difficult man to get to.'

'Difficult would qualify as the understatement of the year.'

Tindal reached into a briefcase and took out some photostats. 'I think I would be correct in saying that your interest in Meredith stems from his status as a victim?'

She made no comment.

Tindal removed a set of half-moon spectacles from his inside pocket and began to read. '"Prevalence of Adult Sexual Assault in an Inner-City area", Vine and Trewyn; "Recovery Rates in Attempted Homicide Survivors", Vine et al.; "Battered women and Resistance to Medicalisation", Wilson, Vine and Falkirk . . . The list is seemingly endless.'

Natalie sighed again. 'My interests are the reactional, emotional and psychiatric factors consequent to violence. "Victim"', she made inverted commas in the air with two fingers of each hand, 'is a slight oversimplification.'

'I'm a simple man, Doctor.'

'Then tell me in simple terms what exactly I can do for you?'

'I'm here to ask for your help.'

'With Meredith?' She guffawed. 'Meredith won't talk to me. He doesn't talk to anyone. You know that. I managed once to get hold of him on the phone. It was a very brief but colourful conversation. He hasn't replied to any of my subsequent letters. But why this sudden resurgence of interest in him anyway? I thought you'd sucked him dry. Surely your own people have –'

Tindal's hard grey eyes stopped her in mid-sentence. 'Your reason for contacting him was purely academic, I take it?'

'Purely.'

'Mind telling me what you know about him?'

Natalie stared for a long five seconds at a February snow-covered Alpine mountain range on Falkirk's Swiss landscape calendar before answering in a bored voice, 'Thirty-three, unmarried, heterosexual. Both parents deceased. Two healthy siblings older than him, both married. He has no record of criminal activity and is of above average intelligence. His current situation is evidence of the practical effects of his depression. His work record was excellent; he was a rising star in the medical firmament until –'

Tindal held up his hand. 'Forget the biog. Tell me about the until.'

'Until he and his girlfriend were attacked by . . .' Natalie paused and looked up at Tindal with distaste. '"The Carpenter"?'

Tindal acknowledged her query with a frown. 'The press love this one, as you know.'

'My understanding was that Meredith had co-operated,' said Vine irritatedly.

'Oh he's talked all right, but nowhere near enough.'

'But he has talked.'

Tindal let some air escape from his mouth in a derisory laugh, his eyes momentarily straying upwards towards the false ceiling.

'A cold, factual account. Cold, factual and harrowing enough to make twenty-year veterans balk at it. I've had to force some of them to wade through –'

'They wouldn't let me see any of it,' she interrupted truculently.

'It's part of an ongoing and therefore restricted. But apart from that, they'd take one look at you and not want to let you anywhere near it.'

'I've done attachments at Broadmoor and Rampton,' protested Vine. 'I've had access to all the files there. Surely –'

Tindal held up his hands. 'I know all that. And I'm sure on paper my colleagues do too. But it's a reflection of the way they feel about this case. Most of them, and I'm talking about hardened murder-squad detectives in Bath, Liverpool and my own patch, have told me unequivocally that it's one of the worst cases they've had to deal with.' He paused, stopping himself from straying too far off the point he was wanting to make.

'Meredith's first-hand account changed everything. Before that all we had were bodies. Mutilated bodies admittedly, but most of us had wanted to believe that he did the bulk of it after death, despite what forensics were coming up with. Now we *know* he does it to them when they're alive.'

Vine frowned. 'So what do you want from me?'

A secretary knocked and entered with a tray of coffee. She poured a cup for Natalie and refreshed Tindal's before leaving as quietly as she had entered.

Tindal hoisted a hip on to the corner of Falkirk's desk and picked up a glass paperweight, twirling it in his fingers.

'Assistant chief constables are usually administrators. High-profile penpushers waiting for promotion. But when there is a crime of this magnitude, one that crosses borders, a senior officer is seconded to co-ordinate the investigation.'

'Congratulations,' said Vine.

Tindal responded with an icy stare, but Vine's mildly inquisitive expression didn't change. Being at the helm of this inquiry was a dubious honour and there was no point pretending otherwise. Still, Tindal was stung to respond by the ease with which she had seen through his mask.

'That's the thing about psychiatrists, isn't it? Always observing. Sometimes seeing a little too much perhaps.'

Vine allowed herself a wry smile. 'Surely you're not one of those people who think we can see through walls?'

'You're trained to see things other people wouldn't notice. Some people don't like the thought of having the way they talk and sit and look analysed into an assessment of whether or not they wanted to sleep with their mother.'

She folded her arms and snorted deprecatingly.

'Sorry,' he said. 'That was uncalled-for.'

She reached forward for her cup and swallowed a mouthful of coffee.

Tindal, unsure as to whether or not she was offended, tried again. 'He killed for the first time in Birmingham eighteen months ago. That's when I became involved. But the way it works is that each separate incident is investigated independently by local officers.' He stopped twirling the paperweight and fixed Vine with an empty stare. 'We are not making progress, Doctor.'

'So where do I fit in?' asked Vine sardonically. 'I'm an academic. To me patients are merely pages of illegibly scribbled diagnoses between ragged sheets of buff cardboard.'

Tindal remained silent, giving Vine her head.

'Surely whoever filled you in on me was thorough enough to have told you that too?' she asked.

'That and a lot more.'

'So?'

'So hear me out. The facts, as we know them.' Tindal sat forward and drank his coffee in two large gulps. And despite herself, Vine listened, her own coffee growing cold and oily in its cup.

'Friday, September twenty-fourth, late evening. Meredith and his girlfriend Jilly Grant were driving home from Bath to Grant's house in Wick, just outside Bristol. They were travelling across quiet country roads, Jilly at the wheel. A police motorcycle patrol signalled them to stop. Jilly was breaking the speed limit and so, naturally enough, they pulled over, expecting a reprimand or at worst a ticket. The patrolman approached and they noticed that he was wearing a Balaclava under his helmet against the cold. Unusual, but after a gloriously sunny autumn day it was bitter that night with a ground frost. Meredith remembers only that he was of medium height. The jacket he wore obscured his upper body. He called Meredith out of the car to check a rear light. His voice was muffled, unrecognisable. The patrolman knelt at the light, and Meredith joined him. It looked perfectly normal and as he turned his face up to question the patrolman, something was sprayed into it. We now know it was chloroacetophenone, more commonly known as Mace. Meredith fell to the ground, blinded, clutching his face. You ever experienced it?'

Tindal's eyes were bright, the corners of his mouth curling in a tight smile. 'You can't do anything. It burns your throat, sears your eyes and nose. Very effective weapon.' There was something almost accusatory in his tone, goading her to respond. She didn't comment and he went on with his harrowing account.

'Meredith was struck several times about the head, not quite to unconsciousness, then gagged and handcuffed. Jilly got out to see what was going on and got the same treatment. They were driven to an empty farmhouse two miles away, only five miles from Jilly's house. The farmhouse had been empty for two years, but a room had been prepared – swept clean in readiness.

'He kept Jilly Grant alive for fifteen hours. It was a Saturday, cold and wet. No one came near the place. She was blindfolded and gagged except when he wanted her to say things or when he was sticking things in her mouth. Meredith was gagged too, but he was kept blindfolded only some of the time. Occasionally, the blindfold was removed so that he could see what was being done to Jilly. The murderer wore a robe, thin and white, tied around the middle. Probably hand-made, something he would burn later to get rid of the bloodstains. It was worn ankle-length and it was hooded. Tall, pointed hood with eyeholes – possibly Ku Klux Klan inspired. Cheap white plimsoles on his feet, again probably used once and burned afterwards.

'The room was blacked out so as to keep the light from being seen outside. But lights there were, so that he could take photographs. Looked like a Nikon to Meredith, tripod-mounted with a hand remote.'

'Tape recorder?' asked Vine.

'He recorded everything,' affirmed Tindal coldly. The tight smile was still there. It was almost as though he was getting some vindictive pleasure from his answers. 'And he was very, very careful. The nails he used on Grant had been removed from the woodwork in the farmhouse. He wore a condom for the rape and gloves all the way through. There were no traceable body fluids except those of Meredith and Grant. No bite marks. All the trauma was mechanically delivered with instruments. Most of the injuries were inflicted before death by strangulation,' he concluded coldly, his eyes still bright and challenging, willing her to respond.

'What did he do after she died?' she asked calmly.

'He took her eyes out. Has done in every case.'

Vine nodded and looked down at Tindal's hands. She watched his thumbnails play against one another repetitively.

'He spent less than ten minutes on Meredith,' continued Tindal. 'The intention was obviously to let Meredith survive, but even so he suffered considerable internal injuries. There was anal foreign-body penetration that was violent in the extreme. Meredith required a defunctioning colostomy until things healed that end. Now I think he's more or less back to normal.'

'Back to normal?' said Vine incredulously.

'Physically, I meant.'

Vine said nothing but her eyes were heavy with scepticism. Tindal added, 'He won't speak to our psychiatrists. Flat refusal.'

'It's hardly surprising.'

'Oh?' said Tindal.

And Vine knew he was fishing. Knew she was taking his bait.

He would have been told all this already by whichever Home Office psychologist they'd have consulted.

'Guilt. He survived, Jilly didn't. It took thirty years for some of the Auschwitz survivors to even begin talking about what they saw. Rehabilitating Meredith is going to take years.'

'We haven't got years,' said Tindal darkly. 'This animal is a torturer. A sexual sadist. He likes what he does. Likes killing people. Your colleagues, even in this esteemed place, have no adequate name for him.' His voice dropped to a lower, slower level. 'And I want to put an end to it.'

There was a pause while Vine tried to assimilate what Tindal was implying by all this.

'You need a profile of the murderer?' she asked.

Tindal shook his head. 'I already have profiles. What I need to know is why Meredith is alive. Why the pattern was broken with him. I need to know what's in his mind. Something he might not even be aware of himself. Something he saw or heard that might help us. But he won't let us in there. That's why I'm here, Dr. Vine.'

He stood and paced, the paperweight still the focus of his attention. 'I've had all the standard spiel. The killer's profile is full of nebulous statistics I can recite off by heart. Afro-Caribbean male, right-handed. Fifty per cent chance of parental divorce, 40 per cent of homosexual experience. Bright, has some anatomical knowledge, but most of them do. We know only one thing for certain, that he's a police buff – the motorcycle, handcuffs, etc. But it's too thin. We need something concrete, something to bite on.'

'Could he be a policeman?'

Tindal shook his head. Vine remained silent for a moment, watching Tindal evenly.

'We've checked every officer. There aren't that many black patrolmen.'

'So, as I said, where do I fit in?' she asked eventually.

'Our people have looked at Meredith from as near as he'll let them get, which is about four miles downwind.' He paused, mindful of her previous outburst over his knowledge of her. He let another slow smile appear before adding, 'I know that you are an academic, and a good one by all accounts. But we both know that you have extensive experience in interview techniques. Also, I have been reliably informed that a female approach might be better received.'

Vine shook her head. 'Have you any idea how patronising that sounds? Female approach? Who on earth have you been talking to, some local radio station agony aunt?'

'We want you to consult for us, Doctor.'

'I have commitments, lectures, a conference in ten days –'

'That can all be taken care of.'

This time it was Vine who stood up and paced. The spectre of Zilvan loomed threateningly on her mental horizon. 'There are other specialists in this field. Why me?'

'I would have thought that someone in your position would jump at the chance of helping to catch this lunatic,' said Tindal smoothly.

'Answer the question. Why me?'

'Because you come highly recommended . . . And the others aren't as hungry as you.'

'Hungry?'

Tindal checked himself. 'You have specialised skills.'

Vine's eyes narrowed cynically. 'Oh, yes. You just give me twenty minutes with Meredith and we'll have a colour Photofit you can transmit on *The Nine O'Clock News*. We'll have our man behind bars in no time at all, Sheriff.'

There was a long pause as they stared at one another calculatingly.

'You're female, separated, thirty-nine years old,' said Tindal finally. 'A reader for the past five of those years. Would you say you have a good working relationship with Professor Falkirk?'

Vine flushed. 'What is that supposed to mean?'

'It means you'll have standard expenses, a fat consultation fee and full access to everything we have on Meredith and The Carpenter – exclusively.'

'I'm a doctor, not a journalist.' The words rushed out, but she could hear her pulse drumming in her ears.

33

'And I can almost smell your frustration in this place. I am told case studies like this are very rare. Isn't that why you were chasing Meredith in the first instance?'

Vine didn't reply. Tindal saw the colour flare in her cheeks. His sources had told him that this last point was the one, if there was one, that would make her sit up and take notice. He could almost see her mind racing, imagining what she could do with such a gold mine of material. He measured her silence and then decided to get tough.

'Fine. If you're too stubborn to admit to me that you're wasting your time supporting a second-rate department in this mausoleum, so be it. You and I both know what this could mean for you, and frankly this holier-than-thou charade of yours is boring me. So let's try massaging your gleaming conscience with this. Think of what's going to happen unless we stop him, because he isn't going to stop himself.'

'You can't be sure of that. It's been five months since –'

Tindal's face suddenly hardened and Vine sensed that she'd touched a nerve again. He regained his composure, then said, 'This is not a game. I'm asking you to go into a very dark place. Whatever you've read or seen before, this is going to be worse because he isn't locked up behind three sets of security doors. He's out there, waiting, planning, loving every obscene minute of it. I've been told that you can do this, that underneath you've got a good, disciplined mind. I hope to God you have, because you're going to need it. This monster thinks this is one huge game. He thinks he's above us mortals, and by normal standards, he is. But he'll make a mistake. My bet is he already has in letting Meredith live.' Tindal's eyes blazed with anger. 'I want you to be prepared to do whatever you have to to get whatever is in Meredith's mind. Now, do you think you can hack it, Doctor?'

'You wouldn't be here if you didn't think I could, am I right?' she responded.

Tindal's firmness didn't waver. 'Are you up to it?'

Vine hesitated only momentarily. It was, she knew, an opportunity that could not be declined without years of self-recrimination. She heard herself say, 'Yes, I am.'

34

Tindal held her gaze, defying her to drop her eyes first.

'What about social encumbrances?'

'You know I'm unmarried.'

'That doesn't answer my question.'

'It's not a problem.' She held his stare steadily.

Tindal relaxed first.

'Jilly was his eighth. That means eight that we know of.'

'Eight?'

'You're going to have to be careful. Not draw too much attention to yourself. We've got the press on a tight reign, but there's always one cowboy out for a story. They've been sniffing around Meredith for months.'

'Surely you're going to tell people about the approach – his disguise as a policeman?'

'We may have to,' said Tindal tightly.

'But –'

'But what? Can you imagine what that could do? No one would stop for a police motorcyclist any more, or any policeman for that matter.'

Vine paused, gathering her thoughts before saying: 'I'll do this. I want to do it. But you're still not happy, are you?'

'You come very highly recommended, Doctor.'

'That's the second time you've said that and it doesn't answer my question.'

Tindal dropped his gaze momentarily, caught out for once. 'I'll be honest with you. Involving a woman was not my idea. And I still don't like it.'

'Oh dear. Haven't you read that little sentence that ends with "equal opportunity employer"?'

'You asked,' said Tindal.

Vine sighed. 'Aren't you making one huge assumption in all of this? I can't make Meredith talk to me if he doesn't want to.'

'Oh yes you can.'

'How?'

Tindal pulled a notebook and an italic felt-tip from his pocket.

On a clean sheet he drew:

6

Vine looked at it. 'Am I supposed to recognise this?'

'Pray to God you never see the real thing,' said Tindal. 'We found it on a wall above the remains of twenty-five-year-old teacher three days ago in Hampshire. It's his signature.'

'It's started again,' said Vine in a whisper.

By thy bloody and invisible hand.

'Policemen are human. When they see something beyond their understanding, they sometimes react to it inappropriately. When they first saw this killer's handiwork, the way he impales his victims' hands with nails, some lag commented humorously that it looked like a beserk carpenter had been let loose. The sobriquet stuck. This is The Carpenter's calling card. When my people found it in Birmingham the first time, they thought it was some kind of code. We know now what it means because Meredith told us. He wants recognition, wants to be admired. Our friend likes numbers. He marks himself out of ten. He gave himself an eight for his work on Jilly Grant. Eight out of ten for torturing a girl to death. This one only merited a six.'

Vine's expression had contracted into a scowl of distaste.

'There's a press conference this evening. It'll be headline news tomorrow morning. You need to get to Meredith with it first.' He paused before adding, 'I'll give you one last chance to pull out.' But he knew she wouldn't. He could tell from her eyes that he had hooked her.

She shook her head firmly and Tindal reached into his briefcase to pull out three folders. He wasn't smiling as he handed them over.

'The hard facts of every incident are in these files. In a nutshell, the evidence is very thin. You may remember the first case in Birmingham,' Tindal smiled wanly. 'That was when he started to lead us up the garden path. We went the whole hog, *Crimewatch*, the works. There was quite a lot of physical evidence at the scene. Red fibres and a matching bloodstained Liverpool Football Club

36

scarf fifty yards away. The blood was the victim's and it looked as if the scarf had been lost as the killer made his getaway. He left his mark on the wall and that too was written in the victim's blood.' Tindal's tone was calm and measured, but his eyes were blazing with anger.

'That first case also yielded some evidence of a struggle. There were marks on the victim's arms. Perhaps, since it was his first time, he was less controlled, I don't know. But we found traces of skin under her fingernails. It was highly pigmented and we were able to get a DNA profile from hair samples in the skin.'

Natalie was staring at him. 'The fact that he's black is unusual. Lust killers usually hunt within their own ethnic groups. Was Meredith able to confirm that?'

'It was a dark night. When the car was stopped, Meredith could only see two inches of face because of the bike rider's Balaclava that covered the nose too. He thought that what he saw was black. After that either Meredith was blindfolded or, when he wasn't, the killer had his hood on.'

'What about the scarf? It sounds almost too good to be true.'

'It does, I agree. At the time we thought we might be dealing with an opportunistic killer. One who could panic and make mistakes.' Tindal snorted. 'Know anything about Premier League soccer, Dr Vine?'

'My father was a Chelsea supporter and he used to watch *Match of the Day*, but it never did anything for me,' she said dismissively.

'Twenty-two teams, all from major cities. Liverpool is one of them. Every murder has taken place in or around a city with a Premier League team except for Jilly Grant's. Bristol and Bath don't have Premier League clubs, but in March Liverpool played Bristol City in a sixth-round FA Cup tie and as I explained, she was killed between Bristol and Bath.'

'But Jilly was killed in September. It's a tenuous link, isn't it?'

'Tenuous perhaps, but the evidence tallied.'

'So you know that he is a black football supporter and can ride a motorcycle.'

'There is more. The skin scrapings had hair and a small amount of blood, enough for us to get DNA and blood typing done. The blood type did throw up an anomaly. A positive, as in forty per cent of the population, but when they tested the sample for other blood groups, they come up with all sorts of problems. There were simply too many of them to come from one individual.'

'Are you telling me that more than one person was involved?'

Tindal shook his head. 'What I'm telling you is that the blood they found under that girl's nails came from more than one person, yes. But the concentrations were small. The lab boys came to the conclusion that it could have come from one person, but only if that person had had a transfusion. In transfusions, the ABO groups would naturally be matched. That was why we only found A positive. There are enough donors around these days to provide almost any combination of A, B or 0 positive or negative blood for those requiring it. And in a blood bank there would obviously be blood from a wide variety of donors. But this matching process doesn't extend to the other, minor blood groups.'

'A transfusion?' said Vine incredulously.

'The DNA probe on the blood sample came up with six separate sources. That means that this lunatic had been transfused with blood from five different donors.'

'Five? Are you saying that he's got something wrong with him? That he was in a hospital under treatment just before he did this?'

'That is one possibility.' Tindal remained grim-faced, watching her.

Slowly, Vine nodded as she realised what Tindal's silence implied. 'Or he transfused himself. There have been cases. It could be a power thing, almost vampiristic. Auto-haematofetishism is not uncommon in drug addicts. They get a sexual kick out of the sight and feel of their blood being drawn up into a syringe. But with this guy it could also be the assimilation of another's life source that turns him on. Very biblical,' she added drily. 'But it would mean that he had access to stored blood, wouldn't it?'

Tindal gave her a sideways glance and nodded before continuing.

'The scarf found at the first murder in Birmingham was new,

sold in thirty or so outlets in the city of Liverpool and in various franchises across the country. There are literally thousands of registered supporters of the club. We started to look for hospital employees, men linked to the slaughter trade, butchers, medical students. We have done extensive blood testing to eliminate anyone we suspected. We came up with nothing. But Premier League clubs have national followings. You're just as likely to find Liverpool supporters in Aberdeen as Plymouth.'

'What about the timing of the murders?'

'Liverpool have played in all of these cities over the last two years. The timing of each killing varies. Sometimes a week, sometimes two months after a visit by the team.'

'He's more measured about it – enjoying the planning as much as the act,' commented Vine. 'What about Meredith's case? Does the transfusion thing tie in anywhere?'

'We did begin wondering about a hospital connection in Bristol. We found some fibres on Grant's body consistent with the sheet Meredith described. It comes from a company called Lockston Textiles. Big company, one of five or six that supply vast amounts of linen to schools, hotels and the NHS. But we couldn't just look at coloured employees. It would have caused a riot. Almost four hundred men in the right age group volunteered for blood testing. We concentrated at first on those with motorcycle licences, but then widened the net. In the course of eighteen months we've taken twenty thousand statements, interviewed fifteen thousand people, mainly in the Midlands and Merseyside, but in Bristol too. I won't tell you how much money it's cost.' He shook his head again.

'And unless you've got another nice biological sample to compare them with, his blood type and DNA profile are useless. There have been no semen samples?'

'Never semen. As I said, he wears condoms. There could be some more skin samples from Southampton. She may have put up a fight as well. It's too early to say yet. But I'm dubious about the whole thing. This man is so careful. He's probably read more pathology books than you have. Perhaps he is a pathologist, or a surgeon, or a medical rep who visits these cities . . . I don't know.

All right, that first time he may have been out of control, made a mistake and dropped the scarf, but . . . I don't know. I just don't know.' Tindal sighed before glancing at the files and adding, 'Have a look through these. If there's anything else you need, you can get hold of me through the local CID either here or in Wales.'

Outside, as Tindal sat in his car, Lyons asked, 'You want me to take her down to Wales, sir?'

'No. She's a maverick. Leave her alone.'

'Should I allocate a minder?'

Tindal paused thoughtfully before answering. 'Not yet.'

Lyons noted the grimace and the involuntary massaging of the lower sternum that was becoming Tindal's trademark.

'If you don't mind me saying so, sir, you don't seem too happy at the thought of her involvement.'

Tindal turned his flint eyes towards Lyons. 'The last thing I need is some bolshy female trick cyclist blundering around. But even I have to do as I am told sometimes, Lyons. Now, where the hell around here can I get some Pepto-Bismol? I ran out of Rennies four hours ago . . .'

Chapter 4

Natalie Vine handed the cashier a pristine blue five-pound note dispensed that morning from a cigarette-burned Link machine in Islington.

It was almost eleven thirty on a freezing Tuesday night in the Flamingo restaurant at the Junction 47 service station off the M4. Glancing at her watch, she realised that she had stood at that Islington dispenser sixteen hours and God knew how many miles ago. She felt grimy and drained. A headache pulsed dully at her temples. Behind her, a coachload of passengers from Stoke, bound, she assumed by their eagerness, for the ferry at Fishguard and then Rosslare, bunched excitedly at the '24-hour Hotspot'. Her thoughts drifted towards Dublin and a happy three days spent at a conference there the previous June. The sun had shone and the Guinness had flowed. She wondered sardonically if the Irish were gastronomically prepared for the Stoke contingent as she watched them peer with depressing enthusiasm at the anaemic pork goulash and a congealed beef curry reminiscent of something she'd once seen steaming in a field.

The cashier studied her tray, rang up coffee and an open prawn sandwich and took eighty-seven pence from the till as change. It was only as he handed over the coins that he deigned to look up. His glum, adenoidal expression brightened as he took her in. She sensed his mind working as he searched for some verbal quip with which to delay her passage.

As he managed an uninspired 'That all you goin' to eat?' she registered that his incisors overlapped unevenly, and picked up her tray. She walked away, angry with herself for letting such a small thing get to her. She wanted anonymity, desiring only a quiet corner to collect her thoughts.

She chose an alcove, mindful of the fact that she was doing exactly what her father had always done towards the end: search for quiet corners in public places. Easier to contain good old Mary that way. Less of an intrusion into others' enjoyment. Natalie had not, still did not understand his determination not to give in to the disease that had transmogrified her mother into a malignant, capricious child. Consumed by the self-consciousness of a teenager, she had suffered her father's single-mindedness with an ill will tempered only by the terrible confusion of emotion that she still felt for her sick mother.

Mary, Mary, quite contrary.

She forced the memory into the compartment of her mind reserved for it and looked around. The service station was conspicuously new. Surrounding her on three sides, trelliswork stretched from waist to eye level, sectioning off areas in an attempt to break up the cafeteria environment. Beds of plastic plants at the corners of each intersection sprouted artificially gleaming ferns and palms. Despite the Stoke coachload, there were few people about. This far west the M4 traffic was light at the best of times. Now, in early February, things were deathly quiet. She stared out of the window at the freezing rain driven against the glass by a gusting wind. Outside, there were woods and landscaped mounds of greenery, invisible now in the darkness. Instead, the glass acted like a huge mirror, reflecting back the bright lights and garish colours of the restaurant. From where she sat, Natalie could see her image. A woman sitting alone, toying with a thin plastic stirrer, preoccupied and tired. Above, from the new PA system in the sloping ceiling, Diana Ross was giving it her all.

It was then that she saw Meredith emerge from the swing doors to the kitchen. He used a paper towel to wipe sweat from his neck and hands as he navigated the narrow space behind the counter. A plump girl in a checked peasant scarf who was serving coffee at the '24-hour Fountain' glanced slyly at him as he walked head down towards her. She pressed herself forward against the stacked coffee cups to let him pass. Natalie saw that he chose to turn away from her, presenting his buttocks to hers and holding his hands aloft in an exaggerated gesture. The natural male response would have been to turn the other way. Women always turned their backs; men preferred a frontal brush.

As he pressed himself away from the girl, he looked to Natalie like a man traversing a ledge above a deep, dark precipice. He didn't speak or apologise as he squeezed past, but Natalie saw the girl turn her face and smile conquettishly. Now that he was drawing closer, she saw that the gauntness of his face belied good bones. His eyes could have been mischievous had he smiled. Now, they looked like the ragged holes left by seal-hunters in the snow; cold and redolent with the aftermath of violence.

He stood next to the cutlery dispenser surveying the seating area, his expression unreadable. Natalie suddenly realised that he would have no idea who he was looking for. She stood up and raised a hand, feeling exposed and a little stupid. The smallest of nods was all he returned before threading his way between the walkways towards her.

Natalie stood to meet him. Immediately she became the taller of the two. She'd deliberately worn heels that afternoon for the seminar but now she was overconscious of the extra height she'd gained. Leaning slightly against the table to bring her eyes level with Meredith's, she held out her hand.

'Natalie Vine,' she said and turned on her professional smile. Tom Meredith looked at her hand but made no move to reciprocate. He stared back into her face with eyes that boiled with suspicion.

'What do you want?' His voice was resonant and deep but edged with wariness.

'You obviously received my message,' said Natalie, still smiling.

Meredith nodded tersely.

'Can we sit down?'

His eyes hardened abruptly. 'If you're a journalist, you'd better tell me now.' He tried to maintain the flat, even tone, but barely disguised disgust filtered through.

'I'm a psychiatrist from the Ellison Institute . . . of Psychiatry.'

43

She added the unnecessary qualifier as a carpenter might hammer in an extra nail for safety.

Meredith's expression didn't change. He said, 'The man from the *Sport* told the police he was a behavioural psychologist.'

'I am a forensic psychiatrist,' repeated Natalie reassuringly.

Meredith watched her, unimpressed. 'Tumours of the third ventricle – what syndrome?'

Natalie's forehead momentarily crumpled in confusion. 'That's organic brain disease. Not something I see very . . .'

His expression remained unyielding.

'I presume', she said evenly, trying to please, 'you mean an amnestic syndrome – short- and long-term memory impairment.'

Meredith persisted, unsatisfied. 'What are the McNaughten Rules?'

She stifled a sigh of exasperation. 'Rules of fitness to plead. To be unfit by reason of insanity, defendants have to satisfy the McNaughten Rules.' She gave vent to a surge of irritation. 'Is this really necessary?'

Meredith held her gaze.

Resignedly, she continued, quoting from memory. 'That by reason of a defect of the mind, the defendant did not know the nature or quality of his act. Or that by reason of such a defect, he did not know that what he was doing was wrong. Or . . .' she paused, glancing at Meredith for a signal to stop. She got none. '. . . where the defendant is under an insane delusion which prevents the true appreciation of the nature or quality of his act.'

'Appreciation,' said Meredith, his lips drawn back in a parody of a smile. 'Odd word, isn't it? Sort of thing you apply to art, not . . .'

He sat down. His face broadened fractionally into a frozen grey January smile that was meant for himself, oblivious momentarily of her presence. But she knew what he was thinking of. It was the reason for her being there. Sitting down opposite him, she said gently, 'You think The Carpenter satisfies the rules? That he's mad?'

Meredith jerked his head up, anger distorting his mouth in readiness for a vitriolic response. But he checked himself, his eyes losing their focus once more. When he spoke, Natalie felt again that he was answering the question for himself rather than for her. 'He . . . *appreciates* . . . what he does. He's outside the rules.'

'Go on,' urged Natalie and before she had finished the phrase she was regretting it as Meredith's eyes hardened again into coal-blackness.

'What do you want?' he asked eventually.

Brilliant, thought Natalie acidly. That's great, Natalie. Absolutely brilliant. He actually mentions the killer in the first sixty seconds and all you can do is stuff a size ten in there and say 'Go on.' *Go on*, for God's sake.

'I'm researching victimisation,' she began her speech. 'The effect of violent crime on . . . survivors.' She hesitated, wondering if the word might offend him, overconscious of the dubious wisdom of her deceptive strategy. He didn't blink. 'I'd like to interview you. All absolutely confidential of course. Whatever you tell me would only be used in the broad context. No names, nothing specific to identify you in any way.'

'Why?'

'It's my field. You must realise how unique your position is.'

Meredith laughed drily. 'The number of times I've heard that . . .'

'I'm sorry for what happened.'

Meredith stared at her.

Natalie continued: 'The police said that you refused psychiatric counselling?'

'I told them what they needed to know.'

'Talking might help.'

'Help who?'

'You.'

'To do what?'

'Adjust,' she said softly.

Meredith stared at her with such unfettered disgust that she felt the colour rising in her neck.

'You can hardly call working the night shift as kitchen hand in this place well-adjusted behaviour,' she flared. 'I've talked with your colleagues in Bristol. They –'

'Live on a different planet,' interrupted Meredith. 'They know nothing. This is my choice.'

'Is it? Truly?'

'Look,' said Meredith, standing, 'I'm sorry you've come all this way to be disappointed. I don't want to talk to anyone. No offence.'

'Denial is not healthy.'

Meredith glared at her. 'Thank you, Doctor. Find somebody else to make you famous.'

Natalie watched him leave, suddenly a thousand times more tired than she had been ten minutes before. Her tiredness was making her light-headed. The setting of the service station didn't help; they fulfilled such a transient function they could almost have been way stations of the mind that ceased to exist the moment you left their vicinity. Nor was her disorientation helped by the people she saw around her. They looked like lost souls. Pale, tired people on the way to perhaps a better, perhaps a worse place.

She thought of following him, but the fight had gone out of her.

She'd been talking to Meredith's ex-colleagues in Bristol at four thirty, sipping bad coffee in a Cardiff police station at six and had almost fallen asleep at the wheel during the god-forsaken journey west through the industrial landscape of Port Talbot. The cloying chemical stink of the place still clung to her. Having arrived, it would have been much more sensible to have had an early night, steel herself for the encounter. But her excitement had got the better of her. She had wanted to see him immediately, familiarise herself with her quarry. She had decided to avoid any mention of Tindal's brief initially, fearful of alienating Meredith. She shook her head, angry at misjudging things so badly.

She got up and walked to the reception desk, glad at least that she had decided on spending the night at the motor lodge attached to the service-station complex rather than opting for the dozen or more miles to the nearest city hotel. Picking up her key, she dragged herself to her room.

She entered a beige and magnolia world. Even the wood, varnished with some polyurethane finish to make all the surfaces easier to clean, looked beige. Twenty-nine pounds for the room, colour TV, tea/coffee-maker, hairdryer, trouser press. Only the counterpane on the bed had some colour, in the form of a pale blue chevron design over a beige background. The overall effect was of a beige womb. She flicked on the light in the ensuite bathroom and saw her stark image reflected in a huge wall mirror.

Weariness stared back at her.

She flicked on the TV for company before kicking off her shoes and stretching out on the bed, wiggling her toes in their newfound freedom. It wouldn't really matter, she told herself, if Meredith didn't talk to her at all. Tindal could go to hell. The Anaheim conference was looming. Sunshine and hours of shop-talk in Mexican restaurants ... She shook her head. It was Meredith and his terrifying ordeal, signed, sealed and delivered, that she truly wanted.

The prospect of going back to the Institute empty-handed and suffering the ignominy of commiseration ate into her. The thought of hearing Falkirk's condescending never-minds was almost beyond bearing ... That and the missed opportunity.

'Go on.' *Jesus!*

She should have asked an indirect question, or said nothing at all. It had only been the opening minutes of their conversation. She could have worked on that. She sat up, switching off the TV in irritation. It was too bloody late now.

She showered and then dialled her own London number, calling up the messages on her answerphone. Two were social calls, friends who, unwilling to leave gossip on tape, would call back. The third, from her landlord, was his offer of a repair to the leaking chimney. He would finally choose to call now that she was two hundred miles away.

The fourth message destroyed any lingering traces of self-esteem she had.

John Falkirk's obsequious Edinburgh accent whined over the line. 'Ah, Natalie. I wasn't sure if you'd be in. Events moved so quickly this afternoon and you left in such a hurry that I didn't have the opportunity to discuss things with you. Ah, I wanted to congratulate you on what is a marvellous coup. I know of at least half a dozen of our colleagues who would have given their eye-teeth for a crack at this, but I was most keen to reassure Mr Tindal that he could not have chosen a more able professional for the task. All I can say is that you deserve it. If there is anything I can do, please don't hesitate . . . Ah, when you return perhaps we could get together and discuss your findings. I will ring Assistant Chief Constable Tindal to instruct him that I would be happy to fulfil a supervisory role . . . Good luck.'

Supervisory role? Falkirk couldn't supervise the ticking of a clock. The gall of the man. The smarmy little shitheel. God, he'd been riding on the back of the real workers in his department for so long, he hardly had an original thought left in his head. Natalie felt her fists clench in a spasm of exasperation. She felt like screaming. It should have come as no surprise to her.

How the hell did he manage it? How could one man get so far under her skin? And yet there was nothing overt – that was never his style. Falkirk's middle name was attrition. Never direct, he wormed his way out of almost every engagement and into every small iota of praise that came her or the department's way.

The main weapon in his armamentarium was the 'note'. They appeared on her desk with depressing regularity, surreptitiously placed for her to find on her return from what might only have been a trip to the loo. Falkirk's secretary was as skilled as he was in spotting a temporal 'window' through which to push the note and avoid any physical confrontation. Never more than five inches square, on thin copy paper, they were typed and neat and a sure-fire way of raising Natalie's diastolic by ten points.

She had thrown lectures together in two hours for him, met visiting foreign academics at short notice, once even deputised at the college meeting in front of two hundred delegates who had paid good money for a didactic teaching session. He had given her twenty minutes' notice on that one. But irritatingly, when it came to the big stuff, he always managed to be around. He had a nose for it. Well, not this time. If Tindal wanted her to do this, it was going to be her and her alone.

The tone sounded again in her ear, signalling another message. This time, static filled the air, pierced only by a gurgling sigh that bordered on a sob. A disappointed, drugged sigh. The noise a drunk made when realisation finally dawned that the person he was phoning wasn't in and all he had to speak to was the cold answerphone.

Natalie Vine knew that sound well enough.

It kept her awake even longer than Falkirk's irritating message.

Chapter 5

The alarm call dragged her out of a deep, cocooning sleep. She came through the layers reluctantly, trapped by her dreams into believing she was in a Birmingham conference centre waiting to present an important paper to her peers. The ringing was transformed with hypnagogic ease into the one-minute warning calling delegates back to their seats while she sweated on the dais, praying that the visual-aids man hadn't messed up her carousel of slides.

Rrrrrrring.

They were streaming in, most of them male, all inquisitive, looking at her legs, weighing her up, leaping with easy discrimination to the conclusion that a pretty woman was unlikely to make a smart psychiatrist.

Rrrrrrring.

And then the lights dimmed and she turned to the projection screen and pressed the button that called up the first slide.

Rrrrrrring.

But her nice blue-and-white diazo heading didn't appear. Instead there was a white-robed figure in a pointed hood with dark pits for eyeholes staring at her. Frantically, she pressed the button again.

Rrrrrrrring.

The image disappeared only to be replaced by a dreadful, graphic slide of a woman, partly clothed, blindfolded and gagged, writhing on hands and knees against her bonds, blood streaming from her crucified wrists, the handle of a blade emerging from her breast. Vine tried to speak, to apologise to the audience, but as she turned she saw that they were applauding, cheering and whistling. Eyeing her appreciatively, yelling for more.

RRRRRRRRRING.

Suddenly, instantly, she was awake. Aware of the stifling heat of her motor-lodge room, aware of the phone ringing, already forgetting the stark imagery of her dream.

'Hello?' she croaked into the mouthpiece.

'Your alarm call. It's seven a.m.' The voice was local and lilting.

'Uh, thanks.' She began to move the phone groggily towards its cradle, stopped and shot it back to her ear.

'Did you say seven?'

'Seven a.m.,' said the girl.

'But I asked for a six a.m. call,' said Natalie, sitting up angrily.

She heard a muted discussion in the background, a hand over the mouthpiece unable to eradicate the expletives that were as good as admission of error as a signed confession.

'I'm sorry, madam, our instructions were for a seven a.m. call.'

'Shit,' said Natalie in anger and frustration and banged the phone down. She was already up and running for the bathroom.

Ten minutes later, in the jeans and sweater she'd bought in the hypermarket clothing outlet on the outskirts of Bristol the day before, partially revived by the shower but still with a feeling that her eyelids had been injected with silicone, Natalie was hurrying through the lobby towards the Flamingo restaurant. Ten people were queuing for breakfast. She pushed through, ignoring the hostile glances, and spoke to a corpulent woman serving eggs from behind the counter. Over one huge breast she wore a white name tag with a wobbly handwritten RITA capitalised on it in red felt-tip.

'Is Tom Meredith still here?' Natalie demanded.

Bovine eyes focused on her slowly. Thrown by this unprecedented departure from scrambled eggs, sausages and baked beans, Rita put down the greasy spatula she was holding and considered the question with undue gravity before finally answering. 'Hang on, love, I'll ask,' she said in a singsong voice.

She lumbered into the kitchen and Natalie could hear muffled yells from inside. When she emerged there was disappointment on her broad face.

'Sorry, love, he finishes half six, see. Gone long since he has.'

'Shit,' said Natalie for the second time, her mouth a thin line of frustration.

With puffy eyes the breakfasters and Rita watched Natalie storm away, unperturbed by her outburst, their expressions dumb and accepting like people in a slow-motion dream.

Natalie bought coffee, gulping it down as soon as it was cool enough. In the shop, she bought two Aeros and a Twix, abandoning her dietary regimen in one chocolate surge.

She returned to her room, finding it in the same state of disarray as it had been when she'd finally fallen asleep the night before. Even then it had been fitful and at three she had been wide awake. For an hour or so, unable to quell the scudding clouds of thought racing across the sky of her mind, she had sat up and poured over Tindal's files.

She retrieved them now from the untidy pile they had fallen into at the foot of the bed. Handling them again in the cold light of day, they appeared deceptively ordinary and banal. Natalie had a sudden image of many hundreds of similar files lying on identical tables in identical rooms as travellers awoke to their day. But she had woken to inescapable knowledge of The Carpenter. He might be waking now, hiding behind the mask of normality. It was three days since he had lived out his fantasy again. He would be in his depressed phase, his blood lust satisfied, the realisation hitting him that indulging himself had not altered anything, had not changed the dreadful reality of the mental traumas that drove killers like him into their homicidal compulsion. But the depressive phase sometimes brought bonuses. Some sadists felt sickened by what they had done, occasionally sending notes to the police 'confessing' their crimes. The phase might last days or weeks and outwardly there would be no sign. But in the incomprehensible mind of The Carpenter this turmoil would slowly ease until the fantasies, the need, the compulsion would gradually return and the phase would change. The Americans had a term for it – when didn't they? – the aura phase. In the aura phase, the killer would gradually slide into a machine-like mental state, thinking only of the ritualistic acts that fulfilled his need. Existing only to fulfil those needs. In the aura he would be unstoppable.

It was a cheerless thought made even more unnerving by the unfamiliarity of her surroundings as she whipped open the curtains on to the first glimmer of dawn outside, knowing that she now had no choice but to venture out into it.

Cursing once more, but this time with an air of resignation, Natalie shook her head and turned back to face the room. It appeared suddenly stark and plastic in the orange glow of the bathroom light as she began to pile her clothes into her overnight bag.

She found the village easily enough.

The name Oxwich had an odd, English ring to it, nothing like the tongue-twisting names full of ls and rs she'd noticed on her drive down. The journey had taken her around the city of Swansea and out on to the Gower peninsula. There, she'd followed signs to South Gower, passing through rolling farmland on the one good road, turned left at the crumbling remains of a castle lodge, and headed along a sunken road through a marshy lowland covered in swaying ranks of common reed to the village itself.

She caught glimpses of the sea between hillocks of grassy dunes, a moving grey mass of water against the lighter grey sky. At a crossroads twenty yards past the one store, she drove up a steep, narrow lane towards Oxwich Green. On both sides she was flanked by ancient stone walls with vegetation behind and more than once she caught sight of signs reminding visitors that the area was a nature reserve. A hundred yards up she saw a turning, too sharp for her to manoeuvre the car around, under a sign indicating a public footpath. She drove on to the brow of the hill and reversed into the entrance of a large caravan park. From her vantage point, she looked down on to the bay and suddenly caught her breath. A vast curving expanse of sand stretched below her, ending in cliffs and topped beyond the marshes she'd driven along by woodland. She'd heard of the Gower coast only in travelogues. Now she was face to face with its rugged beauty and for an instant she almost forgot the purpose of her journey.

Somewhere above her, a wheeling seagull screamed. The noise brought her back to herself and she eased the car down the lane and took the sharp right under the footpath sign. The track she followed was rutted and full of puddles, but it had been stoned and seemed firm enough. Almost immediately, she caught a glimpse of the ruins of a fortified manor house to her left. A sign, hand-painted and faded, read, 'Oxwich Castle, No Entry'. Ahead, the lane wound past farmhouses until it dipped into a large clearing in a patch of woodland. From there, a rickety wooden gate stood open and an even narrower lane led up to a level area where a car – Meredith's she presumed – had parked in the middle of the driveway, preventing access from below. She walked up, noting how the hedges hid the chalets until she had almost reached the top.

There were four in all, squat, ugly, flat-roofed buildings arranged in pairs, each pair joined seamlessly in the middle like Siamese twins. To the side of each chalet was a gravelled area for parking. Two of the chalets were boarded and shuttered against the winter damp, their individuality indicated only by the two different shades of blue their owners had coated them with. The other pair, pale lemon paint flaking off the rough render, were not shuttered but looked equally desolate and forlorn, their bleached wooden doors in need of maintenance, the remains of a hanging basket straggling withered brown tendrils over a window.

Natalie wondered whether during August the grassy lawn echoed with the laughter of children. The place needed children. Without them it was a sad echo of long-lost summers.

There was no sound, no sign of any occupancy. With a pang of guilt, she wondered if he was asleep. She turned away from the building and stared down at the bay and the grey sea breaking against the shore, toying with the idea of returning later. She turned back again. Meredith was standing in the doorway of the right-hand lemon chalet staring at her with his ghost-like face. Natalie jumped involuntarily, and then laughed in embarrassment.

'Sorry. You scared me.'

Meredith didn't smile. He stood in the doorway in his bare feet. She looked down at his toes, white and naked. She saw the scars, whiter than the surrounding tissue. Small and linear, two inches above the cleft between his big toe and its neighbour.

Did he wake up and still feel the nails there?

Meredith kept his hands in his pockets, his shoulders hunched.

'How did you find me?' His voice was loaded with anger, his eyes flickering around, assuring himself that she was alone. 'How?' he seethed.

'I asked,' said Natalie.

Christ, he's scared. Scared of me.

'No one at the service station knows where I live. Who told you?'

'I only want to talk.'

'WHO FUCKING TOLD YOU?' yelled Meredith, his face shaking with emotion.

'The police. The police told me.'

'Great,' said Meredith. 'That's just bloody great.' But Natalie saw that some of his anger had evaporated. Her answer seemed to placate him, albeit reluctantly.

'I think we should talk,' said Natalie.

'I've told you, I've got nothing to say to you.'

Natalie took a couple of steps towards him, as if she were approaching a nervous horse. 'How do you know?'

'I'm tired,' said Meredith, stepping back and beginning to close the door.

'Have you seen the news?' asked Natalie, her voice suddenly lower, more commanding.

Meredith wavered, his expression suspicious.

'Radio?' she asked.

Meredith shook his head.

'Then you'll have to take my word for it.'

'What are you talking about?'

'He murdered a teacher four days ago.' The harsh words steamed out of Natalie's mouth and hung in the air between them. Meredith stared at her. His face matched the greyness of the sea. She thought he was going to stumble but he put out his hand to steady himself against the door. The remaining anger dissolved in him and it was as if his spine had melted. His eyes, already dark-rimmed, seemed to fall back into his skull, lost and unfocused.

'If you're lying . . .' he whispered.

'Do you have a TV?' asked Natalie.

Meredith's eyes hooded in puzzlement.

'A TV?' she repeated.

'Somewhere,' he said vaguely.

Natalie stepped towards the door and momentarily Meredith's face took on a look of panic, but it was transient. She stood expectantly on the threshold and he stepped to one side, letting her enter, confused resignation replacing the panic.

She found the old Philips portable under a pile of ancient magazines in the corner of the small living room. Thick dust coated the screen and the plug rattled loosely at the end of the lead, but, having perched it on a low coffee table and fiddled with the aerial, the black-and-white picture was clear enough as she tuned in to the BBC's breakfast news. A vaguely familiar political face swam into view and Natalie turned the volume down to a barely audible hum. She stood up, satisfied, and consulted her watch. It was five minutes to eight. There would be a bulletin at eight.

Behind her, Meredith watched silently as she took in her surroundings. Worn nylon padded sofa and chairs, a once garish, now faded floral-pattern carpet, shiny blue vinyl wallpaper. The coffee table supporting the TV was the biggest of a nest of three; the other two were loaded with magazines. Natalie glanced at them. *Yachting*, *What Car?*, *Amateur Photographer*. The most recent showed a spring 1988 date. A small alcove in one corner contained shelves. The first and second held paperbacks, Forsyth, Wambaugh, Lodge. She couldn't see a telephone or any radiators.

'How long have you been here?' she asked.

'Four months,' said Meredith. Natalie shivered with the cold. He didn't seem to notice it as he stood with his arms folded across his abdomen.

'Is it me or is it really cold in here?' she asked.

Meredith shrugged. 'It's difficult to keep a fire in.'

The familiar news-signature tune brought Natalie's attention back to the TV. She turned up the volume and sat down on the sofa. It exuded a musty, damp smell as she sat, still wearing her coat. The item made second billing after a record trade-deficit announcement.

'The body of a twenty-five-year-old woman found brutally murdered in the Bitterne Park area of Southampton on Monday has been named as that of Alison Terry, a biology teacher at a nearby secondary school. Her mutilated body was found on Monday morning by colleagues calling to give Miss Terry a lift to work. A police spokesman described the murder as a vicious and harrowingly sadistic killing of a popular and well-respected woman. There appeared to be no obvious motive. It was also confirmed that Miss Terry's death could be linked to that of Jillian Grant who was murdered near Bath five months ago. Police are not ruling out the possibility that Miss Terry is the latest victim of The Carpenter, who is alleged to have killed eight women over the last eighteen months.'

Eight that you know of, thought Natalie.

'His first victim, twenty-five-year-old nurse Barbara Lamb, was murdered in August of last year. This report from John Vickery...'

The scene changed to a panning shot of a Victorian terrace and white-suited men emerging through the front door, followed by a portrait photograph of a girl in cap and gown.

The voice-over was explicit and more graphic than the pictures. But Natalie wasn't listening. She was looking at Meredith. He seemed mesmerised by the screen, by the image of the charnel house.

The picture cut to a harassed-looking CID man who repeated words like vicious, evil and sadistic. The report ended with a shot of Alison Terry's parents' house, a Thirties semi with a manicured lawn. The voice said that they were 'being comforted by relatives'. The couple, bewildered and grief-stricken, were shown in gaunt close-up, the woman crying openly, the man bemused and shocked.

Leave them alone, you bastards, she thought.

She got up and turned off the TV. When she turned around, Meredith was staring at the blank screen.

'It is cold,' he whispered croakily. 'I'll get some wood for the fire.' He hurried, almost stumbling in his haste, into a small hall and opened a door to the rear of the chalet. Natalie followed slowly. The thin rain that had threatened from the lowering sky was finally drizzling. She stood looking out at a small yard area, unkempt and overgrown, that ran into thin woodland behind. There was no sign of Meredith. And then she heard the sound of the axe. Wrapping her coat around herself, she followed the noise to the side of the building.

Meredith was hunched over, his back towards her, his thin T-shirt already damp and clinging to his body from the rain. There was a desperate violence in his actions as he worked the axe out of the remains of a huge tree stump, bracing himself with his foot and jerking the handle to and fro. With a sudden surge, the axe came free and immediately Meredith swung it in a huge arc over his shoulder and back into the stump with a splintering thud, grunting with the effort as he once again worked to free the axe and repeat the stroke.

After several repetitions and one particularly frenzied blow, the axed lodged firmly, and despite all Meredith's efforts it wouldn't budge. Natalie watched as his body heave with a huge sob of frustration that gave way to a moan as he leant his head right over, breathless and spent, his brow touching the tree stump, his knees sinking until they met the wet ground.

Natalie didn't speak. Instead she gathered some kindling from the ample supply stacked against the wall of the building and went inside. A cursory search yielded matches in a cupboard in the tiny kitchen.

It took only minutes to light the fire in the wood burner set in the corner of the living room. She threw on a few extra pages of yellowing newspaper and flames flared brightly. As they crackled and spat, she felt the first vestiges of warmth begin to spread into the four corners of the room.

She went back into the yard. Meredith hadn't moved. She felt his body shivering as she put a firm hand under his arm. He didn't object as she helped him stand and led him inside. She found the bathroom, tiny and cramped, but mercifully with an electric shower. Meredith shivered on the threshold, his eyes still pained and confused.

'You'll have to get out of those wet things,' said Natalie.

Hearing her voice, Meredith looked up, awareness once again impinging unwelcomingly. Shuddering with the cold, he nodded. Natalie reached over and turned on the shower, instant hot water steaming in the cold air. For a moment she wondered if she would have to strip him but, like an automaton, he was already beginning to peel off his T-shirt.

Nodding approval, she went out. Meredith didn't bother to shut the door. As she turned to do it for him, she saw that he was already naked. His pallor emphasised his thinness.

Natalie fed the fire and when Meredith came back from the bathroom buttoning up an old faded blue check work shirt over black jeans, she could see the skin around his neck pink and warm. Almost immediately, he began yawning.

'You need some sleep,' said Natalie.

'Can't,' he said.

'I'll stay if you like.'

He shook his head automatically.

'I meant it when I said I could help.'

Meredith looked at her. His face was sceptical.

'There are techniques . . .' she began.

He turned his face towards her, anger flaming his cheeks.

'You're not here to help me.'

'Yes, I am.'

'Don't lie. You want him. You want me to tell you about him. You used him to get in here. You knew what it would do to me. Don't fucking lie.'

Natalie thought about protesting, toyed with the idea of denial and then threw it out.

'OK. I'll tell you the truth. I do want to know about him. The police are desperate. But that's not the only reason I came down here. I want to find out about you. And I can help. You might as well have post-traumatic stress disorder tattooed on your fore-head. Believe it or not, the only way you can hope to deal with all this is with help from me, or someone like me.'

'The police can't leave me alone. I hate them.'

'I can't accept that. You don't hate the police at all. You hate yourself. You loathe yourself for being able to sit here and listen to the news instead of being one of his statistics.'

'Don't give me any of that psychotherapeutic claptrap.'

'Spare me this, please. You're not some confused bank clerk. Your intellect is fighting with your emotion. You know all of this but you're too scared to admit it to yourself.'

'Scared?' screamed Meredith. 'What do you know about being scared?'

'Nothing. Tell me.'

'Go to hell,' spat Meredith, stung by her trap.

'No.'

'You have no right to do this. No right.'

'Rubbish. You know damn well that you've already made the decision.'

'What decision?'

'To stay alive.'

'What are you talking about?'

'Don't pretend you haven't thought about it. What do you have, a twelve-bore stashed somewhere? A few pills? The safety net, am I right?'

'You bitch.'

'You might as well face up to the fact that you'll never do it. You are by definition a survivor. And having made a decision, you owe it to the others to help. This maniac is not going to stop.'

She let it hang in the air, watching his breath heave raggedly in his chest. When she spoke again it was gently.

'I've seen the police reports on the last eight murders. They're swimming against the current. He's got them chasing their tails. In almost every case they've been reactive, looking for possible connections between him and his victims,' she shook her head hopelessly. 'But how can you blame them? There is nowhere to start. No one is looking at the broader picture.' Again she paused, letting the information settle on Meredith's unreceptive ears. Again he didn't comment.

'I have to return to London today, but I'd like to come back.'

Meredith didn't say anything.

She was encouraged by the absence of a flat refusal. 'I'll contact you via the service station. I'll only be gone a day or so. We'll take it slowly. How do you feel about that?'

He stared at the floor.

'Unless you want me to stay while you sleep?'

'No,' he said. 'No thanks.'

Natalie smiled a professional, reassuring smile. Inside, her heart was hammering in her chest, driven by a bolus of adrenaline; the gambler's high.

She left shortly after, hearing several bolts slide home as the door shut. As she walked down to her car the dull roar of the sea came up from below. Halfway down, she turned and looked back up at the chalet. It looked bereft of life. Curtains had been drawn, shutting out the harsh reality of the day. Meredith, she thought, had done the same thing with his mind. But as she watched, she saw the curtains twitch and a chink appear.

Chapter 6

It took her four hours to get back to London. Four hours on the M4 shrouded in billowing spray under a sky the colour of slate.

As the windscreen wipers beat rhythmically, she began thinking of the killer's ritual. Of all the cases she'd studied, this particular one was unusual. What had set him off on this course? Someone, somewhere had been responsible for planting the seed that had grown into the poisonous weed. There was a strong possibility that The Carpenter's name was on a file somewhere. It might be a police-record file, a social-services abuse register, a psychiatrist's folder. How many times had she read that somewhere in the past of all lust killers there had been a cry for help, a missed opportunity by a professional to spot the telltale signs? Perhaps she herself had already missed the next killer. It was an unhappy thought.

She got back to Highbury at seven, parking under a light, aware of a surge of noise as she opened the car door. She glanced up to her right and saw a yellow-white glow in the sky from the floodlights over the Highbury ground, home of Arsenal football club. It looked as though tonight was a home game for the Gunners. They too were a Premier League side, she mused. Glancing nervously right and left, she quickly crossed the street and went inside.

She made coffee, showered, put on a clean sweat shirt and pants, rummaged in a drawer for some old woollen socks and put a band in her hair to keep it off her face. Thus armed, she took herself and a steaming mug of black coffee into the small bedroom she used as a study.

She worked there for two hours, pouring over the reports from

Tindal's files, searching for the behavioural traits that might give her an inkling as to how to approach the problem of Meredith.

She understood Tindal's conviction that he was the key, but it was a tarnished conviction, and reading the reports she realised that the police were indeed floundering. She knew that they would be looking for patterns, hoping to find some common theme, utilising and collating as much data as possible, plodding along with methods that had worked so well in other investigations. Methods that in this case were totally useless.

Despite all their cross-referencing, there would be no real connection between the victims. They would have been plucked from the ranks of the population at large for no other reason than a way of smiling, the colour of their eyes, tint of their hair, a gesture. From the reports there seemed to be a predilection for dark-haired girls, fine-featured, small-boned. All except for Jilly Grant and now Alison Terry. Aside from these two, it could simply have been the smallness of their frames that had attracted him, making it easier for him to overpower them, but she thought not. Meredith's description, within its limits, indicated a height of just above average. Five ten perhaps. That and the fact that he used gas to overpower them also made it unlikely that he depended on brute strength. So the type could be significant. Necessary if his victims were to fulfil the role he designated for them.

The autopsy reports all bore out her ritualistic theory, confirming her conviction that they were dealing with the uncontrollable episodic violence that characterised such killers.

She looked again at the autopsy report on Grant. She scanned the page for the twentieth time, trying hopelessly to imagine what Meredith had felt as he watched what had been going on.

'... Thirty-five stab wounds to the lower abdomen and perineum penetrating to a depth of 3.5 millimetres on average. Two wounds appear symmetrical and are obviously differentiated from the stab wounds. These are full thickness extending from a mid-inguinal point, curving superiorly and medially to the lower ribs. From bruising and lacerations to the deep structures underlying these wounds, it appears that a larger instrument was involved, possibly with a sawing motion. Haemorrhaging and bruising to the internal organs indicate extensive trauma . . .

Meredith's stark account described all too clearly the weapons used, the methodology employed.

'. . . He was leaning over her from behind. He kept looking back over his shoulder to make sure that I could see. I couldn't, not very well. I tried not to look, but he kept saying it . . . "Look at me, look at me." Like some malignant child. I thought at first he was raping her, but there was no movement in his lower body, just his hands and his shoulders writhing. She was moaning . . . It could have been screaming, but the gag muffled everything . . . And all the while he was looking at me . . . willing me to watch him. I couldn't really see. I didn't want to see, until he took his hand out. The noise was all I heard first, a slick, oily sound before he held his hand up. It was red and glistening. And then I saw the blood dripping from the hole in her abdomen and I knew that he'd been inside her all the time, violating her . . .'

Natalie turned to her textbooks, discarding much of the older works as confused, conflicting rubbish. No one had dared put forward a true explanation for sadistic murderers for years, labelling them as borderline schizophrenics, misapplying all sorts of psychiatric theories to fit their purposes. Ironically, it had been left to a convicted lust murderer to provide, from his own self-examination, a better understanding of the sadistic mind. And even then, the understanding was only partial. A lust killer's description of his murders was often patchy and tenuous. The total lack of empathy in his mind enabled him to dehumanise his victims, to perform the act only for the dreadful compulsion of it. It allowed him to proceed with the ritual that was so necessary for his own psychological survival and then somehow forget the details. This amnesic safety valve was why so many of them took souvenirs and were obsessive in recording the event.

Natalie stared at the passage she had highlighted. Stared at it and tried to assimilate it.

'. . . Absolute mastery over another person – that is the aim. To render that person a helpless object of my will, to become her God to do with as one pleases. Humiliation, enslavement are all a means to the end. The prime objective is to cause suffering and there is no better way than to cause pain, to inflict suffering without the ability to defend. The exquisite pleasure of complete domination is the very essence of what makes me tick . . .'

And yet there could be no generalisation as to why. Was The Carpenter a rat in a cage, responding to intolerable pressures in the broader sense, striking out violently at the society that had allowed those pressures to exist? Or was it purely the manifestation of a primal urge, the dark side of human nature that intellect normally kept at bay? There were precedents in nature, the pleasure cats took in tormenting mice for example, but that answer would only come retrospectively, after he was caught and if, *if* he was willing to let someone delve into his dark past. For a dark past there must have been to create such a mind.

The doorbell rang at nine. Natalie squinted through the peephole, mouthed to herself 'Shit,' and opened the door.

The man who stood there grinned at her, leaning languidly against the doorjamb. Impossibly natural brown curls danced on an olive brow inherited directly from Tuscan ancestors, the nose long and straight between arched cheekbones. His teeth gleamed boyishly in a dazzling array. Behind his back, like a child, he held something.

Natalie spoke first, her greeting tinged with displeasure.

'Mo.'

'Nat,' said Mo, looking her up and down with unashamed and familiar lasciviousness. 'Love the outfit,' he said, grinning sardonically.

He walked past her uninvited into the flat. Helplessly, the objection freezing in her throat, Natalie stepped to one side to avoid contact. Seeing him already upstairs, she turned and ran up after him.

Mo's coat was already off and thrown haphazardly on the back of a chair. He knew she would hang it up for him. It was something that women, *his* women, always did. For him to do it would have been unthinkable. Mo himself was in the kitchen, helping himself to a beer from the fridge.

'So, Nat, how're things?' He moved to the drawer that held the bottle opener, prizing off the top with practised ease.

Natalie stood on the threshold of the kitchen, watching him go through his act, registering the attraction she still felt for him physically, still beguiled by the Wellingtonian accent at such odds with his appearance, hating herself for having actually opened the door and let him in.

'Mo,' she said again exasperatedly. 'What are you doing here?'

Mo, the beer at his lips, let his shoulders sag with reluctant resignation.

'Jesus, Nat. Not this fucking shit again.'

'Mo,' said Natalie with restraint. 'We agreed. Two months was what we said. It's only been three weeks.'

'Three weeks too long, baby,' he said, smouldering at her like a ham actor. He took a long swallow of beer and let his attention fall on one of the photocopied articles Natalie had left scattered around the kitchen. He picked it up and made a face. 'Jesus, Nat. Do you really read this stuff?'

Natalie strode over and snatched the paper away. 'I want you to leave. Now.'

'For God's sake, Nat. I called to see if you were OK. I thought maybe you'd like to have a few beers, maybe go to Galliano's, yeah? Or . . .' He reached out for her and put his arm around her waist, pulling her to him, '. . . even stay here and get naked.'

Natalie put both hands up between them and pushed away. Mo resisted, allowing her to step back a foot before pulling her to him again more forcefully. Natalie smelled tequila on his warm breath. She pushed away again, feeling his arms tighten in resistance, the first vague fluttering of panic beating beneath the anger in her mind. She glared at him, the effort of the struggle distorting her face, and he relaxed, releasing her before swallowing thirstily from the Becks.

'So,' he said deliberately, looking at the far wall with sudden interest, 'you've been away? I tried ringing.'

'I've been in Wales. Research.'

'Wales,' said Mo with distaste.

'And I may well be going back there for a while. Which, from the way you're behaving, is probably a good thing.'

'Why?'

'Mo, don't you ever listen? I need time to think things through.'

'You're always thinking things through, Nat. That's your fucking trouble. Relax.' He moved towards her but she shook her head and stepped back. She saw his jaw working, his eyes moving with alcohol-induced sluggishness. And then his face changed, the boyish grin took on a pout, the violent eyes narrowed in pain. 'What's the matter, Nat. You don't like me any more?'

A month ago she would have fallen readily, yielded to those eyes, let herself be dragged in. But now she saw the trap. The fact was, she didn't like him any more. The fact was, she hadn't relished the feeling of panic she'd felt in his strong, pinioning arms a moment before. The fact was, she felt uncomfortable with him there. She was scared of him and even more scared of what his presence brought out in her.

Involvement had come unexpectedly, at a party she had not wanted to attend. She had been a girlfriend's chaperone, introduced as a 'brilliant head doctor', which she had not forgiven easily. Immediately, she had seen the fascination and the intimidation that had caused. Most of the guests had been young and moneyed, their eyes flicking from her hair to her wrist, checking out whether the timepiece she was wearing was genuinely Swiss or a cheap Malaysian copy. It had fascinated her to watch them strut and brag. Even the beer had been designer Japanese. She'd learned later that all the men (boys?) had been commodities brokers – Mo's exclusive little club. But he had been different, uninhibited and not at all intimidated by her label or her appearance. He'd renamed her the 'rinky-dink shrink'. And she, for her sins, had responded with an alacrity that had surprised her.

Mo's life was dominated by every possible icon of success. He was an advertising executive's dream. Porsche, Rolex and Armani were his watchwords. She had laughed at him, but he hadn't seen the joke. Worse, it had taken her a month to realise that she was as much a symbol of his success as his Vodafone. He had 'pulled' her. And yet she had been prepared to put up with all of this as a delicious physical interlude until he had begun to hint at moving in. She knew then that she had misread the signs. He began turning up at all hours, wanting to stay, always anxious to know where she was or had been. She realised that his upbringing had produced a capricious child totally used to his own way. Summers spent at his mother's villa outside Florence, Easters in New York and Christmases in Switzerland were hardly likely to produce a shrinking violet. And William Peter Mowatt (Mo) Alberini was definitely not one of those.

So she had tried to cool things off, but he had manipulative skills, knew exactly what to say to make her back down. He would, she realised, have made an excellent counsellor were it not for his ego. And yet, beneath it all, there was something that had made her want to go back for more. Something in his make-up, an untapped mother lode that fascinated yet repulsed her. It wasn't simply a bad-boy thing, or even his forced superficial vulgarity. The only excuse she could find for herself for not looking at the situation analytically at an early enough stage was that it had been buried deep. But it had finally surfaced with the heady perfume of a badly preserved corpse.

Eight weeks after they met, she had found herself at another extravagant party. Mo had drunk his usual excessive amount and they had gone back to her flat by taxi. She'd helped him up the stairs as he leaned heavily against the wall, singing in a beery slur.

Propping him in a chair, Natalie had fetched some iced water, toyed with idea of lacing it with salt as an emetic to help him disgorge some of the excess alcohol still sloshing unabsorbed in his stomach, but had abandoned it when she saw him eyeing her through slitted lids. She gave him the water and watched him sip it and spit it out.

'Jesus, Nat. Are you trying to fucking poison me? Give me a fucking beer.'

'Mo, you've had enough.'

'A beer.'

'No.'

He was up out of his chair like a bull, his eyes wide, nostrils flaring. He hit her once in the stomach, hard. The speed and force of the attack took her completely by surprise. She felt the air whistle out of her, felt the deep, paralysing sensation in her stomach. She heard herself gag; she couldn't breathe. She lay there for long moments, her mouth open, grunting tightly in her throat, waiting impotently for the surrounding air to enter her stretched lungs. And then his hand was on her hair, yanking her up as his palm came round in an arc. The slap was sharp and painful.

'Don't ever tell me what I can and can't do.'

He let her head go and it sagged to the floor.

The blow helped bring her round. She took a deep, convulsive sucking breath and then the terrible, sinking, visceral pain came, deep in her abdomen. Waves of it washed over her and the grunt became a moan. From somewhere above her, she heard Mo open the fridge and the chink of a bottle. And as the waves of sickening pain gradually eased, the realisation came to her as to why she wasn't up and running down the stairs, screaming for the police. It was because she had *sensed* this in Mo all along. Had waited for it to happen, had secretly longed for it. The tears that followed were silent tears of shame and guilt because it was her fault that he had hit her.

(*Slut.*)

Unequivocally, illogically her fault. Just as it had been her fault when her mother had started hitting her.

(*Slut.*)

As she lay in pain on her own kitchen floor, her thoughts had flown effortlessly back to the oval-mouthed vegetable in the psychogeriatric ward of the Worthing hospital she had visited so many times in the last few years.

A truffle pig.

She remembered the unbidden, unkind comparison that had popped into her mind one stuffy afternoon by the bedside. That was what her mother had reminded her of. A truffle pig existing only to hunt out the succulent fungus. Except that in her mother's case it was sweets and biscuits that she sniffed out and stole from the other patients, either surreptitiously or, more often, violently. In the three years since her admission, Mary Vine had put on two stone. And once the thought had crept in, it popped up each time Natalie visited. It wasn't her mother fidgeting in the bed, it was some Alzheimeric Doppelgänger.

With hindsight and knowledge, she now knew that her mother had been ill for years. Addicted to alcohol before the sweets were ever substituted. But it was still difficult to forgive the great skill and deviousness she had used to terrorise the teenage Natalie. It was the wrong age for comprehending any illness that might turn a bright, caring woman into a vicious monster.

'Slut' had been Mary Vine's favourite word in those dark days. Waiting for Natalie at night. Waiting for her to return home from an evening out with friends.

Slut.

Waiting with an open hand and that terrible, whispering, accusation.

Slut.

Natalie's father had suffered himself, desperately trying to comprehend the incomprehensible. He had, however, suffered in silence, and for a long time had played down the problem. Blinkered, he refused to hear the words or see the bruises. Her mother would start with a slap, but preferred to knead her daughter with hard, bony knuckles.

Slut.

Dull points that bruised muscles in the shoulders, arms and chest, so much that they ached in the quiet of the dark night hours. Sometimes, if one was near at hand, she used a bottle.

Slut.

Always Amontillado, always the neck. And always Natalie had taken it. Persuaded always by love and obedience not to respond, not to fight back, but to run and hide and pray for her father to intervene.

As the nights became fewer and fewer when she could force herself to spend an evening with friends and thus incur the wrath of her sickening mother, Natalie had suffered the inevitable peer abuse.

Slut.

Whatever was wrong with Nattie, asked the voices.

Slut.

Nattie was becoming *such* a snob.

Slut.

And boy had poor old slutty, snobby Nattie suffered until her father had made the decision that she should suffer no more.

Natalie jerked back through the vivid layers of memory with a jolt that almost made her lose her footing. She kaleidoscoped between that first night after he'd hit her and the present. And Mo was watching her and he knew she was thinking about it.

Clumsily, he said, 'Nat, what's wrong? You ill?'

She toyed momentarily with the idea of explaining. But what would words like co-dependency mean to Mo? She'd see his eyes glaze over and his brows furrow in a frown. He had the intellect to understand, it was simply that he had not the desire to listen.

'Leave,' she whispered. 'Just leave. Please.' And all the while her eyes never strayed from the bottle in his hand.

Wordlessly, accepting defeat, he put down the Becks, walked past her and picked up his coat. He hesitated at the top of the stairs.

'I'll give you a ring at the weekend. Maybe you'll feel better then.'

Natalie didn't reply. She was still standing in the kitchen when she heard the front door slam.

She tried working after he'd gone, but couldn't settle. She was in bed by ten, exhausted by the travelling and drained by Mo's visit.

The phone woke her at ten thirty. She let it ring five times, waiting for the answerphone to click on, certain of who it would be.

'Nat?' His voice was high and loud. 'Oh come on, Nat, answer the fucking phone.'

She lay in bed, listening.

'I know you're there Nat . . .'

He paused, waiting.

'Nat, why are you doing this to me?'

In the darkness, she found herself shaking her head. He was pathetically predictable. Her fault. Always her fault.

'Look, I'll come over on the weekend. We can motor down to Brighton, yeah?'

Pause.

'Nat?'

Pause.

'Nat, you are there, aren't you?'

Pause.

His voice dropped a notch to a harsh whisper. 'Nat. I'm never going to let you go, you know.'

Pause.

'Fuck . . .'

In the darkness of her warm bed, Natalie shivered.

Chapter 7

Tom Meredith heard the noise in his sleep. Or rather a part of his brain that had been permanently altered since *it* had happened, a part that was always aware, even during the time when alpha waves ruled the rest of his consciousness, registered the noise. The effect was the same. He was instantly awake. The wind had picked up, driving horizontal rain against the chalet wall. Meredith lay unmoving, listening for it again. It came, a tugging scrape, repeating itself once or twice, and then silence, bar the moaning wind. He let his mind roam around the building, imagining what there was that could possibly be making the noise, suppressing the panic that hammered in his veins. The scraping came again. Was it a window or a door being opened? No, the repetition argued against that. He focused in on it. It came from the right, the front of the chalet. He heard the rain spatter against the battered windows. There, it was coming from there.

He let his mind drift outside. The empty barrel once filled with marigolds, the loose downpipe he'd fixed with wire, the spreading juniper that had mushroomed since it had been planted years before. He saw the juniper, its blue-green branches stretching towards the house like a crooked hand. He saw the wind take it, saw the branches bow and scrape towards the house, saw the feathery leaves caress the glass. That was all it was, a branch scraping against glass. It came again as the wind moaned a gust. Now is sounded reassuring, not threatening.

In the darkness, he held up his wrist. The luminous dial showed seven p.m. He'd slept for almost six hours, much longer than he normally did. After the woman had gone, he'd wandered aimlessly around the chalet, then chopped more wood in his anger and frustration until exhaustion had driven him back inside to his bed. He'd become accustomed to snatching two hours at the most. Usually some innate self-preservation mechanism woke him up after two hours, before his sleep became too deep, before the dreams began. Groggily, the realization came that he would be late for work, but he knew nobody would mind. They left him alone, grateful for his willingness to stay on whenever necessary, grateful for his presesnce at all on the difficult-to-fill night shift.

He got up, switching on lights as he moved from room to room. He made tea and took it into the living room. The TV startled him, seemed to be watching him with one large, square, blind eye from its new position on the coffee table. Unaccustomed to its presence, it triggered memories of Vine, and in turn the image of the photograph of Alison Terry they'd shown on the news. He found himself thinking of the drawn features of the girl's mother, an unnecessary close-up, the tears a magnet for a media thirsty for any true emotion. He wondered how much the police had told the parents, wondered where they would draw the line. The Terrys would probably press for details, but he found himself hoping desperately that the police wouldn't tell them everything. It would be beyond bearing to know what *he* would have done to her.

Like the sudden flooding of a dry riverbed, he felt the darkness flow into his brain. The all-consuming, viscid darkness that threatened to trample his reason, crush it like an origami crane in the fist of a vindictive child. Outside, he heard the wind moan, mocking him. An ancient standard lamp stood in the corner of the room, crooked from a long-ago accident, its twisted and worn silver twin flex emerging halfway down, repaired and patched with black insulating tape. Meredith's eyes were drawn to the tape like a vulture's to a corpse. Slowly, he walked towards it, pausing only to switch off the living-room light. He stood in total darkness and paced across the floor, reaching out with his hand to grab the flex, running his fingers up until they touched the black insulating tape. He fell to his knees, pushing his face towards his hand, bringing his nose close to the tape. It was old, and dust and fluff had collected on part of the exposed adhesive side, but there was still a faint odour when he got really close.

It had been stronger when it had been strapped across his mouth and under his nose. Every breath he'd taken had reeked of the clean, gluey smell of plastic.

Helplessly, shivering and fearful, he inhaled deeply and in the darkness all around him, he descended like a junkie on a bad trip. He heard the voice: flat, unemotional, oblivious to the muffled screams.

'Say it . . .'

Her eyes were wild, feral from the pain.

'Say it . . .'

Sometimes he thought he saw the light of reason flicker momentarily in her face as she desperately searched for him, for help, for a way out.

Somehow the flatness of the instruction emanating from behind the hood was more terrifying than any screamed abuse.

'Say the words.'

She was squirming, wrenching her body away from his hands, but the nails were firm, hammered in to the hilt.

'Say the words and if it's good . . .'

Meredith could hear himself screaming, shouting, pleading through the tape and the gag beneath.

'. . . I'll take it . . .'

He couldn't see all her face from where he lay, only as she shook and turned and writhed could he get a glimpse of her burning, terrified eyes as she turned to look behind her, over her shoulder, her hands and knees outstretched from the position he'd placed her in. What he could see was his hands working, manipulating, and the blood pumping . . .

'. . . out . . .'

In the darkness of the chalet living room, Meredith crawled across the floor, his conscious mind only dimly aware of what he was doing, preoccupied with the images he could do nothing to keep at bay, desperate only for the comfort of the one thing he knew could release him.

He crawled like a child towards the sofa, feeling behind it for The Box. It was tin and ancient, round like a drum, depth greater than its diameter, its original contents long ago consumed. The image of the rotund Quaker it bore had been synonymous with breakfast for generations. He rolled it towards him over the floor, the solid contents bumping and rolling. He hugged the tin to himself, rocking back and forth on the cold floor like a child with a friendly, familiar blanket.

After a while he stopped rocking and his hands went to the lid and prised it open. Reaching in, he closed his fingers around the objects he needed so badly. Something rustled, his hand fingering paper and Cellophane packaging. Through the paper he could feel the syringe, and he picked up the needle in its plastic sheath, the tourniquet, the small thin Alcowipes for skin antisepsis, and then he felt the vial. And as his fingers fondled the smooth glass sides, the demons, his demons, began to recede. The voices, her eyes, the hood all began to fade gradually, defeated by his own irrefutable knowledge that if they didn't go, if they didn't flee back to their dark little hole, he could make them go away. He could make them go away for ever. He even had the power in the vial to banish *him* for ever.

By touch, in the Stygian blackness, he expertly placed the tourniquet on his arm, tightening it with his other hand and his teeth, feeling the vein swell beneath his finger. He imagined flicking open the needle sheath, pressing it firmly on to the syringe, cracking open the vial, drawing up its contents, pushing the sharp stainless steel into the big, plump vein, injecting . . .

So far, imagining it had been enough. It gave him the power. The comfort of knowing he could kill the demons if he wanted to. But he also knew that this was no game. He would do it if *he* came back to haunt him. Death was his weapon. *He* had no power over the dead.

Later, when he was sure the blackness had gone, Meredith placed everything back into the tin and hid it again. The woman had been very astute. The spark, the desire to live, that primal drive was keeping him alive, keeping him from destroying himself.

If there was a reason for this desire, he had no conception of what it was. Somewhere deep inside was the thought that perhaps one day there might be a healing, a return to a semblance of normality. Perhaps that was the pilot light that kept the flame from dying. He thought again of the woman and her intrusion. Normally he would have turned her down flat. No one had the right to see his demons, but the distraught face of the parents of Alison Terry had disturbed him. If someone could catch The Carpenter perhaps there was a way back for him. Perhaps . . .

At seven thirty, Meredith began the ritual of leaving the house. There were several locks on all the doors, but his was not the security of the worried homeowner. He cared little if he returned to find the chalet ransacked, as long as he came back to an empty shell. The only things he cared at all about were the contents of the Quaker Oats tin, and a backup cache he kept outside in the tiny toolshed. The fear that drove his security was that of the victim. The Carpenter had allowed him to live. But he had not carried out his desires and there was always the threat, the promise that he would return. That was why he worked through the night hours: to be with people. The dark night was a featureless landscape in which he felt exposed and vulnerable. Meredith knew that the threat had been an instrument of terror, but it haunted him as much as, if not more than, the image of the tall white hood with the stark bright eyes and the flat, unemotional voice. And so he took precautions.

Outside, in the torchlight, he began to brush away the superficial layer of the chipped bark that made up the path outside the chalet. Since he had barred the windows, there were only three ways of entering: front door, back door, and possibly through the skylight in the bathroom. All were locked, and apart from knocking a hole through the wall, they were the only ports of entry. On the path outside the doors, and under the skylight and windows, Meredith did the same. Once the little piles of bark had been scooped away, he hurried round to the rear. There, adjacent to his woodpile, was a bundle of inch-wide plywood. It was modelling material, thin and brittle, incongruous amongst the piles of kindling. He picked up the bundle and removed several of the thin pieces, each carefully cut to a precise length. They were three millimetres thick and would easily have blown away in the wind had he not held on to them tightly. Kneeling on the damp bark, he carefully placed six of the strips six inches apart to span the path and covered them with the bark. He repeated the process in front of the rear door and beneath the windows. He knew that the windows were barred, but an intruder would not. There was nothing to see when he'd finished. Anyone standing on the path in those locations would undoubtedly snap the wood and assume it was a twig in the bark that they'd disturbed. It was a simple but effective check on visitors during his absence and it would be the first thing he would inspect on his return.

Careful to avoid stepping on them himself, he double-checked the doors before walking to his car.

Fingering his key fob, he depressed the alarm button. The car chirped twice as hazard lights flashed momentarily. Meredith quickly squatted and shone the torch underneath and inside before opening the boot and finally satisfying himself that there was no one waiting. This was his most vulnerable time, outside, alone in the darkness. When he finally got in, slammed the door and depressed the central-locking device, the shivering that racked his body came only partly from the freezing air outside.

With numb fingers, he gunned the engine, flicked on the head-lights and left for work.

Chapter 8

Natalie got into her office at the Institute at eight forty on Friday morning after the usual tense drive in. Sometimes she commuted by tube on the grubby Northern line, but when she knew she had somewhere to go after work she usually drove.

Her thoughts had been treading dark paths. The police files she had read through had begun to yield some helpful information. Meredith's survival increasingly seemed an incredible risk on the part of the killer. A risk that so far had not yielded any perceptible dividends. She found herself wondering how he felt about that. Was he angry? Affronted? Frustrated? Or had the incident passed out of his mind? Had he forgotten about Meredith as he began to fantasise about killing again

Her parking space was a quarter of a mile from the Institute and her preoccupation with unresolvable questions persisted as she joined the flow of human traffic spilling out of Warren Street Station. In the crowd she felt an odd calm, a soothing of her nerves. The herd mentality, she mused. Safety in numbers.

She went straight to her office and had begun sorting through the hefty pile of paperwork that had accumulated during her short absence when Francesca, the departmental secretary, arrived.

'Ahah,' said Fran, putting down on her desk the inevitable wicker basket she transported sandwiches and magazines in. 'The wanderer returns.'

'Hello, Fran,' said Natalie with a forced smile. Francesca had a vexing trait of being incapable of delivering any message without drama. It could be very irritating and Natalie sensed that this morning would prove no exception.

'Prof. Falkirk rang. He's rescheduled your lectures for next week and don't worry about the Epsom clinic, he'll get Wardell to cover. He also said that he'd probably miss you this morning, but good luck anyway. All rather sweet, really.'

Natalie mumbled 'Very,' and watched as Francesca flipped a page on the pad.

'Oh and Mo rang – at least half a dozen times.' She paused and smiled teasingly. 'He sounds very dishy. When are we going to see him?'

'Not ever, if I have anything to do with it.'

'Oh dear.' Francesca pouted, waiting for Natalie to elaborate. When this failed to materialise, Fran continued with a disappointed sigh.

'Central Middlesex rang asking if you'd chair a seminar next week.'

'Better say no.'

'It's not until next Friday.'

Natalie shook her head. 'I don't know how long I'll be away.'

'Is this a foreign trip?' asked Fran with her usual air of over-inquisitiveness.

'Sort of.'

'Why all the mystery?'

'Certain people want it that way.'

Francesca, unwilling to give up and not a little irked by Natalie's tight-lipped attitude, was on the point of probing further when the phone rang. She answered it and almost immediately held it out for Natalie.

'Hello?'

'Dr Vine. This is Tindal.'

'Hang on.'

Fran had busied herself with some shuffling paperwork and was so engrossed in moving a pile from one in-tray to a more distant in-tray that it was only an embarrassingly long silence in the room that eventually made her look up.

'Should I leave?' she asked, all wide-eyed innocence.

Natalie returned an equally insincere saccharine smile and watched her sashay out of the door.

'Go ahead,' said Natalie as the door closed.

'Did you establish contact with Meredith?'

'Yes.'

'Any progress?'

'He was very disturbed by the news of the latest killing.'

'And . . .'

'And he's agreed to let me go back down. I'm leaving this afternoon.'

'That's excellent news. What did you make of him?'

'It's too early to say.'

'First impressions, that's all.'

Natalie paused. 'I'd rather not on the phone.'

'Of course. Stupid of me. I also have everything we've got on the Southampton case. Shall we meet?'

'Yes.'

'I'll come to you.'

They met in an empty consulting room, bare except for the inevitable couch and a veneered table with a cream phone and matching angle-poise. Against the wall stood a solitary bookshelf with some ancient and dusty tomes.

Tindal sat in the psychiatrist's chair, looking at Natalie on the other side of the table. Behind her, the grimy windows let in grey February light that threw her into silhouette as she sat, still speed-reading the dossier on Alison Terry that Tindal had given her. He watched, searching for any sign of emotion. So far he had seen none.

Either she was ice-cold or she had a remarkable gift for detachment. Tindal had seen it only a handful of times even in the medical profession. In those instances the reaction to the hard life manifested itself in equally hard drinking and smoking as the pressure was released. But he saw no nicotine stains on Natalie's fingers, nor did her hands show any telltale drinker's tremble.

Finally, she put down the folder. He expected some general comment, an expletive by way of release. Instead, she said pragmatically:

'The nailings, identical in every way?'

81

'He likes them in the missionary position. Another of his foibles.'

'Still no semen?'

'Dry as an old bone. The analysis on the condom lubrication in her anus showed a standard make. He keeps the vagina for his props.'

'What about evidence of resuscitation?'

'Not in this case. My guess is that he got a little over-excited, went a little too far the first time and couldn't bring her back to do it again. He's had five months' lay-off. Probably got himself worked up.' Tindal spoke with his face fixed in a hard, emotionless mask, but she saw the anger spark again in his eyes.

'The lab work is preliminary, obviously, but there is no doubt about MO?' she asked, scanning the report again.

'None. There were hair follicles and blood in the nail scrapings and the DNA profile will come in a few days, but it'll be identical, I know it will.'

'So she did put up a fight?'

Tindal nodded. 'And marked him. We can already tell that the skin is not Caucasian.'

She jotted down some thoughts on to a pad, her eyes narrowing as her mind concentrated. When she spoke again it was with a confused frown.

'I'm still trying to get a handle on the evidence in the Birmingham case. The mixed blood sample. Apart from self-transfusion, I'm desperately trying to think why else he might have been transfused – whether he was anaemic or had some surgery.'

'He wasn't anaemic. They checked that.'

'Then –'

'Look, Dr Vine. With all due respect, other experts well versed in forensic pathology have looked at these samples. You're not telling me anything new. Alison Terry was a fit girl. She put up a struggle, scratched him. We have skin samples from under her nails which match similar scrapings from the first murder. They are from the same source. Yes, he may have had treatment prior to beginning all this. We'll know more from the lab work on this case. But if they show a mix too, I'll put money on the fact that he pumps himself with a few units of juice before he kills. All part of the service. He doesn't have leukaemia or any other blood disorder requiring transfusion, and for him to have started all this a few days after major surgery is too much to contemplate. Now if you're truly interested, you are more than welcome to liaise with the lab. The scientific officer who is overseeing all this is very experienced. You'd get on like a house on fire. Her name is Norris, Pat Norris.' He checked himself, pausing before repeating with a hint of impatience what he'd said earlier. 'What you're telling me I know already. What I don't know is what you think.'

Natalie looked up, surprised. 'About what?'

'The Dow-Jones,' said Tindal drily before adding exasperatedly, 'Meredith.'

'There's nothing to tell yet.'

'But you think there might be?'

'It's possible. There's so much guilt and denial that God alone knows what information is locked up inside his head.'

'But you think you can get it?'

Natalie's jaw clenched in irritation. 'I said I'd try.'

There was an uneasy silence until Tindal said: 'What about The Carpenter? You've had time to see the files?'

'What can I tell you that your own people haven't already?' she said sardonically.

'Psychologically, I meant.'

Natalie put down her pencil and massaged her neck. 'Male, Afro-Caribbean according to the evidence, and an obvious erotophonophile.'

'English, please.'

'The Americans are less esoteric, not to say blunt. They have specific forensic sexology terms. Paraphilics, or sex offenders, have many subclassifications. The erotophonophile is the nasty one – the lust murderer. Many paraphilics have fantasies, but rarely do they spill over into lust murder. The Carpenter is a prime example of such a spill over.'

Tindal waited.

Natalie felt like smiling to herself, conscious now how their relationship had shifted, so different from the previous occasion.

She heard herself speak, heard the intellect swing into gear, and not for the first time wondered at it. Sometimes she felt schizoid, convinced that some other force took over when she donned her professional hat. A clever poltergeist that spouted out the big words. She heard Mo say, '*Jesus, Nat. Do you really read this stuff?*' And suddenly the smile died in her head.

To Tindal she said, 'He's using a "con" approach. Impersonating police patrolmen and catching victims off guard. I agree, he's probably a police "buff". May even have tried to join at some stage, and that might be worth pursuing. There is nothing impulsive about him. He will choose his victims and plan his attack very carefully. I presume you've found no pattern linking the victims?'

'Except for the fact that they all come from around or within cities with Premier League football clubs, none so far.'

'You won't. He will pick strangers. They will not be strangers to him, of course, at least not in his warped mind. He will fantasise that they're the same person, totemise them. He'll follow them, perhaps for days or even weeks, find out their habits, pick his location, choose his time and place. He's probably brighter than he appears and unfulfilled professionally.

'He has some medical knowledge, albeit slight. The way he's resuscitated some of them so that he can torture them again implies it. His vampiristic tendencies, if that's what they are, mean he has access to a doctor's surgery or a hospital. Also his mutilative expertise indicates that he's read a book or two.' She allowed herself a distasteful pause before continuing. 'He may be medical, paramedical or merely have taken an interest in first aid.'

Tindal's lips had drawn themselves into thin lines. 'You're really cheering me up, you know that?'

'He likes driving. He'll enjoy the sense of freedom he gets from it. And it's obvious from the murder locations that he's prepared to travel. But it's more than that. He feels in control when he's driving his car or riding his motorcycle. It's a common feature of serial killers.'

'First I've heard of it,' said Tindal.

'Very current. A new study from the States,' Natalie added.

'They have more material to research over there. Anyway, as I said, it's all part of the fantasy. He hasn't sent any notes?'

Tindal shook his head. 'Except for his scores . . .'

Natalie shrugged. 'Some of them do. They enjoy the chase. Our man may well feel invisible, literally. And it might explain why he let Meredith go. My guess is he wanted him to see so that he could tell you about it. Glorify himself in some way. I would guess his biggest thrill might be to see his story in the Sundays. Unfortunately, I think he picked the wrong man.' She had Tindal's full concentration now.

'He'll have a room,' Natalie continued, 'a place somewhere full of his things – his special things – and he won't have let anyone see these. Pornography, detective magazines – the type with photographs of women in submissive, humiliating positions – maybe military publications too. And then of course there will be the totems, the prizes that will enable him to relive the glory. Photographs, momentos.'

'He took their purses,' Tindal said.

Natalie nodded, knowing full well that it could just as easily have been body parts. She shuddered inwardly.

Tindal blurted, 'Do you think someone's sheltering him?'

Natalie sensed the desperation, the straw-clutching hope that they were still dealing with something mundane and comprehensible.

She shook her head.

'I doubt it. I doubt that even the person he has allowed to get closest will have any idea of what happens in that other dimension. Previously, despite the extreme violence of their crimes, many paraphiles were diagnosed as borderline sociopaths. That was like calling King Kong a monkey. These are straight men with fantasy worlds who outwardly appear perfectly normal, perhaps even a little prudish. He may well hold down a job, may even be married with children. The point I'm trying to make is that he is not a one-eyed monster. The extreme sadism he exhibits is the only way he can truly fulfil himself. The Carpenter is not mad in the true sense.' She added quietly, 'He's outside the rules.'

Just like Mo, said a mocking imp in her brain. Mo was outside the rules. Mo was just a nasty piece of work who managed to keep a lid on things until the alcohol freed his inhibitions. When Mo went up before the judge for GBH with Vine lying in a trauma ward bruised and battered, his defence would not be psychosis. The startling premonition struck her like a handful of cold water.

'You talk of that as fulfilment.'

'What?' said Natalie, coming back to reality.

'You said he had to kill to seek fulfilment,' Tindal repeated himself.

'You're making the mistake of applying your own set of norms,' she said with a hint of impatience.

'Isn't that why society has police forces?' It was obvious that Tindal didn't like Vine's train of thought. Everything he had tried so far had failed. What she was telling him now simply added mortar to the brick wall they'd come up against.

'It is, of course. And that's why we are so horrified. But the only way he can survive psychologically now that he has started down the path is to kill again. He's fantasised about killing for years. Now he has a taste for it. He is committing the same murder over and over. The victims he chooses are incidental. They fulfil a role, they're archetypal. The things he does, the ritual, appear beyond comprehension to us in their cruelty. To him they have a totally different meaning in the context of some dark scenario.'

'He's butchering people,' Tindal said heatedly. 'He was down to a two- or three-week cycle before he took a six-month holiday. If he reverts to type, we have three weeks at the most.'

'I'm going back down to Swansea tonight.'

'Then you agree. You do think the answer lies with Meredith?' Tindal wanted reassurance.

'Perhaps. But he's been severely traumatised. He's as good as left society, shutting out the pain. It's going to take time.'

Tindal kept his eyes on hers. 'That's exactly what we haven't got.'

'Don't keep pushing me,' said Natalie.

86

Tindal held her stare. 'Don't feel you're being singled out. I push everybody,' he said, and didn't smile.

After he left, Natalie tied up her loose ends, trying her utmost to shut out the shocking image that had crept into her brain like a sly rat. It had never happened before; never even in her nightmares had she seen Mo as that much of a monster. But there was a precedent in her life. Wasn't it about time she admitted to herself what this was all about? Nothing more than a sexed-up version of what she had gone through with her mother.

Mary, Mary, quite contrary . . .

All of a sudden the trip to Wales seemed altogether less unwelcome. She knew there would be no answers for her own hang-ups there, but at least it would give her time to think. And even as she told herself that little lie, the imp said, *Who are you trying to kid, Nattie?*

She gave Fran the address and phone number of the motor lodge.

'This is for emergencies only. Anything and everything routine can wait.'

'You're on a mission from God, right?' said Fran, chewing a Danish and sipping coffee.

'More like a mission from hell,' she said bitterly. 'I don't want to be disturbed, Fran. Use your judgement.'

And even as she said it, she felt the cold hand of apprehension on her neck.

Chapter 9

Leonard Bloor stood patiently at the theatre entrance beneath the sign that said 'No Unauthorised Personnel'. He was unprepossessing, five feet ten inches tall, running a little to fat, a florid face with small, alert eyes that had a tendency to slide away when forced to confront anyone who spoke to him directly. He had two distinguishing habits that in themselves were hardly noteworthy: when he walked he held his arms close to his sides, which accentuated an already round-shouldered lope, and in quiet moments such as this he would absently fondle his chin with his hand. It gave him a pensive air but was in fact the legacy of a self-conscious teenager when irritating acne had plagued his complexion. Part of his red-faced appearance had sprung from the overuse of steroid ointment on the part of an ignorant GP who had treated Bloor during his formative years.

The doors in front of him swung open with a pneumatic hiss and a trolley came through pushed by a recovery nurse. Bloor glanced casually at the patient lying semiconscious on the trolley. It was a woman, dark-haired, early forties. He could tell from her face and the tautness of her skin over her cheekbones that she was slim.

From the corridor behind the recovery nurse, an obese female auxiliary called to him in a soft Bristol burr.

'Hello, Lennie. How're the sleepless nights?'

Bloor grinned. 'Not too bad, thanks,' he said, straining at the same time to hear what the recovery nurse was saying.

'. . . routine appendicectomy. BP's stable . . .'

Flaherty, the obese auxiliary, had walked up to the entrance and was beaming at him. 'Jessica, isn't it?'

88

'Dani,' corrected Bloor.

'Oooh,' cooed Flaherty. 'How old is she now?'

The recovery nurse was still speaking. Bloor delayed his reply to listen.

'. . . twelve point five of Stemetil. It was quite a nasty one.'

'Uh, six months,' said Bloor, walking behind the trolley, ready to begin pushing it back to the ward.

'It's a lovely age. Make the most of it.'

'I will.'

'Give my regards to Tina, won't you.'

'Sure,' said Bloor and turned away to concentrate on steering the trolley back to the ward.

Ahead, a staff nurse walked slowly towards the lift. In front of Bloor, resting at an angle between the patient and the trolley's cot sides, was a thin set of notes in a green cardboard folder. Bloor reached forwards and pulled them towards him. He read the sticker: Veronica Reuban, D.O.B. 06/07/51. The address was out of town; somewhere near Keynsham. He'd ferried patients to and from the ward all day, and like all the others, Veronica Reuban's head rolled groggily, her lips pale and dry. But even in her sick condition, she was more than attractive. She was a stunner.

They turned abruptly into the approach to the block of lifts. With an exaggerated movement and an ejaculation of surprise, Bloor lunged to one side as the notes spilled on to the floor in the sharp turn. The staff nurse slowed and glanced around. Bloor smiled triumphantly, the notes held firmly in his hand. Dismissively, the nurse turned again to the lift and pressed the call button. Behind her, Bloor swiftly tore the drug chart from where it was clipped to the surface of the folder and threw it behind him into the corridor. The doors of the lift opened almost immediately and Bloor pushed the trolley and Veronica Reuban in. There was no one else inside; it was one of the two lifts reserved solely for patient transfers and as such had only enough room for one trolley plus escorts. Bloor pushed the first-floor button and silently, smoothly, they descended three floors.

At the bottom, the opposite doors opened automatically and

the staff nurse exited, letting Bloor do the heavy work of steering the trolley behind her. As the back wheels trundled over the metal interface between corridor and lift, the vibration completed the work that the sharp turn upstairs had begun and the notes that Bloor had carefully placed on the edge of the trolley clattered to the floor, dispersing like a paper-fragment grenade.

'Oh, God,' said the staff nurse accusingly as she came up behind to help Bloor, who was already on his knees. He said nothing. They both knew that if she had been carrying the notes as she was meant to, it would not have happened.

Bloor gathered up the sheets and handed them to the nurse with an apologetic smile. He watched as she put the folder back together. This one was a real miserable cow. He hated doing transfers with her. He waited to see if guilt would trigger a little more vigilance.

'There's no drug chart,' she said finally. 'Sister'll bloody kill me.'

Bloor began searching the floor as the staff nurse did an ungainly pirouette. It took her a full minute before the thought finally struck home and she gave Bloor another hostile glance. 'It didn't fall off upstairs did it?'

Bloor shrugged.

'Stay here,' she ordered before turning away in a stiff-legged walk towards the stairs. Bloor watched her go and as she disappeared around the first flight, he swung back towards the lift. He jabbed his finger at the button and watched the doors glide open. With one hand, he stepped in and yanked the trolley with the semiconscious woman on it in behind him. From his pocket he pulled out a key and inserted it into the panel. He pressed 'Door Close' and turned the key through forty-five degrees, thus overriding any outside instructions.

Isolated in the eight-by-six-foot space, he turned to the trolley and slowly pulled down the green blanket and the thin white sheet. She was naked except for a large dressing over her right lower abdomen. He moved to the side of the trolley, his breathing deep and controlled. He reached down and began to run his hands up her legs from her shins, delving deep in the soft, satiny feel between her thighs, trickling his fingers over her pubic bone, moving inexorably upwards towards the clean white dressing. It shone like virgin snow against her dark, sun-browned skin. He wondered briefly where she'd got her winter tan. A Caribbean island, or a humid Florida? His eyes were drawn to the dressing. Carefully, he pulled back the corner of the adhesive tape holding the white gauze in position, peeling it back and hinging it across her flat belly.

Swiftly, he removed the pillow from under her head.

The woman moaned slightly at this disturbance. Bloor waited until she settled again – a matter of five seconds. Gingerly, almost lovingly, he held the pillow in the strong fingers of his left hand. With his right, he ran his fingers down over her neat, flat breasts towards the exposed incision in her right iliac fossa. Veronica had been Jackman's patient. Jackman still believed in sutures – four O prolene. Not for him staples or subcuticulars. Bloor's fingers were now at the lateral limit of the gash. He snaked along it, searching for a gap. He found one, big enough for what he wanted.

Quickly, he inserted his finger into the warm, slick wetness of her intestines, searching for the tied stump of her appendix.

On the trolley, Reuban jumped. The scream of pain that wanted to emerge was snuffed out by the pressure of the muffling pillow under Bloor's left hand.

Bloor rotated his finger, feeling her hot insides sliding and slipping beneath it like some frightened animal running from a predator.

The postop narcotic that Reuban had been given would have seen her through the normal discomfort, but now the hot searing pain that was emanating from her belly fired up already traumatised nerve endings. She flexed convulsively on the trolley, her drugged consciousness aware that something was hurting her, that something was dreadfully wrong.

Bloor gave up the search for the stump. He pulled back a little and hooked his finger under her abdominal wall, feeling the firmness of those hard muscles of hers. He felt possessed of a magnificent strength. He felt he could pluck her off the bed with that one finger, swing her around like a rag doll, smash her skull like a shell.

Then, with a deep breath, his eyes glazing over as if in some spiritual ecstasy, Bloor yanked back hard on the wound, feeling the sutures yield under the strength of his fingers, hearing them pop like the stitching on a fat lady's skirt.

Beneath him, Reuban screamed.

The pain was getting past the drugs. The pillow was cutting off her air and the suffocation reflex was kicking in. Bloor watched with bright glittering eyes as her hands came up to her face, straining to remove the pillow, her body thrashing.

Swiftly, he removed his finger and the thrashing stopped. Her hands still clawed at her face and he let the pressure on the pillow ease. Quickly he put back the dressing, seeing the ooze of blood from the previously dry site. He threw up the covers with one experienced hand and, leaving the pillow still covering her face but with no pressure, he turned the key and opened the doors. Reuban pulled off the pillow, her eyes wide and frightened, much more aware than she had been five minutes before. The first person she saw when her eyes focused was Bloor dressed in theatre greens, his face ruddy, his eyes full of concern. He spoke soothing words, stroked her face, calmed her and eased the trolley back out into the corridor.

By the time the breathless staff nurse reappeared, everything was almost as it had been. The drugs had lulled Veronica back into an easy sleep as Bloor trailed behind the tight-lipped staff nurse and helped lift the patient on to her bed. When he left, he parked the trolley in the corridor outside the ward and used the staff toilet.

Tremblingly, he masturbated, the memory of his adventure in the lift strong and stimulating. Then he washed his hands with the nail scrubber he kept in his pocket. The first time it took him a full five minutes. The second and third were shorter. It was only afterwards that the folly of it began to worry him. Rupturing the sutures had been rash, but he had been transformed by the power of it, the sheer ecstasy.

Fifteen minutes after the arrival on the ward, the nursing sister was concerned enough by Veronica Reuban's whining discomfort to call the house officer. His examination of the wound revealed a gaping hole with pink bowel presenting. Ten minutes later, Bloor was standing at her bedside, helping them transfer her on to a trolley back to theatre. The lazy staff nurse was on a tea break, so it was the sister who asked him the questions, almost in passing.

'Anything untoward happen on transfer up here, Leonard?'

He paused for a moment, his face thoughtful, before answering in his customary measured way; 'She was fidgeting a little in the lift. I did tell Staff Nurse Milne.'

The sister nodded. 'She's popped three sutures. She must have had her fingers in there. Either that or Mr Jackman is losing his touch.'

Bloor nodded, watching her smile tiredly. Realising that he was allowed to share the joke, he smiled too.

'Still, with a bit of luck he'll have gone home. Young Stuart will have to tidy her up. Damned nuisance. I can't understand why Milne didn't say anything.'

Bloor and the sister took Veronica Reuban back to theatre for resuturing. It was talked of on the ward for the rest of the shift and then forgotten. Eventually, Veronica Reuban went home and dined out for a month or two on the fact that she had unpicked her own stitches. She and her husband laughed about it, mercifully unaware of how close to death she had been.

Bloor's shift ended at five, just as they were putting Veronica to sleep for the second time. He had gone back to the porters' lodge to pick up his flask and sandwich box from his locker, waiting until ten minutes past to do so in order to avoid most of his day-shift colleagues. Even so there remained a phalanx of die-hards who had nothing better to go home to. Half a dozen blue-shirted men were clustered around the TV. Plumes of blue cigarette smoke billowed up from the huddle as Bloor walked to his locker and removed the flask and the Tupperware box. Newspapers, most of them covered with doodles, lay strewn about. Bloor picked up a couple of the most complete and asked: 'Everyone finished with these?'

A couple of porters looked around distractedly. One of them said, 'Hello, Len. Yeah, go ahead.' He turned back to the set and added, 'Come and take a look at this.'

Bloor didn't move. There were enough gaps for him to see well enough what was showing. The men were oohing and aahing, occasionally breaking out into a cheer as the girl gyrating on the bed performed something slightly more suggestive with the muscular male who was her prop.

'Fucking incredible to think this is on kids' hour. Pop videos? More like porn videos,' said someone.

Bloor knew the name of the woman singing and pouting. The press called her the queen of sleaze.

'Bet you'd like your frenulum flicked by that, eh Lennie?' said a voice from the huddle. The rest tittered.

Bloor watched for a minute and then said, 'She's disgusting.'

'Hey, come on, Len. Doesn't she do anything for you?'

Bloor watched as the girl dug scarlet nails into the male model's thigh and licked her lips lasciviously.

'She's a whore.'

Something in the way he said it made half the group swing around inquisitively.

'Come on, Len,' said one. 'It's only a bit of fun.'

Bloor turned his back on them and walked out of the room. The porters watched him go. Someone said, 'Jesus, he can be a prat sometimes.'

Nobody replied. In response to a yell of delight from those whose eyes had never left the screen, they all swung back to the set. Somebody whispered in awe, 'Look at the pair of tits on that . . .'

Bloor walked out into dank February air, his florid face crimson with embarrassment and a cold anger burning inside him.

Whore.

They shouldn't show things like that to kids. It was appalling. As he opened the car door, his overriding thought was that he should write to the IBA and complain.

He swung into the seat and almost immediately felt better. The

1987 Capri smelled of pine forests from a dashboard turtle. The clean smell heightened the elation he always felt as soon as his hands clasped the steering wheel. He ran his hands around it, enjoying the firm coolness of the contoured black plastic against his palms. The boredom and constraint of the day evaporated as he turned the key and the engine thrummed to life. He drove out of the car park and headed across town towards Temple Meads, away from his home, towards liberation.

He wanted to drive, needing to distance himself from things, but mostly to drive. Driving gave him what he craved, a cocoon in which he was untouchable. A haven in which he could indulge his thoughts, imagine the fantasies he craved and relive those he had made actual. He drove well and automatically. The direction was immaterial.

He wallowed in the memory of being in the lift. He still felt the power coursing through him from what had happened there, the helplessness of his victim. It had been a good week overall. On Monday they had brought in a dreadful RTA with facial injuries and a crushed right leg. When word had got round, he'd hung around Casualty, waiting for it to come in. He'd helped to hold the patient down as they cut off the trousers from his mangled limb, feeling warm blood on his arms, listening to the anguished cries. It had been reminiscent of that first time. When he had been given the gift of knowing that the power was within him.

But watching was not the same as doing.

Doing was what brought the pleasure and eased the pain in his convoluted mind. Effortlessly, like a child who kept the most delicious chocolate until the last, he let his mind explore the very blackest memories. His last sortie had been good, but flawed. He remembered it with a growing buzz of excitement, feeling his erection push spasmodically against the constraint of his flies. He had been in a frenzy, completely unable to control himself, despite the fact that she had not been ideal. He had chosen her because it would make the police think twice. She had been taller, more like Meredith's woman. Not really like Susan at all. His inability to make it last as long as he had wanted had resulted in her meriting only a six. Marks out of ten for pleasure and pain.

As he had been given as a boy by his stepfather.

But six long months of pent-up fury and frustration had been unleashed on her. Six months of dutiful fatherhood, trapped in the house with Tina and little Dani.

He reached down to a small customised cassette holder and removed a tape. The small plastic box had 'Hot Hits from the Sixties' written all over it in psychedelic pink. Bloor deftly removed the cassette and threaded it into the machine. Automatically, he turned up the volume.

No music filled the car. Instead a yawling ululation screeched out from the speakers. The sounds were almost sacred to him. Each one carefully chosen, one high point after another in the slow, murderous destruction of a human being. Like the beating waves of drug-induced ecstasy, the noises washed over and through him.

Suddenly the traffic slowed as he entered a built-up area and traffic lights. A car pulled up adjacent to him and the elderly driver gazed across. Bloor turned down the volume and removed the tape. It was private. Not to be shared. No one to know except himself.

But he had given them something to think about nonetheless. Enough to have kept the media buzzing for months. At least they should have been buzzing. But it had not happened. The police had effectively gagged the newspapers, he knew that. That angered him. But not half as much as Meredith did.

Meredith, who had been granted the singular privilege of witnessing his work in all its glory. He had played his part and it had been better, yet at the same time worse. The better for having the voice there, even though it was forced and cracked, sometimes screaming, sometimes sobbing, often pleading. It was still a voice. A voice that praised, guiding him through the ritual. And when Meredith had spoken words in the right places as instructed, it had been magnificent. Bloor had been transported, elevated beyond anything he had experienced before. He had contemplated capturing Meredith and a separate victim, but that would have been far too dangerous. And so he had used Meredith's woman, and despite her not fulfilling the role exactly, it had been worth it.

He had let Meredith live beyond the part he had given him in the hope that he would instruct the press. Instruct and inform in that voice, that magnificent voice that was so near to the one he remembered so clearly.

But even Meredith had betrayed him. Hidden away like some monk, guarding his little secrets, ungrateful for the mercy he had been shown.

Well, so be it. He had visited Meredith in his little hideaway, finding him through letters addressed to him at the hospital that his loyal departmental secretary had rerouted. During his visits he had contemplated killing Meredith, but he had not gone through with it. One day Meredith might see the light and tell the world. One day, he, Bloor, might consider him unworthy. The balance was a delicate one. And if the scales tipped it would be a simple matter for Bloor to end what he had begun. To a mind that lacked any vestige of real feeling, it would be nothing more than swatting an irritating fly.

Chapter 10

A tiny patch of weed-infested lawn stood outside Bloor's Thirties semidetached. The green patch around an unkempt forsythia made up the twenty or so square yards that separated front door from pavement. Bloor inserted a key and stepped inside, where the smell of cooking oil hit him immediately. Tina was not a great believer in fibre and greens.

Upstairs, he could hear the sounds of cooing and splashing from the bathroom.

'Lennie?' A disembodied voice floated down the stairs.

'Yeah, it's me.'

'Come and look. She's really enjoying it, aren't you, you naughty girl?'

Bloor put his flask and sandwich box on the phone table and sprang upstairs. Tina was kneeling on the floor of the bathroom, her flabby arms reaching in to support the head of a chubby dark-haired infant who gurgled and kicked in the water. A plastic wind-up whale was puttering around aimlessly next to her ear. As Bloor's face appeared above her, the child giggled and splashed excitedly with her hands.

'Who's that?' said Tina in an exaggeratedly low voice. 'Who's that, eh? That's Daddy come to eat you up.'

The child laughed delightedly.

'Pass me a towel, Len.'

Bloor retrieved a towel from the banister outside the bathroom. When he turned back, Tina was levering her large bulk up off the floor with ungainly effort.

Once up, her face red from the strain, she scooped up the child and, swaddling her in a white towel with pink edging and a hood bearing a Paddington bear logo, bundled her to Bloor.

'Hold her while I let the water out.' Tina stooped over the bath again.

'Hello, Dani,' said Bloor enjoying the feel of wriggling bone and muscle in his hands. He loved the warm, responsive bundle. But when he held her, it triggered feelings that he found difficult to deal with. Unaccustomed warmth and responsibility; lost feelings. He had not planned for this child.

Sunday nights after Ruth Rendell, Tina would have a bath and the room would smell of some dreadful cheap and cloying floral odour her mother had bought from a door-to-door saleswoman. He would follow the trail to the bedroom and find the room in darkness. He would clamber in and steel himself. The unbearable silence would weigh heavily as he waited for her puffy hand to close around him and try clumsily to jerk a response from him. Neither of them spoke or moved until he felt erect enough to scramble on to his knees. He would slide over her peach nightdress, which had already been drawn up the prerequisite amount, and find her hand there to guide him home like an oil-rig worker feeding in the drill. The infrequency of the act made him mercifully quick and she would get up and wash herself and the following morning there would be no mention except for an odd sly smile that made the toast crumble to dust in his mouth.

He had not made it to the hospital for Dani's birth and Tina had not expected it. Her sister had been there instead, which had been Tina's choice. But Dani's presence had affected him in ways he had not imagined. Holding her, he felt the old power and urge rush through him. He could crush her with one hard squeeze, smash her rib cage with his powerful fingers until the lungs wheezed into silence. He stamped on the thought as if it were an injured wasp and was momentarily filled with an overwhelming revulsion for the things he had done. It was such an all-encompassing, vehement feeling that he almost stumbled as he stood clutching the child. Immediately after her birth, the feelings had been strongest. His self-loathing had enabled him to keep at bay the dark thing that germinated inside him. But not for long.

He had fed it once since Dani's birth, but it was already hungry again.

Tina finished emptying the bath and held out her arms for the baby. Bloor's face was fixed in an abstracted stare that mirrored the torment within. But she noticed nothing. Her attention was wholly taken up by the child, as it always was. Bloor was nothing to her now except a source of money and food for her and Dani. He had fulfilled his purpose in providing her with a child; she had no great desire for any more as yet, and so sex had become unnecessary.

She had never allowed him to dry and dress the child, despite repeated offers in the early stages. There was always a reason for him not to do it. He waited now for her stock excuse.

'Go on, Daddy,' she said, addressing the child, not looking at Bloor. 'Mummy will do all this. Your dinner's in the oven.'

Bloor was not stupid, he knew she was shutting him out. It was a family trait. He'd watched her father drift increasingly into solitude as his wife and two daughters ignored the quiet man. He wondered sometimes if they'd even breathed a collective sigh of relief when he'd eventually died, broken and bowed from Parkinsons.

Bloor turned and walked downstairs without a word. He was aware of all Tina's wiles. He stopped at the bottom and looked up. Tina had been twenty pounds overweight when they'd married. Since Dani's birth she had added another twenty. He watched her waddle into the nursery, her doughy broad face red and sweating from the effort of bathing the child.

He wasn't annoyed. He didn't let it get to him. He had long ago accepted her narrow-mindedness. It was at least constant and dependable. And he sensed in an autonomic way that it was one of the reasons he had married her. When at last he had found his true spiritual destiny, the reasons for many things had become clear to him. Basking in the cold shadow of his corpulent wife had become a part of the necessary charade. And beside all that there was the knowledge of what was to come, the dreadful, vengeful secret that the darkness harboured inside him. Let the women do what they wanted. Let them plot and chatter, let them exclude and ignore. One day the child would be older and there would be times, special times, when he and she would be alone together and he could use the camera to record his special games with her. Again the pang of remorse stabbed at him, but the memory of the episode in the lift was strong within him, as was his trip to Southampton at the weekend. They gave him power, so much power. He was above all the petty bickering of Tina and her family. So far above the little people that scurried like ants.

The power snuffed out the remorseful emotion like a spark in a hurricane. Smiling to himself he went to the kitchen and began washing his hands. By the time he'd finished and removed the plate of food from the oven, the beans had crusted drily on the plate and the chips were soggy. He unfolded the newspaper he'd brought home and began to read as he absently forked food into his mouth.

An hour later with Dani asleep and Tina gossiping with her mother on the phone, Bloor opened the back door and stepped out into the garden. He wore an old anorak against the freezing wind that tore at his coat from out of the east. It whipped at his collar and stole his breath away. He felt it seep into his flesh like a thousand blades of razor ice and he grinned. It was elemental this wind. Powerful and unstoppable with the smell of a cold, Siberian plain.

The forecast had shown gales streaming down from Scandinavia over the east coast and into the West Country. A grinning weathergirl had given a warning to wrap up warm. But he knew it would do no good. This was an Arctic wind that would find every tiny crack in the woodwork, every loose roof tile, every doorjamb. And the country would freeze over and old men with arthritis would die in their chairs. It felt bitter and powerful in his face, numbing his lips into senselessness as he bared his teeth to it in admiration.

A single bulkhead light on the corner of the house's gable end illuminated the way. Tina looked after the sparse shrubbery and the square lawn, but at the rear Bloor had erected two large sheds. Beyond them the garden ended in a precarious stone wall that separated the house from the paddock behind. Incongruous in what was effectively a residential area, the acre of paddock lay overgrown and open, a dark wilderness between Bloor and the lights of the house on the far side. Previously a formal garden of the large house at the bottom of the hill, it had grown in neglect and succumbed to nettles and brambles. When the house had become an old people's home, they had fenced it off and forgotten it. Bloor liked it because it was a hunting ground for cats. Since they'd lived in the house, Bloor had managed to capture three of the wild creatures. They were buried now where they had once hunted mice, decaying into bundles of fluff; at least what he had left of them was.

He went to the right-hand shed and unlocked the padlock. It was an old, weather-beaten but sturdy cedarwood construction, the wood stained almost black by the repeated layers of treatment Tina's father had slapped on over the years. It was custom-made and Bloor had dismantled, transported and reconstructed it carefully following the old man's death. It had originally been made as a summer house for Tina and her sister, complete with French windows and a porch. Tina's mother had always considered it ugly and had been only too pleased to get rid of it from her own tiny garden. Now he stepped inside and flicked on the light. One side housed all of Tina's gardening tools. Some still bore faded Spear and Jackson labels. These were recent additions. Many had been home-made by her long-suffering father. Heavy, rusting implements that he'd preferred to the gleaming steel of the expensive garden centres.

The middle of the floor space was taken up by a large grey plastic sheet draped over a 500 cc Honda. Bloor lifted off the sheet and gazed at the machine that gleamed beneath it – the symbol of his freedom, the instrument of his ultimate release. The Honda was more than a vehicle, just as he, Bloor, was more than a man. He perceived it as much a part of himself as his arms.

The white fairings and the orange and green luminescent stripes he applied to the panniers were missing, hidden out of sight. The panniers themselves were attached and locked. Inside were his uniform, helmet and the blue rotating beacon he could attach in minutes whenever he needed to.

He thought of Veronica Reuban in the lift, felt the warm wetness of her very being, her inner essence on his fingers again, felt the elation of her helplessness, and felt the hunger grow in him. It would not be long now before he could indulge himself again. Feed and grow.

He put the sheet back over the motorcycle and locked the door on his way out.

He crossed a narrow concrete path and unlocked the other shed. Tina had scribbled 'Den' on the door in one of her lighter moments. Bloor hadn't minded, it was part of the way he was able to play the role she expected of him, hiding in plain sight. He indulged Tina her whims, all the while sure that he was controlling her.

The minutiae of life were Tina's interest. It had always astounded him how she, together with her mother and sister, could know every detail of the real and fake lives of soap stars, and yet not one of them could remove a spark plug or check a tyre's pressure.

It had not been difficult to keep Tina out of the Den. Bloor had simply filled it with things she had no interest in. In fact he had cultured an interest in the things she found stupefyingly boring. As such, they were dismissed from her mind.

He had put a Yale lock on the door. He kept his ammunition in there, so there was need for security. Tina detested guns. She had also not objected to the heavy padlock he had put on to the trunk in the den. After all, ammunition had to be kept clean and dry. He had studded the shed and lined it with plywood, with a rock-wool sandwich between. A small, powerful fan heater sat squatly on the floor. Around him, stapled and pinned to the plywood, were posters of Manchester United Football Club. Between the posters were photographs, pennants and programmes – the whole range of fan paraphernalia. He had, of course, been a genuine Red Devil follower once, almost fanatically so. But now it was a blind to fool Tina. He kept up the pretence and knew that he could even con the two fans he travelled to matches with every other weekend in the Capri. They appreciated him, more than appreciated him. They knew they were on to a good thing. His ability to abstain from alcohol made him the perfect driver, and they were only too willing to chip in a generous contribution towards petrol costs. After all, who else would give them a lift from door to stadium and back again? And as for Tina, she seemed only too pleased to have him out of her hair.

He shut the door behind him, locking it before walking to the rear of the den where the trunk lay. He'd made a shallow tray that took up a third of the depth. In it were the things he showed Tina – his ammunition made up of three boxes of twelve – bore Eleys, his priceless collection of Manchester United cup-tie programmes, rosettes and memorabilia.

Tina had grown up with the understanding that men (her father) did things that kept them out of the home. Since childhood, weekends had been a women's affair, her father banished. Sleeping in Saturday mornings, shopping in the afternoon, TV in the evening and all day Sunday. Bloor had suspected from the way she spoke of their enforced two-week holidays in Devon that without the banality of their weekend ritual they had been bored silly.

Bloor picked up the shells and studied them. The boxes were almost full. *His* Sundays were spent out on the motorcycle. He would be up and out of the house before dawn, heading away from the claustrophobic semi, exploring remote areas of country-side.

His gun was kept in the house; locked in the attic in a steel-plated cabinet, a legal requirement these days. He loved to hold the weapon but it simply wasn't safe to keep it in the den. The 430 side-by-side Baikal was Russian-made with a twenty-eight-inch barrel and was the full ejector model. He had bagged his fair share of rabbits and birds, but he had never taken it with him when he had killed the others. It would have been too risky. He had a shotgun licence and a blameless record. Using the gun would have been like pointing a finger.

He lifted out the tray and placed it on to a narrow workbench nearby. Beneath it, in the bottom of the trunk, Bloor surveyed his real valuables. He reached in and removed a photograph album, cheap maroon plastic, jumbo size. Hardly the sort of thing to keep treasured pictures in, but then the photographs it contained were not for general viewing. Such photographs were normally only seen in police files and scene-of-crime reports. Every page of the album was headed with a date and a place – Birmingham, Salford, Bath – and each section contained twenty-four black-and-white photographs, one roll of film detailing the destruction of a human being.

Bloor unfolded a camping seat and flicked on the heater. He gazed at the album as a connoisseur might gaze at a catalogue of old masters, admiring his handiwork and inventiveness, impervious to the agony and anguish, the frozen, silent screams. The abject terror he had inflicted was the brushwork he judged them by. And he saw not women but merely instruments of his fulfilment. That they had lives and families and grieving, horror-struck loved ones left behind in the aftermath never penetrated apart from a cursory acknowledgement.

The pillow used to smell of lavender as he lay with his young face, hot and red, pressed into it.

Above him, he could feel the girls' hands, inexperienced but effective, squeezing him, sometimes painful, but mostly coaxing him into excitement.

From this corner of his eye, he could see that big shadow sitting in the chair, watching for the moment. Watching and ordering, instructing with that slight, threatening tone that invoked the fear.

'Good boy, Len. Good boy. They won't hurt you. Let them do it. Let them do it. Turn over you little runt, and LET THEM DO IT . . .'

Fear had made him turn over. Fear had overcome the cheek-burning certainty that it was wrong. What was happening was terribly wrong. He had looked up and seen confusion in the elder girl's eyes. A sliver of tenderness shining beneath the blackness of corruption. And then she was at him, instructing the little one at her side, threatening him to keep still as the voice from the corner grew hoarse with excitement.

'Good boy, Lennie. Good boy. Just let it happen, boy. Let her get at you. She isn't going to eat you, boy. Ha ha ha . . . Or maybe

105

she is. Don't struggle boy. KEEP STILL, OR I'LL BEAT THE LIVING SHIT OUT OF YOU . . .'

And above, half hidden by the tumbled bedclothes, he could see the feet of Christ, nailed and hanging, below the face that watched from the crucifix on the wall. In the church his mother took them to he had heard the story of the children . . . Suffer the little children to come unto me . . .

'Lie back and enjoy it, boy . . .'

And forbid them not . . .

'That's it, Lennie, that's it . . . Ah, Rose, that's enough for him. Get over here. Get over here.'

Perhaps there would be a reward after a score was given, his marks out of ten for performance. Praise or punishment depending on how he had done.

For such is the Kingdom of God.

After several minutes of silent viewing, he put the album down on the tray and picked up a child's scrapbook. Innocent, homely line drawings of scissors, glue and tape adorned the bright yellow cover. Inside, each page was stuffed with clippings from newspapers from all over the country. They were the distillation of hundreds that had been scrutinised. Bloor had highlighted in fluorescent green the words and phrases in each clipping that he particularly liked. The earlier clippings contained the best descriptions – before the police had clamped down. Words and phrases like 'night stalker', 'diabolical fiend', 'genius of disguise' and 'police baffled' stared back at him. Some words he had scribbled out – 'pervert', 'monster'. But all of the extracts lacked the real power he craved. There was no mention of his virtuosity or his brilliance. No real acknowledgement of his uniqueness. No admiration.

That was why he had chosen Meredith, to extol his genius. To confirm his true worth.

It had happened so suddenly, the revelation that had transformed Bloor's life. He could still remember the victim's name (how could he ever forget?): Elmore Fisher. It had been an A38 pile-up. Three cars, four killed. They had brought what was left of Elmore Fisher and three others into Casualty. Mr Meredith, the trauma expert, had been called. The injuries were massive: crushed chest, pelvic and skull fractures, dislocated hip, and both legs crushed below the knees. Meredith took one look and just pointed to theatre. It was there that Bloor had picked up the case. He'd been a porter for only three weeks. The theatre was full, busy people running hither and thither, fetching blood, drugs, instruments. And in the middle of it all stood Meredith, calmly conducting the insane orchestra, his gown soaked in blood. Bloor had stood by and watched until Meredith had seen him. There was nothing sterile about the situation; they were desperately trying to stop the bleeding from a dozen points. Meredith looked up and saw Bloor watching. He called to him, bade him don gloves and asked him to hold one mangled, flapping leg as Meredith worked on the large artery under the knee. It was at that moment, with his hands on warm, bleeding flesh and with Meredith's encouraging tones in his ears, that Bloor felt an excitement, a surging, dizzy explosion of ecstasy like nothing he had ever felt before.

And Bloor had stayed, mesmerised as the efforts had failed and Meredith had reluctantly given up. But even then it had not stopped. Long after his shift should have ended, Bloor had stayed and watched the harvesters work. He had remained and seen the liver, lungs, heart and eyes removed for transplant purposes. And all the while Elmore Fisher had lived, albeit with a brain that had no vestige of higher function left. At two a.m., as a 'reward', the tired sister had entrusted the willing Bloor with the body to transport to the mortuary. He had done it alone, taking his own long time about it.

At the bottom of the shed in a freezer, in a Tupperware box he'd labelled 'Rabbit Meat', was a two-pound hunk of Elmore Fisher's abdominal wall. He took it out occasionally, the last time only five days before on his trip to Southampton. He had a lot to thank Meredith for – a lot to thank Elmore Fisher for. Three weeks after Elmore Fisher had died in hospital from his injuries, Bloor had gone to Birmingham and found a girl. *The* girl.

His decision to plant the scarf he'd found outside Anfield at the scene of his first triumph had been inspired. United had lost to Liverpool the day he'd found the scarf. Even then he had known that picking it up was the right thing to do. He had been driven, guided by some inner force. Implicating a Scouser was a subtle and masterly piece of revenge. He'd watched the police run around like headless chickens ever since.

And it was Meredith who had shown him the way.

A bitter rage again welled up in him and he stared at the clippings until his pulse returned to a semblance of normality.

Someone had been sniffing around the hospital. He'd seen a woman asking questions earlier in the week. He'd heard a few of the doctors talking, oblivious of his presence – his cloak of invisibility. One had mentioned the possibility of a book, that the girl had been researching background material. He grinned to himself. A paperback? His exploits written up for all to read. For his father and Rose and Susan . . .

Some time later, when he had had his fill, he replaced the scrapbook and the album at the bottom of the trunk together with his copies of detective magazines and his 'tools': handcuffs, knives, rubber tourniquets and old surgical instruments that he'd salvaged from a renovated theatre and which no one had wanted.

He locked the trunk and glanced at the fixture list on the wall, knowing full well where Saturday's game was, but looking nonetheless, feeling another tingle of anticipation course through him.

Indoors, he made his wife some Ovaltine and sat down with her to drink it. LA Law boomed out of the TV. They didn't speak. At ten, Tina went to bed and Bloor waited until she was asleep before looking in on Dani. Then he put out his clothes for the following morning, arranging them in their proper order on the bed in the spare bedroom. He washed his hands before starting, washed them again when he'd laid out his trousers, and washed them again when he'd polished his shoes. Then he took a shower for fifteen minutes, scrubbing himself red with the nylon brush. When he'd finished he washed his hands again before retiring.

He dreamed of Veronica Reuban helpless in the lift.

108

Chapter 11

The van, a rusting pale blue Astra with 'Roger's Electrical Supplies' peeling off the side, had woken Meredith. It had pulled up on to the gravel hard, standing outside the least decrepit of the two boarded-up chalets. Even with the doors of the van still shut and the occupants busy reading tabloids and smoking, Meredith could hear the bass beat of the radio.

He stood well back in his living room in a semi-crouch, wary and watchful. The initial panic of awakening to an unfamiliar sound had abated, but the curiosity it left still drove his pulse along at a hundred.

The chalets had been boarded up since his arrival and he had taken it for granted that he would not be bothered until the spring at the very earliest.

The van door opened and the radio volume tripled, blasting across the small space between it and Meredith. A tall, painfully thin man wearing skintight stone-washed denims and a filthy purple Levi's sweat shirt got out and stretched.

A new tune had started on the radio and Meredith saw the van's suspension rock as the remaining occupant bounced and swayed around to the Stones' 'Brown Sugar'. The man took a packet of cigarettes from his pocket, lit one and swung round. For a moment Meredith felt that they were looking directly into one another's eyes, but the stranger's sweep of the terrain triggered no response. Instead, he said to the driver, 'Turn that shit off. Jesus, I'm freezing out here.' Neither the van's rocking motion nor the music ceased.

'Twat,' the thin man said before walking to the rear of the van and opening the tailboard. From the back, he removed a heavy donkey jacket and put it on, keeping his cigarette alight and in his mouth while he did it.

'Oi, turn it off, you prick,' he yelled, picking up a crowbar. The volume increased momentarily. Then, abruptly, the noise ceased and a long-haired youth wearing a pair of khaki combat trousers and a skeleton T-shirt got out, smiling challengingly. The thin man shook his head and walked towards the pale blue chalet, where he began to prise off the boards.

They stayed an hour, ripping the boards down from the doors and windows of the chalet. Meredith watched in silence, standing well back, not straying outside, aware only of the nameless anxiety that plagued him over even this small wind of change. He felt little or no relief when they finally left.

He watched TV, unable to go back to sleep. An American talk-show hostess and audience were discussing rape without a tremor of self-consciousness. It took him only ten minutes or so to realise that despite all the confessions and open-heartedness, what emerged was a safe, middle-American opinion that was carefully and meticulously imposed by the well-briefed hostess. She would, God willing, never know the truth.

Outside, the freezing wind of the night before was dying away, leaving a dull, damp afternoon that was sliding quickly towards dusk.

The woman and child arrived at four in a dilapidated Lada. Meredith heard its protesting whine before he saw it, labouring up the steep drive like an injured animal. Immediately, he was on his feet, once again peering through the gap in his closed curtains. The Lada lurched to a stop, the passenger door opened and two small frog galoshes appeared from beneath the doorsill. They hovered there momentarily before dropping down with long, extended necks on to the gravel below. They had yellow eyes and wide, grinning mouths. They capered silently before emerging and revealing their owner as a little girl of four or five years. Clutching over her bright blue plastic raincoat an animal rucksack that bore a raccoon's ringed face, she ran heedlessly towards the door of the chalet. There she stopped and turned an impatiently perfect Miss Pears face back towards the car.

The woman was slower to emerge. Mantis-like, she levered herself out of the car, tossing medium-length platinum-blonde hair in the cold breeze. Even from where he was observing, Meredith could see that the dye was fading badly into dark, almost black roots. She leaned back in and pulled out two bulging Kwik-Save plastic bags. Pausing only to glance around at her surroundings, she followed the child to the door, where she struggled with her packages and a key.

Contrarily, once the door opened the child took off and ran around the outside of the chalet, her feet crunching metronomically on the gravel, fading out and then back in again as she circled the building.

'Mandy, don't wander off now, you hear me?'

The woman's voice, earthy and crusted by a Mancunian accent, fitted her perfectly. He watched as she entered the house and then re-emerged, a cigarette freshly lit in her mouth, to begin unloading the car. The dark jogging pants that she wore were faded beneath a white sweat shirt with 'Orlando' written large in orange above blue streaks. The scuffed-white inch-high stilettos began below pale white ankles that were a perfect match for the pasty canvas of her face. The padding in the shoulders of the sweat shirt gave her thin frame a grotesque appearance. As she opened the boot and leaned forward with her back to Meredith, her pants drew tighter over her buttocks. The flesh there looked sparse over the protuberant bones of her hips.

Emerging laden with boxes and a large green tote, she staggered back towards the chalet.

'Mandy, come on love,' she shouted.

Mandy continued to circle the chalet, but when the woman re-emerged on another foray to the boot, she seemed unperturbed and Meredith realised that the words were mere habit, a reassuring ritual. When, however, after another two trips, the woman slammed the boot shut and entered the chalet for a final time, the ritual changed abruptly.

'Mandy, if you're not back here in twenty seconds, there'll be no crisps or pop,' she yelled.

The ultimate deterrent worked magically and the frog galoshes and the raccoon trotted unprotestingly through the open door.

111

The silence in the clearing seemed suddenly loud in Meredith's ears. Behind him, the TV audience was applauding a woman who had attacked her rapist with a knife after his release from prison. He turned it off.

So he was going to have some neighbours. So what? It didn't change anything.

The fridge was almost empty when he opened it. Irritated, he threw on a coat and quickly set about laying his indicators – fewer this time for such a short time away. Slipping out the back door to avoid being seen, he headed for the village.

Bab's Store in the village exuded a stale aroma of curry powder and bananas. A thin bespectacled girl dangling a small gold ring from one side of her nose stood in front of him in the queue. From the chiffon scarf in her hair to the patent DM's, she wore black. Meredith stood behind her and inhaled cheap perfume. He stared at her nose ring and then away again.

The girl bought a cherry Coke and a Whispa. Jilly had liked chocolate. The Saturday before she'd died, they'd seen *Thelma and Louise* again and Jilly had bought a quarter-pound of Continental Chocolates, which she'd devoured unthinkingly. He thought of the film, remembering the open spaces, the empty roads, the inevitable sunshine bathing the landscapes. Jilly had liked it because it was about women who somehow, despite the downbeat ending, had come out as spiritually superior to men. They had talked about it in the restaurant when they'd dined just before . . .

Beg me . . .

Her eyes, wild and feral . . .

Beg . . .

The woman in the sari behind the counter was staring at him oddly.

'Anything else?'

'Uh . . . no . . .' said Meredith flatly, focusing on the till's LCD, reaching fumblingly into his pocket for change. The sari watched him with impatience rippling over the surface of her eyes.

He finally found a crumpled five and watched, mesmerised, as practised fingers put the tea, milk, eggs and cheese he'd bought into a paper bag and rang up the change he was owed on the till.

He was sweating when he got out of there. For a while he could do nothing but sit in the car clutching the steering wheel, waiting for his hands to stop shaking.

The Lada was still parked outside the blue chalet. Lights burned inside. He drove around to his allotted space and put the groceries on the bonnet while he went through his checks. The front door seemed undisturbed, the sticks unbroken. Flicking on a small torch, he wound his way round to the rear. It was a cold, damp night, the mist dulling the ever-present roar of the sea below. At the rear, he knelt and brushed away the bark. Even with the torch, it was difficult to see clearly but he had done it before without light, judging by touch alone the integrity of the thin sticks. The torch was awkward. He needed both hands to get at the bark so he put the black-and-yellow casing in his mouth. It was difficult to direct the torch's beam. And so he didn't see but rather felt the jagged break in the wood that sent a watery judder of fear through his bowels.

He snatched the torch from between his teeth and pointed the beam downwards, confirming the splintered remnants.

OK, he said to his racing brain. Only one was broken. It could have been an animal – a foraging fox come sniffing. He would have heard the wood snap and run off. Yes, it was possible . . .

He tried with desperation to rationalise, to calm the pounding fear, to quell the scream of terror that threatened to escape from his lips.

With tremulous fingers, Meredith scrabbled away the bark, searching for the remaining strips.

Broken.

He lurched upwards, his worst nightmare unfolding in his fevered mind. Losing his balance, he staggered crazily against the side of the chalet. Flicking off the torch, suddenly aware that it illuminated him as a target, he began to inch his way around, keeping his back to the wall, towards his car. No, it was too far – towards the tool shed.

The tool shed!

There he knew there was a weapon. The ultimate weapon. His breath heaved impossibly loud in his ears, drowning out all other sounds. His eyes flicked up over the silhouette of dark woodland and its secrets beyond.

The tool shed, the tool shed ... The words repeated in his mind like a mantra, but still he could not hear for the roaring in his ears.

Then there was another voice, a high voice breaking through the roaring.

'Hello?'

Meredith yelped like a kicked dog. He lunged away from the side of the chalet, his hands and arms flying up protectively. The woman stood bathed in the yellow light emanating from the open door of the chalet she'd stepped out of. Silhouetted against it, she looked large and ill-defined, a dark, nameless form.

She hovered uncertainly, confused by Meredith's demented behaviour.

'I ... I saw you come in,' she offered nervously. She nodded towards the woodpile. 'I borrowed some wood. I hope you don't mind.'

The words fell like earth on the surface of a coffin. They bounced and danced hollowly, meaningless and unheard in Meredith's singing ears. He had forgotten about his neighbours. The woman and her inquisitive child. Somewhere, he felt the first tingling in his fingers as he overbreathed, unable to help himself as the panic spiralled up. Reflexively, he put his hand over his mouth, trying desperately to stem his gulping breaths.

The woman stared anxiously.

'Mandy was playing near the door. I thought I heard something break but I couldn't see anything.' She paused, fascinated by the whites of his eyes, which showed gleamingly.

'Are you all right?' she faltered. It was the trigger for Meredith finally to find his voice. It screamed at the grotesque shadow in front of him. Burst out with all the desperate fear within him.

'JESUS ... JESUS ...' He moaned, trying desperately to keep his mouth shut as he hyperventilated.

'I'm sorry,' said the woman, stepping back. She was scared now. Behind her, the little girl, dressed in pink fluffy slippers and Care Bear pyjamas, watched round-eyed.

'JESUS,' yelled Meredith again. His chest sucked in gouts of air. Between the spasmodic heaving, he managed to squeeze out the words he wanted to give them.

'*Stay . . . away . . . from . . . here . . .*'

The woman had backed almost to her doorway, her face twisted with anxiety.

'*Stay . . . away . . .*'

Suddenly, Meredith moved. He ran round towards the car, the abrupt motion eliciting a tight little scream from the woman as she turned and fled, the door of her chalet slamming shut behind her.

Meredith grabbed the brown paper sack he'd left on the bonnet, upending the contents on to the floor and crumpling the top into a mouth-sized funnel. He clasped it to his lips, praying the pins and needles that tingled in his forearms wouldn't spread any further.

It took almost five minutes for the attack to die away. Afterwards, he felt sick and drained, shivering in the cold air.

Slowly, laboriously, he put everything back into the paper sack and went back to his front door. From the corner of his eye, he saw a curtain flicker in the chalet opposite.

Once inside, he collapsed on to the ancient sofa, unwilling to accept the nauseating fact that some part of the blackest corner of his mind harboured a pang of regret.

If it had been *him*, at least he might have made it to the tool shed.

Then, it might have been over.

Finally over.

Chapter 12

Natalie's wake-up call on Saturday morning came promptly at six thirty. Her threats after the last time finally seemed to have got through to the motel staff. In fact, the previous night the desk clerk had offered such an icy assurance that she felt sure her complaints had earned her the title 'That bitch in 36'.

She could live with that.

But she still wasn't sure why she'd decided to come back to the motor lodge. Certainly not aesthetics. Probably convenience, in that it did afford her easy contact with Meredith, should she need it. Her plan was to meet him as he came off his shift to make sure he was reminded of her presence. She haboured a paranoia that he would simply decide not to return to the chalet, not be there when she turned up. Not that she knew of any place he would want to go to. During their brief meeting, he had seemed chained to the draughty holiday home. It had struck her as a refuge that he was unlikely to give up easily.

Still, her presence in the motor lodge was at least a guarantee of her keeping track of him. She had travelled down the previous evening directly from work after secreting herself in the Institute library for the afternoon. She hadn't seen the need to go back to the flat, having packed her bag over breakfast that morning. It had made sense not to have to travel across North London before heading west. But beneath the impeccable logic lurked a murky suspicion she was loathe to admit to. There was an ulterior motive for not returning to Highbury, and with the clarity of mind that early morning brought, she knew it to be a far stronger reason for her actions than all her time-saving rationalisation.

She hadn't gone back to the flat because it was a sure way of avoiding Mo.

There, it was out in the open. A nasty, decaying, odorous little truism that felt all the better for seeing the light of day. The likelihood of his being there at the time she returned was small, but there would have been the answerphone and she would probably have listened to it.

'I'm never going to let you go, Nat . . .'

She shivered a little in the stark morning light, telling herself that it was a draught from the window, knowing that it was a lie, but accepting it anyway because the alternative was uncomfortable and irritating.

God, he was just another predatory male, after all, wasn't he? More tenacious than most, admittedly, but that was all.

All?

Bullshit, Nattie. One hundred per cent bovine effluent.

The worst, the absolute worst thing about the whole damn mess was that somewhere in her mind she knew that all her previous relationships –

Relationships? Hah!

- had been leading up to this. Her lousy choice in men had seemed a chapter of unhappy accidents. Wasters, her father would have called them. Fond of booze and drugs and other nefarious activities, but at the end of the day not fond of Natalie Vine at all. What the hell was it with her anyway?

And now there was no denying the fact that her 'relationship' with Mo was unhealthy.

Unhealthy! screamed a voice in her mind. *Natalie, it's bordering on the pathological!*

He was exhibiting all the signs of violent, uncontrollable jealousy. Professionally, she would have counselled herself to be careful, perhaps even suggesting a court order. There was a danger inherent in the condition. A danger that could erupt like a capped volcano at any time.

So it needed a clean ending. Fine. OK. So be it. *Finito.*

But instead of doing the sensible thing, her intellect and training were acting like a soft filter on a zoom lens. She had been trained to handle it. She could handle anything.

117

Thus aided by the twin Band Aids of distance and calm logic, the gaping wound of her relationship with Mo stopped bleeding for a short while.

But what she needed to do was to listen to her instincts for once. To heed them whenever she remembered Mo's black eyes. Eyes that could wound her, as her mother's had once done.

In the Oasis restaurant at six forty on Saturday morning Natalie sat waiting for Meredith. She'd informed a bulging Rita of her presence and had received a conspiratorial wink in return. A few minutes after she sat down, he emerged from behind the soda fountain looking even more haggard than when she'd last seen him.

'Morning,' she said brightly.

'I wasn't expecting you so soon,' he replied pithily.

'No time like the present.'

He sat down, nervous and unsure. Initially, Natalie wondered if it was the open space that worried him, but when he spoke she knew it was more than that.

'Perhaps this is not such a good idea –'

Natalie interrupted. 'I've already decided what we should do. There's some new work going on in this field. You don't want to be confronted with a question-and-answer session, and that's understandable. Your resentment is understandable. But if we could approach your thinking pattern and memory set from the treatment aspect, it'll be far less traumatic. We could take it slowly. No interrogation as such. I'll be able to use what we get out of the treatment for –'

'Treatment?'

'Post-traumatic stress is a wide-open field. There is no definitive method.'

Meredith pinched the bridge of his nose and studied the ripped remains of her Sweet'n'Low packet.

'Nothing more than simple conversation.'

Meredith snorted.

'I think we should try.' There was just the merest hint of insistence in Natalie's voice. Enough to make Meredith lift up his head. She held his gaze and after a moment, as she knew he would, he looked away. She watched him pick up a plastic stirrer and doodle imaginary shapes on the Formica.

'I realise how much this must frighten you,' she said quietly, watching the stirrer bend and yield to his pressure. She imagined his mind doing much the same thing and so she waited. There were few people about. Someone whistled in the kitchen and there followed a yell and the crash of an aluminium utensil.

'Was the last one definitely him?' he asked, his voice full of desperation.

'Alison Terry?' she breathed.

He looked up, his eyes slits of pain.

Natalie nodded gently and saw his fingers flex out and then clench in a white-knuckled spasm. He got up abruptly.

'Not here.' He turned, looking around him like a nomad in a desert.

Surprised, Natalie managed, 'Where?' But in truth she knew exactly where he was going.

He was already striding away. She dropped her document case in her hurry to follow him and had to stoop clumsily to gather it. In the car park, a clear, freezing, magenta sky was predicting a fine day above a white, hoarfrosted landscape of Tarmacadam.

Meredith didn't speak as he strode to his car and began peeling newspapers from the windscreen, revealing a clear, frost-free surface.

'Should I follow you?' she asked.

He did not stop clearing the glass but said, without eye contact, 'If you must.'

There was cold comfort in the small living room of the chalet when Natalie arrived shortly after Meredith. He was on his knees stoking the last embers of a dying fire, coaxing it to life with bits of twisted paper and kindling.

As she entered through the front door left ajar for her, it looked for all the world like a Dickensian nightmare, except that here the austerity was self-induced. Meredith looked like a Victorian consumptive seeking solace from the flames of a fire as

119

his breath sent flurries of steam into the chilled air. She felt like an intruder. An unwelcome inquisitor who would soon be asking deplorably personal questions. In truth, she felt surprised at how co-operative Meredith had so far been.

They both left their coats on and sat around the fire as it finally, begrudgingly began hissing and crackling warmth at them. The February sun, escaping this morning the mist that usually cloaked its reluctant appearance, found the single kitchen window through which to throw a cheering shaft. There was little or no warmth in the orange light that sent motes wildly dancing, but its presence was a spiritual restorative – at least for Natalie. Ridiculously, she took its presence as a good omen as Meredith made them tea.

'I'll start by asking you some general questions,' she began. She sat with an open legal pad on her knees and a Berol still capped.

Meredith stared into his mug, fascinated by the swirling of the brown liquid within. The silence was broken only by the spitting crackle of kindling. She waited for a response from him, some acknowledgement that it was all right to begin.

'General questions?' he breathed finally.

'Background information, that sort of thing.'

'Isn't it all in "The File"?' Meredith's mouth twitched slightly and Natalie knew that for all the sarcasm and bitterness, he was trying very hard.

'I need more than dry facts. I need to understand.'

She was sitting as close as he would allow. He had changed in the few minutes between his arrival and her own into the plaid shirt and black denims.

'How', said Meredith, his lip curling, 'is knowing what school I went to going to help you . . . understand?'

The cynicism was inches thick, but Natalie's reply was still patient.

She sat back, giving him space.

Meredith put the tea down but left a trembling finger on his lip rubbing away an imaginary drop. When he took it away, Natalie realised that it was his lip that was trembling.

'She was a windsurfer. We met on a lake . . .'

The words were enunciated with exaggerated care, his eyes became slits above a smile full of bravado.

'What else did you have in common?'

'We were a medical item. She was a physio. Is that clichéd enough for you?'

'How long had you known one another?'

'Fourteen months.'

'She was an attractive girl.'

'Very,' Meredith nodded, his eyes darting down to where she scribbled something indecipherable in her notes.

'Before Jilly, had you many girlfriends?' Even before she'd finished the question, she realised it was badly phrased and his response came as no surprise.

'Thousands,' said Meredith with thinly concealed anger.

Natalie waited, cursing inwardly.

'I don't know . . . half a dozen? What difference does it make?' asked Meredith.

'I'm merely trying to establish what sort of relationships you were used to forming.'

'Heterosexual,' said Meredith icily.

'That is not what I meant.'

He looked away and Natalie put the cap back on to her Berol.

'I am not trying to catch you out. I know how painful all this must be for you, but believe me, it's a start.'

'The start of what?' demanded Meredith.

'Understanding,' persisted Natalie.

'Sod fucking understanding.'

Things were beginning to degenerate; Natalie could see it. But she wanted to push it as far as she could this first time.

'Did she ever tell you about any odd incidents? Strange phone calls, the feeling that someone was following her?'

'No.'

'Had you or she ever been stopped by the police before?'

Meredith frowned, unable to follow her reasoning. 'Not that I know of. Why should that be of any . . .'

The question hung in the air, heavy with implication.

'Jesus,' said Meredith in disbelief. 'Are you trying to tell me that this . . . this madman might have stopped her before?'

'I would say that he had certainly been following her for some time. In what guise, it's impossible to say.'

The look of loathing and disgust in Meredith's face stunned her. His lips began a spasm of uncontrollable quivering and he put three fingers to the corner of his mouth to stem the trembling.

'What . . .' he faltered, the words like dust in his mouth. He swallowed, his tongue rasping across his palate like a rake. When he spoke again the words came out slowly and painfully, separated by sharp intakes of breath. 'What . . . kind . . . of animal . . . is he?'

'A sick one. He likes what he does. I would say that he is addicted to it. It is the only relief he gets from whatever nightmare existence his past has created for him.'

Meredith frowned, his earlier disbelief intensified by a new, unacceptable truth. Incredulously, he said: 'You're sorry for him?'

She shook her head. 'Not sorry. A certain compassion, perhaps, but only because I know what sort of situations make people like him do what they do.'

'How can you feel anything for him?'

It was obvious that she'd said too much. There was no objectivity yet. He was incapable of it.

'How can you say that?' Meredith insisted.

She saw his breathing begin to increase, anger stimulating the respiratory system.

'It doesn't matter. What does is catching him. He must be stopped, Tom.'

Her use of his first name fell on deaf ears. Meredith still wore the dumb, incredulous expression of total disbelief.

'Compassion . . . Jesus.'

His voice had risen and Natalie saw the tremor flick from his mouth to his fingers and spread to his hands. She got up quickly and knelt next to him. Hyperventilation was something she'd seen many times before.

'Relax,' she said. 'Try not to work yourself up . . .'

She put her hands on his arm and he reacted as if her fingers were red-hot. He yanked his arm away, leaving Natalie's hands in midair, fluttering like frightened birds. He turned his back to her and she could almost hear his teeth grinding.

'I'll be fine. I'll be fine,' he said.

He got up abruptly and went hurriedly to the kitchen. Running water from the tap, he forced himself to drink from a tumbler. Behind him, Natalie sat and listened to the clinking of glass against the enamel of his teeth.

Outside, in the white light of the sun, Mandy had emerged and was playing on the small patch of grass with a large yellow ball.

Natalie stood and watched the frog galoshes leave dark smudges of footprints in the frosted grass. Mandy saw her and waved; self-consciously, Natalie waved back.

When she turned back into the room, Meredith had retreated into the bedroom.

At least she had made a start.

Chapter 13

A hundred miles away to the north-east, as Vine looked out upon the face of innocence through Meredith's chalet window, Leonard Bloor was travelling north on the M5. To the west, the first gentle undulation in the terrain heralded the edge of the Cotswolds as they approached and bypassed Gloucester. Traffic was fairly light, the day bright and cold. Bloor wore sunglasses against the glare.

He was not alone, but his two companions shared the world's ignorance of the truth of Bloor's existence. To them, Len was one of the boys, a stalwart of their own tiny cadre, itself one small part of the vast army of travelling supporters that followed the Red Devils. Even this far south of their destination in Nottingham they were encountering other cars with red-and-white emblems streaming from their windows.

Stan Wrigley was a thin, wiry man with a smart mouth that was always backfiring. He wore milk-bottle-glass spectacles and was blind without them.

'I think we're going to stuff 'em today,' said Wrigley. 'We're going to have another good cup run this year.'

'We will if Sparkie's fit.' The third member of the party added a cautionary note. Known to the others simply as Kev, he was a portly twenty-three-year-old who had never kicked a football in his life and looked as though he hadn't. The nylon United shirt he wore was stretched thinly over his ample gut like a hide tanning in the sun. Beside him he clutched a Tesco carrier full of crisps and beer. At nine thirty in the morning he was having great difficulty suppressing the urge to dip thick fingers into the bag and begin eating.

'How did we do up here last year? One nil, was it?'

'When they were still in the Premier, you mean?' said Kev drily. Everyone laughed. 'Nah,' Kev continued with a shake of the head and a dancing of chins. 'They drew with us one all at home. We shat on them two nil away.'

'That right, Len?' asked Stan, as always unwilling to accept Kev's didactic answers.

Bloor didn't turn around. He said, 'One nil.'

His contribution to the banter was, as usual, limited. He had, if needed, the welcome excuse of having to concentrate on motorway driving, but the other two knew well enough to virtually exclude him unless some statistical point required adjudication.

As for himself, Bloor listened to the diatribe with only half an ear. He drove expertly and with ease, using only the auto-pilot of his brain to navigate. The remainder of his consciousness was lost in a hum of pleasurable anticipation. Whilst Stan and Kev were looking forward to the game, what he was planning had nothing to do with football.

Like all successful predators, Bloor had melded with his environment. Once a month he worked weekends at the hospital and on one of the remaining three, he and Stan and Kev would choose one of United's more glamorous fixtures to attend. They rarely made the trip to Manchester for a home game, preferring instead the adventure of an away fixture, revelling in the atmosphere of the red tide as it poured over a foreign city. They had been together for four seasons and Bloor always drove, much to Stan and Kev's delight.

By midday, they were on the outskirts of Nottingham. Traffic was heavy but flowing. In the rear, Stan was pontificating with relish upon the most recent revelations of yet more police corruption. His voice was slurring from the export lager he and Kev had been steadily consuming for the last sixty miles.

'Stands to reason. You rub 'em up the wrong way, they'll come back at you like a ton of bricks.'

Kev said, 'I heard that juries aren't believing police evidence these days. If you're up, best try and get a jury is what they're saying.'

'Too expensive, mate,' said Stan. 'And anyway, if they want to put you away, they'll find some way of doing it.'

'I dunno. These days –'

'Bollocks,' said Stan. 'All we hear about are the big cases. Them bombers and such like. There may be hundreds in clink who shouldn't be there. The cops just make it up.'

'Unbelievable really, innit. And they still haven't caught a whiff of that fucker, ummmm . . .'

'Who?'

'The Carpenter.'

Stan exhaled and shook his head. 'Never will if you ask me. Off his rocker, but a clever bastard, no doubt about it.'

At the wheel, Bloor allowed himself a tiny smile.

They drove across the Nottingham and Beeston Canal, satisfying themselves that the ground was within walking distance before Bloor headed back into the town. He found a multistorey adjacent to the Broad Marsh Centre only two hundred yards from the railway station where the bulk of the supporters would emerge from. He reversed the car into a space and they went to find something to eat. What Stan and Kev really wanted to do was to find a pub and sink five pints before the game, but they respected Bloor's abstinence and so had established the ritual of the meal.

Today, however, Bloor was not hungry. He was preoccupied and as anxious to shake off Stan and Kev as they were to rid themselves of him. So, they ate quickly at a MacDonald's and made their usual arrangement. Bloor would go off on his pursuit of sporting-goods shops to peruse the guns and fishing tackle, while Stan and Kev would find a pub. Sometime before the game they would meet up and enter the ground together. Bloor chose a newsagent next to the station as the rendezvous.

'If I'm not there by half-past two, I'll meet you at the car at five.'

Stan and Kev nodded. Eight times in the last two seasons they had missed each other and resorted to the car park. It worked well.

Today, it would have to.

Bloor had no intention of going to the match.

He waited until Stan and Kev were well out of sight before swiftly returning to the vicinity of the car. Unlike his companions, he wore no emblem of United on his person. He had deliberately dressed in neutral colours, wishing only to be mute and bland, unremarkable.

He passed shoppers who spared him not a glance. Some dawdled, some hurried, but none of them saw him for what he really was and the feeling of invisibility that he often and genuinely felt crept over him again. The city buzzed with activity but Bloor was oblivious to it. His mind was concentrating itself for the task in hand.

He walked, sticking to pedestrianised areas. He was unfamiliar with the city and the streets sounded odd and a little folky to his unfamiliar ear: Bridlesmith Gate, King John's Chambers, St Peter's Gate. He traced a tight circle back to the large malls of Broad Marsh. After twenty minutes, he found a likely victim. She was not alone. There was an older woman with her and there was enough of a resemblance between the two for Bloor to surmise that he was following mother and daughter. He kept well back but was desperate to get a glimpse of her face. He managed it in Marks & Spencer where she stopped, browsing over some leisurewear. She took off her leather coat, a baggy black mid-thigh affair. Under it she was petite, just the way he liked them. She held up a voluminous sweat shirt, smiling and joking with her mother as Bloor watched. He followed them for twenty minutes until, to his dismay, he realised they were heading for a bus station. Bloor stood anxiously behind as they queued, trying to listen to any snippet of conversation. Things were not going well. He had hoped they would at least have had a car. It was too far for him to get back to the car park and expect them still to be waiting for a bus when he returned. Frustrated, he had to stand and watch as the bus arrived and she got on, leaving him none the wiser and unable to follow.

It was often thus when he was trolling. Things had to come together. Once, on a train station, he had heard the girl give her phone number to the boy she had been with. He had used that to trace her. It was more than luck, he knew; it was destiny. As he watched the bus pull away, the woman faded from his awareness and he turned and began again.

He walked back to the upper mall, pausing in a bookshop where he found and bought a city map. He stood near the plate-glass frontage, perusing hardbacks on wildlife and travel, interested only in the view it afforded him of the street outside.

He saw her after ten minutes.

She walked towards the bookshop carrying plastic bags emblazoned with the logos of several of the city's better stores. Outside the bookshop, she paused momentarily, staring in at the publishers' displays before heading for the walkway back to the car park. In that instant, fatefully, she stood no less than five yards from Leonard Bloor.

The girl who had caught and enslaved his attention wore a plum-coloured duffle with a huge baggy hood that hung around her shoulders. Her legs were sensibly clad in plaid trousers and the warm boots on her feet were flat. That was not to say that she was unattractive. Indeed, her large-eyed, almost child-like face pulled several admiring glances as she strolled along. But for Bloor, she was the epitome of his warped desire.

She was the right height and, from the way the coat hung, he could see that she had a girlish frame. But it was her hair, dark, almost black, cut in a tight bob, that had been the real trigger.

He watched as she strode along with a light, confident step. She must be the one.

He left the bookshop, following at thirty yards. As if to confirm the overpowering feeling of destiny he had, she walked straight to the car park. He let her walk up the stairs, listening at the bottom of the stairwell, hearing her even footsteps, oblivious of the dank smell of urine. Hearing a door click echoingly open, he ran soundlessly up on rubber-soled trainers to the second floor, prising open the door to watch as she walked to her car. Luck was with him; he could see it clearly. An H-registered Golf. He lingered in something approaching rapture as he watched her open the boot and lean over to load parcels, and then he was running up two flights to his own car.

Swiftly, he gunned the Capri's engine and cruised to the down ramp. As he entered the second level from above, the Golf was out of its space, reversing lights bright in the dim half-light. He waited politely for her to complete the manoeuvre and followed her out.

To his surprise, she was an aggressive driver. He stayed two cars behind, afraid of risking a bigger gap for fear of losing her. Once, at some lights, she shot through an orange and forced Bloor to wait agonisingly as she caught up with the traffic ahead. He drove away from the lights frantically, heedless of any risk, to catch her. At the next set of lights he saw her waiting. He had her scent in his nostrils, although he had never been near enough to inhale any of her odours. What he sensed was her vitality. It intoxicated him. He was like some wild cat driven by hunger, aware only of its prey.

She stopped once at a patisserie outside the city centre in an affluent residential area. She emerged carrying a small brown parcel tied with ribbon. An affectation, Bloor thought. A little girl's treat.

Alone in the car, Bloor smiled. It was now ten after three and things were going well. He knew that the odds were stacked against him when he trolled. Finding a victim was one thing, being able to track her to a contact point was quite another. But when it did happen, the feeling was sublime. It was all part of the ritual, this preparation, this stalking of his prey.

She drove south out of the city and as they travelled, Bloor's excitement grew. He reached into the glove compartment for the Dictaphone he kept there. As he drove, he spoke into it, noting road numbers, landmarks, anything that would help him remember the route.

As he followed, the thin veil of sanity that cloaked his mind melted away. His heartbeat filled his head with its rhythm, and he began to dream, to fantasise about what he might achieve with this girl.

This girl.

This special girl.

His sister . . .

*

129

Her name was Susan, she had a perfect face, a flawless complexion and jet-black hair, and she was his little sister.

Leonard the child had for four years lived as happy an existence as any normal toddler might. His father, a Portishead stevedore, had loved his children and their mother. She, a loving but weak-willed woman, had succumbed to stereotype with ease. She let Leonard's father make every decision, but had never complained.

One balmy July afternoon, three stern-faced policemen had arrived on the Bloors' doorstep with the earth-shattering news that Leonard's doting father had been crushed and mangled to death by a thirty-ton container lorry whose driver had not seen the man's waving arms, nor heard his cries above the Willy Nelson tape that had been blasting through the cab. Leonard saw his father only once more. A made-up corpse lying in the family parlour in an oak coffin.

His mother, ill-prepared for even the most minor of domestic disasters, never recovered. But, after six months, she had found it within herself to seek and retain a job packing detergent in a nearby factory. After a year, a neighbour offered to baby-sit the children while the widow had a deserved night out once a week.

Later, the young Lennie would dream of destroying the kind-hearted neighbour in the most gruesome ways. Even at the age of seven, his young mind could appreciate that all his troubles had begun with that misguided offer of succour.

Harry Bloor was unemployed, but a charmer. He met Lennie's mother at a British Legion dance in 1958. Within three months, he was living in the disrupted family's cosy home. Within six, he had, through marriage, become little Lennie's new daddy, and he and his sisters had to learn to write their names afresh.

Leonard was approaching his sixth birthday, his sister Rose was ten and the baby, Susan, was three. Harry was a great one for games, especially during school holidays when the three children were home alone with their chronically unemployed father while their mother was out at work.

Harry had a favourite within the family, as most fathers do, strive as they might to eke out equal measures of affection. But Harry Bloor's conscience was untroubled by such constraints. He made no secret of the fact that he preferred little Susan. What he did hide was his lust for pretty little dark-eyed Susan.

It was shortly after Harry's arrival as a permanent fixture in the household that Lennie started regressing, soiling his trousers and crying in the night for his mother, who never came because Harry would not allow it.

Rose had nightmares. Real, reach-out and touch-them frighteners that began to show up as dark rings under her eyes, as if there was a poison in there that wanted to come out but couldn't, except when she slept.

And as for pretty little Susan, after a few months they all began wondering when she would start to talk again instead of withdrawing into that secret, silent world of hers she'd discovered.

The family's inexperienced GP told an anxious mother and father that what they were seeing was a reaction to the father's death. It sometimes took months, he said.

He, like Lennie's sheep-eyed mother, had no idea of what was going on as Harry had nodded solemnly, revealing nothing.

Lennie and Rose hated summer most of all. During the long school holidays they were trapped at home. Their mother would leave for work at seven thirty and the hot weather made Harry even more of a threat than normal. Even more crotchety and libidinous. But rainy days were the worst; you couldn't even escape outside when it rained.

Harry Bloor's back pain kept him off work for long, long stretches, but never stopped him from leaping out of his chair when a horse actually won on the TV races he was glued to every afternoon. Lennie and Rose would sit and wait for him to stop reading those funny magazines and yell for them. He would usher them upstairs after locking the doors and they would sit on their mother's big bed and watch in silence as he would undo the buckle of his big belt with one large nicotine-stained hand, while the other pulled down the silver zipper.

At first they had cried and reacted, but Bloor was a big man with a hard hand. Still worse, for a child, was his voice.

As well as providing Harry Bloor with a strong body and a warped mind, God had seen fit to give him a voice of immense power, a power that was all its own and had nothing to do with volume. Harry could sing, and often did a little crooning with a local skiffle band. His lust, however, was forever getting him into trouble and out of popularity with the band members, many of whom harboured a nebulous dislike for him that went beyond his obvious philandering nature. When asked they could never quite put a finger on what exactly it was about old Harry. Sleazy and slimy were the best they could come up with usually. Understandable when it was obvious to anyone who cared to look that Harry had little real interest in his talent apart from as a means to entice any female foolish enough to show any interest.

Especially the younger ones.

Even when he whispered, his inflection and timbre and pitch could be the sweetest you had ever heard. When his voice praised it was like the best surprise you ever had, like the cheering of a vast audience. And when it scolded with hot, acid, biting words, it was enough sometimes for the young Lennie to lose the fragile control he had of his bladder.

Harry's voice, like his labile moods, confused Lennie. His hard hand swiping the back of Lennie's head to the accompaniment of those terrifying threats was followed by pleas of forgiveness and promises of treats. Rose, however, would simply do as she was told and scold her brother for not doing it properly and incurring the wrath of the adult.

And always above the bed where he lay in terror, either waiting to perform or actually doing the acts Harry Bloor forced him into, hung the huge crucifix with the image of Christ looking down in agony.

There was one in each room of the house, but it was the lurid plastic one with the Christ pink and bleeding that Bloor remembered. Ever present, deaf to their whimpers and muffled screams, a silent, impotent witness.

When she was fifteen and finally pregnant by her stepfather, Rose confessed to her mother the terrible truth. Too late for the family and certainly for Lennie. By that time the dreadful activity that had become their norm had been etched into Lennie's very being.

Harry Bloor was removed from the family when Lennie was eleven years old and the dye was long since cast. Lennie heard Harry's voice encouraging or threatening him with almost every action he took. He heard it in his sleep, sometimes in the roaring of the storm drain at the gateway to his house, often in the keening east wind, moaning in despicable ecstasy.

Harry's malevolent spirit continued to haunt the family he'd poisoned. Lennie's pliable emotions had been wrenched and bent in a way that was not meant to be. And of all the conflicting feelings in the mind of the ruined child, the most unlikely emerged supreme.

Admiration.

Lennie could not understand why he missed his stepfather, but he did. And then he began abusing Susan himself, continuing the corruption that Harry Bloor had instilled in him, like a dog salivating at a bone, desperate to hear that voice encouraging and rewarding him for the incestuous desires that had been so unkindly awakened.

Inevitably, and continuing the decimation of the family, Lennie was removed to a series of homes, all of which attempted to rehabilitate the boy, and all of which failed.

At fifteen and after three years of institutionalisation, Lennie was fostered by a Gloucester couple with a militaristic attitude towards discipline and a strong work ethic. When at nineteen the boy Lennie became the man, he left their austere home and never returned, but the four years there had instilled in him the ability to survive in the essentially hostile environment of the normal world. He had reluctantly accumulated a handful of basic qualifications under the strict eyes of his foster parents and he gravitated almost unconsciously towards hospitals, drawn by the thought and dreams of blood and bone that had fascinated and preoccupied him as others had been obsessed with screaming musicians or rare birds.

His first day as a theatre porter was one he was unlikely ever to forget. His job that day was a split shift, half of it spent ferrying patients to and from wards, the other inside the theatre lifting unconscious patients on and off tables. In the theatre suite when he wasn't actually lifting, he was free to do mostly what pleased him. And whilst most of his colleagues spent time drinking coffee or flirting with the nurses, Bloor had stayed and watched, transfixed.

When his shift was over, in the smoky, ammoniacal toilet in the porters' changing room, Bloor had masturbated. Holding his bone-hard erection, so very hard that he had trouble walking, he had climaxed in a sticky orgasm that was like the eruption of a long dormant volcano, infusing his mind with dizzying pleasure, the images of the day's surgery etched into his brain.

In theatre, his dreams gradually, inexorably, became real. Then Elmore Fisher came along and gave him the opportunity he had been praying for. To touch and feel all that rendered flesh while Meredith's calm, encouraging voice instructed and his hands cut and sawed. Elmore Fisher was the catalyst for the reaction that had been brewing in Bloor for months.

In Elmore Fisher, Bloor discovered a way to rationalise and justify his existence, and with an almost physical burst of insight, he saw that he needed to become a doer, not a watcher.

The fantasies that had plagued him, left him sweating and uneasy, suddenly clarified, gelled into understanding. There was a way to ease the pain he had suffered, still suffered. A way to erase the hurt. No, not to erase it, to change it, to establish control.

A new fantasy appeared where he was not the one who suffered the humiliation or felt the pain. One where *he* was in control.

The object of this fantasy was a girl, a stylised confabulation of his sisters, the dominant Rose and the dark-eyed, whimpering Susan. The cause of his humiliation, the instruments of his stepfather's demise, the objects of sweet desire. To control the pain, to inflict it, to hear again his stepfather's wonderful voice encouraging and praising. That was all he wanted.

He spared no thought for those who helped him achieve his goal of recapturing the only time in his life that he had felt worthy of anything in his stepfather's dark, evil eyes.

And yet, occasionally, he sensed that somewhere, beneath the layers, there slept a child, uncorrupted and innocent, one who loved his real father, who had never recovered from his death. One who had hidden away for fear of being discovered. But his understanding of this was vague, like the awareness of a storm in the far distance. It usually surfaced in the aftermath of his dreadful actions, accompanied by the dark depression that came over him then.

After half an hour behind the girl, they passed a sign that said Beeston. She slowed and pulled off the trunk road they were on and wound up a hill in a leafy suburb. She drove into the drive of a semidetached mock-Tudor house. Bloor looked at his watch; it was now almost three forty. The local radio station was giving ten-minute bulletins of the match between Forest and United. There was no score. Parkin, the United fullback, had left the field with an ankle injury. He knew enough to get by, but he wanted to get to some of the match if possible. Three times he had not made it due to aborted trolls, once ending up miles away from the city centre while Stan and Kev had waited for him, bored in the cafe they'd arranged to meet at. That time he'd used crowd trouble as an excuse and both his companions had tutted and grimaced in sympathy as he'd blamed the heavy-handed police for rerouting him miles out of his way.

Now, as she got out of the car and took her packages into the house, he let a small smile of satisfaction cross his face. After a few minutes, he drove around the peaceful tree-lined avenues, familiarising himself with the territory, pausing several times at likely vantage points. The street was a long crescent. A cul-de-sac at right angles some forty yards from the house afforded a reasonable view.

He knew there was a possibility that she was visiting friends or relatives. There was no guarantee that this was where she lived, but it was a contact point. He would be back to check it all. But for now, this would suffice.

He watched for ten minutes, seeing no movement, before driving around the quiet streets once more and finally rejoining the trunk road.

An hour after he had left the city, Bloor was returning, re-tracing his steps, checking road signs, speaking slowly into the Dictaphone.

He found a parking space on the same floor in the multistorey and arrived at the match with thirty minutes left of the game and the score still drawn at nil all. He smiled to himself. He had missed nothing.

Chapter 14

Meredith slept into the early afternoon, and Natalie, no longer able to stand the chaos in the chalet, began rearranging and tidying. Although she recognised it for what it was – a compulsive obsessive trait for order – she no longer questioned it. The physical activity soothed her as she cleared the floor space and rearranged the contents of cupboards and shelves.

As she neared the end of her task in the squalid living room, she again saw the little girl outside in the watery afternoon sunshine, arranging pebbles on the gravel, squatting effortlessly in her galoshes.

On impulse, Natalie reached for her ski jacket and gloves and went out into the crisp, bracing air. Seeing the door open, the little girl pivoted to watch her.

'Hello,' said Natalie as soon as the door closed behind her. Mandy looked on in silence, her face neutral.

'Aren't you cold?' Natalie ventured again.

Mandy shook her head solemnly and Natalie saw for the first time that the apparently random play she had witnessed from Meredith's window had been far from that. On the ground, Mandy had constructed a face from the stones, a mosaic of shades made from the blue pennant and the yellower sandstone that constituted the gravel floor.

'Who's this?'

Mandy remained silent, her eyes shy and hooded.

'Is this you?' asked Natalie.

Mandy shook her head.

'Is it Mummy?'

Mandy shook her head.

'Daddy?'

Mandy nodded slowly. There was something in that nod that sent a twinge of sadness through Natalie. On her haunches so as to get closer to the child, she saw the frilly cuffs of pyjamas under a woolly sweater and the too-short arms of the thin anorak that provided dubious shielding from the cold.

As if on cue, a curtain flicked in the chalet behind and the girl's mother appeared, her face puffy from sleep, twisted by confusion and wary suspicion at the sight of the stranger near her little girl. Instantly, the curtain fell back and the door opened to reveal the woman. The unkind comparison that sprang into Natalie's brain was that of a precarious scarecrow on two broomstick legs. The pallor of the flesh against the black jogging suit created a strangely sombre impression and added to the fantasy. Here was a scarecrow attending a funeral.

'I was just admiring her artwork,' said Natalie.

The woman glanced down at the child's playful imagery with disinterest before staring again at Natalie, her mouth hard.

'My name's Natalie,' she offered and saw the woman's eyes flick up over her shoulder towards the other chalet.

'You with him?' she asked with sullen wariness.

Natalie suppressed a smile. It was obvious that the brief impression Meredith had created was not a favourable one.

'Just visiting,' she said lamely.

'He gives us the creeps, doesn't he, Mandy?'

The little girl let her eyes stray from Natalie's face and glanced at her mother in agreement.

'He's been through a lot lately,' said Natalie, not knowing why she was defending him.

'Haven't we all,' said the woman. 'But there's no need for ranting and raving . . .'

Natalie responded with a taciturn nod.

The woman, content at having voiced her criticism and finding no real disagreement, studied Natalie afresh. The possibility that here was an ally dawned on her face like the sun on a grey pond. Instantly, the olive branch was extended in an unsubtle but genuine offer.

'I'm Julie. Brew's on if you want a cuppa.'

Inside, the chalet was cluttered and musty but thankfully warm from a glowing electric fire. In the hearth, half-burned logs lay scattered from abortive attempts at lighting the wood burner. Half-open suitcases occupied much of the floor area and Natalie tried to suppress an urge to stare at the layers of dust that coated tables and chairs and cast a sepia filter over the room. She watched Julie pour herself a second cup and cringed at a sight that explained much of the circumstances. After the milk, but before the sugar, Julie poured in half the contents of a miniature bottle of gin, holding it up and arching her eyebrows in Natalie's direction when she'd finished.

Natalie declined with a slight shake of her head. Having had her offer refused, Julie added another millilitre to her own cup for good measure.

Being in Julie's gregarious presence was the antithesis of the time she had spent with Meredith. Sentences laden with candid and personal facts poured out in a steady stream. By the end of Julie's second forty-proof cup, Natalie had an almost complete dossier of her circumstances and family tree.

She had brought Mandy away for a 'bit of a break'. The chalet belonged to her brother-in-law's family and had done for twelve years or more. Her sister had made all the arrangements to enable them to stay a week or two, or as long as it took for Brian – Mandy's father, but not, as yet, Julie's husband – to come to his senses, or, as Julie had put it, 'grow frigging up'.

Brian, it seemed, was building the nation's transport arteries. Motorway construction meant a lot of weeks away in digs. His most recent return to their flat in Salford had resulted, after eighteen hours of sleep, in a binge of drink, gambling and revelry that had dissipated whatever hard-earned cash he had brought back with him.

'I told him,' said Julie in broad Mancunian, 'if he thinks I'm sitting it out week after bloody week only to end up emptying the bucket he's thrown up in every morning, he's got another frigging thing coming.'

The statement left her mouth quivering and angry and Natalie, reading between the lines of her bitter tirade, found herself wondering if Brian really cared a single jot. It was impossible for her to look at Julie sympathetically. She had already surmised that what calories Julie ingested entered via the neck of a bottle. Food, when it was remembered, was more than likely an unnecessary encumbrance. Meanwhile, the ashtray was overflowing with half-inch stubs, whilst the jogging suit looked as though it hadn't seen the inside of a washing machine for far too long.

All thanks to the booze, God bless it. With a surge of paranoia, Natalie realised that she was doomed to be targeted by alcohol and its victims.

The reason for little Mandy's slovenly appearance was thus nigglingly clear. This morning, like every morning, her mother would have awoken with a hangover the size of a beach ball.

Mandy, Natalie suspected, was becoming a very self-sufficient little lady, and if there was any sympathy lying about it gravitated very easily in her direction.

'What about school for Mandy?' asked Natalie.

'Sod it. Won't do her any harm at this age. Doesn't like it anyway, do yer, love?'

Mandy looked up with that enigmatic expression of hers. Natalie guessed that it didn't do for Mandy to show too much of any emotion. Disappointment was a powerful suppressant.

'Doesn't say much, does she,' observed Natalie.

'Can when she wants to. Proper little chatterbox when she wants to be. Takes her time with strangers, that's all. Probably a good thing too.'

Natalie looked down at the drawing Mandy was manufacturing on a big sheet of yellow paper. A square house with two windows either side of a big red door. In front, on a narrow path, two stick people held hands next to a smaller stick person.

Mandy's subconscious preoccupations were worn very much on her sleeve. Being two hundred miles from her home, it seemed, was not enough to diminish it.

'You just a friend of his, then?' asked Julie.

'Mr Meredith's?'

'Yeah, Coco the Clown over there.'

Natalie smiled and shook her head. 'It's difficult to be his friend at the moment. I'm just helping.'

'Don't look like any cleaning lady I've ever seen,' Julie said wryly.

'He's been unwell. I'm helping him convalesce.'

'You a nurse?'

'A doctor,' said Natalie, strangely self-conscious. Announcing her profession usually signalled an immediate shift in relations. It had led to a guarded reticence on her part. She did not walk about with her stethoscope dangling round her neck, preferring to be seen for who she was rather than what she was. At the same time, she did not want to tell Julie too much of her true reason for being there. A low profile was definitely the order of the day. Thankfully, the news of her qualification had very little effect on Julie, who carried on unperturbed.

'I wanted to be a nurse once. Before I met Brian that was.' Julie swallowed her regret with a large helping of tea-flavoured gin and Natalie again studied Mandy's artistic efforts. A four-legged animal had been added to the nuclear family.

'Have you got a dog?' she asked, deliberately steering the conversation away from Julie's preoccupation with Brian.

'Oh, don't start her off. Always on about bloody dogs. No good, though. Don't allow dogs in our flat do the council.'

Mandy continued to fill in the animal's body in green pencil.

Natalie shifted to sit nearer the little girl as Julie eyed her calculatingly. Suddenly, she said, 'Tell you what, I need to pop out for a few bits and bobs. Would you mind her for half an hour?' Natalie hesitated and Julie added reassuringly, 'I won't be long.'

Shrugging, Natalie said, 'Uhhh . . . no . . . of course.'

Mandy hardly looked up when her mother left.

Julie returned after an hour with flushed cheeks and glary eyes. Her thanks to Natalie were effusive and as they passed one another in the confined space of the chalet, Natalie caught the full force of Julie's breath, close and warm. It wafted juniper sweet and as she registered the fact that Julie's shopping expedition had undoubtedly taken her via a pub or off-licence, she was suddenly back in the musty confines of her mother's parlour, ordered there to await the vitriol her mother had decided to mete out as punishment for any small misdemeanour she could be guilty of. Her mother kept her supplies in the parlour, hidden away in a roll-top cabinet. When Natalie touched it it would tinkle and chime on unsteady legs as the bottles, packed close together, jostled for position inside. Natalie hated that cabinet. How many terrified hours had she spent staring at it, waiting for her mother to appear, praying for her father to come home?

The suddenness and the immediacy of the memory took her breath away as she crossed the threshold of Julie's chalet. Outside, as her feet found hard-packed earth, the stark reality of Meredith's retreat a few yards away crowded in on her. She took in gulps of freezing air. Olfactory triggers were, Natalie knew, some of the strongest, but she had never experienced anything like this before. She kept her memories closed inside a mental strongbox. Something had just found the combination and it unnerved her immeasurably.

Turning halfway between the chalets, she saw Mandy's expressionless face in the window watching her.

Meredith answered the door with eyes swollen from sleep. He stepped aside to let her in without a word. She felt confused and impotent. It was none of her business, she knew that, but even so she felt bogged down by responsibility for a child she had not set eyes upon until two hours before.

'Nice walk?' asked Meredith cynically.

'Visiting the neighbours. The little girl is a beauty. The mother may have been once, but', Natalie shook her head sadly, 'now she has a drink problem.'

Meredith shrugged.

It fed Natalie's ire and she flared, 'Don't you care in the slightest?'

Even as she spoke, her mind registered the fact that it was bitterness at her own past rather than Meredith's callousness that made her react so angrily.

Meredith threw her a challenging look and walked to the kitchen.

'Want some tea?' he asked without conviction.

'No, I don't want any tea.' The anger was still there; she simply couldn't help it.

Meredith put down the kettle he was about to fill.

'What is it with you? Those two prize specimens of the great unwashed appeared here yesterday uninvited. I met them when they were trying to steal some wood from me, and now you obviously expect me to buy raffle tickets for their benevolent fund.'

Natalie felt her cheeks burning. 'If that's your attitude, I might as well leave.'

'Oh dear,' Meredith said with heavy sarcasm. 'What will I do without you?'

Silently, Natalie picked up her briefcase and walked out, unable to resist the compulsion to slam the door behind her.

Back in her car, she drove along the narrow lanes of the rolling peninsula without any real notion of direction. It didn't matter because her mind roared with frustration as images and forgotten emotions from the past floated to the surface of her consciousness. How could she have let herself be so undisciplined? It had never happened before, certainly not to this extent. It wasn't even as if she had never been exposed to such problems. It was what she did, for God's sake.

She had trained herself to resist sentimentality. It was possible to be sympathetic and caring to her unfortunate patients without wallowing in unnecessary sentiment. Without that shield, there was no objectivity. Judgement was clouded; you simply could not function.

So why?

Why now?

She clutched the wheel and drifted through villages, heedless of their beauty, her mind a whirlpool of confusion.

Was it Meredith who had caused this? The sheer horror of his case?

It seemed inconceivable. She was no amateur. She had prepared.

Then what? What?

Mary, Mary, quite contrary.

She lurched to a halt, the wheel shuddering in her hands. Realising that she was in the middle of the road, she pulled over and stopped thirty yards from a pub with a thatched roof. The realisation, or rather the acceptance of it, hit like a hammer blow. There was no blame attached to Meredith, no finger to point at Julie. She had no one to blame but herself.

She had been running away from herself for months. Or, rather, from the true image of herself that had formed in the mirror lately. An image that she disliked. An image that had been made by her relationship with Mo.

It was Mo who was making her begin to see the truth about herself, and it was not a pleasant truth.

Cool, analytical Natalie Vine – the cold academic. An image she had chosen. A mask she had hidden behind.

The career girl, reliable, thorough, destined for higher things. In reality, just a shiny, vinyl cover over a dirty, shabby, un-pleasant mess.

Sitting in her car, as a final insult, Natalie committed the ulti-mate sin.

She began to cry, softly, silently.

Roughly, she wrenched open the glove compartment and reached in for a tissue to stem the flow of tears and wipe the mucus from her nose.

Unforgivable. This was simply unforgivable.

Self-pity was not something Natalie was particularly familiar with and it made a particularly unacceptable companion now. But the tears tapped into a stream of pent-up emotion she was helpless to damn. She thought of her father, impotent for all those years, his face lined with the burden he had taken so long to accept.

Her mother, never far from her thoughts anyway, entered now with vigour. It triggered more torrents as, in her mind, Natalie trod familiar paths. There were no new insights here. She had considered all the permutations many times.

She thought of Mandy, and the sorrow was compounded.

She thought of Meredith and it gave her the handle she needed to put an end to the sobbing.

Innocence. If there was a trigger, it was innocence. No one had asked Mandy if she'd wanted Julie as a mother. Meredith had not applied for a rendezvous with The Carpenter.

The whim of fate. The unkindest cut of all.

The corruption of innocence had been the major influence throughout Natalie's existence. Blowing her nose, she knew she could not walk away from Meredith. It would be too exquisitely ironic. For her to have begun to break through and then to blow it because of her own buried hang-ups was not acceptable.

Hear that, Nattie? Not acceptable!

She turned the car and headed back to the motor lodge, her nose and eyes heavy from lacrimation, but her heart somehow lighter. She felt as though she had met a thorny barrier and crossed it unscathed. The faint prickling in her scalp whenever she thought of it told her that in some undefined way she had been close to failing.

And yet there was no magical notion of how to help Meredith, or of how to get the information that Tindal required. But she was buoyed by a conviction that within her she had a way, as yet unfound, to reach this goal.

The anger had dissipated. In its place was strength. Not the false façade she had built, but an inner structure that felt strong and permanent.

Suddenly she felt, with an almost total conviction, that already he'd given her a clue.

The burning excitement this insight brought sent a surge of energy through Natalie. She felt her foot go to the floor as she pulled on to the dual carriageway that led to the motor lodge. Whatever catharsis this day had brought, it seemed relevant only in terms of this new, bright insight.

For the first time in weeks, Natalie smiled.

She had work to do.

Chapter 15

As Natalie Vine sat in the utilitarian surroundings of her hotel room, trying to convert to words on paper some of the amorphous intuitive feelings she was having, Leonard Bloor was heading down the M5 for Bristol.

The match had disappointingly ended in a one-all draw, neither team able to raise its game sufficiently to provide the necessary spark. In its wake, Stan and Kev were going through their routine of finding blame with officials, management, individual players and the playing surface. Bloor knew that had United won, it would have been effusive congratulations all round. But he put up with the banter, his own mood poles apart from the taciturn, subdued driver of the upward journey. He harboured within him a dark, gleeful anticipation that bubbled to the surface in occasional gregarious remarks.

Stan sat hunched in the back seat, his eyes heavy lidded from alcohol and the heat of the car.

'Wait till we get them at home in the replay. We'll crucify 'em.'

'When Sparkie is fully fit, he'll tear their throats out,' Bloor added.

'Yeah,' breathed Kev in agreement, his eyes gleaming at the thought. They glimmered in the dimness of the car, but nowhere near as brightly as Bloor's. He faced front, his mind half concentrating in that eerie way of his that freed his imagination from the task of driving. Allowing it to travel different roads. Dark, tortuous roads that never saw light.

He'd found *her*.

And the knowledge filled him with tingling anticipation. On the surface, the veils of normality had pulled together and he functioned anew as a carefree, invigorated Lennie who had Kev and Stan chuckling. This was the Len they liked. Restrained by sobriety and subject to a few moods, but otherwise, a good lad.

But beneath the veneer, The Carpenter had awoken.

Kev and Stan gave Bloor six pounds each to cover petrol and just before he dropped them at the Wellington Arms in Horfield they made provisional arrangements for Coventry in a month's time. In between, United would be away to Queens Park Rangers, but the trip to London was daunting and miserable and the unwritten rule was to ignore fixtures in the smoke.

Tina was engrossed in *Blind Date* when Bloor got in.

'Good game?' she asked through a mouthful of crisps.

'Draw.'

'There's plaice and chips in the oven,' she said, already turning back to the TV.

As she did so, Bloor noticed that she had, almost overnight, grown an extra chin. It wobbled wattle-like as she fixed again on the colourful screen. And at that moment, the veils slipped. With harsh and painful clarity he saw his fat, complacent wife and felt nothing for her but contempt. How could he, how could *he* deign to touch this despicable worm? Since Dani's birth, he had not had to perform the act with her and he was suddenly, un-utterably grateful. So much so that he yearned to yell his thanks to the world. There was nothing he found attractive in her. Compared to the girl he had chosen, she was nothing but an ugly weed that required plucking out at the roots and discarding. How she had ever contributed to the formation of something as perfect as his daughter Dani, he could not fathom.

His mind strayed to the baby asleep upstairs and he crept up to look at her, cherubic and silent. He let himself imagine what she would be in seven or eight years – the age Susan had been when their stepfather was finally taken away. An age of innocence.

His hand trembled as he reached in to touch the curling hair, stroke the down-soft cheek. In seven years she would look at him in terror when he commanded her to do the things he wished her to do, just as Susan had opened huge dark eyes and whimpered as he, Leonard, the boy-man, had preyed on her fears.

147

He still heard her whimper in the dark hours of the night and the sound of it was like a memory of opiates. It had soothed his pain once; now it was the only thing that gave him succour. He felt the beating of his hot, fevered brain as explosions of exquisite memory aroused him again.

Not yet. Not yet.

Quickly, he stepped back from the cot. The veils fell back and his mind fell too into acceptance. His life was a mere shell he inhabited, body armour with which to fend off the tiresome routine that assailed him, constantly attempting to thwart his real purpose.

But he felt the power beating within him. The power to achieve what he had been destined for. And with each blow he struck, he felt stronger.

At midnight, as Vine slept an untroubled sleep and Leonard Bloor walked the paths of his unimaginable dreams, Mo entered Vine's flat in Highbury with the key he had cut a month before. He stumbled heavily on the stairs, uncoordinated from drink, driven by a dull, pulsing rage.

She hadn't answered the fucking phone for two nights running. She could be a hard bitch, a hard aloof little bitch who thought she was a cut above everyone else, always on about books and writers he'd never fucking heard of. She could be so fucking irritating. And who was she trying to kid, pretending that she didn't care about money? Every woman he'd ever met had wet their knickers when they knew how much money he had. All except Nattie . . .

If only she knew what she did to him with that offhand tone and that sexy, educated voice. All he wanted was to be with her, to protect her from the wolves. He could only do that if he was there all the time to keep an eye on her, couldn't he? Shit, you could get raped putting the milk bottles out these days. And if he was here she could cook for him, dress for him.

Mo turned to the wall and drove his fist into it. The plaster cracked and dented under the blow. Little bits of dark mortar drifted down the stairwell as he paused, feeling the dull pain in his knuckles and letting it seep into him.

Jesus, talk about hard to fucking get.

She needed 'time' and some 'space'. Well he'd had enough of that. He'd seen the way she'd acted the first time he'd hit her. He'd been annoyed at himself, but she'd made him so fucking angry. All he'd wanted was a drink and she'd said he'd had enough. There was never enough.

He'd suspected something right from the start. There had always been a hint of submissiveness, the suggestion that she'd wanted him to take the lead. Once he'd done it, once he'd thumped her, he could see that it had been right. He'd let fly that night and he'd seen that look in her eye. A gleam that he had been unable to understand, partly because of his inebriation and partly because it was not what he had expected. But it had returned when the threat of violence was in the air, and he'd recognised it then.

Inevitability.

She went so quiet. No hysterics – just that odd gleam, like a whipped dog waiting for more.

Jesus, it had given him such a charge the first time he'd seen it. Inside Miss Perfect was this little Sindy doll just waiting to be thrown across the room. That gleam in her eye as she touched the bruise on her lip, her tongue coming out to touch the place he'd struck.

She'd liked it.

And the rush he'd felt was like the best snort of snow he'd ever had. God, if that was what she wanted, he was her man. Women liked to be treated rough, he knew that. Just that some of them wouldn't admit to it themselves. But it was the way of the world, wasn't it?

He pushed himself away from the stairs, swaying gently, his mind suddenly filled with the image of Natalie's body naked under the sheet upstairs, waiting for him, opening up to him. He crept up to her bedroom, aroused and excited. He would scare the shit out of her and then fuck her stupid.

He pushed open the bedroom door and switched on the light. He wanted her to see him.

Empty.

He stared around him at the order and neatness of the room. A rage like a bush fire engulfed him. His eyes bulged as his face became black with fury. He leapt towards the bed, yanking off the sheets, screaming her name.

'YOU BITCH . . . WHERE ARE YOU, YOU BITCH?'

He turned and ran from room to room, tossing furniture like matchwood, habouring the desperate idea that she had heard him and was hiding, defying him.

But the fridge was empty of milk and the answerphone was on. And as it became increasingly obvious that the apartment was truly, hollowly empty, so Mo's rage blossomed.

In the living room, he kicked over the bookcase, oblivious to the pain in his foot. Grabbing titles he neither recognised nor understood, he began tearing them apart like a weasel in a hen-house, his destructive lust fed by the noise of ripping paper. In the kitchen, he swept all the appliances from the work surfaces, yanked open the utensil drawer and emptied it on to the floor. He pulled a Sabatier knife from its wall-mounted holder and, armed and seething, went back to the bedroom, all the while chanting a mad mantra to a Barry White tune dredged from deep in his brain.

'. . . *I'm gonna hurt you, I'm gonna hurt you. Look out baby, I'm gonna hurt you . . .*'

In her bedroom again, he attacked the duvet with frenzied blows. He'd always despised the fucking Laura Ashley pattern, and now he tore it to shreds, creating an instant blizzard of duck feathers. He was out of control, unable to stop himself. Every item of hers that he saw he destroyed in an almost inexhaustible whirlwind. He went from room to room like an automaton, un-inhibited by alcohol, driven by the need to annihilate what he could not possess. His jealousy went beyond the simply delu-sional. His ego was such that he had never feared she would cheat on him. He could hardly contemplate Natalie in a relationship with anyone other than himself. Mo firmly believed that he was the only person in the world she could possibly find attractive. Her denial of the inevitable was what had driven him to such un-fettered rage. But now, when the thought finally occurred to him that she might, just possibly might be doing something other than 'research' in godforsaken Wales, his anger boiled over into a seething cauldron of confusion.

Pacing, he found and drank a half-bottle of whisky.

There was reassurance in the bottle. And, when the red tension that had been building in his brain for days faded and his thoughts were finally dulled by the huge amount of alcohol he had consumed that day, Mo passed out on the bedroom floor amidst the debris of his havoc.

Chapter 16

On Sunday morning, long before a pale grey dawn washed the sky, as Mo lay unconscious on the floor of Vine's bedroom, and before Vine herself had begun to turn and toss in her motel room with the first stirrings of wakefulness, a light burned in Bloor's garden.

Neighbours, drawn from their slumber by screaming infants or by less vociferous but equally demanding bladders, were used to the chink of light that exuded through the shutters of the shed window at that hour. They knew that Bloor was an early bird. What they had no conception of was what he was contemplating and preparing for behind that chink of light.

In the cold glare of the naked hundred-watt bulb, Bloor was busy. He worked quickly, his arms flying to familiar objects and tools. The hunger was upon him. Everything he looked at stood out with an unnatural distinction and this clarity was mirrored in touch and hearing. He was on a different plane of existence, vaguely aware that this elevated state came with the hunger and that it befitted him. It was part of the transformation, part of the power.

He was already dressed in his leathers, although his jacket was off and draped over a bench. Despite the early hour and minus temperatures, he felt nothing of the cold. Something happened to Bloor on his trolling days. He felt truly invisible and immune from physical discomforts.

In the panniers of the Honda were all he would need that day: camera, sandwiches, flask of tea. The Honda was a bonus. He had declared it stolen two years before. It had been easy to dupe the insurance people and the police about the bike. Dead easy.

He had kept the licence, but was no longer on file as the keeper of a vehicle. The police had known that when they had talked to him after the attack on Meredith had brought them to the hospital looking for a black man who rode a motorcycle. He'd even volunteered for a blood test. Remembering it, Bloor grinned to himself. He definitely wasn't black and as far as they were concerned he didn't own a bike.

The insurance money had come eventually, enabling him to buy the things he'd needed, like the Mace gas. That had come from a United trip to Hamburg. God, he mused, you could buy almost anything in Hamburg. But he wouldn't need the Mace today. Today, he would be travelling relatively light, the Mace against the wall with the other things he would leave behind for another day.

Another special day.

The white fairings, red, green and black tape, and the blue light he'd picked up from a scrapyard looked like innocent flotsam scattered there. And in the other shed, far from innocent, were his instruments. Locked away, awaiting only the murderous hand that guided them.

The motorcycle wore its black tank jacket zipped up, hiding the white paint he'd sprayed on months ago. He chose the blue helmet, carefully packing away the white one with the chequered band around it before wheeling the motorcycle out, enjoying the silent and smooth passage of the machine in the darkness. If he was stopped, he would tell the police that the motorcycle had been returned to him and that the registration documents were in the post. He had nothing to fear.

Locking the door behind him, he didn't even spare a glance for the upstairs rooms where his wife and child slept undisturbed. At that moment, from his perspective, they existed on another planet.

On the street, he gunned the electronic ignition and the machine responded immediately.

Vine woke with the previous evening's resolve still burning within her. By eight, she was crunching along Meredith's gravel in the dim half-light of a tardy dawn. She knocked three times before the door swung open and he stood there, his dark brows lowered in an expression of irritation.

'Good morning,' said Natalie brightly.

Meredith ran his fingers through his hair and looked uncomfortable.

'Before you say anything,' continued Natalie, 'I have an apology to make. I had no right to say those things to you yesterday. If you hadn't guessed it already, I was angry with myself for letting things get to me. Why I should decide to take it out on you, I have no idea. Let's just say that I find it difficult to admit to myself that sometimes my personal life spills over into my work. It should never happen, and I'll try to make sure it doesn't again.' She paused, offering him an olive-branch smile and adding quietly, 'I won't bore you with the details, but I would be grateful if you'd accept my apology.'

Meredith stared at her, his mouth slightly open.

'If you'd prefer, we could pretend that I'm premenstrual. Would that help?'

Meredith's mouth became a momentary oval of surprise before his face crumpled into a confused smile and he stepped back to allow Natalie to enter.

She did so without hesitation.

'Do you mind if I help myself to some coffee?' she asked, fishing out a jar of Colombian-blend freeze-dried and shrugging off her jacket. 'I brought this along because the drain cleaner you serve at the Flamingo is beginning to corrode my oesophagus.'

She busied herself in the kitchen, stealing a glance at Meredith only when the kettle was beginning to hum. He was staring at her, the smile gone and in its place a suspicious hostility.

'I thought we could talk about your work this morning,' she said spooning granules into a cup. She risked another glance, saw his eyes fall away in irritation.

'Why?'

'Background information. Not contentious.' This time her attempt at humour fell short of its target and he continued to frown unhappily.

Natalie poured water from the kettle into her mug and watched steam rise in wisps from the dark liquid. She wanted it black and hot this morning. Meredith stood just inside the door, leaning against the wall. Still smarting, she guessed, despite her apology.

She took the mug to the lousy armchair and sat down. There would be no clipboard today to irritate him.

'Did it fulfil you?' she began.

Meredith looked up and let out a sigh before wandering over to the settee.

Natalie waited, sipping her coffee. Eventually, Meredith said, 'As much as any job, I suppose.'

'But it wasn't just any job, was it?'

Meredith shrugged.

'You were a senior lecturer in orthopaedics. An honorary consultant,' said Natalie.

'OK, OK, I was really special.' Meredith's cynicism was meant as bait but Vine didn't rise.

'Something you'd always wanted to do?'

'Was I bandaging my teddy bear when I was three? I don't think so.'

Natalie sipped her coffee and waited, allowing him to spit out the poison. Finally, he added reluctantly, 'Medicine was always my career choice.'

'Get on with your colleagues?'

'I think so.'

'Liked as well as respected. A rare combination.'

Meredith blurted: 'What is this shit? Some pathetic attempt to boost my ego?'

Natalie said calmly, 'You specialised in trauma, isn't that right?'

'It's what's called a special interest.'

'Bearing in mind what our friend does to people, it's an interesting coincidence, don't you think?'

'Oh come on,' said Meredith disparagingly.

'I knew you'd ridicule it. But the fact is that our friend shows not a small degree of imaginative skill in what he does.'

155

'Skill. Jesus . . .' said Meredith distastefully.

'More than once the police have thought that he's medical. His attire, gloves, his knowledge of and access to blood storage and anatomy . . .'

Meredith's face changed. The derision gave way to doubt. She watched him. His eyes showed the turmoil within. She had succeeded in breaking new ground. It was making him think, something that was essential if she was to get anywhere. He stood up in one jerky movement, his hand shaking badly, the control he strived for gone in one second.

'Am I right in assuming you don't work Sunday nights?' asked Natalie.

Meredith was at the window, staring out.

'What?' he answered distractedly.

'Sunday nights. You don't go in to the service station?'

'No,' he mumbled.

'Would you like to go somewhere. A drive, a pub, anywhere for a change of scenery?'

'No thanks.' It was an automatic response. One that hardly came as a surprise to Natalie. But as he thought about it, Meredith slowly turned, his anger building.

'What is this with you?' he said suddenly, rounding on her. 'First you want to ask questions, now you're inviting me out to a pub. Is this some sort of game?'

'No game at all,' said Natalie. 'It's obvious that talking about it distresses you. I think a change of scene might do you some good. If you prefer to sleep –'

'I can't bloody sleep.'

'Why?'

'Because . . . I dream.'

'Do you want to tell me about it?'

'No.' Meredith's reply was vehement and certain.

'All right,' said Natalie reasonably.

Meredith exhaled in exasperation. 'Christ, you're irritating. I think I preferred it when you were feisty.'

Natalie suppressed a smile. 'I can't make you talk about anything you don't want to. But I'm here if and when you're ready.'

Meredith's reply was more of a challenge. 'I'm never going to be ready.'

'I know that's how it must feel to you now. But I can give you strategies to deal with it.'

Meredith's eyes narrowed. 'What sort of strategies?'

'A form of neurolinguistic programming. Sounds complicated, but it isn't. Not at all. But I can't do anything unless you're prepared to talk.'

'That's the price, is it?' His face had become hard and sceptical.

Natalie smiled reassuringly. 'Not at all. It's an intrinsic part of the process. I told you, the treatment is the thing. Information will come out of it naturally. You have to believe that.'

Meredith sat down again and stared at his feet while Natalie drank her coffee. After a while, he said, 'The girl who died most recently, was she like Jilly?'

'Yes. It's one of the odd things ... Neither Jilly nor Alison Terry fits the pattern of the others physically. All the women before Jilly were carbon copies.'

'Then why? Why Jilly?'

'There are several theories. It could be that his fantasy is changing – he's aiming it at another type. Or, more deviously, that this time he's killed someone like Jilly just to confuse, to mislead. Almost a utilitarian killing, if you like. My guess is that he'll revert to type.'

Meredith's head fell again. He began pushing his cuticles back. When he spoke, it was in a quiet monotone.

'I sometimes think he's in the restaurant watching me, knowing I'm there. No one else can see him, only me. He only exists for me. I have to check the back seats, even the boot of the car whenever I get into it. I only feel really safe here. In the daytime, it's so quiet you can hear everything. No one can come near without me knowing.'

Outside, despite the early hour, Natalie heard a child's gleeful laughter and cursed inwardly. Now was not the time for anything to impinge upon Meredith's train of thought.

Meredith hadn't heard, or if he had it hadn't registered.

'I went back to the hospital once after it happened. It was only

157

to pick up a few things. When people saw me they froze. Something happened to them, as if their brains curdled. They couldn't look at me, didn't know what to say to me. I felt like a freak. Someone asked me how I was and I burst into tears.'

The tinkling laughter outside had died away and the noise of feet on gravel, running, jumping feet, waxed and waned. Natalie heard the door of the chalet slam shut. There followed a tentative knock, the sort a small child who could hardly reach might perform. After a while, as Meredith sat with his thoughts, the knocking stopped and a pleading moan, quiet but definite, began to flow across the space between the chalets and into Natalie's receptive ear.

Come and get her, Julie, Natalie said to herself silently, gritting her teeth. *Come and get her now.*

Meredith looked up, still preoccupied.

'He is real, isn't he? This isn't some nightmare made for me?'

Outside, the moaning turned into silence, followed by a thud and a scream. The noise was hopelessly compelling. A child's scream of anguish.

Meredith frowned, his trance broken.

Cursing, Natalie stood and looked out of the window. Outside the blue chalet, Mandy was kneeling, holding a grazed knee, an overturned bucket next to her. It didn't take a genius to work out what had happened. Mandy had stood on the bucket either to peer in through the window or perhaps to yell through the letter box. The bucket had overturned and the child had fallen.

But Natalie saw other things too. Things that brought back all the anger of the day before. Mandy was wearing nothing but the frilly pink pyjamas. Even at this distance, she could see the pink cuffs were now a dirty grey, having been left on all through the previous day. Bitter anger burst from her lips.

'What the hell is that woman doing letting a child out on a morning like this? It's freezing out there.'

Meredith was looking at her dully. He was waiting for her to answer his question.

Outside, Mandy let out another harrowing scream. One that Natalie could not ignore. Her thoughts rebounded from the child to the man. An odd, disembodied feeling came over her and she saw herself from a distant point, trapped in a web, having to make choices that were simple yet inordinately complex. Her work with Meredith was vital. Thousands lived in fear of The Carpenter. What she could do here might, just might save the life of one, if not countless women. For that reason it was more important than anything she could conceive of.

Her cold intellect now told her to ignore the crying child, turn her mind to the difficult task in hand: to prise out of Meredith the vital knowledge that he held.

But there was a deeper need, one she could not ignore. Mandy had no one but her inept mother. She was not even as fortunate as Natalie had been in having a father as an ally against the disruptive booze. And in recognising this need to do something for the child, Natalie acknowledged a novel, frightening sensation that excited her. For the first time she was following her instincts and it felt exhilarating.

She got up and moved towards the door, registering the fact that Meredith was staring at her, waiting for her to give him the signal to carry on.

'I'm going to see what's wrong,' she said.

Natalie threw open the door and ran to the crying child. She offered no resistance as Natalie picked her up and cradled her, speaking soothing words. She stepped across to the blue chalet and knocked.

No reply.

Through the child's thin clothing, Natalie could feel her icy legs and she pulled the girl closer into her. Mandy had quietened down and was shivering and whimpering softly in her arms as she walked around to the window and stared in. There was only a thin slit in the curtains for her to peer through, but it was enough.

On the settee of the tiny living room, Julie lay with one leg on the floor. Beside her, the TV flickered, unseen and unheard by the unconscious woman. Panic seized Natalie momentarily. Julie was so still, her face unclear through the grimy window, but sickly pale. And then Natalie saw the chest rise as air was sucked in. The breathing was deep and slow – the automatic breathing of the semicomatose patient. Natalie followed the limp hand that dangled over the sofa's seat, the fingers open, pointing unerringly towards the overturned squat green bottle. Anger washed over her in a dark tide.

The stupid, stupid bitch.

In her arms, Mandy whimpered and said feebly, 'Mummy?'

Swiftly, Natalie turned and headed back towards Meredith's chalet. 'It's all right,' she whispered soothingly. 'Everything will be all right.'

Inside, the warmth of the wood burner seeped welcomingly into her body. She looked around for Meredith but he was nowhere to be seen. On her knees in front of the stove, she vigorously began rubbing life back into the child's limbs. Mandy giggled but didn't resist. Then a noise behind them made the little girl start and turn huge eyes towards the bedroom door.

'What the hell is this?' asked Meredith.

'She's freezing.'

Meredith didn't answer and when Natalie turned her head his way, his expression was still incredulous.

'This isn't Dr Barnardos,' he said icily. 'Where's her mother for God's sake?'

'Flaked out from a gallon or two of gin, by the looks of it.'

'Oh great, just great.'

'It's minus five out there,' said Natalie.

'This is no place for her.'

'Why?' asked Natalie quietly, surprised at the control in her voice.

'Because I don't want her here.'

'You aren't the only one in the world with a cross to bear.' Immediately she'd spoken she regretted it, but her voice was calm, not vehement. 'Innocence is not a crime.'

Mandy swivelled her head to look at Meredith again. The big eyes were mournful and pleading. Harsh words between adults were not strange to her ears.

'If our presence offends you so much, I suggest you go to bed,' said Natalie, renewing her limb massage. 'I'll keep her quiet until her mother comes round.'

He didn't protest. Natalie saw his head drop in that defeated way of his and he trooped off towards the bedroom like a scolded child. She turned her attention back to Mandy, whose colour was improving by the second. Behind her, she heard vague shufflings followed by silence. When she got up on stiff joints a few minutes later, Meredith was nowhere to be seen and the bedroom door was firmly shut. On the tiny work surface of the kitchen, she saw that he had put out a T-shirt and an old sweater.

The sleeves of the sweater hung off Mandy's arms like broken branches and the T-shirt reached her ankles, but they were warm. It had been a spontaneous gesture from Meredith, something human he could not deny. It made Natalie think that by following her instincts and helping Mandy she had perhaps prised open Meredith's shell. It had obviously made him feel uncomfortable in the extreme, but at least it had made him *feel*.

It was a good sign. An excellent sign.

Chapter 17

It took Bloor three hours on virtually deserted roads. Once he hit Gloucester, he came off the motorway and branched off for Stowe. From there he took the A429 until it joined the Fosse Way, the ancient Roman road also known unimaginatively as the A4455. It took him up past Stratford, Warwick and Leamington Spa in a straight cross-country run before he took the Coventry ring road and joined the M69 and eventually the M1 for Nottingham.

By eight thirty, he had parked the bike at the corner of the little cul-de-sac on Moore Road in the quiet suburb of Beeston, having experienced no difficulty whatsoever in retracing his route from the day before. The distant sun, although bright, did little to warm the crisp, clear atmosphere. It didn't matter to Bloor anyway; the frosty air was as intoxicating as ice-cold champagne.

Quickly, he found a storm drain and using a small crowbar removed the iron grille. From the panniers of the bike he took out a canvas bag and emptied it of its contents: several eighteen-inch-long pieces of plastic tubing with white connecting pieces. It took two minutes to construct a five-and-a-half-foot-high framework with a triangular roof that he placed over the storm drain. Out of the other pannier he took a second canvas bag, more flattened and square. From it he removed a red-and-white canvas-and-plastic canopy. Draping it over the framework, he tied it in place with the attached straps, which he fed through eyelets at the canopy's base. He had sewn on the canvas roof himself, just as he had sewn together the dozen or so large shopping bags to make the walls of what now passed as a standard workman's hut. The plastic framework had come from a Wendy house bought at a jumble sale.

From inside, Bloor positioned the hut so that he could see *her* house through one of the ventilation flaps.

Satisfied, he went back to the bike and from the back box took out a foldable camping stool, a small Primus stove, sandwiches, flask, and the newspaper he'd bought at a service station. Finally, he checked that his numberplate was carefully hidden from view by the canvas bags draped over the handlebars and seat. Ten minutes after arriving, he was ensconced inside his hide. To passers-by it looked like the power services or Water Board were carrying out essential repairs. If they were curious enough to peer inside the hut they would see a hole in the road, but no one had ever done that. No one had ever bothered.

He sat watching and waiting, his hunter's senses alive to every footstep, every cloud that passed across the sun, every waft of movement in the breeze.

Patiently, but with his brain singing in anticipation, he sat unseen and unnoticed.

Mo awoke an hour after Bloor began his surveillance.

His awakening was not pleasant. A nauseating, throbbing headache competed with a raw, dehydrated throat. He crawled to the bathroom, cupping his hands under the cold-water tap as he knelt weakly against the bath. He gulped down the water and stood, took two shaky steps towards the door, turned and regurgitated the water and the best part of an undigested chow mein into Vine's toilet bowl. Falling to his knees, he continued to retch until bile appeared. But still he couldn't stop his body wreaking revenge on his overindulgence. The vomiting continued with dreadful insistence. The bile became dark and bloodstained.

He hung his head, waiting for the next wave, thinking of the stupid, inane phrases people used to describe throwing up.

Psychedelic yawn.

Talking on the big white telephone.

Retrograde tonsillar tickling.

All of a sudden, none of it sounded the slightest bit funny.

He retched again, but this time it was empty, nothing came. His throat felt twice as raw as before and he stayed where he was for ten minutes until the dull, wretched nausea abated completely.

Finally, he felt able to try some more water, sipping at it this time, lying down on the floor between tentative swallows, praying for no more vomiting, inevitably searching for someone to blame for his predicament. Inexorably, all thoughts led to Natalie.

Stupid, ungrateful little bitch, that's all she was. When she was with him, he didn't drink as much. He still had a few beers, but generally she had a moderating effect. If she wasn't so hell-bent on playing this stupid fucking game . . . Jesus, she made him so fucking angry. Well, that was it – fuck it. Fuck her. She wanted to play games. He'd give her fucking games. Hiding in fucking Wales wouldn't help her. He'd find the bitch.

He lurched upwards, a seething anger chilling the headache. He went back to the chaotic bedroom, his anger redoubling at still being able to find no hint of where she had gone. He lunged at some books that remarkably had escaped his onslaught the previous evening. They stood on a bedside cabinet, thick and heavy. Forensic psychiatry. A tome of long, detailed case histories, her bread and butter. He grabbed the book and held it open between his hands, twisting and screwing the covers, wrenching at it to pull it apart – and instantly stopped.

That was the answer. Somebody at the Institute must know where she was.

Sunday. Shit, it was fucking Sunday!

But Vine often went in on Sundays. Somebody would be there. He inhaled and was immediately assailed by the stale stink of drying vomit on his shirt. He tore it off. He needed to think, he walked into the living room towards the telephone. It stood on a small table in which there was a drawer where she kept her telephone books. He yanked it open. Inside, apart from the thick Telecom directory, was a Liberty-print address book. The Institute was listed and he picked up the phone and dialled. A vague and pessimistic switchboard operator couldn't help.

'What about doctors on call?

Yes, there was a duty doctor.

Mo waited while she made the connection.

'Hello?' said a voice, young, male.

'Oh, hi. I'm trying to get hold of a friend of mine, Natalie Vine. Dr Natalie Vine,' Mo said affably, the epitome of reasonableness.

'Who?'

Jesus Christ, thought Mo. 'Dr Vine. She works there, doesn't she?'

'Does she?'

Shit, what did they give these creeps for brains these days? 'Don't you know?' said Mo incredulously.

'Sorry. There are at least twenty doctors on the staff here. I've only been here a month.'

'Great,' said Mo.

'What's her speciality?'

'Forensic psychiatry.'

'Ah, right. You mean the Reader?'

Hoo-fucking-ray. 'Yeah. But you don't know where she is?'

'No idea.'

'Is there anyone else I can speak to?'

'I suggest you ring tomorrow. Try the departmental secretary.'

'Name?' asked Mo sharply.

'That would be Fran.'

'Fran who?' said Mo through gritted teeth.

'Marks. Fran Marks.'

Mo put the phone down and began thumbing through Natalie's address book. Ms Marks' number was entered in Natalie's neat hand on the second page of Ms. He punched in the number and examined her pretty little book. He despised the neatness, the attractive cover, the femininity of it. Hearing the number ring, he tossed the book away disdainfully.

She answered the phone from her bed.

'I'm so terribly sorry to bother you,' he said with a voice that had inveigled thousands from customers reassured by the note of total sincerity in his voice.

'Who is this?' she asked groggily.

'Mo, Mo Alberini. We've spoken before.'

'Oh, right. Umm. Natalie's friend.'

'Is that what she called me?' he said disparagingly.

Fran laughed, enjoying the sound of his voice, enjoying the joke.

'What can I do for you?' she asked, sitting up in her bed.

'Does Natalie confide in you?'

To Fran, he sounded troubled. No, more than that: heart-broken.

'Sometimes. Why?' she replied, concerned.

'She told me she trusted you. I supposed it would have been you she would have opened up to.' He let the sentence hang un-supported, listening and hearing a small intake of breath in the earpiece before adding, 'You'll know that we've been through a bit of a rough patch lately.'

Fran, always one to stand close to the edge of other people's business, now jumped in with both feet. 'Yes,' she agreed, 'I did know.'

'Most of it was my fault. I suppose I didn't give her enough attention. Pressure of work and my mum being so unwell. Nat has been great, but I suppose people can only ever wait for so long.'

Fran was riveted.

'It can be hard,' she managed. 'And Natalie can appear cold when she doesn't really mean to.'

'You're so right, Fran. But underneath all that, she's desperate for affection.' Again he paused, listening to her breathing, know-ing he had captured her.

'Surely she wouldn't do anything drastic –'

He interrupted. 'Oh, God, don't think I blame her or any-thing. It's just that over the weekend I've spent a lot of time thinking things through. I need to do something to show her how much I . . .' He broke off, letting her imagination do the rest. Pretending to blow his nose, he said, 'I'm sorry. I've got no right to do this to you.'

'Don't be silly,' said Fran.

Shit, the bitch meant it, too, he thought to himself.

'I know she's gone away. Didn't leave me her address. After last Thursday, I can hardly blame her. But I want to send her some flowers. I want her to wake up tomorrow to a huge bunch of tied freesias. They're her favourite. I just want to send the flowers with a message.'

Fran didn't hesitate. 'Ohhh, I think she's very lucky. Hang on, she gave me a phone number, will that do?'

'That would be just marvellous,' said Mo, wiping a piece of regurgitated noodle from his chin as he waited for her to come up with the goods.

'Here we are,' said Fran after a moment. 'O seven nine two seven one two eight three.'

'Fran, that's terrific. I'm going to do this right away. If there's an engagement party, you'll be top of the list.'

'Don't mention it,' she said.

Fran put down the phone and turned over. She usually didn't get up until eleven on Sundays, and she drifted back into sleep easily, with a balmy sense of romantic achievement. The nagging doubt that Natalie Vine might not approve only served to heighten her sense of matchmaking. Someday she would thank her.

Mo dialled the number he'd been given and the motor lodge desk answered. The desk clerk was only too happy to oblige when asked for directions.

He guessed it would take him about four hours maximum, but he wanted to wait until the afternoon. He wanted to get there under cover of darkness.

'Got you, you bitch,' he grinned with dry, cracking lips, and went in search of something to drink.

Shit, he felt fucking better already.

At eleven, the girl emerged just as Bloor was inconveniently pouring tea from his flask. He stopped when he saw her, paralysed by the adrenaline charge that shot through him. He peered out of the viewing hole in his workman's hide, his eyes unwavering like an ornithologist tracking a red kite. He watched as she opened her car door and shut it with a careful clunk, and looked on as the car began reversing out of the small, neat drive surrounded by a small, neat privet hedge.

He was already outside and helmeted as she completed the reverse and put the car into forward gear. By the time she had reached the junction between the crescent and the next street, he was nosing the big bike in the direction of her steaming exhaust fumes.

The traffic was very light and he stayed well back. She drove at the same aggressive pace as the day before and as he followed, Bloor began to feel the heightened awareness return. He could taste her in the air, smell her warm blood, feel her very thoughts coursing through him like ripples on a still lake. The sharp breeze of the air whistling past his face felt like a caress, and with the big bike thrumming beneath him, he felt his erection bulge against his leathers.

Open countryside stretched to the south. They passed through a few small villages and a couple of miles after Monkford, she turned into a narrow lane with a concealed entrance. A sign above read 'Weobley Riding Stables'. He turned in and after twenty yards stopped. The lane curved and opened out into a much broader access that led directly to the stable yard. Pulling back slightly, he got off and crept forward, keeping close to the fenced hedgerow.

He watched her park the car, get out and wave a greeting to someone. She wore jodhpurs and carried a hard hat. Five minutes later she was trotting away from him down the yard on a large chestnut gelding.

Bloor drove back out of the lane. She looked as if she did this type of thing often. He guessed that she would be at least an hour.

Time enough for him to find somewhere quiet and deserted.

Somewhere suitable.

Chapter 18

Meredith resurfaced at midday looking hollow-eyed. He glanced at the small bundle on the sofa under Natalie's coat and said nothing, but his mouth looked set in a thin line of petulance. Natalie was sitting on the one armchair busily filling up an A4 pad with large handwriting.

'Feeling better?' she asked and did a good job of saying it without any sarcasm.

'I woke up before things turned really nasty,' he answered enigmatically. He looked over at Mandy asleep on the sofa but didn't comment.

'She's fine, but you're down two bowls of cornflakes,' said Natalie.

'The village store isn't far,' he said evasively. Picking an apple out of the shallow cardboard box that served as his fruit bowl, he added, 'Shouldn't somebody look in on her mother?'

'Why don't you?' said Natalie.

He didn't reply.

Natalie watched, cataloguing the acts. But he didn't wear this indifference well. She realised with an uncomfortable pang that she would like to have known the true Meredith. The discomfort sprang from a certainty within her that, as an entity, that person no longer existed.

'What was your childhood like?' she asked impulsively.

Meredith stopped chewing momentarily and looked at her, but then took a large bite and through it said, 'Healthy. Normal.'

'Happy?'

'Yes, happy.' His eyes began to narrow.

'You seem unsure.'

'I didn't walk around singing Zip-a-dee-doo-dah.'

'Happier than hers though, you'd say?' Natalie let her eyes stray to Mandy on the sofa.

'Oh, please. Look, I am not a bloody social worker, all right?'

The knock on the door took them both by surprise. Meredith dropped his apple and was on his feet immediately. Natalie watched as he stared at the door, making no move to open it. The knock came again, this time accompanied by an anguished cry. Natalie got up and went to the door.

Julie stood there in her stained sweat shirt sobbing hysterically. She was incapable of words and tears had blotched her face, making red, swollen continents traversed by rivulets of mascara.

'I've lost her . . .' she managed finally.

Natalie tried a reassuring smile and pulled her inside.

'No, she's here, safe and sound.'

Julie took one stick-insect step over the threshold and the cries died immediately on seeing her daughter. Her face was transformed into one of Madonna-like rapture. She stumbled forward, not giving the frowning Meredith a glance as she fell to her knees at the child's side and scooped her up into her arms.

Mandy stretched before opening her eyes and proffering a sleepy grin. The sheer emotion of the scene was too much for Meredith. He saw Natalie smiling, and, curiously, the urge was there for him to smile too. It was an overwhelming feeling. To avoid it, he turned and walked out into the bathroom. When he returned, mother and child had left and Natalie was reaching for her coat.

'I'm starving. I saw a sign on the pub that said bar meals. Why don't you come too?'

Meredith shook his head.

'Why not?'

'I don't want to ruin your lunch,' he said sardonically.

Natalie shook her head in exasperation. 'Have a day off from punishing yourself, eh?'

'Thank you, Doctor.'

Her eyes blazed momentarily. God, he could be bloody exasperating. But anger wasn't the answer. That was what he

170

wanted – another fight. Another opportunity to run off into a corner.

'OK, I promise, no inquisition. A drink and a sandwich. Maybe a walk on the beach?'

'Sounds wonderfully romantic.'

'OK, OK, stay here.' She began putting on her coat again.

There was a long silence as Meredith watched her. Finally he said, 'What'll we talk about?'

She gave him a sideways glance, fearing yet more sarcasm. But his tone was different, almost anxious.

'I'll tell you Julie's life story,' she said quickly.

Meredith nodded and reached for his coat. 'I can hardly wait.'

Natalie turned away to hide from him the small smile of satisfaction that crept over her lips.

They ate crisps and cheese rolls. Natalie drank mineral water and Meredith orange juice.

'Who's going to carry us home?' he asked.

Natalie told him about Julie. She had explained away her unconsciousness as a migraine and a little too much alcohol mixed with her analgesics.

'So what's the diagnosis, Doc?' he asked when she'd finished.

Natalie registered the sarcasm, but this time it was good-natured. 'Inadequate personality. A good-time girl flattered into bed. An unwanted pregnancy and consequently an illegitimate child.'

Meredith whispered, 'Wham, bang, thank you, mam.'

'Now she's trapped. No skills, living off her relatives. Outlook bleak and negative. Consequently she's depressed and escapes into alcohol.'

'Sounds terrific.'

'Whatever you think of the mother, the little girl is a cutie.'

'For how long?'

Natalie shrugged. 'You never know. Perhaps she's a survivor.'

Meredith held his drink and stared into it. 'Like me, you mean?'

Natalie looked around the pub, ignoring the challenge. The

place was half empty, barely twenty people in the bar clustered around a real log fire clutching mugs of frothy beer and murmuring remembrances of last night's drinking with rasping voices and hooded eyes.

Why had she come here?

Pubs brought back to her what alcohol could do, the number of lives it could reach and corrupt: Julie, Mandy, her own mother.

Slut . . .

Where have you been, you little slut?

With difficulty, Natalie swallowed the remains of her roll; suddenly it tasted of her pillow. The one she had chewed in misery during the dark hours of the night after her own mother had threatened and screamed at her.

Why had she suggested the pub? She hated pubs.

'Want some more?' asked Meredith.

She shook her head. 'I need some fresh air.'

'It's cold out there,' he observed.

'I can't stay here.' She was up on her feet and walking out before Meredith had time to finish his orange juice.

Outside, the clear, chilled air washed over her, blowing away the stale smell of the pub. It was fifty yards to the beach. After twenty, she could feel her face begin to tingle from the wind chill. A wheeling gull squawked nearby. It sounded terrifyingly human. She stopped and turned, and saw that Meredith was behind her, looking at her strangely.

'What's the matter?' he asked, his lips unable to respond quite as normal as the cold bit.

She shook her head. 'I have this thing about pubs. It's the booze. I hate booze.'

'Booze?'

'Look, let's walk. I promise not to ask any questions if you do the same.'

'Suits me,' he said.

The wind picked up the sand and hurled it along in swirling bands at knee level as the grey surf churned and lapped its constant rhythm against the long beach. It was deserted except for a

172

man throwing sticks for his dog. Meredith and Natalie trudged along like inmates from a Gulag labour camp, their exposed faces white and purple. Both welcomed the numbing cold. It virtually eliminated conversation and instead both were left with their own thoughts to contemplate. But it was the wind and the spray and the sea that preoccupied them, and despite the cold it was exhilarating.

When they got back to the chalet Meredith appeared more wasted and exhausted than ever.

'Most exercise I've done in months,' he said, rubbing his hands in front of the fire, cajoling life back into his fingers. Within minutes, he was yawning repeatedly.

'Why don't you sleep?' asked Natalie.

'I can't. I mean, really sleep.'

'Why?'

'I can't control what I think when I sleep.'

'There is a way –' She stopped when she saw the pleading in his eyes, but it wasn't a plea for her to stop. It was more than that.

He nodded, barely.

'It won't be pleasant. It's a self-confrontational technique – neurolinguistic, as I said. The aim is to release the victim from the involuntary emotional responses that come with memory of the event. Things like nightmares, dreams, the terrors. It isn't an amnesia trick, not hypnosis. You'll always be able to remember what happened, but you'll be able to establish sensorial control so that you can prevent an emotional overload when something triggers the memory.'

'What's the catch?'

Natalie paused before saying, 'It means you reliving it in graphic detail. Recounting it as a running commentary.'

Meredith's face fell.

'We use a TV allegory. But it's all controlled by you. You can switch it off whenever you like.'

He looked up, confused and lost and exhausted.

'I suggest you get some sleep now, whatever you can manage.' She smiled. 'Go to bed with the realisation that you're over the worst hurdle.'

He stared at her.

She explained softly, 'Wanting to do it is the most difficult thing. You've made that decision. We can start tomorrow. Early.'

Meredith still stared dubiously.

'This technique has been very successful in post-traumatic stress.'

Meredith said, 'I hope you're right. I really do.'

'It'll be a new beginning. I promise.'

Chapter 19

She left the riding school at two and drove back the way she had come. Bloor was waiting for her fifty yards from the entrance. She passed him without a backward glance.

The hut was still standing exactly as he had left it. He lit the Primus and brewed himself some hot tea, having long exhausted the supply in the flask. He felt well pleased with his afternoon's work. On the outskirts of a tiny hamlet he'd found an abandoned petrol station attached to a small transport café. The station's awning had collapsed and the Shell sign hung at an improbable angle, but behind it the café was solid and well boarded-up. Judging from the vegetation that had encroached, it appeared that few people went near it. Inside it was dry and windowless except for two grimy skylights that he could clean and which would give him enough light for what he had to do. He would need plenty of batteries for the flash photography. It had almost been disastrous last time; some of the photographs had not turned out well. There was no electricity, but he was learning to do without. The Primus would give him enough heat; he hardly felt the cold anyway.

The room he had chosen was a small space with access from the rear and surrounded outside by abandoned cars and vans that afforded excellent cover. Conveniently, it was only three miles from the stables. In the forty-five minutes he had spent there, he had neither seen nor heard another living soul approach within half a mile.

At six, she left the house and drove towards the commercial centre of the suburb. Bloor followed her to a cinema complex, leaning in the dark doorway of an empty boutique across the street, watching her pace back and forth in the freezing night, trying to keep her circulation moving. To his right, a dark access road ran behind to service the shops. He stared across at her, enjoying the way she moved, graceful even in her shapeless winter coat.

And then, quite suddenly, the unthinkable happened. She seemed to look across at him, stare at him. He pulled back involuntarily, holding his breath as she ran across the road and stood, bathed in the light from a jeweller's window not fifteen yards from where he lurked in the shadows. This was the closest he had been to her and he saw now that she was a pretty girl by any standards. And as he watched, the hunger began to grow and ache inside him. He knew she couldn't see him. This was partly his own deluded belief in his invisibility and partly his hidden position, but what was new was the conviction he suddenly had that he could simply walk over there and take her. He had never felt it so strongly and it troubled him because of its incredible intensity. All his well-laid plans were evaporating in a junkie's rush of extreme craving. His mind became a roaring flame of blood lust. Desperately, he hunted around for somewhere he could take her.

Yes, there to the rear. The access road was dark, mottled with huge tracts of shadow and darkness, perhaps there might even be a way in to one of the buildings where he could hide her. To one part of him it felt all wrong. It was too risky, too messy. His clothes would get torn and bloodstained and he didn't have his instruments, his camera, his tape recorder. But to another part the hunger was not to be denied. She was sweet meat waiting to be taken as she stood, unaware and innocent, not forty feet from him.

He felt it taking over, felt his feet begin to move him out of his hiding place. Still she didn't turn around or seem to notice anything. Now he was within five yards and he could smell her, really smell her perfume. He felt the muscles of his arms tense. They felt like rods of powerful steel. He knew he could snatch her up with one of them and he took his hands out of his pockets, clenching them into claws. And then he was a yard away, within striking distance. The street was almost empty. His heart thundered in his chest. He would be quick, pull her into the shadows and –

Across the street someone shouted.

The girl turned, her face smiling, her hands raised to wave to whoever had hailed her. He was so close that a collision was inevitable. Caught off balance, Bloor fell to the pavement clumsily, her hand knocking him aside. In that instant he knew it was over, despite the fact that her arm was upon him as she knelt over him, staring into his face, apologising. But he was pulling away, mouthing some platitude, hearing only the screaming voices of frustration and disappointment in his head. He lurched to his feet and ran off, his face burning with embarrassment. At the corner, he looked back and saw her in front of the cinema laughing with two companions who were looking and pointing.

He slumped against the side of a building-society office, his breath ragged in his throat, his heart pounding at the nearness of his triumph and the narrowness of his escape. It had been stupid to try it, but he had lost control. Lost control for the first time.

He could still feel the pressure of her hand on his arm. Still smell her perfume. He pushed away from the building and made himself walk. He wanted to scream out into the night air, but the feeling gradually passed as he strode back to where he had parked the motorcycle. He couldn't afford to lose control. Without control there were mistakes. Tonight he had almost made a bad mistake.

But that face! That hair!

In a week, it would all be his. His patience would be rewarded as it always had been. He had already laid the ground, already tracked his prey. One week would make no difference to the ecstasy when it came. He got to the motorcycle and the trembling of his hands almost made him drop his keys.

By seven thirty, he had packed away the hut and was on his way home. He had a week in which to dream and fantasise, to anticipate what he would achieve with this one. This special one who looked as if she would be the best, the nearest yet.

He had seven days in which to rise above the uninitiated fools who surrounded him. But he had to be careful, play the role, not let anyone see the change that pulsed and galloped within him. And then, after this one, it would be time to look for Susan.

Little Susan.

He didn't spare a thought for being caught. He was certain the police had no inkling of who he was. He had given them no cause to even begin to think of him in any guise. He was invisible. He thought of the girl, of her small features. He thought of her writhing and squirming, speaking her part. Her voice was tinkling and musical, a small girl's voice. How, he wondered, would it sound when he hammered in the nails and began telling her what he was going to do?

How would it sound when she said the words he would teach her to say? Pretending to her that by saying them it would help ease the pain.

He thought of blood and of eating her pretty throat. The throat that contained her voice. If he cut it open while she was speaking would he see it there? Would her voice be visible to him, or would he merely see the vibrating cords of her larynx and be disappointed – as he had been before?

The thoughts sustained him as he journeyed home. He would not be able to face Tina's congealed roast. He would not need it. He could feed on his dreams.

At home, he packed away the hut and carefully double-checked the bike before unlocking the trunk. He poured over the photographs, admiring his handiwork, barely able to contain himself at the thought of more to come.

Natalie got back to the motor lodge at eight thirty. Unable to face more service-station food, she'd driven into the city and found an Italian place that made its own pizza dough and had feasted, lingering over it as she scribbled down her strategy for the following day.

A single sheet of A4 paper joined the thirty or so she'd covered with her jottings over the previous few days. They were observations of Meredith's behaviour, of the small and very few things he'd let slip about The Carpenter. They were meagre pickings, but they all helped. She was beginning to assimilate her intepretations into what she knew from the police reports and what was emerging was indeed an alternative profile. The outline of the man they were searching for.

She found her thoughts straying to him. Had he been out trolling that day? He killed mainly on weekends. Which meant he had a steady job that kept him busy weekdays and evenings.

There were gaps, vital pieces of information that she needed. Her notes were a travelogue without a destination. But with luck, they would complete the journey tomorrow if Meredith could overcome the final barrier. The image of his drawn face was difficult to erase. He was a shell of a man, a hologram, devoid of everything that had made him the person he was before.

And what had that been, Natalie? a mocking little voice asked. The doctor. The carer. The lover?

My God, Natalie, how can you even think it?

But she knew how. It was an irrevocable part of what she had learned.

Meredith had been – was attractive. She'd sensed it in the reactions of the female members of the hospital staff in Bristol.

She allowed herself a wry smile.

She was vulnerable, she knew.

The thing with Mo ... God, she cringed now even thinking about it. She supposed she was rebounding, although she would hardly have called her relationship with Mo a *true* relationship. She wasn't sure how she would describe it if she had to. An accident? But not the happy kind, more like a motorway pile-up. She ordered some ice-cream cake and forced herself back to the notes. She didn't want to think about Mo. Didn't ever want to see him again. And then a new thought struck home.

Had Meredith done this to her? Made her want to forget Mo?

She caught her image on a mirrored print on the wall. It shocked her to see that she was smiling.

There were no messages when she got back and she went directly to her room, flicked through the channels on the TV, found nothing of interest but left it on as background noise before once again turning to the police file on Jilly Grant. She wanted to be able to correlate Meredith's story to the crime as seen by the authorities. That was what she told herself. And yet, she found herself dwelling on the brief, succinct profile of the dead girl. What was it about her that had marked her out as a victim? Why had The Carpenter picked her out? Were they the same features that had made Meredith choose her? Was that the link between the two men?

Natalie studied the photograph of the girl. A vibrant, candid shot of her against a sunny backdrop. She wore a baggy Gap T-shirt and yellow shorts above tanned legs and blue Nikes. Her hair was pulled back under a baseball cap as she posed with hand on hip and a golf club slung over one shoulder. There were other prints, formal poses of a younger girl, probably supplied by the family, but the golfing shot breathed life. It was the one that Natalie would have chosen and she was willing to bet that Meredith, or the man in her life before Meredith, had taken it. The composition had male written all over it. She looked more closely at the long, straight legs, the strong teeth, the large, made-up eyes. She had been an attractive girl, the tallest of the victims at five eight, and had the lightest hair.

Natalie took out the other files she'd been given and studied the photographs of Alison Terry and Jilly Grant. The resemblance between the two was remarkable.

She searched out the computer correlation of physiognomies. There was a correlation of 80 per cent between the early victims. And then came Jilly and Alison, who went way against type. So what? she thought to herself. If truth be told, Grant was very attractive. She would have stood out anywhere. But that was not the way the killer's mind worked, and she knew it. In the past, there had been deliberate attempts by lust killers to kill against type just to throw off the police. If that was his motive in this instance, it had certainly succeeded in confusing the issue.

Or was she and everybody else missing something? Some vital detail that was staring them in the face? She had pondered this point many times before and still there was nothing she could come up with.

The knock on the door startled her and she remembered

Meredith's expression when Julie had knocked that morning. She dragged her legs off the bed and self-consciously slipped them into shoes before walking to the door.

The knock came again.

'Who is it?' she asked, her hand on the door.

'Housekeeping.'

A high, unfamiliar male voice. She opened the door a crack. The shock delayed her the few milliseconds it took for him to get a foot and a knee inside the door before she could slam it in his face.

For a wild moment they struggled with Mo's cheek pressed to the door, his teeth bared in a fixed grin as Vine tried to squeeze it shut on his intruding leg. But then he found some strength within him she could not compete with. He shoved hard. The door flew open and she shot back into the room, almost losing her footing. She didn't even see his hand until the back of it mashed her lip into her bottom teeth and she spun around like a wind-up clown, staggering against the TV, grabbing it crazily to stop it and her from toppling.

And when she stood and turned to face him, she knew everything had changed. Mo was out of his closet with his hand balled into a fist. He stank of stale booze and stared at her with the grin that she'd seen in her kitchen when he'd looked up at her from the seat drunk as a dog and hit her that first time.

Hit her and grinned.

He saw the fear in her face and the grin widened.

'What's the matter, Nat? Aren't you glad to see me?'

She wanted to say that she'd been startled, pretend it was all a mistake but then she realised what it would sound like and she would be apologising for the fear on her face. He'd hit her for God's sake! She saw her hands shake and felt stupid and frightened.

'Yeah,' said Mo answering himself and shutting the door behind him with one foot. 'Well . . .'

They eyed each other and when Natalie moved slightly to her left, Mo did the same, his hands coming up to stop her. They were too far apart for him to touch her, but she flinched away almost as if he had. She heard his breathing, shallow and rapid, saw the pupils huge in his eyes and her fear doubled.

And in that doubling, her mind slipped inexorably back. She was catapulted to the parlour in Esher, sixteen years old, still dressed up and painted with borrowed Boots No 7 from the school Christmas disco, still tasting that one rum and Coke Jane had brought mixed up in a Pepsi bottle and insisted she take a hit from. Shivering from the knowledge that her mother was sure to smell it, like a wolf smelling a rabbit. Shivering in anticipation of those gleaming eyes. Flat mirror eyes with nothing behind them but sorrow and apology and alcohol – pickled hate. She remembered the feel of warm urine on her leg as she'd gazed into those eyes, certain she would die of embarrassment and shame at the names she was being called and the false accusations that were being hurled at her. She had wished her mother dead for the first time that night as the slapping hand crashed down on her ear and that terrible angry voice . . .

'*I should have done this . . .*'

'*. . . a long time ago.*'

Mo was still grinning as his words penetrated and shattered the waking nightmare Natalie was remembering. She looked up almost quizzically.

'We were made for each other, Nat.' His voice was controlled and she knew he meant it. She shook her head in denial, but it was unconvincing, a timorous shake weakened by self-doubt.

'What do you mean?' she said, and surprised herself by sounding fairly normal.

Mo laughed. A full-throated, head-back cackle. And then it stopped abruptly and he said, 'You fucking love it. Come on, Nat. A little bit of pain. Come on.'

Natalie felt the repulsion rise in her. It was rich and black, full of fear and loathing and doubt and it coiled about her like a flatworm, oozing its paralysing juices into her, threatening to overwhelm her. How easy it would be to close one's eyes and succumb to the numbing blackness.

And worse, worst of all, was the keening voice that asked: *But is he right, Natalie? Could he be right after all?*

He came at her as she procrastinated, caught her off guard with her arms at her side. He was breathing all over her. Natalie smelled the stink of her own hell there: stale gin. Her mother's smell.

He grabbed her arm and twisted it behind her, jolting it up. She felt something stress in her shoulder with a deep beating pain. His hands were all over her, squeezing her hard, pinching flesh, hurting her. And then the realisation came to her with belated terror that yes, this was going to be rape. And with it came the blinding recognition that this was what he had always wanted.

He would throw her down on the bed and hit her again. Probably hit her several times before tearing off her shirt and dragging off her jeans. And she would plead, her cries full of humiliation and misery and she would see then in his eyes the thing that had drawn him to her from the beginning. She would see his disbelief, his total contempt for her and her words because he was convinced they were a lie. He really believed that they were meant for each other. That this was her destiny.

A moan leaked from between her gritted teeth as a massive kaleidoscope of confused images exploded in her head. She saw within herself the dreadful thought that perhaps one small iota of her did not want her to struggle any more.

The terrifying unfairness of it jacked up her heart rate and she felt it swell with emotion. Her mother's face swam in front of her again.

Slut.

The face yelled at her. It told her that what was happening now was only what she deserved for being a . . .

Filthy little SLUT.

And yet, at the back of her mind was the true voice of reason that had managed time and again over the years of her training and her meaningless relationships to say to her:

Don't, Natalie. Don't be so bloody stupid.
You were fourteen when it started.
Your mother was ill.
It was all some sick joke. None of this is real. Only you are real.
You do not deserve it.

Then why did you encourage him? Why? said her mother's voice.

No answer.

In one final rush of self-contempt, Natalie started to cry.

Mo's fondlings had become more frenzied. He was pressing himself against her and she felt his groin harden against her hip and the numbness inside her began to yield to it. It would be so easy. Let him do what he wanted, get a shiner, a fractured jaw at worst. Defeat stared out at her mixed with garbled tit-bits of her training. Let him do it, give in to him. And then when it's over and he's snoring beside you, run a mile and call the police.

But ah, Christ, she didn't want to. She didn't want him touching her at all.

Mo let go of her arm and the relief from the pain was like a river bursting its banks. But respite was short-lived. He swung her around to face him, his eyes dark pits, his mouth still grinning wildly. He seized a handful of hair and jerked her head back and she felt his lips grind against hers, felt his tongue trying to probe its way roughly into her mouth.

She jerked her head back even further, his hand convulsively mauling her breast, causing her own lips to fish-mouth in pain as he yanked hard on her hair.

'What's the matter, Nat?' he spat. 'You been getting it from the fucking loony, is that it?'

He jerked downwards with his hand. She uttered a small yelp as the pain drove her to her knees in front of him.

But the mention of Meredith had confused her. He had no place in this scenario. And yet he was the reason for her being in this godforsaken motel room, wasn't he? New thoughts began to flood into her head. She somehow felt totally responsible for Meredith. What was going to happen to him if Mo put her into the hospital, which he well might? When she failed to rendezvous in the morning, she knew he would simply accept it as yet another act of betrayal by a member of the human race that, collectively, he felt had long ago abandoned him.

And with that odd, misplaced thought, Natalie knew that there was much more at stake here than her own self-preservation.

Whatever shadowy spectre had reached out from the past to put her in Mo's sphere of influence had no place in her life any more. A shard of light and reason shot through her confused agony. To see herself as the saviour of another being was grandiose in the extreme, and yet she knew there was more than a grain of truth in that thought. Meredith was going to have one shot at this, or end up in an institution or with a tag on his toe as a suicide.

Her eyes, driven up to Mo's contorted face, slid down over his expensive silk shirt, across his Gucci belt and alighted on the zipper of his chinos.

Mo saw it and she felt his grip relax.

Gingerly, she put her thumb and index finger on the little silver toggle and pulled, letting her eyes stray back up to his face. And Mo did not see the puffy eyes, or the blood trickling from her crushed lip. All he saw, as he always did, was the acquiescence, the yielding in her eyes and face, together with the small voice she used to say, 'Let me do it.'

He eased most of the pressure on her hair at that point and she stretched her neck and shook her head in relief, rolling her head on her shoulder as she reached in for his prick, letting her eyes scan the room and locate her keys. They were still there on the small bureau.

Mo had taken both hands away to put them behind his head. He was getting ready to enjoy himself. He'd known all along that she'd see reason. He had seen it in her, had been right all a-fucking-long. A firm hand, that was all she wanted, all any fucking woman wanted.

He felt her fingers probing in his shorts, saw her arch her neck in that arrogant, sexy way. And then her nails were tickling his testicles her fingers curling around . . .

He opened his mouth to moan, but what emerged was a strangled cry of utter agony.

Natalie had cupped both sacs in one hand, holding her thumb across the anterior surface like the safety bar on a fairground ride. And then she had squeezed and jerked with all the power her arm could muster, feeling the hard testes roll against her pincer fingers. She lurched to her feet, still yanking at his balls. She took one look at his face before she let go. Pale, twisted and with those dark eyes full of an unbelievable betrayal above the screaming maw of his mouth. She let go and thrust him back with her free hand as she turned and grabbed for her keys and coat.

Halfway through the door, she glanced back. He lay foetal on the bed, his hands clutching his bruised anatomy, tears of pain squeezing from the corners of his eyes.

She was three miles south when the shaking started. The roads were clear and quiet on a freezing black moonless night and Natalie's arm was trembling so much that she couldn't even hold the tissue paper to wipe the steam from the windshield. The tremor ran down her arm and into her legs and she jerked the accelerator spasmodically a couple of times before she hit the brakes and pulled over on to the hard shoulder of the dual carriageway.

She left the engine running and the heater blowing as she tried to steady her hands. She had to get out, the shakes were intolerable in the confined space of the car. She stepped out into the dark night air. Her teeth chattered, not from the cold but from the adrenaline surging round her body. She stood in front of her car in the headlights and began jumping up and down, swinging her arms up to shoulder height like a maniacal gym mistress to rid herself of some of the terrifying energy her body had pumped up in response to her fear of Mo.

The stars above bristled in the night sky. And as she looked up she shouted at them, like a dog baying at the moon.

The image of herself, instantly crystal clear, stopped her in mid-yell. Here she was, a thirty-nine-year-old psychiatrist screaming at the stars. She didn't, couldn't think about what she had done. Coherent thought was impossible in the sudden tidal wave of wellbeing that coursed through her. She sat on the bonnet of her car and leaned back, basking in the cold night air, tossing her head, tasting again the blood on her lips as her mouth split the wound afresh in a grin. But this time, she felt no pain. Pain had no place in that ecstatic moment. Instead, as the blood flowed again, she tasted in it something that had been hidden from her all the years of her adult life.

In it, she tasted *freedom*.

Chapter 20

Her arrival near midnight had startled him. She had driven through the city for an hour, unable and unwilling to relinquish the immense exhilaration that bubbled away inside her. Eventually, the adrenaline had faded and a semblance of reason returned. She needed somewhere to stay. There was a Holiday Inn she'd seen in the city centre and she pointed the car in its direction. At the first set of lights she hit after deciding, she realised with numb panic that she had nothing with her; no bag, no wallet, no credit cards. They still sat on the dressing table of the motel room. Normally, it would have terrified her to be without those essentials of survival, but instead the panic faded. She could, *would* cope.

It didn't matter. It didn't matter at all. In the overall scale of things, where did a wad of crumpled bank notes rate? It could have been her crumpled up on that dressing table. She wound down the window and inhaled huge draughts of frozen air.

The stinging in her chest sobered her somewhat. It was too cold to sleep in the car. Dimly she realised that she had only her ripped shirt on beneath her coat. Did they take itinerant psychiatrists in at the Sally Army? She ran her tongue over her bruised lip and felt a wave of anger stir inside her for allowing even the merest hint of self-pity on such a momentous night. Feeling sorry for herself wasn't in the script. She would not allow Mo one iota of satisfaction.

There was someone she could stay with – it was Meredith's night off. But the thought was an uncomfortable one. What would he make of her turning up on his doorstep? Only one way to find out. Natalie put the car into gear and turned south towards the ocean.

The tousled hair and fearful owl eyes had made him look like a small confused schoolboy when he opened the door to her insistent knock. She had stood apologetically with her hands thrust deep into her coat pockets, shivering, wondering where to begin her explanation.

'I ran into a storm,' she said. 'I need a safe haven.'

Her words made no impression on him. He stood blinking in the light of the room until his eyes focused on her bruised lip, but he said nothing.

Natalie's shivering redoubled. 'I've never had to do anything like this before. It isn't easy to beg, but could I borrow your sofa for the night?'

Meredith stepped back warily, nodding dumbly. Almost immediately, he busied himself by making the inevitable pot of tea.

'You want to talk about it?' he mumbled as she sat clutching her mug, uncomfortable with this sudden reversal of roles.

'I met a bogeyman in my hotel room,' she said with a wavering half-smile.

'You seem unnaturally happy about the fact.'

'As happy as anyone who walks away from a major disaster alive and well.'

'As bad as that?'

'Could have been.'

'Have you been to the police?'

She shook her head. 'I will, but not tonight. Tonight I want to enjoy my freedom.'

Meredith glanced at her strangely. 'You know this bloke? I presume it is a bloke?'

Natalie nodded and sipped the tea he thrust at her. 'A boyfriend. An ex-boyfriend.'

'You've split up?'

Natalie surprised both Meredith and herself by laughing out loud. 'If I ever began to tell you . . .'

Meredith shrugged.

She caught herself. He deserved some sort of explanation.

'Why we do things is often not obvious . . . not at first. I'm supposed to know the reasons, the hidden reasons why people behave the way they do, it's my job. All I can say is when it comes to self-analysis, I'm about as much use as a hole in a bucket.'

Meredith raised his eyebrows. 'You don't look like someone who's too confused by what's happened.'

'You're right.' She smiled. 'Tonight I caught a glimpse of the answer. It wasn't a very pretty sight, but I do feel better for it. Anyway, now is not the time or the place. I need to let you get back to bed on your one night off.'

'It doesn't bother me.'

'No, I insist. Tomorrow, we can swap stories.'

Meredith's face took on a fearful expression. She cursed herself. She had sounded flippant, blasé almost. But her impish mood seemed infectious.

The beginnings of a smile played at the corners of his mouth. A smile that had been absent in recent months. No one had made a joke at his expense since it had happened. No one had dared. And he had not thought that laughing at himself would ever again be possible. He turned away to hide the smile that felt so odd on his face.

'You'd better take the bedroom. There's a sleeping bag. I'm afraid there are only two sets of sheets and one is in the laundry . . .'

Natalie woke from a deep exhausted sleep to the unfamiliar whorls of an Artexed ceiling. She rolled on to her back but found it a difficult manoeuvre to perform, requiring an energetic arching of the spine and rolling of the shoulders. She felt constrained, confined almost. To be expected, she supposed, in a nylon sleeping bag.

Sleeping bag?

Memory flooded in, almost explosive in its intensity.

She looked at her watch. Ten a.m.

She did a quick physical check. Her lip felt a little sore but remarkably not too swollen, and her shoulder hurt where he'd wrenched at it, but otherwise she felt surprisingly good. And mentally? She couldn't suppress the exciting little buzz she felt in her head whenever she thought about what had happened.

Humming to herself, she found the tiny bathroom and showered. It was an ancient affair worked by an electric wall heater. It looked as if it had originally been metered, judging by a disconnected box adjacent to the heater. It had once accepted fifty-pence pieces but someone had ripped out the wires and re-connected it to the mains. The shower head was huge and brass, like some massive watering-can rose attached to a copper pipe running up the wall. She had to stand in a yellowing plastic bath-tub, the shower curtain held in place by only three rings. But the water was hot and the bath, although ancient, was clean enough. She dried herself and dressed in some old jeans and a work shirt she found in the one battered wardrobe.

In the living room, Meredith still wore the owl-like expression of the night before, this time coloured by a tinge of concern. Outside, grey skies hanging down in misty veils of fog had begun to empty cold February drizzle into the earth.

'You OK?' asked Meredith.

She smiled affirmatively, buoyed up by the huge surge of positive feelings that bubbled away inside her. She strolled to the window and looked out at the black, naked trees in the woodland beyond. Across the way, Julie and Mandy's chalet looked deserted, but the Lada was still there.

'How did you find this place?' she asked.

'It's mine,' he said. 'An uncle of mine bought it years ago. God knows how they ever got planning permission. I was left it in his will because he knew how much I loved this place; the beach and the woods.'

'Have you ever thought of modernising?' asked Natalie, looking around her.

'Perhaps, some day.' He shrugged and smiled. 'I spent many happy summers here. I like to remember it as it was. My family used to come here; it was like a foreign holiday. This peninsula was colonised by Normans and then West Country folk. It's not really Welsh at all.'

190

'Hence the names?'

Meredith nodded. 'There's a long history of fortification, defence against attack.'

'That's why you're here, isn't it?'

He looked at her, holding her gaze. 'Yes, it is,' he said simply.

She turned and walked back to the fire.

'Thanks for putting me up.'

'Not exactly five-star accommodation.'

Natalie laughed. 'It's good to see you like this.'

'Like what?'

'Not so defensive.'

Meredith shrugged.

'It might be a good time to start the journey,' she said casually.

'To where?'

'To wherever your hell is.'

Meredith's face, relaxed a moment before, suddenly filled with trepidation.

'Look,' he hedged. 'Perhaps we should delay this. You're obviously not yourself.'

Natalie's eyes crinkled. 'It's no good, Mr Meredith. We are going to do this.'

Meredith's shoulders slumped. He knew he was fighting a rearguard action and losing. 'You want some breakfast?'

Natalie shook her head.

He sat down, his hands trembling.

She moved a chair so that she was sitting out of his view to his rear. 'Stare at the TV screen, if it will help,' she said.

The room was still and quiet. Outside there was hardly a breath of wind. It felt as if the world was waiting for Meredith.

'I want you to look at the TV screen. Imagine that it is switched on and that what you see is in colour. No one else is here besides you and me and I want you to ignore me. I'm here if you need me, but essentially, you're watching the screen alone. I'd like you to imagine that you're standing behind us in the kitchen. You are able to see this room, see yourself sitting on the sofa watching the TV. In effect you are watching yourself watching the TV.'

Natalie spoke softly and earnestly in measured tones. She had never used this technique before but she knew how essential it was for him to believe it was routine. She was depersonalising the event for him, trying to establish a detachment, something he clearly had been unable to do himself.

'What you see yourself watching is a replay of what happened to you in Bath. See yourself as if someone had been there to record the event unbeknown to you. The programme starts as you leave the restaurant with Jilly. You are happy. I want you to watch and tell me what you see.'

Meredith was staring at the screen, his face frowning in concentration.

'Don't be afraid,' said Natalie softly. 'Let it roll in front of you. Watch from the kitchen. Tell me what you see.'

It was almost a full minute before Meredith started to speak in a halting, disjointed voice. To begin with it was a mumble, barely audible.

'The car . . . underground car park. Music . . . Jazz . . . one of the Dorsey brothers . . . she loved the melodic trombones . . . I'd bought her the tape for Christmas . . . Over Lansdowne . . . Past the racecourse . . .'

He began to sing in a tuneless disjointed whisper and suddenly he was there, in the car, in the past.

'Eyes like stars above . . .'

Jilly drives, singing softly to herself as she negotiates the traffic.

Tom sits in the passenger seat humming along. He doesn't listen to the words, they register subliminally; he has heard them so often. It is a Friday evening. Tom feels content. He is not on call this weekend and it looms long and relaxed in front of him.

His thoughts flick briefly, as they often do, to something he must do before Monday. A young woman seen that morning in his clinic. Odd symptoms, back pain, occasional numbness in the legs. The referring physician had reported a normal CT scan, but he needs an MRI and a look at the CT himself. Physicians are not infallible.

But he clamps his thoughts down at that point. It can wait until

Monday. What can't is the boner he has from looking at Jilly's legs. His eyes flick down to her thigh. The car's motion, Jilly's short skirt and three-inch heels showing off those incredible legs have all contributed to old Peter pecker standing to attention. There isn't much space in the Renault Clio and old Peter has stuck his head out of one side of Tom's M&S jockeys.

He continues to hum and drags his eyes off Jilly's delicious pins in an attempt to alleviate his discomfort. They have eaten lightly, neither opting for hors d'oeuvres, both choosing large, crunchy salads in big fruit bowls as entrées. Neither wanting to feel bloated – full stomachs blight their sexual appetites. And although they have not spoken openly of it that evening, they both know that once they get back to Jilly's house they will be in bed within ten minutes.

They pull up at some lights and as she depresses the clutch, the movement of her leg pushes the skirt another centimetre up her thigh.

She turns to Tom and puts a long-fingered hand on his leg, her eyes smiling in mock surprise as she encounters the hard, protruding flesh there. As the lights change, she says, 'I think I'd better put my foot down.'

Tom moves her hand across to her cool thigh, relishing the smoothness. Jilly smiles and Tom feels his cheeks burn in anticipation.

Jilly drives on through the night. Tom feels the wine mellow in his mind. He tries to relax but leaves his hand on her thigh. The roads are empty although it is still relatively early at half nine.

It is Jilly who first notices the flashing blue light in the rearview.

'Oh, shit . . .' she says and immediately relieves some of the pressure on the accelerator. The car slows naturally as drag and friction begin to exert their inevitable effects, but the blue light continues to approach until it is only a few yards behind. Jilly doesn't quite know what to do and she has slowed to twenty miles an hour, but still the motorcycle is behind them, almost daring them to take off.

'What's he playing at?' asks Tom.

But almost as he speaks the motorcycle overtakes and signals them to pull in, swinging out again to give them room. Jilly stops, seeing the policeman slow to a halt some way behind them. Tom has removed his hand from her thigh, the mood shattered. Jilly appears crestfallen. They sit in the car, motionless. Behind them, the policeman is off his motorcycle and coming forward.

'Shouldn't I get out?' asks Jilly.

Tom says, 'No, wait. Perhaps he just wants directions.'

It eases the tension. Jilly smiles gratefully.

Oddly, the policeman approaches the passenger door, nearest the road. But there is no traffic on this cold September evening. The road is deserted.

No one sees the policeman squat down as Tom winds his window low.

The policeman raises his visor and shines a torch into the car. His face is dark and unreadable behind the light. He wears a riding mask high over his nose and down over his brow against the cold.

'In a hurry are we, madam?' His voice is muffled by the helmet.

'Sorry,' says Jilly, contemplating a lie, but deciding against it.

'Before we talk about your speed, madam, I should also tell you that you have a faulty near-side brake light.'

'Do I?'

The torch sweeps back towards Tom's face. The light partially blinds Tom. Behind it, the patrolman's features are hazy, dusky, almost patched.

'If you'd step outside, sir, you could confirm it.'

The policeman stands up and Tom gets out. It is a clear night and a northerly breeze hisses through the branches of large oaks in the fields nearby. The policeman is studying the rear of the car as Tom joins him.

'Brake,' he says and Jilly presses hard. In front of Tom's face, both brake lights burn brightly. Tom blinks in surprise and turns with a bemused little laugh towards the policeman, who is leaning and pointing. Tom hears a serpentine aerosol hiss before the Mace hits him from eight inches. His hands fly up, the liquid searing his nostrils and eyes, burning his mouth and throat. It is an excruciating pain. He feels something hard strike his head from the back; the pain and noise reverberate through his skull twice. It stuns him as he stumbles to the ground, writhing, hitting his head once more against the car's rear, burning his hand on the exhaust pipe. His face is soaked from the tears that pour out of his blinded eyes. Something cold grasps his wrists and he hears a metallic snap and he can no longer move them from behind his back. He jerks and a new pain makes him yell out in terror. Something is tearing at his hair, yanking his neck back, and then there is a dry musty material in his mouth and he can no longer scream. From nearby he hears the car door open and Jilly's concerned voice. He risks a glance through his streaming eyes and sees the blurred image of Jilly coming around to the rear of the car, her face unclear but her voice full of horror and concern before the aerosol hisses again and she screams in agony. He hears the noises above him as she is overpowered and then there are hands dragging him to the car, thrusting him in to the rear seat. He feels something writhe and sob beneath him and realises it is Jilly. The door slams behind him and seconds later the motorcycle roars off.

His hands are immobilised but still, momentarily, hope flares briefly in his head. Someone must have seen. Someone must have disturbed the lunatic.

After a few moments there are footsteps, but they are rapid, without trepidation. He hears the car door open and he redoubles his muffled cries. For an instant there is quiet and then the engine fires and hope evaporates with the realisation of who the footsteps belong to . . .

They drive in jarring agony for what he later learns is a mere three miles. His mind rages with confused terror. His thoughts are disjointed and illogical, defaulting always to the known terrors he reads about daily. He believes for an instant that it could all be a dreadful error. He has never been to Ireland, but wonders if the IRA might have targeted them by mistake. Worse, if it isn't a mistake. Did Jilly have any relatives out there? The screaming voice of reason yells at him that this is the rolling country between Bath and Bristol, not Ulster border country, and yet . . . what else is there to believe?

For half a mile the journey worsens as the car jolts and bumps along a rutted track, throwing Tom and Jilly against one another like rag dolls until, finally, it stops.

Strong hands drag them from the car. Tom is taken first. He peers through slitted eyes at vague outlines. A building – a doorway – a dimly lit room. He is thrown down roughly on to a bare floor of coarse concrete. Something is pulled down over his head and his hands are freed momentarily, pulled roughly in front of him and then handcuffed again. He pulls and yanks but there is no yielding. Whatever object he has been attached to is solid and immobile.

He listens to the harrowing sobs as Jilly is brought in. Tom throws his head from side to side trying desperately to shake off the sack. Something strikes his head with stunning force. He falls on to his side, his head literally ringing.

After that, he stays silent, listening to the noises. His silence is broken only by his own sobs of frustration and desperate, bottomless anguish at what he imagines is going on.

He hears clothes ripping, fearful, terrified moans and then, loud in the night – the hammer.

THUD

Jilly's scream emerges through the gag such is its intensity, modulated into the keening howl of some unnameable animal. It continues unabated while the second . . .

THUD.

. . . and third . . .

THUD.

. . . blows are struck. In the silence that follows, the howling agony begins to diminish, but it is merely a cruel sham.

THUD.

A fourth blow redoubles the noise.

Tom begins to tear at his bonds with renewed vigour. It is partly anger that drives him, partly an all-consuming certainty that he is next in line to receive whatever is being meted out to

Jilly. He stops only when something pointed and hard is driven into his ribs, knocking the wind out of him. For an instant he can not breathe, his lungs scream out for air but nothing enters.

Now the silence is complete and a new fear rushes in to replace the old. He can't hear Jilly. There is no noise at all.

THUD.

As if in response to his waiting, the hammer strikes and Jilly's scream returns. Relief and horror flood him as at last his shocked chest muscles forego their spasm and suck in air. She is not dead. She is not dead, but ah, the screams are dreadful to hear, despite their muted volume. To Tom, they sound as loud as a landing jet.

THUD.

Jilly . . . Oh God, Jilly.

Thud, thud, thud, thud.

Natalie got up, irritated. Reluctantly, she turned off the tape recorder while glancing at Meredith. He seemed confused, disjointed.

Thud, thud, thud.

The insistent knocking intruded again. This time an urgent, imploring voice accompanied it.

'Please, open the door. Please!'

Natalie went to Meredith and put a hand on his shoulder. Unbelievable that it should happen now, of all times. He was doing so well.

'There's someone at the door,' she said softly. Behind her, the knocks grew louder. Natalie saw Meredith's eyes blink in time to the noise.

It was obvious that he was in shock, bewildered and dazed by the suddenness of the transition, still hovering between the reality of the present and the horror of his past.

THUD, THUD, THUD.

'Please . . .' the voice outside implored.

Cursing, Natalie stepped towards the door and threw it open with barely disguised irritation.

Julie stumbled in spluttering incoherently, her hatchet face white with terror. She reached out and grabbed Natalie's elbow in a steely grip.

In her peripheral vision, Natalie saw Meredith's face swing up. It bore a vague, lost expression that she didn't like the look of and she cursed inwardly again. His gossamer connection with reality needed gentle reinforcement, not a jackhammer confrontation. But her anxiety was a transient flicker in the glare of whatever nightmare Julie had stepped out of and Natalie found her eyes held and riveted by that blubbing face.

'Calm down,' she said. 'What is it?'

But Julie was already pulling Natalie out of the door, dragging her along to the other tawdry chalet, unable or unwilling to waste time on explanations.

Natalie resisted. 'Stop this. Tell me what's wrong.'

But all Julie could do was continue to drag Natalie towards the open door.

Resolute and angry, Natalie threw off the strong sinewy arm. *'Tell me.'*

Julie blinked, her wild eyes focused, and the words burst out of her like air out of a pierced dirigible.

'Mandy . . .' she blubbered. 'Can't breathe . . . choking. I fell asleep . . . The noise woke me . . . Choking . . . *please.*' The last word was a wail of fear and pleading.

Natalie stared for one horrified, frozen moment before sprinting for the open door, galvanised by the picture she had in her mind of the mother in an alcoholic haze, the child free to indulge in innocent and sometimes not so innocent activities unsupervised.

The child neglected.

Mandy lay on the floor, but there was nothing reposeful in the figure. Mandy's body was in constant flailing motion, her hands clawing at her throat, her face a livid and impossibly purple-blue. Her feet drummed a tattoo on the hard chilly floor, a bizarre accompaniment to the creaking bray that was emerging from her mouth.

Stunned, Natalie stared without comprehension, an impotent paralysis gripping her. She knew that she was looking at a medical emergency but she also knew that Natalie the doctor was hopelessly unprepared. It had been years since she'd done any physical medicine and though some of the knowledge was still there, it was unpractised and vestigial.

Instinctively, she fell to her knees at the child's side, trying helplessly to calm the convulsing limbs.

Stridor – the braying noise was stridor. Pieces came together with agonising slowness in Natalie's rusty memory. She saw the straining, sucking thorax attempting to vacuum in some air. But Julie had said choking?

Natalie put her fingers in the child's mouth. The tongue was free and anterior. Damn, it wasn't that.

Mandy was tossing violently from the asphyxiation reflex that was pumping adrenaline around her body and Natalie knew that she was looking at a body in its death throes.

She felt her own fear explode inside her. Mandy's face was turning black in front of her eyes, her neck bulging, straining from the effort of attempted breathing, the failing effort. What? What to do?

And then she was up on her feet and running out, throwing off the clutches of the wailing Julie.

Entering Meredith's chalet was like crossing into another dimension. All was calm. Meredith sat where she had left him, his hands folded in his lap, his expression unreadable.

Natalie went to him, knowing it was the last thing she should do, but driven by the image of the child's blackening face. Effortlessly, she pulled him to his feet.

'We need help. The little girl, she's choking on something. I don't know what. I don't know what to do . . .' She was yelling in her frustration, but all Meredith could do was gaze back at her, as if considering the gravity of her statement before formulating a careful reply.

'Tom,' she screamed into his face, shaking him. 'Can you hear me?'

He didn't answer. Confusion reigned in his eyes.

Natalie hit him. Open-handed and hard. The slap echoed loudly and Meredith's cheek flared with the imprint of her fingers.

'Please,' she screamed. 'For God's sake.'

Meredith swung his head back to look at her. His hand went up as if to reciprocate, but Natalie didn't flinch. The hair shirt of her intellect half wished that he would hit her; she felt she deserved it for what she was putting him through. But then she saw his eyes focus, pupils constricting on to harsh reality.

'You must help us,' she pleaded.

His hand, poised to strike, came back to his own face. 'You hit me?' he said, surprised.

But Natalie was already dragging him out and across the freezing earth, thanking a God somewhere for his return.

Chapter 21

Julie was on her knees, rocking back and forth, the little girl struggling in her arms. Natalie noted with alarm that the paroxysms seemed to be diminishing, not worsening, as if the tortured body was finally giving up the struggle. Meredith stared in horror, as Natalie had done.

'She can't breathe,' Natalie said superfluously.

'She's convulsing,' he replied grimly.

'Do something,' she implored.

Meredith stepped forward and reached out for the little girl. Julie's head snapped up. There was no trace of reason in the dark-rimmed eyes that stared back defiantly at him, only malevolence and dreadful acceptance.

Meredith hesitated.

'Julie, you must let her go. We can't help unless you let her go,' said Natalie.

The woman spat back at her. 'You ran away. You ran frigging away.'

'I ran to get help. Better help than I can give. Please Julie. Give her to us now.'

Julie continued to rock, humming a lullaby in a pitiful attempt to comfort the dying child.

'Julie,' ordered Natalie angrily. 'Let her go.'

Julie stopped rocking, then turned her terrified face up to them and with dumb, harrowing acceptance, held out the writhing child.

Meredith took her. He held her by her feet, dangling her before throwing her bodily over the back rest of the sofa. He squatted behind her, threading his arms around her, balling his hands into fists. Straddling her limp, inverted form, he hugged her violently and thrust his fist into the soft hollow beneath her sternum, squeezing with all his might in one spasmodic movement.

Natalie recognised the manoeuvre. It was textbook stuff and she felt guilt burn her cheeks. Meredith repeated it and then sat back, dragging the child upright, checking for any change. None.

He cursed. She was like a rag doll now. The life force eeking out of her with every second. Natalie's nostrils were suddenly assailed with the smell of faeces, and she saw a dark patch appear on the child's inner thigh.

Julie, her face puckered and angry, screamed at him.

'No, you bastard. Leave her alone.'

Meredith ignored her. He had his fingers deep in the child's throat.

'She's obstructed,' he said. 'I can't get at it. It's lodged.' Suddenly he was up and running out of the door, much as Natalie had done, but faster. She saw him blur past her but she was beyond words. She was watching the little girl in ghastly fascination. She was dying, horribly.

Natalie felt tears of frustration and sorrow burn her face. Her ineptitude gnawed away within her. The child's only hope had been Meredith and he had run off like a demented rabbit. To hide again, she supposed. Hide in his little hole. She knew she had absolutely no right to point a finger of any sort at someone in his mental state. But she knew she would. Even more than she would at the hapless and inadequate Julie who seemed to her as much a victim as the child was.

And she knew that after this she could not go on with Meredith. It was a tarnishing even the most coldly professional of relationships would not withstand.

She dared risk a glance at Julie. She had hobbled forward on her knees and taken the little girl's faintly moving hand. She was rocking and chanting again, emitting that wistful lullaby that was by now a lament. Above her head, on the table, Natalie saw two empty vodka bottles. She suddenly had to turn away, unable to withstand the pathos.

She didn't see Meredith return. All she heard was his panting voice from the doorway.

'Bring her to the table. *Quickly!*'

The urgency in his voice brought her instantly to her feet. She glanced around and saw that he had things in his hands, odd, strange things that didn't gel in her mind. But there was no time for her to wonder. Already he was sweeping the table clean with his arm as she took Mandy away from an unresisting Julie.

'Quickly,' yelled Meredith again from behind.

Mandy's limbs dangled as Natalie transferred her to the table.

'Pull her head back and arch her neck,' he said.

She saw in his hand a yellow-and-black linoleum knife. Objections registered and were discarded in her brain as automatically she put her arm under the child's neck, exposing the throat.

He worked quickly, searching with his fingers, feeling for her Adam's apple, working his fingers further down, stretching the skin.

The first cut was superficial, down on to cartilage. He prised open the vertical slit with the fingers of his left hand. Blood welled there and he looked around for something to swab it with. He pointed at a bedsock on the chair. Natalie reached for it dubiously and he snatched it from her.

'What do a few germs matter,' he hissed without looking up. Beneath the red and pink flesh, silver cartilage glistened. He thrust the knife in horizontally, splitting her windpipe.

The change was instantaneous and miraculous. It was a noise Natalie would never forget; the moist, whispering whistle of fresh, life-giving oxygen as it was sucked through the one-centimetre opening that Meredith fashioned as he prized the cricothyroid apart. With three breaths, Mandy's lividity disappeared to be replaced by a bright, healthy pink as her straining heart sent oxygen to the starved tissues.

Meredith was still working, swabbing the blood away.

'Try and control this bleeding,' he said.

Trembling, Natalie swabbed the wound while Meredith picked up the other instrument he'd brought with him. Natalie recognised it as a pen torch, the sort drug reps had given her dozens of when she was still in hospital medicine. Working quickly, Meredith unscrewed the bulb with deft fingers and tapped out the batteries.

'I need the knife,' he said to Natalie. 'You'll have to use your finger to keep it open.'

Mandy's flesh was warm and the cartilage surprisingly resistant to her prizing fingers as Natalie complied. It felt slick and greasy and unreal. If there was ever a reason why she had chosen not to contemplate surgery, this was it.

She watched Meredith slice through the plastic housing of the torch to make a cylinder three inches long.

'OK,' he said and Natalie took out her fingers as he replaced them with the simple tracheotomy tube he had fashioned, sliding it in at an acute angle so that it jutted out beneath her Adam's apple, adjusting it slightly as it triggered off a wheezing cough.

'I'll have to hold this until she gets some proper help. She'll probably try and pull it out. We need an ambulance. There's a phone in the village, next to the store.' He spoke calmly, with practised authority.

Natalie found herself nodding and made as if to leave. She was almost at the door when she remembered Julie. She was still on her knees, staring up at Meredith and the child still supine on the table, her eyes flicking between the two.

Natalie stepped across, relief surging through her.

'It's all right. She's all right.' She stooped and helped Julie to her feet, then around the disarranged furniture to the table.

Julie stared down at the healthy tinge in the child's face, saw the steady rise and fall of the chest, and the floodgates opened. Tears sprang forth, cascading down the pale, hollow cheeks as she wiped a stray curl from the child's forehead.

'I'm going for that ambulance,' said Natalie.

Julie nodded and looked up first at Natalie and then at Meredith. He didn't meet her gaze, preoccupied as he was with controlling the thin trickle of blood that still oozed from the skin wound. But Natalie did, and in Julie's face she saw unadulterated awe and idolatry.

The hospital was modernised Victorian but, as was so often the case, beneath the peeling paint and scuffed furniture there was expertise and kind words. The admission process took a surprisingly short time, but then Julie would not be left alone while Mandy underwent surgery. Natalie spent long, dragging hours staring at outdated magazines and wallpaper TV until the little girl, a small silver tube in her throat instead of Meredith's white plastic torch, returned to the children's ward, reposeful from the anaesthetic and breathing quietly and regularly.

Natalie was exhausted but oddly triumphant when she got back to the chalet in the early evening. As such, she was unprepared for Meredith's sullenness when he opened the door to her. Natalie followed him in disconcerted. She had vaguely hoped that somehow the morning's activity had been cathartic, but in Meredith's face she did not read any alteration.

After several moments, Natalie broke the silence.

'She's fine, thanks,' she said drily.

He said nothing.

'Don't you even want to know what it was she'd inhaled?'

Meredith shrugged.

'A screw top. Probably from a lemonade bottle. It was wedged just above her vocal cords. The surgeon said that it was uniformly fatal without an immediate tracheotomy. They implied you deserved a medal.' She paused, waiting for his reaction.

When none came, her anger flared.

'Don't you care that you saved her life?'

'For what?' he said in a despondent tone.

'For what?' repeated Natalie incredulously. 'She's only four years old. Maybe she'll turn out to be a poet, or invent the light bulb.'

'With a mother like that? Come on. I might as well have saved her the trouble.'

'What right do you have to prejudge things?'

'Every right. I've seen people like that before. Her mother is an alcoholic, for Christ's sake.'

'People survive. They even survive alcoholic mothers.'

Natalie's tone was sharper than she'd intended. It caused Meredith to cock his head, intrigued.

'Yes,' said Natalie with a mirthless grin. 'I know all about it too. I'm an expert, first-hand experience. And I'll tell you something else. You did something this morning that was enough to transform anybody's life. Even yours. You couldn't help yourself. You're angry because this morning you cared. You cared more about keeping that little girl alive than anything. I saw it.'

He had his back to her now, trying to shut her out.

Behind him, Natalie sighed, trying to retain control. Eventually, she said, 'Look, I know what this is about, but you can't go on blaming yourself.'

He swung around. 'What do you mean?'

'You're angry at yourself for doing something for Mandy because you were unable to do anything for Jilly.'

'That's crap.' But even as he said it he knew that it wasn't.

'You have to try and work through this guilt, otherwise it will burn you up.'

'Oh for Christ's sake, give it a bloody rest.' Little flecks of spittle escaped from his lips as he shouted.

She walked up close and said earnestly, 'We can do this. I had my doubts up until this morning, but now I'm more certain than ever. There is a way back for you, Tom. Truly there is.'

She waited for the volcano but it never came. Instead, his head came up, daring to believe.

'You started so well this morning. We could do it again, now.'

'I have to go to work.'

'Work,' she laughed derisively.

He swung around and she saw then the other reason for his sullenness. It was there in his eyes, black and shiny fear.

'I can't.' He shook his head violently.

She'd been through this twice before already. Thwarted by delays and excuses, by his moods and Julie's ineptitude, she fought down the urge to be confrontational.

'But you can do it, you know you can.'

His head was still shaking. 'Not now. Not at night.'

Realisation hit her. He was scared of the darkness. It was illogical and yet this was a primal fear and for that reason perhaps understandable. The darkness contained a power. The power to confuse and conceal, to feed fear and ignorance. That was why, she reminded herself, he had chosen a night job. To shield himself from the darkness.

'Tomorrow then,' she urged resignedly. 'Say you'll try again tomorrow.'

He looked into her eyes and she saw there the guttering agony of indecision that tore at him.

'Perhaps . . .' he mumbled.

They left for the service station together, a little earlier than his shift demanded. She wanted him to come with her to her room. So many things had happened that she had almost forgotten about Mo until the practicality of returning made her think about what could have been. It was a chilling thought, and in its wake a cold dread had surfaced. She could not believe in all honesty that he would still be there. He would realise that she would take precautions, might even have called the police; nevertheless, she could not face the prospect of returning alone.

They went in Meredith's car, just in case Mo was watching for her. He drove down the narrow lane that exited on to the village road and stopped suddenly. 'Forgot something,' he muttered and got out.

Natalie watched him with suspicion. Meredith had become a man of frugal habits, living very much on his nerves. She saw almost every action he performed as in some way connected to his understandable preoccupations and this current little charade had all the trappings of a badly staged play.

She waited until he was out of sight before quietly slipping out of the car and creeping back up the lane towards the chalet. In front, she saw the bobbing beam of an industrial torch, moving towards the rear of the building. Staying on the frozen grass, she edged her way around, but by the time she reached the corner of the building he was on his way back and she had to run to the cover of the nearby trees in the lane and watch as he stooped near his front door. In the beam of the torch, she saw him casting the runes. At least, that was what it looked like as he arranged thin sticks in some intricate pattern. It wasn't until he went on to check the doors and windows twice that she realised what the business with the sticks was all about.

They were his early-warning devices.

He was protecting his back from the predator that stalked him every minute of his waking and, she suspected, sleeping hours. It filled her with a sudden anger. He was still out there, stalking, contemplating his atrocious fantasies, and she seemed no closer to finding the key factors that might help pick him out from among the crowd.

She slipped back to the car and sat shivering from the cold, waiting for Meredith's return.

'OK?' she said as he eased in.

He nodded and gunned the engine. To distract herself, she asked, 'How did you know what to do this morning?'

'I went to the right lectures.'

'Oh come on.' She was glaring at him, his flippancy irritating and inappropriate.

'We had a policy. Anyone on the Major Incident team had to be useful in more than one sphere. What use is an orthopaedic surgeon at a train crash if he can't perform emergency trachies?'

Natalie nodded. It made sense, but she wondered how many of his colleagues had taken that policy seriously. How many had mucked in and learned techniques that were totally foreign to them? How much easier would it have been simply to leave it to the experts – that dreaded phrase that so often meant indolence and buck passing? For Meredith probably not easy at all, she realised. It probably hadn't even entered his pragmatic head to do anything but get stuck in. And that sort of thing usually instilled in colleagues nothing but admiration. It usually transcended envy and petty jealousy. Meredith was the man you wanted on your team all right. No wonder she'd seen that odd light in people's eyes at the hospital in Bristol. They genuinely respected him. Genuinely missed him. And she found herself wondering how her colleagues might have reacted if she had been in Meredith's shoes. The thought sat uncomfortable and imponderable on her mind as they drove on under the sodium lights of a built-up area, the yellow glow waxing and waning on her hands resting in her lap as the car sped between the lamps.

Room 36, when they arrived, was empty. It had been made up by the maid and bore little or no evidence of the previous night's violence. Natalie, however, was not reassured. After a few moments she began searching, opening drawers and cupboards, tearing back the bedcovers.

'What?' exclaimed Meredith exasperatedly.

'The bastard,' she said eventually. 'He's stolen my notes. Police files, everything.'

'Could have been worse,' said Meredith philosophically.

'No,' said Natalie. 'Not really.'

Meredith waited for clarification, but Natalie simply shook her head. 'I have a bad feeling about it, that's all.'

He looked at his watch and said, 'I have to go.'

At the door, he paused and half turned. 'You, ummm, know where I am if you need me.'

'Same here,' said Natalie. But he was out of the door before she could give him sight of the little smile of appreciation that sprang spontaneously to her lips at his concern.

As soon as he was out of the door, she phoned Tindal. Someone answered the number that Natalie had been given, but it wasn't the man himself. Instead, she waited to the accompaniment of tinny Strauss while her call was rerouted. When he eventually came on the line, it sounded as if she had interrupted him dining; his response to her greeting came through several hurried swallows.

'Dr Vine, you have some news for me?'

Natalie hesitated fractionally. Again she sensed his desperation. He wanted her to name The Carpenter for him. But all she had was a minor squabble to report, hardly earth-shattering.

'Dr Vine?'

'No, no news,' she said hedgingly. 'What about you?'

'Nothing.'

Natalie let out a sigh. 'Does that mean he's abstained this weekend?'

'Looks like it,' said Tindal. 'Unless his victim simply hasn't been found yet.'

'It's not his style.'

209

'No,' agreed Tindal. 'Hardly likely.' He paused, letting her continue and prompting her when she didn't. 'I'm listening.'

'Problems,' said Natalie.

'What sort?'

Natalie explained about Mo and Tindal listened without interrupting her. Nothing, it seemed, surprised him as far as this case was concerned. Natalie hurried to finish, relieved and embarrassed by his pragmatism.

'And this Alberini,' said Tindal, 'is he short of money?'

'No, not at all. Why?'

'His motive for stealing your notes could be to sell them to the highest bidder.'

'No. This is pure maliciousness. Utter vindictiveness.'

'You think it unlikely that he'll go to the press?'

'He'll probably throw them into the nearest dustbin.'

'Then why are you telling me all of this?'

'In case he doesn't,' said Natalie sheepishly.

'I see,' said Tindal with the air of a man used to painting the darkest possible scenario. 'Should we pick him up?'

'Not for my sake,' said Natalie hurriedly. 'I mean . . . I don't want to press charges.'

'Is he likely to try to get at you again?'

The question floored Natalie. She hadn't thought for one moment . . . 'I . . . I . . . don't know.'

'He sounds a little excitable,' Tindal said. 'I'll get someone to pay him a visit. Get your property back, have a little chat with him. We'll need an address.'

Natalie gave it to him and Tindal continued: 'In the meantime, I'd be happy to get on to the local people and get them to allocate some manpower.'

'No. I don't want to make Meredith nervous. I'll be very careful.'

Again there was an awkward pause, until Tindal said laconically, 'I take it you have little to tell me on that front.'

'I'm close,' was all she managed. 'What about your end?' Anything else on the forensic work-up?'

'Confirmation that the skin samples we found under Alison

Terry's nails are identical to those found in Birmingham eighteen months ago. He's black, and has A-positive blood.' There was the faintest of pauses before he added, 'And this time too there was a mixed sample.'

'More transfusions?'

'It appears that way. The DNA work-up is being pushed through as quickly as possible.'

'This one is a real ghoul, isn't he?'

'That's one word for it.'

'No convenient Liverpool scarf though?'

Tindal heard the scepticism in her voice. 'All right, I admit that was probably a deliberate ploy to mislead us on his part. We had no idea of the sort of thing we were dealing with that first time. And stranger things have happened in murder investigations.'

'They have indeed,' said Natalie. 'Could you fax the forensic report through to me here? I'd like to see it. That and copies of what Mo took.'

'I'll get someone to do it now.'

'You sound tired,' she said suddenly.

'Do I?' His tone was loaded with sarcasm. 'I don't sleep well on weekends any more. If our man did abstain yesterday, it means we have six day's grace before he feeds again.'

'Of course.'

'Then I'll wait to hear from you. And thank you for your input, Dr Vine.'

After she put down the phone, Natalie rang the desk and arranged for another room. She wasn't expecting Mo to come back, but the room, despite the maid's efforts, made her feel unclean and uncomfortable.

That night, as she drifted towards sleep, she wondered if the police might talk some sense into Mo. Somehow she doubted it. His contempt for the fuzz was all part of his macho image. And it made her realise that far from being over, her little problem with Mo was unresolved and would remain so until she did something about it.

Like what, Natalie? An injunction?

Was that what Tindal had meant?

She couldn't think straight; too many other problems were impinging.

Six day's grace was all she had before The Carpenter struck again.

Six days in which to get her act together.

Tindal kept the phone in his hand and with the fingers of the other depressed the plunger in the cradle before punching in a new number. Quickly, he issued instructions to one of the duty officers assigned to the case before returning to his congealing pork chop. He ate alone in the kitchen, pondering this new turn of events.

Upstairs his children were blissfully asleep and in the next room he could hear the TV brainwashing his wife. On the table in front of him lay the *Independent*, bought seventeen hours before as he'd left for work and still unread. He glanced at it lying there and wondered for the fiftieth time why he bothered with a daily newspaper at all.

The food was cold but Tindal was hungry and ate quickly. There had been no time for anything but a cheese sandwich bought in a moment of weakness and against his better judgement from a Texaco garage in Pinner. Someone had found a body in a field there. Tindal had driven down only to hear the forensic people announce that it was at least three days old. Any interest it might have held for Tindal had evaporated then. A quick glance at the modus operandi confirmed it. It looked like a nasty one, but not The Carpenter's work.

He frowned.

He shared little of Vine's relief. He knew only that this butcher was going to strike again. Sunday was his killing day. He had killed once on a Friday, and once on a Saturday, but Tindal knew he preferred Sundays. He was not a good Christian, they knew that about him at least.

He shook his head in frustration. That was just about the only thing they did know. How in the name of God could they know so little after all these weeks and months?

He felt the burning discomfort behind his sternum. He was

heading for an ulcer, there was no doubt about it. Cheese sandwiches from Pinner and no leads on The Carpenter were sure-fire ulcer fodder.

He dropped the last forkful of pork and fat and shoved his plate away, his appetite suddenly gone as a wave of irritation washed over him.

Bloody woman. He had enough to worry about without having to sort out what amounted to a domestic disturbance. If it wasn't for the fact that there was still a chance she might unearth something he would have told her to forget the whole thing. He shook his head. The truth was, they were scraping the barrel for ideas and it looked like Vine was right at the bottom of it. Maybe Falkirk had been right after all. He hadn't liked the man but perhaps behind all the posturing and subterfuge was a large dollop of truth.

His mind drifted back to his first visit to the Ellison Institute. Falkirk's treacherous words rang clear and loud in his ears.

'*Natalie has a complicated personality. She has difficulty sustaining relationships. Her colleagues find her, ah, challenging.*'

'*Are you telling me she's not up to this?*'

'*Far be it for me . . . Academically she has shown signs of brilliance, but on a personal level there are problems.*'

Tindal sighed. This was looking more and more like the waste of time he had thought it would be. Bringing in a woman always complicated matters, and a screwed-up woman, psychiatrist or no psychiatrist, was the last thing he needed. The last thing anybody needed.

Forty-five minutes later, after three Rennies, Tindal had moved to an armchair, pretending to doze with the paper folded in his lap. His wife got up when the phone rang although both of them knew it would be for him.

'Regarding Alberini, sir,' said the duty officer.

'Yes?'

'No trace, sir. Sorry, sir. He rang in sick this morning and it doesn't look as if he's been home. Place looks unoccupied. Neighbours haven't seen hide nor hair.'

'Keep looking. We need to lean on this character. And put

some feelers out amongst the tabloids, but be careful. If he's tempted, I need to know the minute Fleet Street gets a sniff of this. But go easy, for God's sake. We don't want to shoot ourselves in the foot. They can smell a story ten miles downwind.'

If the papers got hold of this, the whole thing was going to blow up in somebody's face. And he didn't need two guesses whose face it would be.

He groaned inwardly. Who was he trying to kid here? He wouldn't have a hope in hell of muzzling the newspapers once they got their teeth into this. Damn and blast that stupid little cow, Vine. And then there was the thought of how The Carpenter might react . . .

Tindal's wife carried in two mugs of drinking chocolate as Tindal rang off. She stopped on the threshold of the living room when she saw his face.

'Martin, what ever's the matter?'

Tindal looked up, preoccupied. 'Eh?'

'Not another body?'

'No, nothing like that.'

'Then what? You look as if you'd heard some dreadful news.'

'It wasn't the news that was dreadful. It's the idea that's come into my head following it that's so bloody awful.'

'What idea?'

He shook his head. 'I can't . . . I can't talk about it.' He reached across to the inside pocket of his jacket, still hanging on a chair back.

'If it's that awful, forget it.'

'Trouble is, it's the only idea I've had in weeks.'

'Then talk about it,' she offered.

Tindal was up on his feet and searching through his diary. He said distractedly, 'No. I won't drag you through the mire. It's what they pay me for.'

'I'm beginning to believe it isn't worth it, Martin.'

When he didn't answer, she added, 'What on earth are you looking for?'

But he was already on his way to the phone, and largely to himself he muttered in reply, 'A phone number. A reptile's phone number.'

Chapter 22

On Tuesday evening, Natalie sat alone in room 25 staring at her notes and the tape recorder she'd placed in the middle of the bed. It was nine p.m. She'd left Meredith in the lobby on his way to the kitchens. It had been a long, harrowing, exhausting day for both of them. But Natalie was having difficulty quelling the small fanfare of triumph that threatened to burst out of her at any moment.

Meredith had completed two full run-throughs of his ordeal using the externalising viewing technique. The first had taken almost two hours and he had broken down several times. But she had made him go back to the point where he had stopped and begin again. He had done well, better than she had dared expect. When he'd finished he'd been physically drained, pale and sweating, his eyes feverish and swinging between dread and relief as he'd sat for fifteen minutes hunched forward in his chair, clutching his abdomen as if the memory had been vomited out of him.

'Now what?' he asked.

'Now is the most important part. Remember, you've been watching it all from the kitchen, seeing yourself watch what's happened on the TV. Now I want you to rewind the film, but this time as it rewinds you're not just watching, you're in the picture.'

Meredith stared at her dumbly, his face emotionally battered from what he had just relived. 'I don't understand,' he said defeatedly.

'Yes you do,' said Natalie firmly. 'It's vital you do this now. Hear his footsteps fade as he leaves you and rewind it from there. Do it quickly, half a minute at the most, as if you've pressed the

rewind button on your VCR. Go on, do it now.'

She watched his face struggle with it, saw his eyes lose focus as they concentrated on the inner horror. She saw them shut and saw his chest rise as he inhaled deeply. After a while he opened them again, looking around him as if at an unfamiliar landscape.

'Done?' She spoke anxiously and told herself to calm down.

He nodded.

'That's excellent.' Natalie was on her feet congratulating him. 'Really, you did very well.'

Meredith shrugged. 'I'm still not sure what the hell I've done.'

'An exorcism, of sorts. We'll need to do it once more this afternoon. There are one or two areas you're still loath to contemplate. That's understandable. If we can work through them I think you'll feel the benefit.'

'Benefit?'

'The idea is that having confronted your memory in detail, the rewind technique will kick in whenever memories trigger off bad feelings. It'll scramble events, mix them up. But what it will also do is bring you back to a new starting point each time. A good memory.' She thought for a moment. 'You and Jilly in the car together, singing.'

Meredith looked away, pondering Natalie's instructions. He spoke hollowly. 'How will I know if it's worked?'

Natalie smiled. 'We'll know.'

Suddenly, in the solitude of her motel room, Natalie felt isolated and a little scared. She half listened to noises in the corridor. Footsteps approaching. Would it be a knock, and then 'Housekeeping?' with Mo's leering face forcing its way in through the half-open door . . .

She felt the muscles bunch in her neck, felt them relax as the footsteps receded.

Silly, this was silly, she told herself. And yet there was reason enough for her nerves to be stretched. She looked at the tape recorder. Innocent black-and-grey plastic. Inside, it contained almost three hours of the most graphic description of lust murder anyone had ever heard. A first-hand account by an eyewitness.

216

A hundred things went through her mind. Thank God that Mo had not stolen this. It was worth thousands to a variety of interested parties. Academics, tabloids . . .

She laughed to herself. There in front of her was what she had wanted, what she had hoped for when she embarked on the project. Now that she had it, she knew that she would never use it. Meredith was inside that black-and-grey plastic. The ultimate degradation and humiliation of one human being forced to witness the inhuman destruction of another. Anyone getting hold of it would crucify him.

An image of a hack thrusting a microphone into Meredith's terrified, lost face and asking *the* question threw itself up in her mind. *The* question that made her boil inside whenever it was asked, and by Christ it was asked often enough by hungry journalists lunging at the chance of a little real emotion to replace the make-believe stuff they saw each day on the soaps.

'How did you feel when you saw what was happening to your girlfriend?'

In the subtext was all the slime of true pornography. The real stuff of snuff movies.

'Tell us about how he stabbed her and throttled her and raped her, sir. Tell us because you were there and we would love to know, just love to know so that we can sell more papers and pull in more viewers, because you're the best TV we've had in ages, oh yessir, by God, sir.'

She couldn't do that to him. Not even wrapped in the cellophane of academia.

But there was work to be done. Because the cause of it all was still out there, rampaging. Somewhere, there was a girl walking around who in a few day's time, through no fault of her own, was going to be brutalised unless . . . Natalie shivered at the thought she had shied away from. Unless she could find something in the middle of Meredith's horror that just might point them in the direction of The Carpenter.

Reluctantly, she pushed her finger towards the button and depressed it. This morning she had been the doctor, getting Meredith through his crisis, giving him succour. Now she had to be the analyst, picking over the bones of the thing, finding the hidden meanings that would yield the psychological fingerprints everyone was searching for.

From her notes, copious and flowing from the two sessions with Meredith, she had marked out certain sections. Much of the account was an elaboration of what had been given to the police. But there were additions. How important, she didn't know – yet.

Next to her on the bed was an unwrapped bar of chocolate. She popped a piece into her mouth as she pressed the fast-forward button, stopping at random and listening momentarily to snippets of the nightmare so that she could orientate the tape.

'. . . on all fours. Blood was still running from her feet where the nails stuck out. He was cutting the rest of her dress off with a knife, slitting it up . . .'

The tape whirred forwards.

'. . . sitting on her. The sheet he wore was soaked in blood as he rode her like a bloody rodeo horse. He had some sort of tight-fitting trousers on underneath, shiny, plastic – possibly a tracksuit. He was pulling on the flex around her neck, throttling her. But never enough so that she would pass out. He had his hand inside her . . . there was a hole in her side and he had a hand inside her gut, working it back and forth . . . All the time chanting that stupid rhyme . . . Chanting and calling her Susan.'

Natalie depressed the button.

'. . . at first I wouldn't read them. I was staring at him, scream-ing at him to let her go.'

She sat back. This was the part she wanted.

'He'd rigged the ligature through a hook on the wall so he could move around the room and still pull it whenever it . . . whenever he felt like it. She had two knives in her by then. They stuck out of her side. They quivered when she screamed. The torch was inside her . . . I'm sorry, I . . .'

'Go on. You must.'

And then he was in front of me, pointing at this piece of paper. I couldn't believe it. I screamed and shook my head. So he swung around and just stuck another knife in Jilly's leg. Oh God . . . Oh God . . .'

218

'Breathe slowly. Just breathe in and out slowly.'

'Ahhhhhh ... So then I did read it. They were just words printed over and over again. Typed, black words ... Good boy ... Good boy ... Don't tell anyone, not even ... not even your mother or I'll tear off your ears. Good boy ... Good boy. Kiss your sister there, boy. Do it, do it ... That's a good boy. That's a good boy ...'

The tape hissed on in silence until Meredith's voice came on again.

'Sick words. Horrible, sick words. I wasn't looking at him when I read them. He made me do it at least three or four times. And when I did look I could see it was turning him on. I was turning the bastard on. He was leaning over Jilly with his bloody hand under the sheet playing with himself and pulling on the bloody ligature. When he saw me watching, he looked at me and I knew he was grinning underneath that stupid mask. I could feel him grinning. I screamed at him, I screamed and screamed until he came over and hit me. He pushed me over and stuck the thing over my head and in my mouth. All I could do was lie there and listen to him grunting like a pig, hear Jilly choking to death while he –'

Quickly Natalie stopped it. She'd heard enough. The Carpenter's psychological wounds had been inflicted deep and early, that was obvious. She tried to imagine what Meredith must have felt, tried to capture even one iota of the impotence and horror. It was impossible, beyond rational thought. The brain was an adaptable thing, it enabled people to survive even the most traumatic of events, but at what cost to the psyche? She began to realise just how remarkable Meredith truly was. He had abandoned society, yes. He had gone into himself in search of some form of sanity. And although it seemed on the surface an unhealthy introspection, he had found strength from somewhere. His survival was, she realised, incredible. And something told her that perhaps The Carpenter had known this too, had seen something in Meredith that had appealed to him.

She frowned, examining this new, idiosyncratic thought. There was no logic to it. No shred of evidence, but it appealed to her.

Somehow it seemed right to think it. She let her mind wander down a few of the dark corridors that radiated from this startling new concept, but they led nowhere and after a few moments she found herself doubting the wisdom of her wool-gathering.

She needed more. She needed to sit down and think it through and ask her questions.

She was waiting for him at seven the following morning in the Flamingo restaurant.

'How do you feel?' she asked brightly.

'Tired.' He yawned.

'Then I prescribe sleep. Cheap but effective.'

'Sleep,' said Meredith wistfully.

'Go home,' commanded Natalie. 'Go to bed and pull up the sheets. I'll pick you up at midday. I want to visit Mandy. Think you're up to it?'

'Fine. But why wait until midday? I won't sleep more than a couple of hours.'

'I have things to do,' she said.

Chapter 23

By nine a.m. Natalie was back in her motel room, sitting cross-legged on the bed, pouring over the reports Tindal had faxed and studying with growing confusion the one she'd picked up from the desk on her way to meet Meredith earlier. It had arrived at midnight. Someone had obviously thought she ought to see it.

But no matter how hard she tried, the reports left her cold and dissatisfied. And it wasn't merely her lack of familiarity with the jargon. This was something she simply could not put a finger on. It was illogical and enigmatic, but nevertheless there.

At the bottom of the typed report she read a name below a scrawled signature. On impulse, she dialled the number she found adjacent to it. Dr Pat Norris was already in her office dictating reports. When Natalie was put through to her, her voice had a clipped Irish brogue that somehow managed to make her jargon-littered vocabulary far more easy on the ear.

'ACC Tindal warned me you might call,' she said after Natalie had introduced herself.

Natalie tried to imagine the face behind the voice. Late forties, she guessed. Not much make-up, dark hair cut short, and intense blue eyes.

'I have your report on the Southampton killing in front of me.'

'If there's anything I can explain to you . . .' offered Norris helpfully.

'You can tell me what you make of it all,' said Natalie in exasperation.

'It's very simple really. The nail scrapings taken from Alison Terry in Southampton contained a small amount of blood. The ABO grouping came up with A positive, nonsecretor, just as we found in the Birmingham case. Ummmm...' Natalie heard papers being shuffled. '... Barbara Lamb I think was the victim's name. And just as we found in the Lamb case, there were blurs on the supplementary groups.'

'Could you run through that for me in English?' asked Natalie.

'Of course,' said Pat Norris cheerfully. 'After typing for the major ABO groups and rhesus, we routinely do MNS grouping as well. Although everyone knows about A, B and O, there are many other subgroups. And what we found were far too many reactions for one single blood type, although they were faint, indicating a diluting effect, as would happen in a transfusion. You have six litres of blood inside you; one transfusion unit is just under half a litre. It gets very lost in amongst the other six litres in your body, hence the diluting effect. The transfused blood becomes far less concentrated. But once we did some DNA analysis it got interesting, not to say bizarre.'

'I'm all ears,' said Natalie.

'The amount of blood in the sample was small. That was one of the reasons we used a single-locus DNA probe. Normally, multi-locus probes are used which effectively identify repetitive sequences within each individual's DNA molecules. A specifically unique bar code, if you like, which is just what it looks like on the X-ray film we take of it finally. Single-locus probes look at one specific location on the DNA molecule and yield just two bands on the bar code, one from your mother, and one from your father. It is some fifty times more sensitive than the normal test. The beauty of it is that it can be used on pinhead-size samples and also allows us to analyse mixtures. In the Lamb case we knew we had a mixture and the DNA probe came up with twelve bands. Divide by two and that tells you that the blood in the Lamb case came from six different people.'

'So the killer had five different donors' blood inside him.'

'Exactly. Forty-two per cent of the population are A positive, so in any blood bank you are going to find a lot of different donors with A-positive blood, but each one will differ in its MNS groupings. These minor groups aren't matched in transfusions because a mismatch doesn't cause any adverse effect.'

'What about Alison Terry?' asked Natalie.

'Curiouser and curiouser. As mentioned, we also found a mixture of blood under her fingernails. The bizarre bit is that we came up with twelve bands on the single-locus probes and they were identical to what was found in the Lamb case.'

'So what you're saying is that not only did the killer transfuse himself, he used the same five donors the second time round?'

'That's exactly what the test shows.'

'But how?'

Pat Norris paused only momentarily before continuing. 'Well one scenario might be that he works for the Blood Transfusion Service. He could wait until his favourite donors' blood comes in. He might work centrally, or at a collection point.'

'Does knowing that help us?'

'One way of tracking down the blood would be to ask A-positive donors to come in for DNA testing. It would allow us to trace the blood through the system. See where it was collected from and where it ended up.'

'You don't sound too enthusiastic.'

'Have you any idea how many units of A positive are collected across the country every week? Anything between fifteen and twenty thousand.'

'Have you told Tindal this?'

'Of course. It's daunting, but it is an option he's considering.'

'Are there any alternatives?'

'Only bad ones. It is possible that the killer might have his own supply of donors. Possible even that his sources are not voluntary. Perhaps he has them locked up somewhere. In which case blood testing would be a waste of time.'

Natalie shivered. 'I don't think I want to hear any more of your theories.'

Pat Norris ignored her. 'My assistant came up with one. He calls it his living-dead theory. But only he and Bram Stoker really believe in it.'

Natalie didn't reply. The silence stretched for half a minute before Pat Norris broke it.

'Do I deduce from your silence that you too think the killer is from Transylvania?' Her tone was light, belying an undertone of inquisitiveness.

'It's all so convenient,' sighed Natalie.

'Convenient?' said Norris. Natalie could hear a trace of impatience creeping in. 'You've seen that the DNA match on the dermal samples found in the nail scrapings in the Alison Terry case is identical to the Lamb case. There's no doubt that it was the same man.'

'Yes, but . . .' Natalie was floundering, voicing her thoughts out loud. 'Alison Terry was against his usual type. The evidence of a struggle, more skin samples and blood – all just . . . convenient.'

'It's all evidence,' said Norris frostily. 'Are you suggesting we ignore it?'

'No, I'm not suggesting that, I just wondered . . . Look, I don't know what I mean, but is there any way you could look at this evidence afresh?'

'Look at it afresh,' repeated Norris slowly. 'Have you any idea of our workload? We're down by 30 per cent from a flu epidemic.'

'I meant you personally,' said Natalie quickly.

'My staff here are all highly trained.' Norris seemed to be holding her temper remarkably well.

'Please, don't misinterpret this. I'm not implying anything. I'm simply suggesting a fresh look by yourself without any preconceptions. I may be a hundred miles off the mark, but for example, is there any way he could have done something to his own skin to make it appear black?'

'No, it's impossible.' She paused before adding, 'But I hear what you're saying and frankly I can't accept that this is manufactured evidence. So far we haven't come across anything to suggest that what we've found hasn't occurred through anything other than the natural course of a violent assault.'

'I know,' said Natalie tiredly. 'I know.'

'But despite knowing that, you want me to "take another look"?'

'Yes please.' She could hear Norris breathing on the line.

'Well, I know you're at the sharp end of all this.' She sighed heavily. 'I'm in court all day and tomorrow morning, but I'll see what I can do. Although knowing what I'm supposed to be looking for would be a help.'

'If I knew that, I wouldn't be asking.'

'I suppose not,' said Norris. 'I'll be in touch.'

William Peter Mowatt Alberini woke up at eight on Wednesday morning feeling mean and sick. Both sensations were becoming depressingly the norm. Following Vine's attack on him in the motel room, he had left with all her papers, reacting with a blind spite, doing the only thing he could to retaliate. He had driven back to London, back to her flat, to wait for her. The place remained a bomb site from his previous destructive efforts.

For two days a black rage had occupied all his waking thoughts and he had fuelled those thoughts with five bottles of tequila.

He pushed himself off the bed, groaning, his head spinning. He stumbled to the kitchen and took a cold Becks from the fridge, gulping from the bottle greedily. He drained it in one, feeling the liquid rehydrate his parched throat and the alcohol take the edge off his hangover.

He had never been so cut up about a bloody piece of skirt before. No one had ever got to him like Natalie had. Shit, he'd even missed two days of work. Guiltily, he glanced at his watch. If he wasn't careful he was going to miss another one. Well, what the fuck. The truth was he couldn't function anyway until he got this out of his system. The bitch! She was tearing him apart.

Standing in the kitchen in his underpants with the beer cooling in his throat, the stark realisation hit him that she was not going to come back to him on her knees. There would be no fawning apology, no begging for forgiveness. And anyway, he mused truculently, now he didn't feel like taking her back. She had blown it.

His mind went back to the previous afternoon when he had wandered around the flat with the tequila coursing through his veins. He had strayed down to the ground floor, scrunching up her mail vindictively before throwing it out into the garden behind. He had seen the door to the basement flat open. It had been lunch time and the workers who were gutting it had left the door ajar and a dusty trail leading to the front door while they adjourned to the nearest pub. Curious, Mo had wandered down into a filthy, chaotic world and the idea had come to him then. He had gone back up to the maisonette, had drunk and plotted until after dark when the workmen left, and had then returned, prizing open the door with a crowbar from his car. In the dim light from one of Vine's decorative candles, he had stood there intent upon collecting the splintered laths, broken furniture, paper and rags for her 'funeral pyre'. In his imagination, he drooled over a picture of Vine's face when she arrived to find the house a black, smouldering shell.

But standing on the threshold of the basement, the candle sputtering in the freezing, dust-filled air, something happened that had never happened before. He broke down. He broke down and cried like a baby, thinking of Nattie's smooth skin that he would never taste again, never gaze at in unbridled lust. Jesus, Jesus, he loved her, didn't she know that?

The emotion of it drained all his energy. He had left the basement untouched and clambered back up to the maisonette, blubbing and stumbling and cursing through the tears.

Now, sober and in the cold light of day, his weakness revolted him. But he couldn't torch the place. It would be too obvious and the last thing he wanted was to be thrown into jail over her.

He opened another beer and wandered back into the living room. On the floor in front of the TV was the pile of files and notes he'd brought with him from that accursed motel room. He glanced at them now. They had been so important to her. More important than him. They had changed her, turned her against him.

He strode across the room and picked them up. He hadn't read them; he had been too angry, too preoccupied, too drunk. He flicked open the cover of the police file on Alison Terry and read. After three-quarters of an hour, the angry frown on his face had turned into a feline grin.

This was dynamite. Mo had always had a nose for money and

was good at his job, but this stuff, shit! He let out a roar of laughter. The irony of it. In his hands was the way to really get to Vine. Get to her through what she held most precious. Her all-consuming fucking work. And, *and!*, he would make some money into the bargain. The press would shit their pants over this.

And then his eyes lost focus, his imagination going off on another tangent.

He took another pull on his beer. Shit, life could be good sometimes.

Natalie had to knock three times before she heard footsteps hurrying to the door.

'Afternoon,' she said with a mischievous smile.

Meredith stood there in a thin dressing gown, blinking against the light, his face creased and puffy from deep sleep.

'What time is it?' he croaked.

'Two p.m.' Natalie walked past him, shutting the door behind her against the cold.

'Two? Jesus, I've slept for six hours.' He paused to throw Natalie a suspicious glance. 'You knew, didn't you? So how? Was there something in my tea? What?'

'What tea?' asked Natalie scathingly.

Meredith sighed in confusion.

'But it's true that this smile you see before you is one of self-satisfaction,' said Natalie, grinning.

Meredith continued to frown in puzzlement until realisation dawned.

'You mean that stuff we did yesterday?'

Natalie nodded. 'That stuff.'

'But that's unbelievable.'

'Not really. Your insomnia has merely been a subconscious safety mechanism that has wakened you whenever memory threatened. Now you have a better mechanism, a conscious mechanism. You no longer fear to dream.' She waited, watching his face. 'What did you wake up thinking of?'

Meredith thought. 'Jilly. Jilly and me . . . in a car . . .'

227

Natalie raised her eyebrows and let him have a sideways glance in reply, to which Meredith could only shake his head in perplexity.

'OK, Mr Van Winkle,' she said. 'You have precisely twenty minutes in which to perform your toilet and dress. I said we'd visit Mandy at two thirty.'

Still dazed, Meredith trotted off to the bedroom. It was only as he stepped through the door that her joke registered. He stopped and half turned his head before shaking it.

Behind him, he heard her laugh.

Much to his acute embarrassment, several of the ENT team that had performed surgery on Mandy shook Meredith's hand when Julie introduced him to the doctors clustered around an X-ray viewer at one end of the ward. Mandy watched from her bed, a smile on her lips as she cuddled a huge teddy bear. In her throat, a small silver tube glistened amidst white gauze swabs. Her mother, munching grapes from an overfull wicker basket at the foot of the bed, looked on in amusement.

'Mandy,' she whispered dramatically as the doctors finally released Meredith, 'here he comes. Where's your card?'

The little girl reached awkwardly behind her and from beneath her pillow removed a much-folded sheet of paper, which she handed to Meredith as he approached. He unfolded it carefully and studied the drawing. Three stick figures were clustered around a smaller, supine figure. Below, in an uneven scrawl, was *Thank You* and several kisses. Meredith studied it with Natalie looking over his shoulder. It was childish and devoid of detail, but loaded with meaning for the four people in and around the bed. Meredith looked up and smiled at the little girl.

'It's very good. Especially my purple hair.'

Natalie laughed, glad of the opportunity to swallow the awkward lump in her throat.

'I didn't get a proper chance to thank you for what you did. I'll never forget it.' Julie was up on her feet, staring with passionate sincerity into Meredith's eyes. 'I haven't got much I can give you . . .' she said falteringly.

228

Natalie was watching Meredith. He looked terrified. Having shut himself off for months, he was finding these deep, heartfelt emotions difficult to handle.

'You don't owe me anything,' he stammered. 'Anybody would have done the same . . .'

But Julie shook her head. 'I know that's not true. I asked Mr Cripps, the surgeon who put the silver tube in. He said you saved Mandy. He says they usually die if something gets stuck in the cords. Four, five minutes at the most.'

Meredith looked away, but Julie took his arm. 'Please, I just want you to know how grateful I am. She's all I've got. I don't know what I would have done . . .'

Meredith turned towards the little girl who watched him with large round eyes.

'I know a little bit about what you've been through. I'm no angel, but I know it weren't right, what happened to you,' continued Julie, 'and I'm sorry for the way I acted towards you.'

Meredith shook his head, still avoiding her gaze.

'I suppose all I really want to say is that as well as being for ever in your debt, I'm sorry.'

Mandy was listening. She held up her arms towards Meredith. He moved towards her like a man in a trance. When he was within reach she pulled herself up and kissed him on the cheek.

Natalie felt tears prick her eyes as Julie said, 'You have a gift. Please don't waste it.'

Largely to escape some of the emotional overload to her system, Natalie asked, 'What have you got planned for her?'

'Mr Cripps said she's still quite swollen inside. A deema?'

'Oedema,' said Natalie, nodding.

'So they're going to take the tube out tomorrow. I won't be able to hear her speak until then. Hopefully, she'll be home by Saturday and we're going back to Salford on Monday. Her father came down yesterday. Took a day off work for the first time in ten years. Says he's going to throw a big party for her next week. I'll believe it when I friggin' see it.'

The words were laden with cynicism, but Natalie saw an odd sparkle in Julie's normally listless eyes. As she turned back towards Meredith, she felt Julie's hand on her arm.

'What can we get him?' she whispered.

Natalie shook her head dismissively, but Julie was insistent. 'Mandy wants to. Something small.'

Natalie nodded reluctantly. 'Let me think about it.'

Chapter 24

Back at the chalet, Meredith threw a few extra logs on the fire as Natalie peeled off her coat and removed her pad and pencil from her case. In response to Meredith's puzzled frown, she said: 'I need to ask you some questions.'

Meredith poked the fire. 'So what's new?'

'These might hurt a bit.'

'You're the doctor,' he said, standing and brushing sawdust from his trousers.

It was late afternoon. A damp freezing fog had come down, shrouding everything in a dense blanket. As Natalie glanced out of the window at the fading light, the chalet seemed like a boat adrift on a silent sea, isolated from the world at large. She felt oddly at ease with the sensation.

'I'd better sit down for this then, eh?' Meredith's bravado was tenuous, but Natalie nodded in agreement and waited while he seated himself on the battered sofa.

'I want to ask you about the things he made you say.'

Meredith waited.

'Listening to the tape, it sounds as if it was all part of his ritual. And you're sure he recorded it?'

'He recorded everything. He had two cameras set up with a re-mote shutter release as well as a microphone on a home-made boom.'

'Did he ask you to speak in a particular way? More slowly, louder?'

Meredith shook his head. 'He just wanted me to say it over and over.'

'And just the one name?'

'Susan.'

'You said that when you read the thing he'd written down, it excited him.'

Meredith nodded.

'After he put the sack over your head, did he play back the tape?'

'I don't know. I couldn't breathe properly because of the gag. I wasn't concentrating . . .'

'Try and think.'

'I was rolling about, hearing Jilly choke. All I could hear was Jilly choking . . . And yes, yes, I heard the name. Susan. But it wasn't in his voice. It must have been the tape playing while he . . .'

Natalie let him settle. 'What about when he assaulted you. Did he play the tape then?'

'No. He didn't dwell on it. It was over quickly. It was more like something that he had to get over and done with.' She saw his eyes drop.

'Why do you think that?'

'I felt that he was just trying to intimidate me, use his power.'

'Did he say anything to you before he left?'

Meredith's voice dropped. 'Just the threat.'

'The threat of returning?'

'Unless I told the world . . .' Meredith shook his head.

'What about when he asked you to read the things he'd written down? Was there an accent, any trace of a stammer?'

'Nothing through the hood. Nothing.'

Natalie took a deep breath and asked, 'Why do you think he didn't kill you?'

Meredith's eyes flicked up to hers. She read pain there. The pain of a suddenly exposed and festering wound.

'You tell me,' he said and his words were raw.

Natalie shook her head. 'You've thought about this for much longer than I have. Please, I'm not trying to catch you out. Tell me what you think.'

Meredith hung his head as if the weight of his fearful perception might break him. 'I think he gets a kick out of knowing that

I'm alive having seen what he does. He's secure in the knowledge that I can do nothing to stop him, do nothing to help anyone catch him. I think it gives him a huge thrill.' He looked up challengingly and saw her nod in agreement. 'I think he would just about wet himself if I stood up on TV and told everybody what I'd seen.'

'He does crave notoriety, I'm sure of that,' said Natalie. 'But there are other ways. Photographs to the press, phone calls to TV stations. What I mean is that there are easier, less risky ways than gambling on capturing a second victim. A witnessing victim.'

Meredith was shaking his head. 'All I know is that I'm never going to give him the pleasure. I'd rather pull the plug than talk to the press.

'No one can make you.'

'No, no one can make me.'

She put down the pencil and stared at the fire.

'Does this really mean anything to you?' asked Meredith suddenly.

'I suppose it should do.' She smiled wanly. 'But I'm damned if I know what.'

'In time perhaps?'

'That's exactly what we haven't got.'

'Don't be too hard on yourself.' He hesitated. 'Five days ago we could never have had this conversation.'

Natalie shook her head. 'You've done it yourself.'

'I was pretty sceptical, wasn't I?'

She followed his gaze to a tall wooden standard lamp that listed in one corner. Someone had tried repairing the worn flex with insulating tape where it had frayed.

'That', said Meredith pointing at the lamp, 'has haunted me for months. I couldn't look at it without . . . It's the tape . . . I used to sniff the tape, although the last thing I really wanted to be reminded of was the smell. Bloody stupid really.'

'Just your guilt. A hair shirt.'

He got up and walked swiftly to the lamp, stooping and sniffing the tape wound around the flex as Natalie watched, transfixed. After a moment, Meredith looked up, his face confused and a little disappointed. 'It just smells of tape.' He stood, laughing nervously. 'Look, no paper bag needed.'

Natalie smiled. 'We should celebrate. Toast you and Mandy.'

'I'll crack open a bottle of orange squash.'

Natalie said brightly. 'Let's go out. An Indian.'

Meredith hesitated only fractionally before his face lit up. 'An Indian. I haven't tasted a *Kheema naan* in months.'

They drove into Swansea and found a Nepalese restaurant wedged between a furniture warehouse and an insurance broker. It was early and they were alone under a woven mural of a red palace.

'Mmm, this is great,' he said through a mouthful of rice.

Natalie smiled. The food really was good. But the change in Meredith was much, much better. She felt oddly privileged at being the one present at this 'coming out'. For that was increasingly what it was looking like. He was behaving much as one would expect of a man released suddenly from solitary confinement. Everything was savoured, each mouthful a delight. And in the quiet ambience of what was, she realised looking around, quite an elegant restaurant, devoid of any trace of flock wallpaper or wailing singers, something else magical happened. Whether it was the aroma of the herbs or simply the spontaneity of his decision, it didn't matter. The fact was Tom Meredith forgot himself. He relaxed, enjoyed the food, enjoyed her company and without realising it, he began to talk.

He told Natalie about his work and about the odd, serious, silly, important and trivial actions and events that constituted Tom Meredith's life. And Natalie listened. At first with what she thought was a professional ear, but increasingly with a fascination that was anything but professional. His voice charmed and beguiled her. It held an odd resonance that seemed to reach in and massage her mind, like someone scratching a difficult-to-reach spot high between her shoulder blades.

Outside of the austerity of the spartan chalet, he was bright, self-deprecating and amusing; the complete and utter antithesis of Mo and of all those sad encounters before Mo.

234

Mo? Why was she thinking of Mo?

Had she met anyone like Meredith before? If she had, she hadn't noticed. Buried beneath her coverlet of insecurity and dodging behind the ample screen provided by her pursuit of a 'career', Natalie Vine, good old Nattie, hadn't noticed. Correction, hadn't wanted to notice. And all because of the constant shadow that lurked behind each encounter, that whistled at the end of each exhaled breath in her body, that dogged the ticking seconds of every waking and sleeping moment. A shadow with the silhouette of a bottle raised to a bitter, angry mouth beneath cold dark eyes that once had loved and cared.

. . . *SSSLUT* . . .

Her mother's eyes.

And she responded to Meredith's outpourings, hearing the noise of her voice and not, for a while, recognising it. For the noises that emanated were as foreign to her as an Algerian folk song, although the language was as English as Shakespeare's sonnets. It was the sheer novelty of voicing those terrible, haunting thoughts that made them appear so foreign. She told him about her mother, her father, her work, Mo. They lined up like lambs for the slaughter. Several times she halted and listened, hearing a silent mental scream that yelled, *What the Holy Christ do you think you are DOING?*, fighting the urge to squirm away, but not once did she make herself stop. It was a necessary release, she told herself. A verbal cleansing of the system after her confrontation with Mo. But it was oh so easy with this man who listened. Listened without criticism, listened without offering anodynes to soothe her troubles. And that in itself was a refreshing novelty after her colleagues, whose armour plating of platitudes always seemed to offer nothing but an impregnable, shallow, selfish barrier. One she had never dared penetrate.

Later, during a lull in the conversation, Meredith glanced at his watch. It stared back at him and said nine thirty.

'Looks like I've missed my shift,' was all he said.

'They'll survive.'

'What about me,' he laughed nervously. 'Will I?'

'I'll stay . . . if you like,' she said and he smiled.

235

They drove back to the chalet in a quieter mood. The night was cold and still. As they approached the coast, the fog thickened, rolling in over the roads, silent and unstoppable.

Meredith stared out at it, remembering the last time he had been in a car alone with a woman. The radio was playing something pianissimo and unrecognisable, not like the last time when Jilly had turned up the volume, had sung along. He glanced in the wing mirror, half expecting to see a flashing blue light suddenly loom up from behind. He fought down the rising tide of panic that suddenly threatened to engulf him. This was not Jilly, this was Natalie Vine, here and now. He glanced across at her, noticing the smooth lines of her face as she concentrated on her driving. The sight of it soothed him. She was oblivious of his terror, but he knew that she was the cause of his ability to contain it.

At the chalet, Meredith soundlessly went through his bedtime ritual, unable or unwilling to contemplate Natalie's amused stares. When he'd finished, she stripped in the darkness of the living room and put on one of Meredith's faded and creased denim shirts that smelled of medicinal soap and him. She paused on the threshold of the bedroom, seeing him lying there on his bed, staring up at the ceiling. She paused only to consider the base self-critical thought that had nagged her for most of the evening before finally dismissing it. This was no ordinary doctor-patient fling. It was part of something much, much more. What she was doing went beyond a kindness, beyond lust, beyond attraction, beyond intellect. It was a whole greater than its parts. She shut off her mind, which sometimes simply got in the way, and eased into the bed. She saw him reach up for the dangling pull switch and saw the room go dark and then the white-yellow afterimage of the naked bulb turn green and purple in the darkness of her shut eyes.

'Who sent you to me?' he whispered, still rigid on his side of the bed.

'The police. I've told you . . .'

She heard the rustle of the pillow as he shook his head.

'I'm no guardian angel,' she protested.

'But you are here.' He turned and threaded a strong arm

underneath her, slowly pulling himself close. She felt his long body smooth against hers as she pulled his head on to her breast, stroking his hair gently.

There was no sound outside. No traffic, no hoot of owl. It was as if the fog had been sent to cocoon them. And in that utter, dead silence, they slept an innocent sleep. Meredith content in her simple touch, and Natalie basking in the glow of an odd, inexplicable peace for which, she realised, she had been searching all her life.

Meredith awoke before dawn, refreshed by seven or so hours of unbroken sleep, untroubled by the visceral nightmares that had violated his sanity for so long. Natalie stirred as well, restless in the strange bed. She felt his hand on her breast, felt the fingers trace her collarbone and travel up her neck, his palm gentle over her eyelashes as she blinked into wakefulness. When she opened her eyes, she saw his face inches from hers, alert and hungry.

He made himself aware of her soft, firm body. He heard her breathing change, he felt her pulse quicken. He had forgotten how warm a woman's body was in the morning. He reached over and felt for the bedside lamp, blinking against the harsh light before placing it on the floor so that it threw long shadows but gave them enough light to look at one another. And in the early hours of that February morning, the major part of Tom Meredith's healing took place.

He abandoned himself in Natalie and she received him with a generosity that was gentle but insistent as her desire grew. And afterwards, as they lay with sweat cooling on limbs thrust out from beneath bedclothes, they both spoke of feeling a strange purity in what they had done together. They felt made over, like emerging metamorphosed pupa who had shed their hard, waxen skin. As the cold dawn crept in through the thin curtains, they were new people. Aliens with things to say to one another, feelings to expose, memories to share. And later, when the talk died a little, they made love again, more urgently this time, more innovatively, with a hunger that bordered on the ravenous.

They got up at ten and Meredith made eggs and toast and they laughed at one another until the food was mere crumbs and yellow debris on their plates and Meredith suddenly grew quiet and contemplative.

'What?' asked Natalie.

'How many days do you have?'

'Until what?'

'Until he strikes again.'

She heaved a sigh. 'Today's Thursday. Two. Three if you include today. He likes Sundays.'

'Is there anything in what I've told you that might help?'

She looked away, troubled by the need to think and suddenly by what she had to do.

'There is something that isn't clear. You said he wore gloves. The forensic analysis revealed a nonstarch lubricant found in a particular make: Cambridge Surgiglove. Have you ever used them?'

'Yes, but not often. They're not my choice; a little tight at the wrist for me.'

'You said in the police statement that you thought he might be wearing two pairs. Why?'

'These gloves are not completely transparent. They're pale flesh-coloured, but once they're stretched you can usually see through them. I remember seeing him glaring down at me, pushing down the webs between the fingers, adjusting the fit. I remember seeing how pale his hands looked with the gloves on. I would have expected his hands to appear darker under the stretched gloves, but they were pale, a ghost's hands. If he was wearing two pairs, they would look like that.'

Natalie was nodding, her face inscrutable, not giving anything away.

'Does that help?' he asked.

'Possibly. One of my hang-ups over this case.' She sighed before adding apologetically, 'I have to go back to London to do some thinking. But I'm going back via Bristol. You've told me so many things. I have to sift through it all, throw away the chaff.'

'What's in Bristol?'

Natalie shrugged. 'Hopefully some answers to some vague

questions. I'll know what to ask when I get there.' She paused before adding, 'Why don't you come with me?'

He hesitated and then shook his head. 'I'd be too much of a distraction. Besides, I need time too.'

'There's nothing to keep you here.'

'I know.'

'Tom,' she said reaching across the table for his hand, 'last night was not charity on my part. I don't give freely. When this is over, I'd really like us to . . .'

Meredith smiled. 'You don't have to explain. But he's there, like the bars of a cage. Everywhere I turn.'

'But it will be over, Tom.'

'I believe that now. I didn't used to, but I do now.'

Natalie smiled and Meredith noticed not for the first time that it changed her completely. The spontaneity added warmth to the icy beauty.

'There is one thing I'd like you to do,' she said.

'Yes?'

'Give me your weapon, whatever it is. The weapon you keep in case he comes back.'

Meredith felt the blood rise in his face. Was it that obvious? He shrugged and laughed quietly.

For a long moment he sat there, staring at his plate before thrusting himself up with his arms and squatting on all fours under the table, reaching behind the sofa. He emerged with the Quaker Oats tin, which rattled as he put it down in front of her.

Natalie took it and prised open the lid. She peered inside and saw the vials and the syringes. After a moment, she said, 'You don't need it any more. I mean that.'

She watched his face. For a fraction of a second, the eyes became hooded again and she saw something dark pass behind them. But then it faded and he said, 'Whatever you say, Doctor.' Twenty minutes later they were walking out of the door, heading for the city and lunch. This time Natalie waited while Meredith set his sticks, which he did without a qualm. He was healing, but it was incomplete. Even so, his progress had been incredible.

God, he was resilient. She felt something swell in admiration inside her and she looked at him again with something more than affection.

The fog had cleared somewhat, but it still hung in damp veils around the hill.

Even if the fog had not been there, it was doubtful that either of them would have seen the long nose of the telephoto lens poking out from beneath the shadow of a dark cedar up to the left of the clearing. The fog did damp down the whirr of the power wind, but it was professional and barely audible at the best of times. They were laughing as the camera picked them out against the chalet getting into Meredith's car.

They were still laughing as they sat at the table in the Italian restaurant they had chosen. Their visitor took two rolls of thirty-six before walking back to his car, which he'd parked audaciously close to Meredith's.

It was two p.m. on Thursday by the time the photographer drove off and pointed his nose east towards London.

It was another sixteen hours before Natalie felt able to leave Meredith and do the same.

Chapter 25

Bloor reached down and began adjusting the foot rests of the wheelchair again, moving them back and forth as if to confirm or refute a mechanical fault. There was nothing wrong with them, but only Bloor knew that and anyone glancing his way would be hard-pressed to say so from the effort he appeared to be putting in. Not that anyone was paying him any heed as he squatted down in a quiet recess off a corridor of the hospital. Around him, nurses hurried to and fro, intent on their tasks, ignoring his presence, all silently thankful that he was not bothering them for anything. No one asked why he was there, the wheelchair and his uniform were his credentials and he was a familiar face around the hospital. Bloor himself was the only one who knew he was there under very false pretences.

He'd seen Vine in the corridor, recognising her instantly as having been to the hospital asking questions about Meredith before. He'd followed her with the wheelchair, which had ostensibly been bound for the gynie ward to pick up someone for an abdominal ultrasound. He'd travelled up in the lift with her to the trauma unit, close enough to touch her. She'd smelled expensive in the lift as he'd stood behind her, listening to her explain her requirements to the hospital administrator she was with. She just wanted to clear up a few things, she said. Some details about Meredith's work situation. She'd looked like a barrister. He'd been shocked to hear that she was a psychiatrist. What was she doing sniffing around Meredith? Perhaps he was ill. Perhaps that was why he hadn't done what was expected of him. Spread the word about his talents, given the world the truth they so longed for.

He watched as she disappeared into the ward with the lackey in tow, then stood up, pivoting the wheelchair with practised ease as he pushed it and himself back towards the lift.

The little pang of doubt hit as he depressed the call button. Perhaps this was all some subterfuge, but who by? The police? He shook his head and smiled. No, it was too subtle for them. Besides, she didn't look like or talk like a policewoman. No, it didn't ring true. Not the police.

As he pushed the chair into the lift, he felt his confidence and his power return in a giddy surge.

She knew nothing. The police knew nothing. Fishing, that's all she was doing. Fishing in a dark lake with the wrong bait. He had a half-day of work left, and then there was the weekend. He would give them more to think about this Sunday. He allowed himself a brief smile. Insects, tiny meddling insects, that was all they were. As irritating as persistent flies, but just as harmless and ineffectual.

Natalie thought Tindal looked somehow older as he stood next to the window in her flat on Saturday afternoon. The two policemen accompanying him hovered behind the settee.

'Sergeant Edmundson and DC Bridger from Gillespie Road,' said Tindal by way of introduction.

Natalie nodded in their direction, Edmundson portly and scruffy in a sport's coat, Bridger, black and athletic-looking in a sage suit. They continued to stand nervously polite until Natalie sat.

Tindal was restless. He paced the room, pausing at the window to look down at the street below and the houses opposite, noting the scaffolding.

'Up-and-coming this part of London, is it?' he asked.

'Until the recession hit,' said Natalie. 'Several of the bigger houses haven't had any work done on them for months.'

Tindal pivoted, his eyes sharp and penetrating. Bridger and Edmundson, who had been gazing around the flat in admiration, swung their heads towards his point of focus, like kittens following a ball of wool. All eyes finally came to rest on Natalie, who sat with the jotted distillation of days of solid thought in her lap.

Arriving back from Bristol late Friday afternoon, she'd called in for two carrier bags' worth of provisions from an 'Eight till Late', and then scattered them all over the floor when she saw the state her flat was in. For a while, perhaps as long as fifteen minutes, she was convinced she had been burgled. But search as she might, she could see nothing missing. It was only when she found the empty bottles that she thought of Mo.

For one wild, sphincter-weakening moment, she thought that he was still there, hiding, ready to leap out at any moment. Why had she come back to the flat alone? She hadn't been thinking. Nervously, she armed herself with a heavy, medium-sized Le Creuset saucepan and tiptoed around the flat. When she was satisfied that she was truly alone, she went down to the front door and put the chain lock on. Then, in defiance of Mo and all he stood for, she cleaned the flat.

It took her three hours.

With the place finally woodland-fresh from potpourri, and with two sackfuls of what he had destroyed that was beyond salvage, she had made herself something decent to eat, unplugged the phone jack and let it all wash over her.

She had read and reread her notes and the copied police files Tindal had forwarded to replace those Mo had filched, opening her mind like floodgates, letting her subconscious be the filter.

Now, in the living room, Tindal took two steps towards an armchair and sat down expectantly.

'I think', said Natalie without waiting to be asked, 'that our friend knew Meredith. Knew him before he killed Jilly Grant.'

In the silence that followed, it was Bridger and Edmundson's open-mouthed expressions that gave her the most gratification. Tindal remained impassive, the slightest narrowing of his eyes the only sign that here at last was a real piece of the jigsaw.

Natalie went on. 'Jilly doesn't fit the pattern. She's unlike all the other victims. Taller, fairer, more angular.'

When Tindal finally spoke Natalie received the impression that he was voicing things for the others' sake, to help them understand.

'So are you implying that this was a whim killing?'

'Far from it. But the real victim was Meredith. It was Meredith he was stalking.'

'You saying he's a shirt-lifter?' Edmundson's voice was gravelly and sceptical.

Natalie shook her head. 'The Carpenter wanted Meredith's voice on tape. He wanted it to augment part of the ritual that makes up these murders. The transcript of praise and the naming of the girl, Susan. It all fits. Susan is the girl he is killing each time. From the phraseology and the alternation between goading and approval in what Meredith was forced to say, I would guess that our man is reliving some sort of childhood episode. Meredith represents an older brother, a parent, someone in authority.'

'Then why kill the girl?'

'Because he wanted Meredith to see it. He wanted Meredith's admiration.'

Bridger and Edmundson were staring at her.

'He killed the girl to try and impress Meredith or whoever he was trying to make Meredith into. As he might try and impress some role model in his childhood.'

Bridger said incredulously, 'Do I detect sympathy?'

'He was a child once. In groping for understanding, I constantly have to bear in mind that there is no such thing as understanding in these cases. He does it because he likes to. He's addicted to it. To the screams, the blood, the ultimate power of taking a life, and even that is only part of it. He has to do it to survive. Killers like him do it not only to take a life, but to ingest it. The killing is almost a spiritual thing. It has nothing to do with the victims themselves. They become something else in the killer's eyes. Something that somehow makes them more whole, or worthy. And I suspect that in Jilly's case he was showing off to his peers, as any child might.'

'Jesus,' said Bridger.

'Something did puzzle me for a while. The reason as to why he attacked Meredith afterwards. Now I think he did it to cover his tracks. He realised he had let someone see. In that, he was unable to help himself. But outside the ritual he is also cunning and intelligent. So he brutalised Meredith to confuse you. He probably felt a little angry with himself too for allowing himself the lapse. But mixed up with all of this there is ego as well. How tempting it must have been for him to let an eyewitness back into the world. Someone who could tell of his skill and power.'

She saw that Bridger was about to bark out a question, but Tindal held up his hand.

'How does this help us?'

'It's important we look at his most recent killing. As I said, Jilly Grant was a utilitarian killing, and I think Alison Terry was too. I think he chose her because she was like Grant and he knew what that would do to the investigation. Also, he needed another vehicle to carry his false trail of evidence.'

'What false trail?' asked Tindal, leaning forward.

'I was never happy about the fact that he was black, nor the transfusion aspect of the samples. When both blood tests revealed the same mix of DNA grouping, indicating that the donors were all the same, I felt that this must be a contrivance. So I asked Pat Norris to take another look at the evidence and she rang me back last night.' Natalie shuffled some papers in her lap before finding the one she was looking for. 'Normally, the laboratory doesn't do much in the way of histological testing; they're not looking for diseases. They could tell that the skin was not Caucasian, that was obvious. But when she looked again, Pat Norris found some artefacts.'

'Artefacts?'

Natalie nodded. 'Nail scrapings often provide fairly ropy samples. But on further examination, she found large spaces in the tissues. Holes, if you like. Added to that were changes in the cells themselves. Some of them looked cracked, the nuclei larger than normal.'

Tindal was looking at her with uncomprehending eyes.

'But this wasn't due to any disease. The holes and the cracking were consistent with changes caused by ice crystals. Yet these were trace samples, remember. All fixed in formol saline preservative before being examined by paraffin section. Sometimes tissue is frozen for later examination – there's a specific technique called a frozen section used in hospitals. But the skin samples found under the nails of Barbara Lamb and Alison Terry were never frozen for forensic examination. The samples were taken fresh, there was no indication for freezing.'

'What are you trying to say?' asked Bridger, perplexed.

'I think it's very suggestive that this skin is from previously frozen tissue. I think it may not be from the real murderer at all.'

Tindal's face was rigid with concentration. 'Are you telling me that he may not even be black?'

'If I were him and I was planting evidence, I would certainly choose a different racial group as my source material. Meredith commented that he thought the killer was wearing two pairs of gloves because his hands were pale under these semiopaque gloves and because you'd *told* Meredith that he was black. But if he was Caucasian and was only wearing one pair, they'd naturally look pale.'

'But the night Grant was killed, he told us that the killer's face was black,' insisted Tindal.

'Meredith saw two inches of face around the eyes. The killer is into dressing up, we know that. It would have been pretty easy for him to have blacked his face. This was a "night manoeuvre" after all.' She paused again, letting it all sink in before summarising. 'Therefore, I do not think he is black. I think he targeted Meredith, not Grant, and I think he is undoubtedly allied to the medical profession. I also think that he may work or has worked in Bristol, perhaps in the same hospital as Meredith.'

'Why?' asked Bridger.

'It would explain the fibres from the white sheet he wore; that manufacturer supplies the health service extensively. Also the timing of the Bath murder. It is the only one that took place other than on a weekend. The others are all geographically disparate as well. To kill on Sundays, he has to travel. If he lived in Bristol or the surrounding area, he could have got across to Bath in half an hour.'

'We've checked Meredith's colleagues,' said Tindal tersely.

'But you were looking for a black man then.'

Tindal flinched and responded in anger. 'If it isn't his blood and skin we've been looking at, whose is it?'

Natalie nodded. 'I don't know. And I'm afraid I have nothing else that's of much use. There was no speech defect according to Meredith, no particular accent. The hood and the sheet could be an affectation worn just for Meredith, or they may be a throwback to the period of his own abuse as a child. There were no particular physical features.'

'How, might I ask, did you break through?' Tindal was forcing a smile on to his face.

I slept with him, screamed a voice in Natalie's head. It sounded hysterical and reactionary.

'I treated him. He has done very well.'

'So have you.' Tindal was shaking his head. The fixed smile hadn't slipped and for some reason it unsettled her.

'None of this is definite,' she heard herself say.

'No, but it makes perfect sense, damn it.' Tindal glanced across at Bridger, who returned the look with a pained expression. Tindal massaged his eyeballs. She'd seen him do it before and it seemed starkly at odds with the plastic smile.

'You have a written report?' he asked, suddenly on his feet. Natalie handed him ten pages of A4 fresh off the WP that afternoon. Tindal motioned to Bridger and stood up. 'We have a lot to do.'

The phone rang as they were walking through the front door and out into the street. Natalie picked it up, hardly recognising the high excited voice which answered as that of Pat Norris.

'I've found him,' she said, blurting out the words.

'Who?' asked Natalie.

'Our black A-positive nonsecretor.'

'What?' This time it was Natalie's voice that took on the high octave. Desperately, she banged on the window until Bridger looked up. She motioned with excited gestures for them to come back in and trotted downstairs with the portable to open the door. The policemen exchanged puzzled glances as Natalie motioned for them to return to their seats in the living room, her face glowing with excitement as she concentrated on Norris's voice.

For five minutes, the policemen remained on tenterhooks as

they watched Natalie scribbling on a pad, her expression giving little away. Finally, she glanced across at Tindal and grinned. 'Don't bother, he's standing right in front of me,' she said into the receiver. 'Oh, I'll tell him, don't you worry. And congratulations.'

Trying to calm her galloping pulse, she put the phone down and turned to the three expectant faces.

'The skin belongs to one Elmore J. Fisher. Forty-four-year-old West Indian from Portishead in Bristol.'

'Edmundson, get on the phone,' ordered Tindal.

Edmundson was on his feet in an instant, but Natalie was holding up her hand and shaking her head.

'Wait, you must hear it all. That was Pat Norris. She's been trying to fit all these pieces together. After we spoke, after she found the artefacts, she began thinking what if the blood really could have come from someone who'd been transfused – the one thing that we've discounted all along? So she played a hunch and did a barrage of tests. One of them included a tissue type on the skin sample, which she then fed into the data base.' She paused for breath. 'The match just appeared on her screen. It came from UK transplant in Bristol.'

'Why wasn't it done before?' seethed Tindal.

But Natalie shook her head again. 'The only people who are tissue typed routinely are those who require transplants, or those who supply organs. It's not done routinely on forensic cases for that reason. But Elmore Fisher was on file as a *donor* – heart, lungs, kidneys, eyes.'

They were staring at her now, their faces bewildered.

'Elmore Fisher died after a road traffic accident nineteen months ago.'

'What?' yelled Edmundson.

'At the Bristol Infirmary,' nodded Natalie. 'The Carpenter has been using Elmore Fisher's tissue. That first time in Birmingham, he didn't use his skin and blood, he used a victim's.'

'Are you saying that he killed Elmore Fisher too?'

'Not necessarily. But it's possible that there is something about Elmore Fisher's case that triggered him off so that he perceived him as a victim. Certainly he would have had undisturbed access to the body if he has taken tissue samples . . .

Tindal rallied. 'Edmundson, get a squad out to that hospital. I want everyone involved in that case questioned.'

Edmundson took the sheet on which Natalie had scribbled Norris's information, went to the phone and began barking orders. Natalie was beaming. A silly, happy grin that she couldn't shake off.

'Congratulations,' said Bridger and his eyes were shining. This was the breakthrough they had been praying for.

Natalie shook her head deprecatingly, but still she couldn't stop smiling.

Tindal was on his feet again, pacing. 'Have you any idea how he has been doing this?'

Natalie shook her head. 'It's beyond comprehension. He probably puts it there after death. He probably lets them fight him a little when they are alive so as to mimic bruising and defence injuries.'

Tindal grimaced. He turned, glancing testily towards Edmundson issuing orders on the phone and looking to Natalie like a man anxious to be somewhere else all of a sudden. Turning back, he strode over to where she was sitting and held out his hand.

'Dr Vine, I am extremely grateful for this.'

She shook it. Then, for the first time since meeting her, he dropped his gaze, concentrating on a point halfway between a potted plant and the TV.

'You will be available for the rest of the weekend?'

'Ummm, yes.' She answered hesitatingly. It wasn't something she'd given much thought to.

'I might need to talk to you again.' Tindal let his eyes return to hers slowly.

'I'm not going anywhere,' she said in reassurance.

'Good.' He turned away as Edmundson put down the phone, motioning to the sergeant impatiently.

'I'll be in touch,' he said over his shoulder as he walked out of the room.

Bridger was the last through the door. He turned and smiled at Natalie, clapping his hands silently and grinning.

When the door shut behind them, Natalie fell back into the chair exhausted. It was done. And God, it *was* a breakthrough. A real breakthrough. And then a frown creased her face. Bridger and Edmundson had almost danced a jig, but Tindal had acted very strangely. Was it the presence of the other officers? Or merely the strain he was under?

What a terrible burden this must be for him. He was right, there was still a lot to do, but even so she had expected a little more emotion after all this time.

Shrugging, she went back to her notes and began amending her report.

Her watch showed four p.m.

What, she wondered, would the world be like twenty-four hours from now?

Would there be a corpse, or a killer in custody?

She looked down at the hand holding the pencil. It was trembling. There was too much adrenaline pumping around her for her to sit still. She needed to do something. Something physical. Her thoughts flew to Tom. If he was there now, they would find a way of dissipating her energy. A very old, satisfying way. It was a deliciously lewd thought, one she kept in her mind as, grinning, she donned her ski-jacket and walked briskly out into the afternoon for some celibate fresh air.

Meredith phoned at nine that night.

His voice, rich and deep, seemed to flow into her ear and down into her spine. It was the first time she'd heard his voice in intimate isolation without seeing him and the effect was disconcerting. He had to speak her name twice before she could release the breath that had locked in her throat.

'Tom, it's you.'

'Yes.' He sounded subdued.

'Where are you phoning from, work?'

He hesitated before saying, 'I didn't go. I told them I wouldn't be in any more.' He paused and then said, 'I think they were quietly relieved.'

She tried to imagine his taciturn, dark-eyed presence in the kitchens and smiled. 'So what now?'

'I thought I'd try some locum work. A general medical job for a week or two. Ease myself back in. Maybe in my old stomping ground in Mortimer Street.'

'Oh Tom, that's fantastic. I'm so pleased for you.'

'I rang an old boss today. There's always someone on holiday. He told me to come up on Monday, take a look at it. No pressure.'

Neither of them spoke for some moments, both too busy weighing up the implications of what he was saying. Eventually it was Natalie who broke the silence. She took a deep breath and told him what had happened, trying to keep the excitement out of her voice and failing miserably. He took it with remarkable calmness and she supposed that this was just a safety mechanism for him. He would accept it only when it was truly over and The Carpenter was either dead or in prison.

'How do you think he does it?' asked Meredith finally.

'The mind boggles.' She had tried answering this question once for Tindal.

'What did Tindal say?'

'Tindal disappeared down a hole like the White Rabbit.' She giggled.

'To Bristol?'

'I expect so. He only has until tomorrow.'

'Tomorrow?'

'Sunday, bloody Sunday.' She regretted it immediately. It sounded hopelessly callous. She heard him repeat it.

'Bloody Sunday . . .'

'Tom, if you don't want to be alone, I'm here. You can come up at any time.'

'No,' he said curtly and she felt her stomach churn. 'I'm sorry,' he added. 'I didn't mean it to sound so . . . There are things I need to do, and . . .'

She heard him falter. He was no fool. He knew what this conversation was all about and it wasn't his job.

Come up here, Tom Meredith, I'll find you something to do, you big dumb klutz.

'I wanted to say thanks,' he said.

'Pleasure,' said Natalie throatily.

'Was it?' he asked with slight desperation.

'Yes. Of course it was.'

'There really are things to do. I have to pack and let some people know I won't be around, otherwise I would come up tomorrow, but I'll definitely be up by Monday.'

'Monday,' repeated Natalie, confirming it.

'Perhaps we could meet up for lunch . . .?'

'Tom,' said Natalie, 'shut up and listen. I don't sleep with my patients as a reward for them taking their medication. What happened between us was real. I want you to come and stay with me, sleep in my bed, eat my lousy spaghetti, take a shower with me. Are you listening?'

There was silence and for one fearful moment she wondered if she'd said too much, moved too fast. Frightened him away.

'Tom? Tom?'

When he spoke, it was with a warmth that set her fingers tingling. 'I'd like that, Natalie. I'd like that very much.' Then they were both laughing, relieved at having broken through a silly, awkward barrier.

'God, Meredith. You make me feel like a bloody schoolgirl.'

'Sometimes you look like one.'

'Come up early on Monday, please?'

'I'll take the seven a.m. Be in Paddington by ten. Your place by eleven.'

'I'll keep something warm for you.'

She heard him laugh and the stupid smile it brought to her lips made her feel as though her face would crack open.

She was still smiling as she waltzed back into her living room and drew the curtains.

Bridger registered that smile through his binoculars as he huddled in his chair. Despite the fan heater next to him, he had three blankets up to his chin. His was the graveyard shift. Saturday night in a bloody empty house in Highbury was not his idea of a fun time. But this was a big one, he knew that. They hadn't told

252

him much but from what he had learned from Tindal and the meeting with Vine, it was the real thing. And nothing came if you didn't put the graft in, or so they kept telling him.

He sighed and reached down for the radio at his feet. It felt as if it was going to be a long, long night.

Chapter 26

At six a.m. on Sunday, Tindal was drinking his third cup of tea from a green thermos his wife had prepared at midnight. He sat in the rear of a white transit van in one of the two comfortable seats that swivelled to allow easy access to the banks of communications and surveillance equipment that took up much of the room inside.

For the hundredth time, he cursed the fog that had steadily thickened the further west they had travelled. Now it hung all around them like some thick, damp curtain. Visibility, he estimated, was down to thirty yards or so. Perhaps with the dawn, he mused optimistically. But still the fog pressed down on him, a dense depressing omen. It was bad enough being in completely unfamiliar territory, even with the total co-operation of the local divisions. He was gambling, he knew that. And the stakes were high: someone's life, his career. Some would see it as the desperate act of a desperate man. So be it. He had not consulted. It was all on his head. His would be the one to roll should things not work out as he hoped.

He trod on the thought. He had been over and over it in his mind. The simple fact was that he could not face another call this Sunday. The call that would drag him to some remote area of countryside or derelict inner-city building, to another example of The Carpenter's handiwork. Left for him to inspect like some mangled bird mauled by the family cat.

The meeting with Vine had surprised them all. He hadn't expected anything from her, least of all the link with a corpse in Bristol. He had left her flat in Highbury numb and full of doubts at the wheels he had set in motion before she had so calmly delivered up her nuggets of information. Wheels upon which his career and the fate of the investigation now rode.

Granted, his reaction to Vine's revelations had been commendably swift. He had dispatched Lyons to Bristol. His men were working now, but already there had been problems. The hospital was running out of space and they had decided to delete the files of everyone dead for more than eighteen months. The duty clerk Lyons had dragged in to root around in the labyrinthine filing system in the bowels of the hospital had spent hours searching. It was only when they finally managed to track down the medical-records manager at eleven p.m. on Saturday on his return from a wedding that they had finally got hold of Fisher's notes. They had escaped incineration by a matter of weeks.

But despite the wealth of information in the file, it had only delayed the investigation further. From the wages department they had requested time sheets. The list of medical and nursing staff on duty the night that Elmore Fisher had been brought in was extensive. And that was just the beginning. There were mortuary attendants, porters, operating-department assistants, cleaning staff, pharmacy staff, domestics – the list was large and still growing. Tindal knew that Lyons would have them working through the night, but it all took time, the checking and double-checking and then the interviewing. And blast it, he didn't have any time, that was just it.

The tepid fluid trickled down his throat and he felt a twinge as it entered his stomach. He ought to eat something, feed the hungry animal that gnawed at him. But the journey down through the early hours had left him with a low-grade nausea that prodded away his appetite.

They had neither seen nor heard any traffic for over two hours. It was a quiet, almost desolate spot near the entrance to the beach car park. The only road out of the village and up to the chalets ran not fifteen yards away. At dawn, someone would move into the wood behind Meredith's place and the waiting and the watching would begin in earnest. He felt a sick wave of doubt wash over him.

He prayed to God that it had not been a mistake to go back to Professor Falkirk on this. He remembered it now with distaste. Falkirk had revelled in the chance at concocting a 'potentially cathartic scenario', but Tindal knew that the man had enjoyed the knowledge that they were betraying Vine just as much, if not more.

He sighed. Why did he have such a bad feeling about the whole thing? Falkirk had been deliriously confident, listening to Tindal with a glittering bead of excitement in his eye. He hadn't said as much, but there was obvious satisfaction in his face as Tindal had explained Vine's predicament. The violent boyfriend had come as no surprise, the stolen notes merited nothing more than an arching of the eyebrows. But there had been constant, lurking smugness. When Tindal broached the subject of his idea, there was no hesitation. Falkirk had leapt at it like a chained dog at a paperboy. He had couched it in acceptable, psychiatric terms and Tindal had listened with a traitor's obsequiousness.

It had felt obscenely hypocritical. He had been prepared to cajole Falkirk, to urge him into co-operation, expecting a degree of resistance out of loyalty to Vine, or at least from the standpoint of professional ethics. To find both completely lacking should have disturbed him, but it hadn't. There was no surprise in Falkirk's sickly grin, merely a sly understanding. Tindal had felt like wiping that grin off, but it was no use. The truth was, they were the same, he and Falkirk. Neither of them trusted Vine. Neither of them gave a toss about her as long as they got what they wanted out of using her.

Well, there was no room for personal feelings in an investigation like this or so Tindal told himself. But his words rang with a hollow echo as he recalled issuing Falkirk that one simple directive.

A flush.

What they needed was a flush . . .

It was little enough consolation to Tindal knowing that there was probably no one better suited for such a dirty job.

They had conferred again after Tindal's meeting with Vine on Saturday. Falkirk hadn't blinked, merely nodded with slitted eyes, a grudging admiration showing briefly through before he had assimilated the information with a shrug. And so it had been Falkirk who had suggested editing the hours of taped police interview into a statement from Meredith. One they could run on national TV and radio. One that would trigger a reaction from The Carpenter. Tindal and his men were in Wales watching and waiting for that reaction.

Lights suddenly loomed out of the fog. A car approached and stopped behind them. The front door slid open and cold air rushed in, followed by an overweight, bespectacled man with a thin moustache and an improbable centre parting.

'Sorry, sir, I had to go to a service station for these.'

Tindal nodded and his eyes fell on the bundle of newspapers the man carried.

'Where do you live, Williams?'

'Killay, sir.'

To Tindal's ear, it sounded almost Irish. 'How far?'

'Seven, eight miles, sir.'

'If I let you go home for breakfast, Williams, d'you think you might spare a bacon sandwich?'

The man beamed. 'No problem, sir. Kath makes cracking bacon sandwiches.'

'Off you go then.'

The policeman began backing out of the van.

Tindal stopped him. 'Oh and ummm, think you could refill this?'

Williams took the flask, still beaming.

'And I'll take these,' said Tindal.

Williams looked down at the huge bunch of newspapers still slung over his arm. He held them up awkwardly. Tindal had to get up out of the seat to grab them.

'Manage, sir?'

Tindal nodded, manhandling the awkward bundle on to the floor before picking up the top copy.

Later, over breakfast, whilst their children ran from room to room and the TV churned out cartoons, Williams's wife spoke over her shoulder as she poured hot tea into Tindal's thermos.

'You probably imagined it, Roy.'

'No, love. I tell you, his hands were shaking so badly he could hardly hold those newspapers.'

'Perhaps he was cold?'

'You didn't see his face, love. You could swear I was handing him a piece of rotten meat, or one of Dafydd's dirty nappies.'

'But why?'

'Dunno, love. Our's not to reason why like.'

'It's too bad they can't even tell you when you're dragged out of bed at four in the morning. You could swear you were looking for some mass murderer.'

'Mass murderer?' Williams laughed. 'Now who's imagining things?'

At seven thirty, Bloor pulled into the Aust service station on the east bank of the River Severn. It was famed for its view of the suspension bridge, but today there was no view through the all-encompassing fog. He'd decided to travel up on the A38, consciously avoiding the motorway. He knew that the police would be looking for motorcyclists and he'd chosen the lesser road at that hour because it was quiet and it would be dark for most of the journey. He had planned the rest of the route carefully. The Fosse Way again, eventually linking up with the M1. The motorways were easy to patrol, but even on a Sunday the M1 would be so busy that the police could not possibly hope to watch all the traffic. He allowed himself a smile as he dismounted the bike. He sniffed the air. Not a breath of wind to blow away the fog. Luck was with him today, he could feel it. There would be accidents by the score. Today, the fog would keep the police fully occupied.

He strode into the building and headed directly for the shop. It was quiet and half empty, the early hour and the fog keeping most people off the roads. His only purpose was to empty a bladder that he'd overfilled with tea, and then to purchase a newspaper.

They were neatly stacked on the bottom shelf, the tabloids one end, the heavier papers the other. He stooped and picked up his usual three, scanning the headlines as he did so.

Two of the tabloids had offered rewards for any information leading to his arrest. They had stood for some three months unclaimed. But there was usually something in most of the Sundays: ridiculous Identikit photographs from eyewitnesses who had never seen him, inevitable comparisons with real and fictional killers, and once a clairvoyant who suggested that he lived in a caravan in Winchester. He had laughed at them all, revelling in their ignorance. But there was something about this headline that sprang out at him.

'MAULED BY THE BEAST.'

Underneath was a grainy photograph of Meredith leaving a building and next to him, waiting expectantly, the woman he'd seen at the hospital on Friday. He felt a tingle of excitement stir inside him as his pulse quickened.

At last.

He let his eyes fall to the text underneath the photograph.

'This is the man who holds the key to the identity of Britain's most wanted man. Turn to page 3 for story.'

He hurried to the till and paid, hardly able to contain his excitement. Could it be that at last Meredith had broken his silence and told the world?

Stuffing change into his pocket he found the toilets and locked himself in before tearing open the newspaper.

Thomas Meredith is the only survivor of the brutal serial killer known as The Carpenter. Seen with him is forensic psychiatrist Dr Natalie Vine, whose thankless task it has been to release the dark secrets buried in Meredith's mind. For ten days, Dr Vine has been locked away with him in a remote holiday chalet on the Welsh coast. Meredith required major surgery after being attacked by the killer who tortured to death his girlfriend in front of his eyes. Dr Vine has been in a race against time to provide the police with clues as to the identity of the sick monster who has murdered nine women over the last eighteen months.

After months of enforced silence, highly confidential documents leaked to the press this week have at last revealed the harrowing details of the depraved psychopath's gruesome ritual. A psychopath who continues to prowl our streets. And in a tape recording taken directly from police interviews with Thomas Meredith, the silence has finally and explosively been broken over the case that has terrified a nation.

He felt himself grinning. This was more like it. But underneath, he caught sight of a subheading that turned the smile into a frozen grimace of puzzled trepidation.

'*Deformed Beast Masquerades as Policeman.*'

The first pang of disquiet hit him then. This was one of the more restrained tabloids. As he read, his disquiet grew into disgust and then anger. Veiled hints at ugliness and physical deformity were rife. Worse, an implication of ineptitude in the sublime act of power when he offered himself to his victims. It was wrong. All wrong.

They described him as a 'crazed baboon'. That was the phrase that stuck like a fishbone in his throat. He felt the blood rush to his face as he discarded one and picked up another.

There it was again. More insults. More depraved hints and jibes. 'Crazed baboon' was there again, surrounded by inverted commas. Obviously lifted from a phrase or paragraph. But those words? Whose Judas words? Vine's or Meredith's?

The thought of Meredith uttering such filth made Bloor nauseous. He looked for the *Sport*. The most lurid, the most outrageously fictional. It had in the past provided him with the most ludicrous reports. The ones that had made him laugh the hardest. But it was with some trepidation that he opened it now. Trembling, he unfolded it and read the heading:

'MAN OR MONKEY? THE DIRTY BEAST REVEALED.'

Inside were the sketches. The invention of some cheap artist. A hunched semihuman form with simian features on the back of a motorcycle.

The *Sport* had gone to town. Next to adverts for the Swedish Exchange, real imported dirty sex talk and a list of 0898 numbers, they described him as a semi-impotent, misshapen Neanderthal.

He felt tears sting his eyes. How? How could Meredith have

done this to him? He had seen his power, witnessed the control, been part of the majesty of his work. He felt his world blacken, a deep pit of dark anger appear in his mind.

He struck out at the door in front of him, beating at it in his frustration until, through the mist of his fierce, affronted fury he heard a voice outside.

'Oi, mate, you all right?'

He stopped, his breath catching in his throat.

'Yes, fine,' he mumbled.

He heard steps wander away and sat down on the closed seat, unable to move, his head bowed. Hot tears of rage began to fall from his face into a little pool on the filthy floor.

He sat there for a long time, his mind a dark swirl of thought until his anger faded enough for him to move. He stood, emptied his bladder and stepped out into the tiled toilet area. The attendant stood out from his little cabin and stared across. But what he saw made him duck back in again quickly. There was something about the man who emerged that didn't invite conversation or comment, despite the scattered sheets of newspapers that lay strewn all over the floor. When he dared look at Bloor again, he was already on his way out of the door.

Outside in the damp air, driven by an undeniable need to know whether or not his humiliation was complete, Bloor took out the small portable radio he carried in the pannier. He tuned it to Radio 4 and waited for the eight o'clock bulletin. The item came third in the morning's list of newsworthy events. He listened to the report, delivered in impeccable English, staring at the outlines of the supporting towers of the suspension bridge, glowing eerily with lights as they disappeared upwards into the fog like the spindly legs of some massive alien spaceship.

'Scotland Yard have been quick to respond to newspaper reports detailing as yet unreleased facts surrounding the multiple murderer known as The Carpenter. The reports reveal that certain pieces of information have been withheld in the interests of public safety. The information, contained in confidential police files, was leaked to journalists last week, it was revealed this morning. Many of today's newspapers have run the story, in which allegations as to the murderer's physical appearance are rife as are details of his method of approaching his victims. In several instances this has been in the guise of a police motorcycle patrolman. This from our home affairs correspondent, James Wilson . . .'

Bloor listened to a catalogue of his crimes, statements from victims' relatives and the inevitable voice of officialdom. But it was near the end that the damning words were heard.

'Thomas Meredith, the doctor at the centre of the controversy, whose survival has always been something of a mystery to police, was unavailable for comment. But the BBC has received a tape recording purporting to be an appeal to those sheltering the killer. Sources have confirmed the voice belongs to Thomas Meredith.'

After a moment's silence. Bloor heard *his* voice reaching out across the airways. The words were stilted and oddly disordered but chokingly full of weary emotion. To Bloor, it felt as if Meredith were speaking directly to him, the deep tones reaching in to his very being.

'. . . I wouldn't call him human. What he does, what he did to Jilly was more like an animal. A crazed baboon. No, worse than that, worse than an animal. Someone, somewhere knows something . . .'

If Bloor noticed how disjointed the statement was, the thought that it might have been a contrivance didn't show on his face as he turned off the radio with trembling hands. His world had changed in the space of twenty minutes. Nottingham was out of the question now. No one was going to stop on an isolated road for a solitary police motorcyclist after reading the Sunday papers and listening to the news. But that no longer mattered to Bloor. There would be other Sundays.

His mind was completely focused on the searing injustice that had been done to him. Between them, Meredith and that bitch Vine had cheapened and diminished what he did. Their lies had crucified him.

He leaned against the parked bike, his head bowed, a statue in the fog. Unmoving except for the stinging tears that trickled down his cheeks, now purple from the cold. His mind was a black whirlpool in which dark forms struggled to the surface.

Harry Bloor was there, now chiding, now mocking him for his stupidity.

And Susan. Sweet Susan. She could have heard those damning words. Might even have seen them repeated on the TV news. Might be reading about him at that very moment. His Susan, cursing him, judging him unfairly.

He leant there, numb with shock and pain as the mist swirled around his feet and limbs, like a traveller on the far bank of the Styx awaiting the boatman.

He leaned until finally his confused mind cleared and settled into an icy calm and then into a diamond-hard resolve. When he finally looked up, what he saw was not the shadowy form of the service station and the bridge beyond. What he saw was something no other man had ever seen or, if sane, would ever want to see. What he saw was his revenge.

In one movement, he pushed himself off the bike, wiped his eyes and clamped the helmet down.

So be it.

They would suffer as he was suffering. There was need for a cleansing. He was still invisible. His power was still within him.

He thought of being so close to Vine in the hospital lift. Close enough to smell her, to reach out and touch the body beneath the expensive suit.

And then he thought of Meredith. Meredith, who had praised, who had seen the glory, betraying him in such a way.

For an instant he hesitated, torn by indecision. It was a difficult choice, but one that troubled him only momentarily. There really was only one thing to do.

Pushing down the visor of his helmet, Bloor gunned the powerful engine and eased the bike out on to the road.

Chapter 27

The crowd began to grow between one thirty and two. When Arsenal played on Sundays the games were usually showpieces for national TV, but Vine barely heard the raucous laughter and loud excited voices in the street outside her window as they streamed towards the ground. She was only vaguely aware of the steadily increasing volume because of her preoccupation with the contents of the newspapers spread out on the floor in front of her.

She had risen late, stiff and sluggish from nine hours of sleep in her own comfortable bed, and had then pottered about, trying not to think of Meredith and failing. A few minutes before twelve she had gone out for the *Observer*. Waiting in line at the newsagent's, her mind in neutral, her attention had suddenly been riveted by a cursory glance at the tabloid headlines. She had returned with every tabloid and broadsheet she could find. Back in her living room, her thoughts kept returning to one and only one source.

Mo.

It could only have been Mo. There were details that could only have come from the files she had read and he had stolen. Her photograph was poor but still recognisable. She felt surprise and then anger as she realised it had been taken on their way to lunch in the Italian restaurant three days before. They had been spied on. Twice already she had phoned Tindal, only to be told that he was unavailable.

The only consolation she felt in it all was that at last people had been warned. It was little enough solace for her affronted privacy, but no one seeing these newspapers was going to stop for a police motorcyclist today.

And then she had heard *him*. The radio was providing background noise; *Desert Island Discs* with a precocious violinist and his informed reminiscences. And then the news had come on. At first she'd only half listened, but when Meredith's voice came through, she had almost jumped out of her skin. The deep warmth was strained and cracked with emotion. She hadn't heard him like that before. And the words – so strange, so unlike him.

She got up restlessly. She wanted desperately to speak to Meredith but he was incommunicado. What would he think when he saw the stories? When had he issued that strange statement? God, what was she thinking? He would run a mile from any newspaperman. It couldn't have been him . . .

Pensively, she found the bulging envelope folders that held all Meredith's case notes and began rummaging through them. She found what she was looking for on a photocopied transcript of his early police interviews. The date placed it a few days after the event; he would, she realised, have been in a severe state of shock. He was describing the attack on Jilly in response to a question as to whether or not her killer had spoken.

> . . . screaming, screaming. I couldn't hear anything else. She was in agony, howling like a crazed baboon. I wouldn't have heard him even if he was shouting. All I could hear was her begging and screaming . . .

She knew she had read it somewhere! But he had been talking about Jilly. His words had been taken completely out of context. But why? And by whom?

Groaning, she walked across to her midi system and found some Vaughan Williams, craving the distraction. As the music grew in volume, she wandered into the kitchen and started percolating some strong coffee.

Across the street Edmundson was on the day shift and he was not happy. He was a Gunners season-ticket holder and a league game against West Ham was not something he wanted to sit out in a draughty abandoned room, even if the target of his surveillance was very easy on the eye.

She had worn a loose-fitting T-shirt when she had got up that morning and Edmundson was still congratulating himself for resisting the urge to take a few close-ups of her stretching at the bay window for the squadroom file.

Well, at least he had a radio and a stack of newspapers. Tindal had warned them to expect something 'a little spicy' in the press that morning, but God help those poor sods on bikes in the traffic division.

He peered down at the street. A steady flow of red and white humanity marched past. Edmundson sighed wistfully. They would all have spent an hour or more in the pub setting the world to rights. And they were by and large a good crowd. He had begun to take Jason, who at five had been completely overawed by the numbers and especially by the seething tide on the north bank.

He glanced at his watch. Fifteen minutes to kickoff. Too early for a beer?

Nah.

Reaching down into an Oddbins carrier bag he let his hand roam around, searching for the familiar smooth, cool, cylindrical shape and felt nothing.

Shit. He was sure he'd pulled them out of the cooler, hadn't he?

He groaned. Three lovely cans of draught Guinness languishing in the icebox in the boot of his car. It had been a little extravagant to stick them on ice bearing in mind that it was brass-monkey weather, but he couldn't stand tepid stout.

He would have to go down and get them, that was all there was to it. He picked up his binoculars and stared across at Vine's flat. She was still in the kitchen, out of his view. She'd gone in a few minutes before and hadn't come out. Probably heating something up. The thought made him hungry and his hunger made the absence of the beer even more keenly felt.

Some industrial polythene had been hung up to try to keep in the heat. It hung in the doorways like blue mist. Edmundson swam through, his feet clattering echoingly on the stairs as he tripped down. He had parked twenty yards down the street

266

behind a skip and it was freezing outside. Why hadn't he bought his coat? Cursing, he ran towards his car.

The scene-of-crime people would argue about it a great deal later, and Edmundson, aware that his job was on the line, stuck to the lie with the desperation of a mongoose on the back of a cobra. It was possible to see the steps leading down to the basement flat of Vine's building from Edmundson's vantage point opposite, but there was indeed a blind spot as the steps turned through ninety degrees at the bottom. And with the volume of human traffic as it had been, it would have been difficult to track one person quickly slipping down. Only Edmundson knew that he had not seen it because he was in the street retrieving the Guinness from his car, but somehow that little fact didn't find its way into his report. Thus it was his own conscience that tried him and found him guilty. He didn't give up Guinness, but he vowed he would drink it warm in the future if he had to.

If anyone in the passing crowd saw anything, no one payed any attention. If anyone heard glass shatter in the door of the basement flat, no one stopped to wonder.

It was as if *he* was invisible.

It was almost five minutes to three when Edmundson got back inside. He picked up the binoculars and saw Vine come back into the room with a tray bearing a pot of coffee. He sat back, satisfied. Time for a beer and a sandwich.

In the street, they were running now, desperate to get there before kickoff. Edmundson flicked on the radio and took a bite from a white cheese-and-onion roll before popping the can and watching it froth into the plastic glass he had brought with him. Thank the lord for Draughtflow, he thought to himself.

He took a long swallow, sat back and let the commentators transport him into his seat in the stand as the teams took the field.

Natalie was never quite sure what it was that drew her attention. The soaring strings of the *English Folksongs Suite* filled the room with its shanty tones as she read an article in one of the more respectable Sundays by one of her old bosses from Rampton. His normal, rambling style was evident and she grimaced as he ranged his discussion from lust killers to berserkers like Michael Ryan. It was sloppy, sensational and offensive to her precise mind.

Was it a flash of movement out of the corner of her eye, or a prescient alarm that made her swing round and glance at the doorway behind her? Whichever it was, the result made her literally jump, her legs convulsing in horror and shock and sending her body up and back into a fighting crouched stance. The coffeepot and its tray went catapulting upwards, the cup performing a graceful arc before bounding on to the carpet and emptying its contents in a brown swirl.

She saw all of this in her peripheral vision because her eyes were fixed on the figure in the doorway who seemed to fill that space. The top of the hood touched the doorframe, the dark eyeholes stared back at her. The white cassock hung in folds above plimsoled feet. She saw it tremble slightly and she realised he was laughing, enjoying the drama of the moment.

Instantly, she was backing off, stumbling over a magazine rack, almost collapsing into the settee, performing a crazy backward tango until she hit the wall. Her eyes darted around the room, searching for something to protect herself with.

He saw it, and from behind him where he had kept it in a belt around his waist, he brought out a knife. Ten inches of glistening triangular steel: a chef's knife with a sharp, wicked point.

To Natalie's right was the window. She could see people down there, intent on their stupid game, unaware that death lurked only feet away. She wanted to scream, wanted to bray for help. Again, he saw it and he came forward, forcing her to move left, away from the window.

A voice, clear amidst the hubbub in her head, screamed at her: *What are you doing, you stupid bitch? You can talk to him Natalie, you're trained for it, aren't you?*

But her eyes were on the knife. Photographs of his victims from the police files kept popping up in her head, getting in the way of logical thought, feeding the primal fear that gripped her. She moaned. You couldn't talk to something that did those things.

He moved quickly again. Nimble, lighter than the bulky cassock suggested. She half turned, ran behind the settee. He stayed in the middle of the room, stalking her. Suddenly, he feinted right and then left. It wrong-footed her and he came forward, only the settee between them.

Talk to him, Nattie. Talk. Talk.

'I know what happened to you.' Her voice was shrill and high. It stopped him for a moment. 'Something terrible. Something unforgivable.'

And then he was lunging at her with the knife and she was backing away again, trying to get the coffee table and the armchair between them. He pivoted and watched her go. Not rushing, biding his time, waiting for the right moment.

With one hand he threw the coffee table on its side and came forward, thrusting out. She saw the knife nick her shirt, felt the fabric rip. Looking down, she saw a dark stain prick the surface and grow.

Blood.

Her blood.

She stood with her hands on the back of the chair, shocked but ready to run, whichever way he went. He straightened, the dark holes in the white-hooded mask never leaving her face. Desperately, she looked about her. She was next to the bookshelves laden with paperweights and useless trinkets, African heads, Singapore lions, letter racks she never used, gathered over the years from aunts with insatiable appetites for souvenirs. She shot out her hand, grabbing for something, finding a glass paperweight emblazoned with an etched thistle and *Memories of Dundee*. She had time to get off one good throw. He ducked, but she hadn't aimed for him and it flew four feet to his left. The heavy weight sailed across the room and hit a three-by-five pane in the bay, shattering it loudly.

She didn't see his leg shoot out until it was too late. With a powerful thrust, he pushed the seat forwards. It took Natalie unawares, sliding into her midriff and lifting her off her feet. She hung there precariously, on the brink of toppling headfirst into the seat itself. And then he was coming again, driving the seat forward with his arms, his face inches from her own until Natalie and the chair hit the wall. She heard a thump and an agonising crack from somewhere on her left side.

In the street, the paperweight landed and shattered into a thousand pieces. A few stragglers stopped to look up and curse, but most continued on their way, heedless of the incident and of the panting man who emerged from the house across the street and sprinted towards the building where the glass had been smashed.

Edmundson ran to and fro on the porch, hammering on the front door like a mad thing until he thought about the basement.

He almost went headlong down the steps, finding the door already open and the flat empty. He had a gun in his hand as he swung from room to room, noting the gutted devastation, his breath heaving in his chest as his heart hammered along with it. Eventually, he found another door ajar and through it steps leading up into the hall.

Natalie stood pinned to the wall, clutching her side painfully as each breath sent a new shard of agony lancing through her. He pulled the chair away, letting her slump down against the wall before yanking up her hair so that she was looking into those terrifying eyes.

And then he had the knife under her lower lid, pressing inwards until she felt the skin break. He pulled her head back suddenly and she heard it crack against the wall. The noise seemed to please him.

He moved the knife down to her bloody shirt and slit it open before again smashing her head against the wall. It sent purple and yellow lights flashing before her eyes, and beneath it all, beneath the pain and the terror, there still was the question: *Why? Why so terribly violently angry?*

Again her head thudded against hard plaster. The pain there seemed to be melting into what was coming from her ribs. She could see him in front of her, frenzied now, the knife at his feet, his free hand fumbling under the folds of the cassock.

But beneath the pain and the nausea and the buzzing in her

270

head, the thin voice of her intellect asked: No nails? What about the ritual? Where was the sound of Meredith's voice?

Her eyes drifted down with agonising slowness. His hand was on the knife again. This time he hardly lifted it from its position on the floor. He merely rotated it so that it pointed towards her crotch. The cassock folds were cumbersome, making him fumble beneath with his other hand. She caught only one glimpse of his erect penis before the knife was through her jeans, chaffing as he slit the denim open like gutting a fish, nicking the tender skin of her thigh and labia. And she knew why there was going to be no ritual. This was revenge, pure and simple. She could feel it, smell it.

He spoke then for the first and only time, his voice rasping and muffled.

'Don't pretend, you bitch. You love it.'

She felt the cold caress of the knife against her thigh as he wrenched her legs open but the pain of it dissolved into the pressure of his crushing weight above her.

Suddenly the room exploded in a deafening roar. Natalie believed that something had burst inside her own head, flooding the soft white matter with crimson clot. Something warm and wet spattered against her face . . .

And then there was silence.

No rustling of clothes, no panting, grunting white shape above her. Was she unconscious or dead?

She took a breath and the shard of agony made her groan.

She wasn't dead. Not yet.

Above her, she heard rapid footsteps. She couldn't open her eyes, she didn't want to see him.

Something touched her face and she screamed. '*Do it, you bastard. Just do it.*'

'It's all right, miss. It's all right. You can open your eyes.'

Natalie opened one eye. A figure was leaning over her, and she flinched away involuntarily, fearful for a moment that it was a cruel trick before recognition dawned. Edmundson was leaning over her, a gun in his hand. At his feet the white robe lay in a lumpy mess. Most of it was stained bright crimson. She wiped away the fluid from her face and her hand came away dark and purple and sticky from *his* blood.

'Is he . . . dead?'

'Oh yes, miss. He's dead.'

Natalie struggled to sit up but stopped in agony. A radio hissed and crackled in Edmundson's free hand.

'Lie still, miss, the ambulance is on its way.'

She heard his voice trail off and the scene began to melt in front of her as the pain in her head returned black and strong and she floated away into unconsciousness.

She woke up groggy and disoriented. She fingered her swollen lip gingerly. It felt huge and numb. On her right temple an egg-sized lump throbbed and as she turned carefully, her ribs tweaked a warning stab of pain. The only cuts she could feel were a crusting slash above her left eye and the small hard nicks beneath her eye and over her sternum. But she could see normally and, her eyes now open, she focused on a uniformed policewoman sitting not five yards away. The WPC stood and hurried to the door with a promise that she would return in a minute.

Natalie's brain spun in mad circles. Something was wrong. Totally wrong, but she was too confused to think clearly. Five minutes later, as she struggled to put her thoughts together, the WPC returned with a nurse and Edmundson.

'You OK?' he asked.

She nodded. Her left side ached but not as badly as before. Obviously they'd given her something for the pain. The nurse busied herself with checking pulse and blood pressure.

'Where's Tindal?' croaked Natalie.

'Crawling up the M4 in a peasouper.'

'M4?'

'Sick as a Norwegian blue he is.'

Natalie frowned. 'You were watching for him, weren't you?'

'Yes, miss. We've been watching you ever since your friend Alberini paid you a visit in your motel room.'

'Mo,' she said vaguely. 'Have you found him yet?'

'Nah, but we will, miss. Don't worry.'

The nurse was pumping up the BP cuff on the patient's arm. As she lifted it to position her stethoscope, Natalie winced as another twinge shot through her side.

'Tell me,' she asked, trying to take her mind off it, 'did you know about the newspapers this morning?'

'Mr Tindal gave us the nod, miss. I knew there was something up, but no details.'

'It must have been Mo who gave them the story. I'm surprised Tindal let it go out in the way it did.'

'The press are usually pretty co-operative miss. But when they get their teeth into something as big as this, they'd rather risk the courts.'

'That's not the impression Tindal gave me.'

Edmundson shrugged. 'I wouldn't worry, miss. It'll all be forgotten tomorrow. We've issued a statement already.'

'Then you know who he is?'

Edmundson looked suddenly uncomfortable. 'Uh not quite, miss. No ID. Younger than I thought he'd be, though.'

'Don't pretend . . .'

The voice, muffled through the hood, echoed suddenly in her ears. She started, the disquiet of earlier redoubling in intensity.

'Late twenties, I'd say . . .' Edmundson trailed off, his eyes narrowing as he saw her eyes open wide.

'. . . you bitch.'

He hadn't used any Mace. Why hadn't he used Mace? Why hadn't he done what he had in all the other cases? He could have subdued her in seconds. Why the dangerous cat-and-mouse?

'You love it.'

There had been no ritual. No real ritual, just the terrible anger and what, what had she thought? Revenge?

'Don't pretend you bitch.'

How did he know that about her? How could he possibly have known about the shadow of the past that haunted her?

'You love it.'

Natalie felt her mouth fill with blotting paper. 'Where is he?' she blurted out, brushing the nurse to one side.

'It's all right, miss, you're quite safe.'

273

'Where is the body?' she demanded, struggling up to a sitting position.

'In the morgue, miss. Downstairs. Once we've ID'd him they'll start the autopsy.'

'I want to see it.'

Edmundson laughed. 'You can't do that, miss. They tell me you'll be laid up for a couple of days.'

'Why is Tindal on the M4?' Her thoughts were racing now as she fought to contain the terrifying idea that was snowballing through her mind.

'It's the only road back from Wales, miss. Another surveillance job. Big one, I think.'

'Who?'

'Don't know, miss. Keeps his cards close to his chest does ACC Tindal.'

Natalie shook her head. 'I can't believe it. I can't believe he's done this.'

Suddenly, she reached up and grabbed Edmundson's jacket. Little flecks of spittle leapt from her mouth and spattered into his blinking eyes. 'How did he get in?'

'Uhhh, the basement, miss.'

Natalie hissed out a sardonic laugh. 'He knew about the basement being empty, knew things about me . . .'

Don't pretend you bitch. You love it.

He knew about her pain and weakness. He had *expected* her to cower and submit to his blows.

'Knew things only one other person could possibly know.'

Edmundson's face blanched underneath his already pale skin. 'Do you want me to get the doctor, miss?' he stammered.

'I must see the body, do you hear me?' She was sitting up now, her face wild.

Edmundson stood up, his eyes never leaving Natalie's face. 'I'll get the doctor, miss,' he repeated nervously.

'No,' she screamed and then made herself be calm. 'Listen to me, please. When you took the hood off, he had brown hair, right? Brown curly hair?'

Edmundson's brow crumpled in perplexity.

'How did you know –'

'I have to see the body. I have to see it now!'

Edmundson was shaking his head. All of a sudden he didn't understand any of this. 'You know who he is, don't you?' he said incredulously.

'Let me see the body, please,' implored Natalie, her seething anger barely constrained.

Edmundson, his eyes wide with confusion and doubt turned to the policewoman.

'Quick as you can, get us a wheelchair, will you?'

Tindal sat staring out at the dense fog. He had been doing the same thing for three hours as they crawled along at forty. They had just passed the Newbury turn-off. They'd be lucky to make London in another two hours.

He'd miscalculated, he knew that. But he had covered it, thank God. It bothered him immensely as to how The Carpenter had managed to get Vine's address. He had made absolutely sure that the newspapers had not been stupid enough to do that. Maybe he had followed her back from Meredith's place. He should have had her tailed. But at least she was alive, he had that to be thankful for.

He drummed his fingers on the van door.

Blasted fog.

The static burst of the radio broke the dark silence. The handset was hot from continuous use. Mostly they had been incoming calls, congratulations from colleagues and senior officers, one from Whitehall. For the first time in weeks Tindal felt hungry, the gnawing pain in his lower chest gone almost completely.

'For you, sir,' said the driver.

Tindal picked up a handpiece from its neat compartment in the rear of the driver's seat.

'Tindal.'

'This is Edmundson, sir. Uhh, I have Dr Vine with me, sir. We're in the morgue. She has –'

Tindal heard Edmundson's apologetic tone cut off and a new voice came on the line. An angry, urgent voice.

'You bastard.'

'Dr Vine, I am sorry for what has happened.'

'I trusted you, do you know that?'

'I know that you merit an explanation, Doctor. Just as soon as I get back, I can assure you.'

'Keep them. Keep your assurances. Your sergeant killed the wrong man, Mr Tindal.'

'What?'

'How was it done? Did you just let Mo go ahead with the press leak, or did you get John Falkirk to embellish it you for? This has his clumsy pawmarks all over it. He would make sure they got every little detailed lie.'

'Put Edmundson on.' Tindal's voice was tight and unhappy.

'You *set* Tom Meredith up.' The accusation screamed out of the telephone at him and there was real raw emotion in that impeachment. An incredulous, harrowing disbelief of what one human being could do to another. It hung in the silent electronic air between them for a moment, heavy as lead. When Vine continued, it was with more control but with an acerbity that made Tindal wince.

'I know where you've been. You've been skulking outside his chalet all day, waiting for that monster to take the bait. How could you do that to Tom?'

Tindal heard her use his first name and it battered at his conscience. Tom was such an ordinary name. It destroyed the depersonalisation that had seemed so necessary for both himself and, he had thought, for Vine. But she had called him Tom . . .

'Hasn't he suffered enough already?'

The line hissed in silence as Vine trembled on one end and Tindal listened on the other.

'I've seen the body, Mr Tindal. It's *Mo*. Mo dressed up as him. He fooled us, didn't he? Fooled us both right down to the hood and plimsoles. Brilliant impersonation, wouldn't you say? But then he had all the details from the files, didn't he?'

'Why?' croaked Tindal and his voice sounded like air escaping from a long-shut crypt.

Vine exhaled an unhealthy laugh. 'To scare the daylights out of me. And perhaps to do the things he really wanted to do to me. Maybe Mo had more in common with the real monster than I gave him credit for.'

Listening, Tindal thought he almost saw her shudder.

'Dr Vine, I –'

'He's *alive*. The bastard is *alive out there*.' Her voice broke into a terrifying wail. 'And you've left Tom all alone . . .'

The other passenger in the van tapped Tindal's arm. He was wearing earphones and he held another phone in his hand.

'It's Bristol, sir. Superintendent Lyons.'

Tindal put the phone down on Vine as if suddenly it had turned into something alive and writhing in his hand.

His stomach roared into a furnace of sudden pain as he listened to Lyons' excited, triumphant voice come on the line.

'We think we've found him, sir.'

'Found him?' said Tindal, and the words tasted of ashes.

'His name is Bloor, sir. Leonard Bloor. He's a porter at the Infirmary. He stayed on after his shift the night Fisher was admitted to help out. He has a motorcycle licence but no vehicle according to the DVLC. We found his locker, sir. He's a Manchester United supporter, not Liverpool. So we were right about the football connection, even if he did try and sell us a dummy. Travels to most of their away games apparently. We've found programmes, sir. Birmingham, Southampton, they're all there. He also has a shotgun licence, sir. According to the few people who know him, he spends most Sundays out hunting.'

'Jesus Christ,' breathed Tindal.

'I thought you'd want to be here when we went to his house, sir.'

'No,' ordered Tindal. 'Get out there. See if he's there. Bring him in now.' His voice was full of a desperate hope that he knew in his aching gut to be forlorn.

'But I thought we'd bagged him in Highbury . . .'

'We all did, Jack. But we thought wrong. It wasn't him. He's still out there.'

'I'll get some people out to his house now, sir,' said Lyons, the shock registering in his voice.

'Keep me informed, Jack.' Tindal put down the phone.

'Turn around,' he said to the driver. 'I don't care how you do it, just turn around. We're going back.'

'Sir?'

Tindal screamed. 'Just bloody well do it, do you hear?'

'Sir.'

But Tindal didn't hear the hurried reply. He had already picked the phone up again.

'Get me the Chief Constable of South Wales police . . .'

Chapter 28

Meredith spent the whole of Sunday afternoon wandering around the largely deserted town, his legs moving automatically, his mind soaring on a different plane.

A restlessness had overtaken him as he'd packed his few things into a bag that morning. The chalet seemed claustrophobic and musty. He had toyed with the idea of a walk on the beach but it had seemed pointless in the fog, although it still held a certain wistful attractiveness. But the restive energy had continued to burn inside him and so he had driven slowly and carefully into Swansea, oblivious of the men in the surveillance team dotted around the grounds outside the chalet. He'd parked on an empty street under a sodium lamp that had not been turned off during this twilight day. He needed to walk. The damp air seeped into his body but he didn't mind as he stared sightlessly into the shop fronts.

Dusk came early and with it he found himself standing against the black iron rails of the marina quayside, staring across at a three-masted square-rigger that floated ghostly in the water. The Black Swan had been anchored and stripped out before being refitted as a pub/restaurant. But as Meredith stared at the black mast looming upwards into the rigging above the shrouded deck, he was overtaken by a surreal moment of hallucination. He felt becalmed in a sea, standing watch, observing the enemy drift past, powerless to alter the fate that had brought them together.

He shook his head and smiled. Why was he always thinking in terms of enemies and confrontation? Still, at least he was *thinking*. His vivid imagination had been a loathsome curse over the previous months. Glancing again at the ship before finally turning away, he realised that it wasn't his imagination that had altered, but his ability to control it.

As he walked back to his car, he passed a telephone box and found himself hesitating, seduced by the thought of walking in and dialling, hearing Natalie's surprised voice. He fumbled in his pockets and swore when he found no change there. The disappointment was acute, but in that moment he realised what she had become to him. In her embrace he had found a peace of mind that he had not thought he would ever attain again. He craved it now. Why had he hesitated the previous night when she had offered him her bed?

He mulled it over and came up with a couple of dubious little gems of which he was not proud: a fear of admitting to himself that he needed someone else's strength, and a fear of frightening her off with overkeenness. He felt the shadow of the old self-loathing creep back, but he had enough insight now to realise that it need not be like that. He could go to her – now. His bag was packed, it was still relatively early. He could make London by ten if the fog was kind. He felt his energy come back in a reviving surge as he turned his face into the drizzle. The beginnings of a faint breeze washed over his face. He took it as a good omen: the wind would lift the fog. He smiled to himself and hurried to where he had parked.

The little village was quiet when he got back. Tindal's interlopers had faded silently away following the news from Highbury. He parked behind Julie's Lada, not wishing to draw attention to himself by driving round to his usual space. Lights burned in the blue chalet. He would put his head in, say goodbye, but he wanted to do it with his bag in his hand. It would give credence to his story of haste. What he didn't want at that moment was to be buttonholed by a well-meaning Julie for half an hour or more.

He stepped stealthily across the grass, avoiding the gravel, feeling in his pocket for the torch he carried as a matter of course. He stopped automatically at the door, kneeling without thinking to examine the arrangement of thin plywood under the bark. He was halfway through doing it when the ludicrousness of it struck him. It was unnecessary, all completely unnecessary. Natalie had shown him that. He wouldn't be needing them again. He would collect them up and throw them on his wood-burner. He continued clearing away the bark hurriedly, smiling to himself until, abruptly, he stopped and stared in disbelief into the pool of light thrown out by the torch.

Three of them were broken. Crushed just as if someone heavy had stepped on them.

An animal, he told himself.

No, no, stupid, it would have been Julie and the little girl anxious to pay him a visit.

He felt his turbocharged pulse slow to a racing one twenty, felt the raw air sear his trachea as he gulped it in involuntarily.

No, not now, Meredith. Not now. Just a grateful, rake-thin woman who thinks you're Superman, that's all.

But still his breath heaved.

Check. Check the others, you cretin.

He moved five yards to the part of the path beneath the sky-light. Squatting down and pulling his coat about him, he scrabbled away the bark. The plywood was broken there too.

She might have walked round. Looked for a light, a sign of activity – natural thing to do.

He wanted to believe it, but there was a dreadful hollowness in his gut. He flicked off the torch and stood with his back to the wall, the skylight above him. He kept it shut at all times. It was an old-fashioned type, hinging on one side of a metal frame and could be held open by a steel cockspur and stay, allowing access to the flat pitch roof. Months ago Meredith had gone up there and tied a length of two-pound strain fishing line across to straddle the skylight. It wasn't meant to make it difficult to open, but if somebody tried they would break the line.

Meredith turned his face to the wall. The middle bracket of a downpipe stood ten inches to his right. He put his right foot on it and levered himself up, feeling his belt buckle scrape against the rough render of the building, praying that the fog would dampen the noise. He clung limpet-like to the wall, feeling with his right hand along the weatherboard for the staple he'd hammered there. It felt smaller than he remembered. He let his thumb and forefinger grasp it and extended his finger to feel for the twine stretching up and over.

But his finger felt only air. Again he felt for the knot. It was still attached, but the twine hung limply down, broken eight inches along its length.

Although he was only some three feet off the ground, he clung like a man on the side of a high-rise building, feeling the same vertiginous darkness clamp down upon him.

Someone had been there.

Someone might still be there, inside, waiting for him.

He scrambled down, his eyes wide and staring, all the rationalisation and hard logic of earlier vanishing in an instant. Meredith was back in the jungle of his mind. It wasn't meant to be this way. He hadn't meant to get caught outside. Inside, he knew the territory, he had strategies, he had means . . .

Memory hit him like a sledgehammer.

She had taken it. He had given her the tin when she had asked for it. There was nothing for him inside.

Panic flared briefly. And then he remembered the tool shed.

He circled the house in a wide arc, avoiding the crunch of gravel. There was a chance that he might already have been seen. He swore at his stupidity at flashing the torch, but he hadn't known then.

Hadn't known . . .

The thought churned through him like a riptide.

If he had been seen, then whoever or whatever was in there might come looking. Might already be opening the door.

He was running by the time he reached the tool shed.

Its rattling door shuddering in the south-west wind was one of Meredith's acceptable noises. Lying awake in the small hours it had reassured him, a sign that all was well. Now, as he fumbled with the wooden peg that held the latch, too scared to risk the torch, he prayed that it wouldn't creak and rattle too loudly.

The squeak it actually made on opening sounded cacophonous to his frayed nerves. Inside, in a three-foot-square space reduced to one foot by a kindling stack that spilled out on to the floor, he knelt and began removing sticks one by one until he could feel the smooth sides of the plastic ice-cream carton he'd hidden there.

Kneeling uncomfortably, he pulled the door to before risking the torch. With trembling fingers he prised open the sealed lid and frantically began ripping open the paper packaging around the syringe. Snapping open the plastic sheath of the needle he rammed it home, missing twice before the male to female connection was made.

His hands were shaking badly as he felt in the box for the vials. The thin necks snapped open easily but he almost dropped the syringe as a raw edge plunged into his overanxious thumb with the fifth vial. Cursing, he balanced the torch precariously on a pile of kindling and in the pool of light it sent out, he began drawing up the contents of the vials into the syringe.

An odd feeling of calm descended upon him as he let the last vial drop to the floor and held up the full syringe. It had been old stock someone had been intent on throwing away. A vet friend had used Meredith to mediate with the pharmacy of a closing hospital. In return, Meredith had obtained enough phenobarbitone for the vet to sedate a small herd of cows. Three vials in twenty-four hours was the maximum human dose. Meredith had calculated that ten vials in one huge bolus should be enough to permanently sedate a human.

He stared at the needle as it glistened in pristine sharpness in the torchlight. Instant oblivion. His weapon against the monster.

But there was something wrong. Suddenly he felt empty. This was as far as he had dared think.

And what if it wasn't the monster?

Doubt sank its teeth into his neck and would not let go.

Flicking off the torch and sitting momentarily with his eyes tight shut, he opened the door and peered out into the gloom. The scene that greeted him made him want to scream.

The woman and the girl were closing the distance between the two chalets, the child clutching something small in her hand.

Even as he drew in a breath to screech a warning, they were at the door, knocking, Mandy skipping excitedly.

And then the breath seized in Meredith's throat as he saw his own front door swing open.

No light spilled out into the damp air.

He saw Julie step forward in confusion, calling his name the instant before she screamed and her hands flew to her face as the Mace hit her eyes. In the tool shed, Meredith's hand flew involuntarily to his own.

Then there was a blur of movement and she toppled forward, yanked inwards by an unseen force.

Mandy made a grab for her mother, but then she looked up and whatever she saw kicked in her own survival instinct so strongly that she swivelled and started running. She made two yards before a white blanket lunged outwards and caught her by the arm. Meredith saw her feet leave the ground still pumping at a run as one large pale arm lifted her up bodily. He heard the first millisecond of a howl emerge from her lips before she disappeared inside and all noise abruptly ceased. It was all over in less than ten seconds. Like the strike of a rattler.

Meredith lurched to his feet, his apathy gone.

Not the little girl. Ah, Jesus!

He felt his breath roaring again, in and out like the pistons of a lunatic engine.

Shit, not now, not now, not now.

His fingers began to tingle. It spread up to the hand that held the syringe. It felt numb. At this rate it would be only a matter of seconds before he would pass out. He felt his eyes darting around in the darkness. There was nothing to breathe into. There was no way of stopping his stupid bloody brain from playing this last obscene trick on him . . . He fell to his knees impotently, arching his neck to look up at the black sky. A desperate primordial scream threatened to surge out of his mouth but was lost in his frantic attempt to gag his pumping lungs. He threw his head up into the night air entreatingly, and whether it was the wind chasing the thinning fog or whether it was his own imagination, he would never know. But in that instant he saw through the mist that clung to the earth. Above it there was a clarity and a purity in the air. A rent in the vapour made a window through which he glimpsed the dense, silent blackness in which hung the stars.

Into his mind, clear but distant, came the sound of a tune he had heard in a car with a woman he had loved. A woman who had been innocent of all but the crime of beauty, for which she had offered by being his companion on a night when a devil had stalked him.

Eyes . . .
like . . .
stars above . . .

Innocence was not a crime.

His mind leapt to the car – Jilly laughing – and the sequence began. Roars of pain, the noise of rending flesh. The sight of gushing blood, the dread of realization, police, Vine . . . The images exploded into his mind, in a crescendo and then a decrescendo as they began to play back at unbelievable speed until . . .

Jilly's laughter tinkled in his ears again.

He blinked away hot tears. He was still kneeling, staring at the chalet. But his breathing was normal and steady, his mind sharp and clear, his eyes adapted to the darkness.

He got up and ran.

At the rear of the chalet was a galvanised bucket. Upending it, he used it to step up on to the kitchen window ledge, not daring to stop and look inside. He didn't need to, the terrified sobs and muffled screams were enough.

On the roof, he tiptoed across to the skylight. A perfect six-inch circle had been cut into the glass. Reaching in, he felt for the cockspur and lifted, mindful that someone else had done the same thing that evening. It came easily, hinging silently.

He let himself down, thankful for the one piece of luck that had allowed the bathroom door to swing half shut, shielding him. He landed on the threadbare rug and half slipped, his hand shooting out and finding the sink before he toppled completely. He sprang up, crouching at the door, peering in on a nightmare scene.

A single torch at ground level illuminated the room, casting long bizarre shadows that cavorted on the walls in a *danse macabre*.

Mandy cowered whimpering in a corner, still clutching the rumpled package. The hooded figure loomed over Julie, straddling her as she lay on her back. His billowing cassock in folds on either side of her body gave Meredith the bizarre impression that he was growing straight out of the floor, a white iceberg of evil. His knees pinioned her arms as she shook her head from side to side, her face wet and streaked from the Mace. He moved forward inch by inch until his knees were either side of her head, preventing it from jerking. He waited while she opened her mouth to scream and then slapped on the thick insulating tape. It took him three attempts.

In between her yells and shouts, Meredith could make out very little that was coherent. But he did hear quite clearly the words, 'My baby, my baby . . .'

The slap came solid and hard, stunning Julie into silence. The tape was on in a moment and then *he* was looming upwards, flicking Julie over on to her stomach like a rag doll. The blow had taken much of the fight out of her. She still struggled but there seemed less frenetic desperation in her writhing.

As he leaned over on one knee to wrap more tape around her wrists, Meredith saw him look up and fix the little girl. The eyes glinted in the odd half-light and Meredith knew he was looking at a predator's stare.

Bloor was grinning under the mask.

It was a deliverance. His destiny. And when he finally released her from her anguish she would be part of him. Perhaps then he would be free of the hunger for a long while.

He wound the tape around the woman's wrist, impervious to her whining, feeling her squirm beneath him, revelling in his power.

Now, and only when he wished it, they saw his true majesty. The render of flesh, the eater of souls.

*

It was the girl that gave Meredith away by her terrified glance as he eased open the bathroom door a little further.

Bloor reared up, spinning as he did so, a knife already in his hand, its serrated edge catching the light and drawing Meredith's eyes like a magnet. He came without hesitation, silent death in an ivory sheet, his arm outstretched with the knife pointing forward as if willing Meredith to fall upon it.

As he stepped out of the bathroom, Meredith flicked on the light. Bloor blinked, caught off guard, but Meredith was expecting it and seized his chance. Bloor did not see the arc of the shower head still attached to its copper piping tremblingly unscrewed by Meredith as it whipped sharply down on to his extended wrist, sending the knife clattering.

Bloor howled in pain. Howled and then roared, his hands coming up like the paws of a great bear. He stood, defying Meredith before lunging forward.

Meredith stood his ground, waiting until the last moment before bringing up the hand that still held the syringe. He aimed for the chest, but Bloor feinted into a crouch, ready to pounce, and Meredith felt rather than saw the sharp stab of the needle entering the monster's throat. Reflexively, Bloor pulled back, but Meredith went with him, pushing the plunger up to the hilt.

The effect was almost instantaneous. Ten millilitres of phenobarbitone entered the nasopharynx and larynx. Bloor began heaving and spluttering, the intense irritation setting up paroxysms of coughing.

Meredith had aimed for the chest, hoping to hit a blood vessel. The barbiturate would be useless in soft tissue. Absorption would take too long. He remembered in an instant of ludicrous clarity his medical-school warnings always to double-check that it was in the vein. Every year there were litigations against hapless medics who missed. In the soft tissue it was nasty stuff; very alkaline, it caused severe tissue reactions and even necrosis. . .

The noise began almost immediately; a gagging, retching, stertorous gasping as Bloor fell to the floor, tearing at his throat. Meredith stumbled backwards, remembering where he had heard the noise before. He glanced across at the little girl, who had hidden her face. He tried to imagine what effect the drug was having in The Carpenter's throat: irritation, swelling, blocking off the airway, choking the life out . . .

He ran across to Mandy, sweeping her up in his arms and depositing her near the door, one eye on the writhing form on the floor.

Quickly, Meredith bent to Julie and released her wrists, his fingers trembling as behind him Mandy watched goggle-eyed. Once, when Meredith risked a glance at her, he saw something in her face that stopped him dead.

She knew.

She knew what Meredith was capable of.

She knew that he could save the monster.

She knew too that he would not do it.

When he ripped the tape off Julie's mouth, she sobbed and reached for the child, clambering for the door with her daughter under one protective arm, leaving Meredith suddenly alone.

Bloor's writhing had risen in a crescendo as he whipped his body to and fro like a landed fish. He clawed at the hood, tearing it asunder. It was then that Meredith finally saw the face of the monster. What he saw was a rasping toad's face, purple and bloated, the tongue protruding, the eyes bulging impossibly. And it came as no surprise to Meredith to see it thus. Beneath the mask, Meredith had never considered that there was anything remotely human. He watched until the movements slowed and the noise that emanated was a single continuous whistling croak that neither rose nor fell. It was interrupted only by the high revving of an engine outside: Julie was making good her escape.

Meredith got up and moved to a chair – the same chair Vine had sat in to supervise him. He sat and watched as The Carpenter's legs began drumming against the floor in an involuntary tremor, rising in volume and tempo until it gradually subsided again into the faintest twitch.

Finally, there was silence broken only by the muted roar of the distant tide. Something caught his eye. In the corner where Mandy had cowered was the rumpled parcel she had been clutching.

He reached over and picked it up. In a childish scrawl, he read his own name in bright yellow.

With leaden arms, he tore off the paper.

Inside was a tinsel star.

Holding it tightly, Meredith stood and walked towards the door and out into the darkness of the night.